"A smooth, flowing tale that entices the imagination."
—*Huntress Book Reviews* (4½ stars)

CodeSpell

"A hint of cyberpunk, a dollop of Greek mythology, and a sprinkle of techno-magic bake up into an airy genre mashup. Lots of fast-paced action and romantic angst up the ante as Ravirn faces down his formidable foes." —*Publishers Weekly*

"One long adrenaline rush, with a few small pauses for Ravirn to heal from his near-fatal brushes with the movers and shakers of the universe, all while trying to figure out how to survive the next inevitable encounter." —*SFRevu*

"Imaginative, fascinating, with a lot of adventure thrown in . . . Mr. McCullough has followed his first two books with a worthy sequel. *CodeSpell* will keep the reader on edge."
—*Fresh Fiction*

"This third book featuring hacker extraordinaire Ravirn is every bit [as much] of a fast-paced, energetic page-turner as its predecessors. Ravirn continues to be a fascinating protagonist, and the chaotic twists of the plot carry the reader through to the end." —*Romantic Times*

Cybermancy

"McCullough has true world-building skills, a great sense of Greek mythology, and the eye of a thriller writer. The blend of technology and magic is absolutely amazing, and I'm surprised no one has thought to do it quite like this before."
—Blogcritics.org

"This is the second book in McCullough's series that fuses hacking culture with ancient gods, and it's every bit as charming, clever, and readable as its predecessor." —*Romantic Times*

continued . . .

"It's smoothly readable, vivid, and fun . . . highly recommended."
——MyShelf.com

"McCullough has the most remarkable writing talent I have ever read . . . Not satisfied to write a single genre or to use a subgenre already made, he has created a new template that others will build stories upon in later years. But know this: McCullough is the original and unparalleled."
——*Huntress Book Reviews*

WebMage

"The most enjoyable science fantasy book I've read in the last four years . . . Its blending of magic and coding is inspired . . . *WebMage* has all the qualities I look for in a book—a wonderfully subdued sense of humor, nonstop action, and romantic relief. It's a wonderful debut novel."
——Christopher Stasheff, author of *Saint Vidicon to the Rescue*

"Inventive, irreverent, and fast paced, strong on both action and humor."
——*The Green Man Review*

"[An] original and outstanding debut . . . McCullough handles his plot with unfailing invention, orchestrating a mixture of humor, philosophy, and programming insights that gives new meaning to terms as commonplace as 'spell-checker' and [as] esoteric as 'programming in hex.'"
——*Publishers Weekly* (starred review)

"A unique first novel, this has a charming, fresh combination of mythological, magical, and computer elements . . . that will enchant many types of readers."
——*KLIATT*

"McCullough's first novel, written very much in the style of Roger Zelazny's classic Amber novels, is a rollicking combination of verbal humor, wild adventures, and just plain fun."
——*VOYA*

Ace Books by Kelly McCullough

SPELLCRASH

Kelly McCullough

ACE BOOKS, NEW YORK

THE BERKLEY PUBLISHING GROUP
Published by the Penguin Group
Penguin Group (USA) Inc.
375 Hudson Street, New York, New York 10014, USA

Penguin Group (Canada), 90 Eglinton Avenue East, Suite 700, Toronto, Ontario M4P 2Y3, Canada
(a division of Pearson Penguin Canada Inc.)
Penguin Books Ltd., 80 Strand, London WC2R 0RL, England
Penguin Group Ireland, 25 St. Stephen's Green, Dublin 2, Ireland (a division of Penguin Books Ltd.)
Penguin Group (Australia), 250 Camberwell Road, Camberwell, Victoria 3124, Australia
(a division of Pearson Australia Group Pty. Ltd.)
Penguin Books India Pvt. Ltd., 11 Community Centre, Panchsheel Park, New Delhi—110 017, India
Penguin Group (NZ), 67 Apollo Drive, Rosedale, North Shore 0632, New Zealand
(a division of Pearson New Zealand Ltd.)
Penguin Books (South Africa) (Pty.) Ltd., 24 Sturdee Avenue, Rosebank, Johannesburg 2196,
South Africa

Penguin Books Ltd., Registered Offices: 80 Strand, London WC2R 0RL, England

This is a work of fiction. Names, characters, places, and incidents either are the product of the author's imagination or are used fictitiously, and any resemblance to actual persons, living or dead, business establishments, events, or locales is entirely coincidental. The publisher does not have any control over and does not assume any responsibility for author or third-party websites or their content.

SPELLCRASH

An Ace Book / published by arrangement with the author

PRINTING HISTORY
Ace mass-market edition / June 2010

Copyright © 2010 by Kelly McCullough.
Cover art by Christian McGrath.
Cover design by Judith Lagerman.
Interior text design by Kristin del Rosario.

ISBN: 978-0-441-01888-8

ACE
Ace Books are published by The Berkley Publishing Group,
a division of Penguin Group (USA) Inc.,
375 Hudson Street, New York, New York 10014.
ACE and the "A" design are trademarks of Penguin Group (USA) Inc.

PRINTED IN THE UNITED STATES OF AMERICA

10 9 8 7 6 5 4 3 2 1

For Laura,
who holds my heart

Acknowledgments

Extra-special thanks are owed to Laura McCullough, Stephanie Zvan, Jack Byrne, Warren Lapine, and Anne Sowards.

Many thanks also to the active Wyrdsmiths: Lyda, Doug, Naomi, Bill, Eleanor, and Sean. My web guru: Ben. Beta readers: Steph, Ben, Sara, Dave, Sari, Karl, Angie, Sean, Laura R., Norma, Warren, and Angela. Keith Spears for his comments on introducing hands. My extended support structure: Bill and Nancy, James, Tom, Ann, Mike, Sandy, and all the rest. My family: Carol, Paul and Jane, Lockwood and Darlene, Judy, Lee C., Kat, Jean, Lee P., and all the rest.

I also want to thank some of the many people who have worked on these books at the Penguin end of things and made me look so good in the process. My fabulous series copy editors: Robert and Sara Schwager. Cover art I love: Christian McGrath. Likewise, cover design: Judith Lagerman. Anne Sowards's assistants: Cameron Dufty and Kat Sherbo. Publicists past and present: Maggie Kao, Valerie Cortes, and Rosanne Romanello. Interior text design: Kristin del Rosario. Production editor: Michelle Kasper. Assistant production editor: Andromeda Macri.

Finally, I'd like to give a big thank-you to my readers of this series. I wouldn't have gotten very far without you.

CHAPTER ONE

■ ■ ■

Pop quiz, multiple choice: When is having a gorgeous naked woman coming after you a major problem? (A) When she's your ex-girlfriend. (B) When she's there to tear your arms off. (C) When she's a Fury.

Why do I always have to be an "all of the above" kind of guy?

It can't be Fate, the family I left behind. I've been off Fate's roster ever since the goddess Necessity decided to transform me from a sorcerer of the hacking-and-cracking variety into an aspect of the Trickster. The Trickster . . . Yeah, that's probably it. Nothing is ever simple for the Raven.

Which is why my involuntary vacation in the land of the Norse gods had ended with an equally involuntary deportation back to my MythOS of origin, the Greek pantheoverse. The process ended with my rather abrupt return to the Garbage Faerie Decision Locus, carrying my clothes rather than wearing them. I was accompanied on my trip by one small sarcastic blue goblin, one giant god-wolf recovering from an unfortunate piercing, and one disembodied but very perky hand. Dignity and grace in all things, that's my motto.

I'd just managed to get my leather pants and one boot on, and was struggling with the next boot, when the unmistakable sound of someone tearing a hole in the universe announced the imminent arrival of one of the Sisters of Vengeance.

Since I was none too sure of where I stood with the Furies at the moment, I dropped the boot and reached for my shoulder holster. Not that I believed a .45 was going to do anything against one of the baddest goddesses on the block—I just wanted something vaguely threatening to hang on to by way of a security blanket. My magic sword, Occam, would have made a better choice if I hadn't recently managed to break it. Sigh. They don't make them like Excalibur anymore.

"Is Ravirn always this dignified?" asked the wolf from off to my left.

"You have no idea, Fenris. You have no idea." My webgoblin familiar, Melchior, shook his head sadly.

"Said the laptop with delusions of grandeur," I replied. I wouldn't trade Mel for anything, but sometimes I wondered if we shouldn't tone the sarcasm down with his next upgrade. Yeah, that was going to happen.

I'd have defended myself further, but the incoming Fury picked that exact moment to pass through from wherever she had been before she sliced a doorway in space and time. An ice-clawed hand was the first thing that emerged, telling me that this must be the replacement for Tisiphone—whom I loved and had been forced to leave behind in the land of the Norse gods when she chose freedom in exile over servitude at home. I couldn't blame her; she'd seen a chance to shed the mantle of a power forever and taken it. I'd probably have done the same if I'd had the opportunity.

The new Fury entered my world fully, and I let out an

involuntary gasp. Like her sisters, she disdained the use of clothing, going naked before the elements. She was tall and slender, with hair and wings that seemed to have been carved from living ice. Beautiful, too, beautiful and cold and deadly. More than capable of tearing me in half if she wished it. She was also desperately familiar.

"You!" I said, in the exact same moment as she did.

"Well, dip me in garlic butter and throw me to Cerberus," said Melchior.

"Raven," said the Fury, and her voice dripped scorn.

"Cerice," I replied, giving her my best court bow. "How lovely to see you again."

My ex-girlfriend Cerice had become the new Fury. Just as the ex-Fury Tisiphone had become my new and already-much-missed girlfriend. Naturally, I'd ended up close and personal with the wrong one.

She sniffed disdainfully as she alighted in front of me. In almost the same moment that her nostrils flared, her eyes narrowed. I couldn't help but remember just how keen the Fury sense of smell was and relate that to the fact that I was barely ten minutes out of bed with Tisiphone. This was not going well, which meant I might as well up the ante. That's how a trickster plays the game . . . whether he wants to or not.

"Oh, and you might recall that I prefer Ravirn," I said.

"That name was taken from you by your grandmother. You remember her, right? Lachesis, the Fate who measures the threads?" Cerice's voice sounded acid etched. "It no longer belongs to you. You are instead what my grandmother Clotho named you, the Raven, a power of chaos and a traitor to the Houses of Fate." She picked that moment to snatch the pistol from my hand and twist it like a dishrag.

"Sounds like you two have some history." Fenris's tongue lolled as he gave a wolfy laugh.

Cerice turned a hard glare on him. "Who . . . or what in Necessity's name are you?"

"I'm the big bad wolf and, unless I'm totally mistaken, you have to be Little Red Flaming Hood's new baby sister."

"If you're referring to Tisiphone, you've hit one mark. As to the rest, I'm not impressed, Fido."

I took the ensuing glaring contest as an opportunity to slip on my remaining boot. I'd forgotten my shirt back in the Norse MythOS, so I had to slide my jacket on over bare skin. It wasn't the most refined fashion statement in the world, but I liked it a whole lot more than the half-naked state it replaced.

"Look, Cerice, I've had a really shitty week. Did you have a point in coming here, or are you just out for a lark? Because if you've come to kill me, I wish you'd go ahead and make the attempt so we can get it over with. If you have some other purpose, say one that doesn't involve you spitting and snarling at me, then you're wasting both our times in a pretty boorish manner."

She spun around and stomped over to glare into my face from a distance of inches. If I'd had any sense at all, I'd probably have backed up or given some other sign of submission. But no one has *ever* accused me of having any sense. I leaned forward and kissed the tip of her nose.

Ouch.

The punch took me in the solar plexus with near-surgical precision—hard enough to fold me up and leave me gasping on the ground, soft enough to inflict zero lasting harm. I was still trying to remember how to breathe when Cerice knelt and took the tip of my nose between two claws.

"Would you like a nice new nose ring, Raven? Because that could be arranged." She released her grip and flicked the end of my nose, drawing blood. "I'm here because Shara wanted to see what had made its way into this multiverse from elsewhere. That done, I'm a free agent for the rest of the visit. If I wanted to kick the crap out of you, I could. I'm not going to do that because of what we used to mean to each other, but don't bet on past relationships saving your skin a second time.

"I used to be Cerice," she continued, "a wayward child of House Clotho and your onetime lover. About a week ago, Shara offered me a new job, and everything changed. I'm a Fury now, and my temper is not something you want to trifle with. It owns me, and it doesn't give a damn about your continued welfare. Piss me off enough, and I might kill you before I have time to change my mind. I'm going to go away now. Think about it."

Her claws flashed out blindingly fast, slicing a line that ran from about a half inch in front of my eyes to a hairbreadth in front of my groin. Smiling grimly, she slipped through the cut she'd made into somewhere else and was gone. I'm almost certain the reason I didn't come back with a snide remark before she departed was because I couldn't breathe and not because she'd scared the bejeeburs out of me. Almost.

"You're an idiot, you know that, right?" Melchior's normally pale blue face had darkened to something in the neighborhood of indigo. "Why are you always trying to get yourself killed?"

"*I'm* not," I said, "but the Raven might have other plans."

Melchior looked away.

One of the problems with becoming a power is the loss of some degree of autonomy. Take Cerice's comment about her temper. Among the things she would have inherited when she became a Fury was an extra-large helping of little-f fury. In my case, becoming the Raven had amped the daylights out of all of my worst tendencies toward risk-taking and mischief-making. Ravirn the hacker and cracker was a trickster. The Raven is a mask of *the* Trickster, one that all too often wears my face rather than the other way around.

Take my response to Cerice as Fury. The old Ravirn

would probably have been appalled on her behalf and at least tried to think before speaking. The Raven? Not so much. The part of me that was the Trickster didn't care about whatever madness had driven Shara to use her position within Necessity to offer Cerice Tisiphone's place as a Fury. Nor about the madness that had convinced Cerice to agree. It cared about winning the conversational duel no matter how much of a callous ass that painted me.

On the lemonade-from-lemons side, the Trickster isn't big on self-doubt, so I have trouble hanging on to morose. At least, when no one is actively shooting at me, I do. I rolled backwards and up onto my feet.

"Forget it, Mel. I'm sure life will drop a bucket of bricks on us soon enough without my help."

"Now, that's reassuring." Melchior shook his head and started to pace. "Do you think she really meant that about Shara?"

"The hiring-decision thing?" I shrugged. "I don't see how else you arrive at Cerice as Fury. We still don't know what happened with Necessity to get us sent off to the Norse MythOS. It's possible that was a symptom of a complete and unfixable crash, and that Shara's running the show now."

"Care to clue a guy in here?" Fenris asked me.

"Sure. Necessity is our version of MimirSoft—the goddess in computer shape who keeps track of the gods and all the infinite worlds of probability. Because of a couple of minor miscalculations on my part, she caught a virus that just about ate the entire multiverse."

"To say nothing of the hardware damage your duel with Nemesis inflicted," said Melchior.

"Well, yeah." I looked at my feet. "There's that, too, but that wasn't really my fault."

"So that mess you made with Mimir and Rune wasn't exactly outside your normal mode of operations," said Fenris.

"More like his specialty," said Melchior.

The wolf whistled. "No wonder Odin wanted to get rid of you. Between that and your little self-aware laptop buddy here"—he indicated Melchior with his nose—"you're something like the ultimate biological malware."

I shrugged. "I prefer to think of myself as a hacker and cracker, but you might have a point there."

"So who's Shara?" he asked.

"That's complex. She used to be Cerice's webgoblin and familiar. Laptop by day, miniature purple Mae West by night, or something like that anyway. Now the part of her that's really her is trapped inside Necessity and—if what Cerice said is true—she may be running the whole show."

"Should I assume that's your fault, too?" asked Fenris.

I looked away.

"Wow."

"I hate to interrupt," Melchior said, coming to my rescue, "but I'm thinking this might not be the safest place to hang out for any length of time. Shall we move this elsewhere?"

"Good point," I said. "It's always harder to hit a moving target. How about we start by introducing Brer Wolf around? I suspect that if we don't do it now, we're going to get way too busy with other issues."

There were a million things I needed to be doing, starting with finding out what had happened to Necessity and how we'd ended up in the Norse MythOS, and moving right along to finding out what the hell Cerice and Shara were thinking. But just for today, I was going to play hooky from responsibility.

"Did you have anyone in mind?" asked Melchior.

I was about to answer when I felt a squeeze on my ankle. I glanced down. A severed hand clung there. Laginn.

"I'm sorry. I didn't mean to forget you. We'll introduce you around, too."

Laginn used to be the hand of the Norse God of War,

Tyr. That was before Fenris bit the hand off and a few hundred years of marinating in the Norse-style chaos that lives in the giant wolf's belly gave it new life. Now, *it* is a *he*, as well as Fenris's constant companion and occasional chew toy. They have a strange, semisymbiotic relationship. Which I suppose could be said of me and Melchior as well.

"Introduce us around?" Fenris canted his head to one side, managing to look simultaneously confused and hungry. "Why?"

"Well, I figure it's my fault that you're stuck here in the land of the Greek gods. That makes it my responsibility to help you get settled. You're welcome to stay at Raven House for as long as you like, but that's a pretty isolated corner of reality. I'm sure you'd like to make some friends beyond yours truly and find a better place to hang your"—I tried to think of a suitable substitute for *hat*—"collar?"

"I *hate* that word; you should watch . . ." The huge wolf stopped and made a series of slow turns, looking rather like a dog chasing his tail at one-tenth speed. "Gleipner really is gone, isn't it? I don't think I fully understood what that means until this very second."

Fenris threw his great head back and let out a howl that probably terrified everything remotely edible within a ten-mile radius. "I'm *free*!"

Then he actually did start chasing his tail. Just when that looked like it might be starting to lose its appeal, Laginn bolted past, running on tippy-fingers. Fenris leaped in pursuit, barking like a puppy the whole time.

I couldn't help grinning as the two dodged in and out among the weird detritus that dotted the surreal landscape. The worlds out at the edge of the Greek MythOS can get very strange, and Garbage Faerie is one of the oddest I've ever visited.

It looks rather like what you might get if a high urban civilization turned over a hundred years of its trash and junk flow to a really twisted designer of Japanese formal gardens. Big-screen TVs lie cracked screen up, with delicate arrangements of pebbles tracing the fractures. Old train engines have been planted like the menhirs of Stonehenge, their original shapes all but obscured by the wild grape and morning glory that grow on them. It is beautiful and bizarre and I love it.

The exuberant game of chase played between a wolf roughly the size and shape of an anorexic Clydesdale and the bitten-off hand of a god made it all the stranger and more wonderful. I laughed aloud for the sheer weirdness of existence. Fenris was a power, too, or had been in his home MythOS. Here, he would be much weaker but also free. Free of the mantle of a power and free of the silver cord of Gleipner the Entangler, which had bound him for more than a thousand years. What would it be like to shake all that off?

I was feeling pretty good about that and my whole Big Fat Norse Odyssey up until Laginn leaped over the edge of the large and very fresh crater that dominated the scenery, and Fenris followed him down. That was when my smile died. The giant hole in the ground had once been a hill with a home under it, the home of a dear friend whose life had paid for the freedom of Fenris and his fellow Norse deities, a friend I had killed.

"You miss Ahllan, too, don't you?" Melchior walked over to stand beside me.

"It's more than that," I said.

Melchior looked up at me, his expression shrewd. "You believe you're responsible for her death, and you're feeling guilty."

"I *am* responsible for her death, Mel. I killed her as surely as if I'd put a bullet in her heart. I may have had the best motive in the world, but the details don't change a thing."

"Bullshit." Melchior's voice was flat and the coldest I'd ever heard it.

"What?"

"I said, 'Bullshit.'" Melchior glared up at me. "That's guilt talking, not sense. Details mean everything. Shooting someone because you don't like the color of their jacket is senseless murder. Shooting someone who's about to kill you is self-defense. Shooting someone as part of an honest, trial-generated execution is justice."

"No matter how you slice it, somebody ends up dead and somebody else ends up a killer."

"Look, I don't know exactly what happened there at the end," said Melchior. "But I do know you and what you're capable of. I also know, or knew, Ahllan. She was the closest thing I have to a mother. The computer that absorbed her memories told us that Ahllan believed what you did was right. Between the two, I know enough to call bullshit on all this 'I killed her' angst. There was a lot more in the balance than just Ahllan's life. Can you look me in the eye and tell me that what you did didn't have to be done?"

I looked away. "I could have saved her."

"That wasn't the question."

How could I explain it to him? Yes, I'd done no more than what I had to, but that didn't make it any better. Ahllan's life was over, and it *was* my fault.

I was still trying to figure out what to say when Fenris bounced to a stop in front of me. "I feel *better*! So, where to next?"

"I know just the place," I said.

It was the strangest game of Risk I'd ever played. The board lay on a huge gray slab of granite. On one side lolled Cerberus, or more accurately, Mort, Dave, and Bob, since the heads were each playing individually. Fenris sat to their left, looking rather like the world's scariest puppy by comparison. The wolf of Asgard is the size of a draft horse and looks like he eats busloads of children as often as he can get them, but the hound of Hades is built more along the lines of what you'd get if you crossed the great-granddaddy of all bulldogs with a carnivorous elephant. Add a disembodied hand and me to the picture and place the whole thing on the banks of the Styx with the Gates of Hades in the background, and you get something that makes *Dogs Playing Poker* look downright Norman Rockwell by comparison.

"You cheat," growled Bob, a Doberman, and my least favorite head. He'd just lost a battle for Iceland.

"How could I cheat?" replied Dave, the rottweiler middle head whom I usually partnered at bridge. "It's luck. You roll the dice and take your lumps."

"He's right," said Mort, the mastiff.

"He cheats," said Bob.

"Are you going to keep repeating that all night long, or are you going to finish your turn and pass the dice?" asked Fenris.

The big wolf looked like he was having the time of his life, and maybe he was. I'm pretty sure that growing up in a place where everyone treated you as a monster because a prophecy said you were inevitably going to turn into one would have a distorting effect on your sense of fun. It might also turn you into a monster.

That it hadn't spoke to the innate resiliency of . . . people? Giant wolves? Gods? Don't get me wrong; he was still a giant, slavering deity in wolf shape, if a much less powerful one. And he was potentially capable of all sorts of harm and horror, but none of that makes him stand out particularly from the rest of the divine crowd, Norse or Greek. Take my extended family for example . . . please. There's plenty of ripping people to pieces, involuntary transformation, and old-fashioned warmongering to go around, and none of it for particularly admirable reasons. Speaking of that last, it was at about that point that Laginn and Mort formed a temporary alliance and drove my game armies into the sea.

After I'd boxed my pieces up, I headed down to the water's edge, settling near where Melchior was sitting with Cerberus's webpixie, Kira—think iPhone meets miniature goth chick, and you've pretty much got the right picture. In pixie shape, she's about three inches tall, blazingly hot in a dye-job black and pancake white sort of way, and straight from the capital city of bad-attitude land. The two of them were chattering away in machine language at about seven thousand times the data-transfer rate of English, and neither looked up as I passed them.

The Styx is a looped river that surrounds Hades the place. Both lie in a gigantic cavern somewhere under the roots of Mount Olympus. The underworld gates, which lay just across the water from me, were huge iron monstrosities set in a stone arch. As usual, they stood open, offering both a threat and a promise. I felt it on an extremely personal level—Hades the god has promised me a special place within. I shivered at that thought but couldn't look away. Just outside the gates is Hades' main concession to modernity, a check-in line taken straight from the heart of America's dysfunctional airport-security system, complete with a full five acts of security theater.

"Hey, Boss," said Melchior from behind me.

"Yes?" I didn't turn around.

"Are you all right?" he asked, his tone shifting from demanding to concerned.

"Why do you ask?"

"Because you're not arguing about the 'Boss' thing. That only happens when you're in too much trouble to take the time, or when something's really bothering you."

"Would it make you feel better if I grumped at you?" I asked.

There was actually quite a lot bothering me, starting with Cerice. The more I thought about her becoming a power, the less I liked the idea.

Mel sighed. "Forget it, *Boss*. The reason I spoke up is

that you've got an incoming visual transfer protocol request from Eris. Do you want to answer or not?"

"How'd she find out I was home so quickly?" The idea of Eris keeping a close eye on my comings and goings made me nervous. I turned around. "Initiate Vtp. Please."

"Done." Mel opened his eyes and mouth as wide as possible. From each came a different beam of light—red, green, and blue—meeting about a foot in front of his face and forming a golden globe with a somewhat misty miniature version of Eris standing at its center.

"Ravirn, dear child, I'd like to have a private word."

"I'm kind of in the middle of something at the moment," I replied. The "dear child" made me *very* nervous—Discord is never sweet or gentle. "I can give you a couple of moments of Vtp time or maybe stop in a bit later in the week."

"You make it sound like I'd made a request. Silly boy."

Her hand suddenly shot forward out of the globe, taking on weight and substance as it grew impossibly long. Before I could do so much as yelp, she caught the collar of my jacket and jerked me forward into the globe. As I became one with the projection, I could actually feel myself shrinking and growing more diffuse. It was one of the stranger experiences of a rather strange life.

I have traveled through the chaos between worlds many times. I have done it as a string of digital code moving along the carefully guarded channels of the mweb or as a deadweight dragged by a Fury. I have gone the route of curdled probability that lies at the heart of a faerie ring, or stepped straight from point A to point B by the fixed gate of a magical portrait. I have even flown the pathless infinities on my very own Raven's wings.

None of that felt half as strange as my current means of locomotion. It was as if I had become a field or wave function that somehow propagated itself through the stuff of chaos, an impulse encoded in the very motion of the

Primal Chaos. When I arrived at the other end, I had the distinct feeling that none of the me that had started the trip had any kind of direct connection to the me that ended it. Deeply, deeply creepy.

"What the hell did you just do to me?" I demanded of Eris in the instant that my mouth reconstituted itself.

She stood atop a waist-high white marble pedestal in the shape of a fluted Ionic column at the exact center of a circular colonnade and temple. A bronze plaque on the plinth said DISCORD, in case I had any doubts. In the moment of my arrival, she wore the aspect of a white marble statue in the classical mode, complete with the traditional clingy dress and strappy sandals. She stood as still as stone, and for reasons unclear, she had on a blindfold and was holding a set of bronze scales in the mode of Justice. Well, mostly in the mode. A severed thumb firmly weighted the left side of the balance, and the blindfold didn't fully cover her eye on that side. Her left arm was partially hidden behind her. By stepping around to that side, I could see her hand, sans thumb, held discreetly open. A cascade of coins fell from nowhere into the hand, where they vanished.

"What do you think?" Her voice seemed to issue from the air about a foot to my left. "It's sort of a commentary piece."

"Subtle," I replied. "Almost as much so as usual."

She snorted with amusement, and the whole statue routine vanished. In its place stood Discord.

How to describe a goddess whose stock-in-trade is change? Start with her height. Without the ever-present stiletto heels, she usually stands in the neighborhood of six-five, and today was no exception. Her skin shifts from onyx black to eighteen-karat gold in the blink of an eye and back at the next blink, or occasionally between blinks— think taffeta and hallucinogens. Her hair, equal parts midnight and blond, hangs to her waist, thick and straight and silken. Her body is perfect, no matter what your definition of perfect might be—that's part of her magic. She wants you to want her so much that you're willing to ruin yourself chasing after her though she can never be caught—again, part of the magic.

For me, today, she wore an elegant face with high-arched brows, sharply defined cheekbones, and bee-stung lips, though that almost certainly said more about my current appetites than it did about her real appearance. The goddess dress was gone, replaced by black leather pants, tight but not obscenely so, and a thin gold turtleneck that made the pants look baggy. The sandals had become a pair of knee-high boots with delicate golden chains around the ankles.

Her eyes . . . were my own, only more so. The tumbling madness of chaos fills the eyes of Eris. Knowing the same disturbing effect looks out at the world through the slits of my pupils is one of the things that makes meeting her gaze one of the least comfortable aspects of any encounter between us. Doubly so now that I know that Loki comes equipped with the same package. It says things about my place in the cosmic scheme that I don't particularly like to hear.

"How's tricks . . . ter?" she asked.

She always knows exactly what not to say. Hence, "Discord." I sighed. She laughed and winked again.

Finally, I laughed, too. "You're impossible, you know that, right?"

"Honey, that's my primary job description."

"What do you want?" I asked.

"What makes you think I want something?"

I raised an eyebrow. "I'm not anywhere near as stupid as I look. So far you've called me 'dear child' and 'honey,' and you haven't yet done that whole magical come-hither thing you do when you're trying to get my goat."

"Are you saying I'm losing my sex appeal?"

She gave me a pouting look that would have made a

monk regret his vows of celibacy. It certainly redlined my libido gauge, but it did it the old-fashioned way, with moist lips and artful posture and none of Eris's patented magic-most-sensual special effects. Once I'd put my tongue back in my mouth and my eyes back in their sockets, I was able to shake it off easily enough.

"Not in the least," I said. "We both know exactly what I meant; it's just that one of us is playing games. If that's how it's going to be, could we at least move this to a poker table. I'm used to you fleecing me at cards."

"You're getting harder to manipulate," she replied. "That's quite unfair."

As she finished the sentence I found myself seated at a round table covered in green felt. Eris sat across from me wearing the traditional green eyeshade of a house dealer and holding a deck of cards. Around us the temple had become a cross between a high-end Riviera-style casino and a thoroughly equipped video arcade. On my right, slot machines shared wall space with the latest successors to the PacMans and Galagas of my childhood. On my left, a roulette table backed against a sunken pit holding a giant-screen TV, a couple of couches, and a suite of gaming consoles. Castle Discord is an infinitely mutable Greatspell taking whatever shape Eris wants at the moment.

"What's your game?" she asked, flicking the cards from one hand to the other in a fancy cascade.

"I think that's my question actually, and I'm not playing anything until I know the stakes."

"You want stakes? All right, I'll show you."

Eris bent the deck between index finger and thumb, then flicked the center with her middle finger so that the cards shot straight across the table at my face. One by one, in the instant before they would have hit me, they turned into butterflies, each patterned in the suit of the original card. Soon fifty-two red and black butterflies were dancing around my head.

"And every one a potential hurricane," said Eris with a wicked smile, "but only if I weight the odds right." She snapped her fingers, and the butterflies vanished—off to cause havoc-weather if I knew her at all. "Those are the stakes."

"Ooh, obscure *and* portentous. What more could a guy ask for?" Now it was my turn to snap my fingers. "Oh, that's right, specifics."

She sighed and shook her head in the manner of a teacher with a particularly slow student. "You want to know everything?"

I nodded, and the world changed around me. I sat in a high-backed leather chair and was wearing a tweed suit. A pipe was tucked in the corner of my mouth, and a notebook rested on my knee. Eris lay at full length on a chaise beside me, one arm thrown dramatically across her face.

"I had a very unhappy childhood, Doc," she said. "My father was a dominating bastard who thought he should be the king of the gods. My grandfather was worse—he *ate* my aunts and uncles one by one and would have eaten my father, too, if the old man hadn't gotten him first. Not surprisingly, I began to act out as a teenager. Wild parties." A ghost of a bacchanal manifested itself around us. "Skimpy clothes." Eris's outfit went briefly as ghostly as the bacchantes. "Attention seeking, really." The party went away, replaced by a heavy golden apple thudding down on a long marble table. "But I was just a product of my environment." A hundred scenes of divine Greek depravity flashed by in an instant. "My family is the very definition of dysfunction and abuse." She caught my eyes with her own. "Or should I say *our* family, cousin mine?"

I spat out the pipe. "Is this going somewhere?"

Eris shook her head sadly and sat up. "You really ought to be able to read between the lines by now." She touched the side of her head. "This is going to give me such a migraine, and I promise that I'm going to take it out of your hide later."

"I don't understand," I said.

"I know. I am Eris, but also Discord, both goddess and power. Straightforward hurts me when it aids order against chaos." Her brow wrinkled in pain.

Eris snapped her fingers and produced a butterfly wearing the jack of hearts on its wings. "A storm is coming." She let out a little gasp.

Snap. Wind filled the room, tugging at my tweeds. "It will be the biggest blow our world has seen since the Titanomachy, a *hypercane*. And you are the butterfly who gave birth to the winds." Her eyes closed.

Snap. Lightning struck the butterfly in her hand, burning it to a crisp. "You must not trust Zeus." Her free hand went to her forehead.

Duh, I thought.

Snap. The thunder came, and a golden apple replaced the ash on her palm. "You must not trust any of us."

Double duh. Family.

She gave a little gasp. "Not even me."

Wow, the hat trick of duh.

Eris handed the apple to me. "The stakes are—no." She gagged, then doubled over and vomited behind the couch, clutching at her head the whole time. "That's all. Go!"

I glanced at the apple and swore. On it were the words, "For the specialist."

CHAPTER TWO

"Cryptic metal fruit, you gotta love that." Melchior held the apple up in one hand, peering thoughtfully at it like Hamlet with Yorick's skull. "Especially the kind that starts wars. I wonder whatever happened to the original." He sat on the rail of the main lanai of Raven House.

"I don't know, Mel. Aphrodite's not the most thoughtful of goddesses. I'm guessing that ten seconds after the contest was over, she forgot all about it in favor of the next shiny thing to catch her eye. It's probably playing doorstop in one of her thousand and one bedrooms."

I leaned forward and rested my elbows on the deck rail beside Melchior, looking past him to the sea. Raven House sits on the Island of Kauai in a Decision Locus that is largely devoid of people for reasons I've never bothered to look into. It's a beautiful and bizarre place, a product of my somewhat twisted subconscious messing with the stuff of probability by means of the faerie-ring network.

The style lies somewhere between Tiki-Modern and Neohedonist. The world's fanciest Hawaiian-themed hotel rendered in acres of black-veined green marble and vast expanses of tinted glass.

The view is fabulous. The half-moon of white sand and blue sea that is Hanalei Bay is backed by the near-vertical tropical forest of the mountains beyond. The latter provides a great sweep of velvet green punctuated here and there with ragged patches of rusty soil and waterfalls like threads of diamond. Breathing the air is like drinking a really good piña colada, sweet, heady, and pure tropics.

Speaking of which . . . I reached a hand back behind me. A cold drink filled it a moment later. I took a big sip, then choked and almost snorted it out through my nose in the next instant when it tasted nine kinds of wrong and far too strong. I managed not to drop the glass, but only just.

"Absinthe?" I hacked, and turned half-around to face Haemun.

"Not right?" The satyr shook his head sadly and looked contrite, though a tiny twinkle of mischief in his eyes made me doubt his sincerity. "Then yours must have been the piña colada." He plucked the glass from my hand and exchanged it for another on his tray.

Haemun is the spirit of Raven House made manifest, a combination butler, cook, valet, bartender, and wicked commentary on my subconscious. From the waist down he's a goat. From the waist up . . . He's got a lot in common with the traditional satyr there; human head and torso, curly hair, tiny horns. But his beard is a very sixties soul patch, and his aloha shirts are loud enough to violate most urban noise ordinances. The current one showed a complete luau scene, only all the participants had tie-dyed octopuses where their heads should have been. It made for a sort of Jerry Garcia dropping acid with Don Ho and H. P. Lovecraft vibe. Haemun can also read the needs of the house's occupants . . . most of the time. Witness the replacement drink I was even then lifting to my lips.

"I'll take the absinthe," said a deep, growly voice from the direction of the stairhead that led down to the beach.

Fenris, back from his latest attempts at surfing—I'd shown him the basics the previous evening after Eris released me. He seemed to have fallen in love with the sport despite the obvious handicaps involved with being a giant wolf. I turned toward the stairs, took a swallow of my piña colada . . . and then went to my knees when pain lashed my eyes and clawed at my right hand when my glass exploded.

"Down!" Melchior yelled somewhere behind me, followed by the sound of more shattering glass.

"Mine." Fenris's voice came out as an angry snarl, and I heard claws scrabbling on marble before a blurry gray streak raced past me.

Melchior arrived at my side in the next moment. "Boss, are you all right?"

I wanted to say yes, but I didn't know yet. While the pain in my eyes had stopped getting worse, the signals from my hand had a shocky feeling I didn't like one little bit.

"What happened?" I demanded.

Melchior didn't answer immediately. Instead, he whistled a binary spell string that I recognized as "Better Living Through Chemistry" before jabbing a hollow claw freshly full of morphine into my right wrist. Not a good sign, that.

"Just hang on, Boss. I don't think it's as bad as it looks."

"I can't see shit, Mel. What happened?"

"Assassin. High-powered rifle, I think. If you hadn't turned when you did, we'd be picking up pieces of your skull. As it is, the bullet hit your drink, and maybe your hand. It's hard to tell what's what with all that blood."

Damn it, damn it, damn it. "Should I be scrambling for cover?"

"I expect Fenris has it under control, but getting off the balcony sure couldn't hurt."

"Guide me." I closed my eyes to minimize distractions.

Melchior caught hold of my right wrist and tugged. I followed on hand and knees.

"Let me give you a boost." Haemun wrapped a helpful arm around my waist.

After we slipped into the shadow of the roofed portion of the lanai, I let my next worry surface. "How bad are my eyes?"

They felt like they were getting better but . . .

"I didn't see any blood or glass fragments, but why don't we have a closer look now." Melchior halted our forward progress, and I felt his tiny fingers tugging at my eyelids.

I let him open them, and a blurry version of my inner lanai materialized. Mel's attentions hurt, but I tried to hold still.

"I think they're fine. You just got sprayed with alcohol when your piña colada exploded. That's bound to sting something fierce, but I don't see you going all Oedipus Rex anytime soon."

"You have no idea what a relief that is, Mel."

"Actually, having met the bundle of spite and bile that is your mother, I rather think I do. Just a second." He whistled another string of binary, something extemporaneous this time. A moment later, I felt warm saline washing out my eyes.

"Much better." I blinked several times as something like normal vision returned.

Haemun had flipped over a Hawaiian-print sofa, putting at least a visual block between us and anyone pointing a gun in our direction. So, temporarily out of the line of fire, check. Eyes functional, check. Time for item three on the triage list.

My right hand was a mess. Reflexes are a wonderful thing, except when they aren't. Mine had closed the hand

into a tight fist when the initial pain hit. Not the best plan
in the world when your drink has just been converted into a
rapidly expanding cloud of alcohol and broken glass.

"Ugly." I rotated my half-open hand this way and
that, trying to ignore the blood and focus on actual tissue
damage.

"Can you move it?" asked Melchior.

"I guess I'd better try." Not that I wanted to.

*Pinkie? Ow. Ring finger? Ow! Middle fi—aieee! Grit
teeth. Index—owowow, not good. Bite tongue. Thumb? . . .
Okay.* I flipped my right hand over and looked at the back.
After a moment, I pointed at it with my left.

"You see that bloody spot, just inside the knuckles, between the index and middle fingers? Exit wound?"

Melchior nodded. "I think you're right. Haemun, hold
his wrist."

The satyr did as told, and I turned my head away. Even
through the morphine, what Melchior did next made me
want to scream.

"Small-caliber, high-velocity," he said after a while.
"Very clean shot, and it doesn't look like it hit the bone or
any major tendons. About as good as you could hope for,
but once we get all of that glass out of your hand, we're
going to need to get you to someone who stitches better
than I do. Hands are touchy."

"I can do it," said Haemun.

The satyr sounded as surprised by that as I felt. His reaction turned me back to face him once again.

"Really?" asked Melchior. "I didn't know that about
you."

"Neither did I," I said.

"That makes three of us," said Haemun. "It wasn't until
Master Melchior said what he did that the knowledge came
into my head. Though, when you consider the way you
two live, it's no surprise that Raven House would come
equipped with a decent field surgeon."

"Fair enough," I said. "Where do you want to work? I think I can crawl a bit farther now."

"No need for crawling," said Fenris from somewhere beyond the overturned couch, his voice sounding strangely muffled. "I got the shooter. I had to kill it, and it's the weirdest damned thing I've seen in a very long life."

I'm not sure what I expected Fenris to drag around the couch, but I know I got something entirely different. Different, and deeply unsettling.

"Why is a spinnerette trying to kill you?" asked Melchior.

That was a good question. Fenris dropped the limp body of the spider-centaur on the ground at my feet in a grim parody of a Labrador bringing a duck to its master. This one was longer and thinner than most, reminding me almost of a scorpion. I'd never seen one quite like it. It was also rougher and less refined than the normal model.

"I take it from your reaction that you two recognize this thing?" he said.

I nodded. "The spinnerettes are part of the network Fate built to control destiny in the days before Necessity created the mweb."

"They work for Fate?" The huge wolf settled back on his haunches and started to scrub his mouth with his tongue like a dog eating peanut butter. "That'd sure explain the taste." Fenris and his family disliked their version of the Fates every bit as much as I did mine, if somewhat less personally.

"Not exactly," I replied. "They used to, but once Necessity's network came along, Fate decided to surplus the lot of them."

"Is that a fancy word for kill?" asked Fenris.

"I guess it is," I said after a moment's thought. "The whole thing happened years before my time, and with mixed results as you can see. It's how my grandmother

Lachesis always talked about it, as though the spinnerettes weren't really alive—I guess I picked it up from her."

"Have I mentioned recently how very screwed up your family is? Especially your grandmother and her sisters?" Melchior got up and went to walk around the dead spinnerette, leaving the job of picking glass out of my hand to Haemun, who had produced a pair of tweezers from . . . well, somewhere.

Lachesis isn't really my grandmother. There are actually quite a number of generations between the middle Fate and me, but no one sane could argue that the great sprawling family of the Greek gods is anything other than monumentally screwed up. Witness Eris's little game of psychologist. Or, more to the proximate point, the fact that the Fates still hadn't publicly acknowledged that the various webgoblins, webtrolls, and webpixies are fully autonomous individuals. An awful lot of Melchior's friends and relations had also been "surplused" by my grandmother and her sisters over the years.

"Do you want to jump in here?" I asked Fenris. I wanted to distract myself from the way Haemun's sharp little tugs seemed to transmit themselves all the way up my arm, as though he were actually pulling yard-long threads out of my flesh. "Melchior's absolutely right."

"Nope." He wrinkled his nose. "My father is the god of mischief. My mother is a Jotun. My brother is a world-girdling snake. My sister is *literally* half-dead. I don't throw stones at anybody's family. The 'kill' question was strictly for clarification's sake. I want to make sure I understand what's really going on around here." With his nose, he indicated the corpse. "If these things don't work for Fate anymore, whose side are they on?"

I shrugged. "Necessity, maybe. At least the only one I've had dealings with was." The thought gave me a nasty little chill. "Back then, it saved my life. Now . . ."

"Now we have to wonder if the goddess that really runs our MythOS wants us dead," interjected Melchior.

"Well, that's no—" Fenris gagged abruptly, swallowed noisily, then started coughing. "Oh hell. Not this again."

The coughs got harsher and harsher, quickly reverting to gagging. Tail down, and looking more than a little embarrassed, the giant wolf turned away from me and quietly threw up—splash, thud. The raw chaos that served as Fenris's answer to stomach acid immediately began eating a hole in the marble floor, while the severed hand that came up with it just lay there and twitched for several seconds. Finally, Laginn rolled over onto his palm and walked toward the spinnerette, leaving little smoking fingerprints in his wake.

"I wish you'd warn me before you do that," Fenris said to the hand. "That's the second time we've made a mess in Ravirn's home."

"Don't worry about it," I replied. "Raven House seems to self-repair."

"Yeah, right, it does," humphed Haemun, as he kept working on my hand.

Laginn seemed fascinated by the spinnerette—walking around and around the corpse. Then he stopped, and it started to circle him. Or maybe that was just the room spinning. Oh. Morphine and blood loss. Right.

Good night, Gracie.

When the world came back, I found that it had put me neatly away in my very own bed and tucked the covers in around my chin. Very considerate of it.

My room is on the second floor of Raven House and about three times as big as I would have picked out for myself if it had been a front-brain decision. Like the rest of the house, the décor is all black and green, with living moss where someone sensible might have picked out a carpet, and walls of gem-quality malachite. In recent months the ceiling has transformed itself into some sort of light-absorbing black stone pinpricked with about a zillion naturally phosphorescent spots that perfectly mimic the constellations of the night sky as they appear at midnight on midsummer's eve. The furnishings are simple, stark almost—sort of IKEA meets and starts dating really expensive tropical hardwoods, and together they move into an old Spanish mission.

The room has two lanais, or balconies if you prefer, though the Hawaiian word is more versatile. One faces the center of the island and the bulk of the mountains to the south. The other looks west over the bay. At the moment, a turn of my head in that direction showed the low-hanging sun above the waters. The door was open, and the evening breeze felt cool on my sweaty forehead.

Melchior had returned to laptop shape and settled himself on the nightstand. The steady dim/bright/dim cycle of his indicator lights told me he was sleeping, though he'd left his lid open—a clear invitation to wake him when I got there myself. I paused before doing so to admire my handiwork. I'd built his current laptop body from my own specs, rather than following one of Lachesis's recipes as I had for Melchior 1.0, and I was pretty proud of the results.

He is currently the multiverse's only quantum-processing, webgoblin, subnotebook—less than half an inch thick and weighing in at just under a pound. His top surface is a very pale blue with an outline of his face etched into it, an outline that doubles as an exterior monitor. He is deeper blue underneath, with loops of LEDs like dragon scales that throw off an eerie glow.

I'd given him bands of blue anodized aluminum around the edges, and surrounded his screen with a frame of brushed aluminum broken only by the blue goblin-head logo on the bottom right. His keyboard was a block of underlit white surrounded by more blue aluminum. A goblin-head trackpad sat beneath that, and I tapped the right ear to bring him awake. The motion brought a twinge from somewhere deep under the bandages wrapping my right hand.

Whazup, printed itself across the screen, and the logo blinked blearily at me—all a put-on, of course.

I grinned and carefully typed, *Me for one. Did I miss anything?* One-handing it wasn't much fun, but neither was it a totally unfamiliar experience.

Not really. You didn't want to be awake for the stitches anyway. Fenris backtracked the spinnerette to a fresh faerie ring, which cut the trail dead. We decided to leave the next move till you woke up. How do you feel?

I paused to stretch my right hand, then started typing. It involved a lot of backspacing but ultimately came out as: *Pretty good actually. There's some pain, and the way that stitches tug when you move them always creeps me out a little bit, but I seem to be able to straighten my fingers all right. Give me a chance to take a bath, and I'll be ready to go have a look at that faerie ring. I'd rather not have any rogue rings on the island. Can you shift over and give me some help with bagging my hand?*

"Done," said Melchior, flickering from laptop to goblin in an instant. The quantum shift was less elegant but much faster than his old morphing transformation.

The bath was wonderful even if I did have to take it with my injured hand duct-taped into a plastic sack. Once I was out, dry, and free of the sack, I hit the closet for a fresh set of motorcycle leathers. I don't get to ride my bike nearly as much as I used to, but I really like the armor factor. Especially since the Kevlar lining that Tech-Sec puts in all their stuff will stop small-caliber bullets. By the time I got all geared up, the sun had touched the horizon, which meant putting the hurry on if we wanted to get this done tonight. Kauai, without people, gets damned dark after the sun goes down.

We made a nice little group of weirdos on our way down

to the faerie ring, even without Haemun. One giant wolf with a disembodied hand riding on his back, one knee-high bald blue goblin peering out of a new Tech-Sec laptop bag, and me—a pointy-eared, cat-eyed, goth refugee from the Houses of Fate. The ring itself had opened about a mile from the house in the place where the Tropical Taco van used to park on most of the main bands of Decision Loci that make up the Greek MythOS. The ring itself was a neat circle of taro plants in the middle of an ankle-deep pond.

"What's the plan?" asked Fenris.

"Enter the circle and wing it." I got a good grip on a handful of his fur—lose contact with someone in a faerie ring, and you may never find them again.

"Why is it that 'wing it' is always part of the plan with you?" Melchior glared at me from his seat in the bag.

I pointed at my face with my good hand. "Hacker."

"I know that, but sometimes I feel like it might be nice to at least think about the next step."

"I have, and this is it." I stepped forward into the ring and elsewhere.

Faerie rings are a by-product of the chaos that divides the multiverse, intrusions of raw magic into the workaday world. Though no two rings appear exactly alike, they are all a part of the sea of Primal Chaos from which everything came, and so, in a fundamental way, there is actually only one ring. Step into any ring, and you have entered *the* master ring. The real questions are where and how and *if* you will ever step out again.

As I entered, I drew the power of the Raven around me, a power of and over chaos, reaching through it to twist the ring to my will. I had once used the same power to summon the world of Raven House into existence. Or possibly, to take me through to a world that already contained the refuge I needed. The result was the same either way. Now I commanded the ring to find the place the spinnerette had entered and to bring me there.

* * *

The sunset jungle vanished, replaced by . . . disorientation. I stood in a circle of blackened silver spoons atop a slightly larger circle of congealed yellow fire, the whole surrounded by the endless churning irrationality of the Primal Chaos. Direction and motion ceased to mean anything. There was no way to tell if I was hanging upside down from a star or standing atop a thrown stone skipping across the great sea of beginnings.

"Where are we?" demanded Fenris in a voice that held more of the animal than anything I'd heard from him before, as much wolfish whimpering as words.

I had trouble focusing enough to answer. Chaos hits me like a combination of strong drink and pure bottled happy. I stepped to the edge of the ring and peered out over the side of our tiny platform. Direction reasserted itself.

We were up. What lay on the underside of the circle was down. Best of all, I knew right where we were. Walking on the sun. Castle Discord is an ever-changing island floating in chaos. Most of the time, it pleases Discord for her home to have a sun in the form of a fiery golden apple. Our ring was on the back of Discord's sun. But how had the spinnerette gotten here?

No sooner had I formed the question than the ring offered its answer. This time we stood in a tiny circle of corroded copper coins on the shores of a great black river. A little shiver ran through me as I recognized our point of arrival.

"Hades." The dark walls of the multiverse's largest infinite security prison loomed just across the river.

"Is that where we played Risk?" Fenris pointed with his nose.

"It is," replied Melchior. "Someone standing right here would have had a perfect shot at Ravirn's back."

"And afterward that 'someone' could have paid my fare with one of the coins from this ring." I didn't like the implications of the spinnerette's route thus far. Not at all. "Five will get you ten our next stop is Garbage Faerie."

"That's a sucker's bet," replied Melchior, "at any odds and even with money found on the banks of the Styx."

For years, the only ring entrance to Garbage Faerie had opened out of a circle of crushed beer cans on the slope above Ahllan's home. Now both slope and home were gone, devoured by the chaos I had unleashed in my duel with Nemesis. So was Ahllan, likewise devoured by something I had unleashed, though in another time and place.

With Ahllan's ring closed forever, I had opened a new one yesterday to take us to the near shore of the Styx and Cerberus, a circle of three-dimensional circuit-board sculptures of forget-me-nots. Someone else had built the one that brought us back to Garbage Faerie now.

"I think somebody really doesn't like you," said Melchior.

I had to agree. We had arrived high in the canopy of the graffiti-oak forest that lay not far to the west of the crater where Ahllan's home had stood. The broad limb provided a perfect sniper's post. That was grim, but not nearly so grim as the circle of crucified ravens that made up the faerie ring. Each was pinned by its wings to the simple cross hilt of a short sword driven deep into the limb. The only good thing about the tableau was that the nature of faerie rings meant the dead ravens had probably been spun into existence without ever actually having lived. Even so, I felt an anger building in my heart at the sight.

"The dislike is mutual, Mel. I'd very much like to have a word with whoever set that spinnerette to this task."

I reached into the faerie ring again, commanding it to take me back another step. Nothing happened at first, and I felt great resistance, as though some other power of chaos opposed my will. In fighting the resistance, I realized that each step of our path back through the spinnerette's past had come a little harder. Perhaps we were finally getting close. I pushed. Hard.

Breakthrough.

The bottom dropped out. The four of us were tumbling through darkness, falling away from a bright ring of candles and black frosting roses circling the rim of an enormous cake stuck upside down to the ceiling of a great cavern. Across the center of the cake, written in black frosting, was the legend "Happy Deathday, Raven. Die, Die, Die!"

"Boss—" Whatever Melchior wanted to say was lost as he ducked down and zipped the case over his head just before we plunged deep into icy water.

I let go of Fenris so that I could swim. He immediately pulled away from me, heading back toward the surface. I kicked after him, but no matter how hard I paddled, I just kept sinking. I told myself to stay calm and *think, damn it*.

That was when something hard and heavy clipped me between the shoulder blades. It felt like a bowling ball rolling up my spine and drove the breath out of me in one huge gasp. My little remaining composure left me with the last of my air. I'd have screamed if I had anything left. But all I could do was watch the bright bubbles shooting up and away from me. All but one, that is.

A single silvery bubble hung between me and the others, began moving back toward me even. As it got closer, I saw a dark and distorted reflection of myself growing on its surface.

What in the . . . Oh shit!

I threw my left arm up protectively in the instant before the falling bubble would have caught me full in the face. The impact still broke my nose. Blood gushed out into the

water, darkening my vision. Somehow I managed not to
suck in a lungful of water despite my anguish, but if I didn't
get air soon, I would die.

I looked around frantically, hoping for some inspiration.
All I saw was the bubble, which slipped up a few yards and
off to my left. It turned as it moved, somehow giving the
impression it was staring at me like some disembodied eye,
despite its lack of features. I wanted to ignore it, to focus
solely on the more immediate problem of drowning, but I
didn't dare let it out of my sight. Besides, it reminded me of
something . . . though I couldn't think what. Then it began
to rapidly expand, and I had it.

The chamber of the abacuses on Necessity's world. A
silver ball stained with streaks like smoke had attacked Tisiphone and me right before the abacuses went berserk and
tossed us all into the Norse MythOS. The ball had taken
everything an enraged Fury could throw at it without so
much as a scratch. This was the same one, or its identical
cousin, and . . . it was coming straight for me.

CHAPTER THREE

I jackknifed and dove. The ball passed above me close enough that its wake tugged at my feet. I kicked harder. The edges of my vision began to darken from oxygen starvation. It was just the message I needed.

Reaching inward, I found a second darkness in the shadow of the Raven. It enfolded me in black wings as I bent my will on the frozen chaos that makes up my physical form. After my destruction in the duel with Hades, I had shaped myself anew from the raw stuff that churns in the place between the worlds, creating a body that was 99.9 percent as real as anyone else's.

I used the remaining .1 percent now as an entry into shape-hacking, like a command line for my own personal reality. It was a sort of time travel, really, taking a magical snapshot of the current configuration of my body and physically reverting it to an earlier version when I had worn another skin. It was exquisitely painful, severing the bonds between the atoms of my body, rearranging them all, and creating new links, all in the instant be-

tween intent and the universe's catching on and calling
me to account.

Three things made this time different from almost
every other time I'd been forced to shed my normal shape.
First and foremost, I did not become the embodiment of
the Raven, shifting rather into the skin of the giant otter
shape I'd learned in my encounter with the Midgard Serpent. Second, I kept one thing stable from form to form,
the shoulder bag bearing Melchior—Tech-Sec's bullet- and
waterproof laptop-protection system. Third, I added an entirely new twist, converting some of my body's mass into a
reasonable facsimile of the air I'd had in my lungs the last
time I took this shape. I would be a slightly skinnier Ravirn
when I returned to myself. *If* I returned to myself.

The thing I was coming to think of as the giant evil
gazing ball of doom took another run at me. This time, I
twisted aside as easily as Loki evading the truth. While
the ball was recovering, I started heading for the surface.
Whatever magic had been responsible for my earlier un-
stoppable sinking, I'd shed it with my skin. The ball and I
played tag all the way up, but it simply couldn't catch the
otter me. When I finally popped my head out of the water,
the ball followed, shooting high into the air.

It hung there, a featureless, lidless, mirror of an eye
glaring down at me for a couple of seconds. I could feel
malice and a very personal sort of hatred regarding me
from within the sphere, and I fully expected it to take at
least one more shot at me. While I waited, poised to dive
again at the slightest hint of attack, I took my first real look
around.

I was in the center of a dark cavern nearly as big as the
one that held Hades. About a hundred yards to my right,
a small island provided the only visible land. What little
light there was came from the upside-down candles embedded in the cake faerie ring high above. I spared a moment to wonder about the mechanics of flames that burned

downward but was distracted when the great mirrored ball suddenly rotated 180 degrees vertically and shot away from me.

It must have been going a hundred miles an hour when it struck dead in the middle of the deathday cake. The faerie ring sent the sphere elsewhere in the very moment of the ring's explosive destruction. Frosting and other debris splattered outward in a wide circle before beginning the long fall to the water below. I took advantage of the intensifying light provided by the falling candles to roll onto my back on the surface and pull my laptop bag onto the tiny dry island of my fuzzy belly.

I expected the lights to go out when the candles hit the water, but, though they quickly began to sink, they kept right on burning. I giggled at the sight—a side effect of the otter transformation. Shapes have consequences, and otters are easily amused.

"Are we all clear, then?" Melchior asked as he poked his head out of the bag.

"I think so. I do, I do, I do!" I followed that with more giggling, which Melchior waited out. "Sorry, Mel. If you'll whistle me up some night vision, I'll see if I can't find Fenris and get us out of here."

"Fair enough." He whistled the binary for "Redeye." "If he's got any sense at all, he's on the island."

He ducked back into the bag and rezipped the top behind him. Then I flipped over and headed for the island, where I could make a new faerie ring.

"Now what?" asked Fenris.

The great wolf sat across the table from me in the inner portion of the lanai. Haemun had prepared us all a lovely dinner of fresh-caught ono on a bed of rice with asparagus. A half dozen bottles of sauvignon blanc—served in glasses or bowls depending on the drinking apparatus of the diner—

rounded out the meal. My injured hand and nose were both much improved by the healing effects chaos had on me because of the several transformations and faerie rings I had been through. Even so, I wanted nothing more than a couple of days of peace to recover. Days I wasn't likely to get.

"That's an interesting question," I replied. "Your family's conflict with the Aesir was not the only god war worrying me last week."

"Was it really only last week? Oy." Melchior took a long drink of his wine.

Laginn bobbed a lazy yes from his place at the table. Though he neither drank nor ate, the hand genuinely seemed to enjoy soaking in a big goblet of wine.

"It's been ten days exactly since gazing ball one sent us all off to play the starring role in the Ragnarok pinball machine," I replied.

"God war?" prompted Fenris.

"Right, sorry. While we were in your pantheoverse, a number of intrusions from this one suggested that whatever it was that sent us your way was part of some larger problem or conflict within Necessity."

"Necessity being your version of MimirNet?"

"Exactly. The elevation of my former girlfriend from programmer extraordinaire in House Clotho to Fury is a really bad sign on the Necessity front and one reason I'd been hoping to avoid having to plunge into the mess, at least for a little while." I sighed. "But the fact that I've already had a spinnerette try to kill me suggests my days of playing Switzerland have already ended. I just wish I knew who sent it and what the hell that gazing-ball thing represents. The cake faerie ring was obviously built as a trap for me, and if it hadn't been destroyed, I might have been able to follow it another step or two back or get something else out of it. Since that avenue is closed, I need to—"

"Set another place for dinner," interrupted a voice from the outside.

I about jumped out of my skin, which elicited a laugh from the woman standing in the archway. She was short and red-haired, with deep smile lines around her eyes and at the corners of her mouth. She had something of Madeline Kahn about her and something of Catherine O'Hara. But every bit of her appearance was a matter of artifice. A goddess can look however she chooses, and she was every inch a goddess. Thalia. The Muse of Bucolic Comedy and my grandmother. Why, yes, I do descend from Fate and Slapstick. It explains a lot, doesn't it? I rose to make introductions.

"Fenris, this is my grandmother, the goddess of off-color humor, among other things. Thalia, my friend Fenris, sometime Norse god of hunger."

"Shake?" she said, extending her hand.

Fenris rolled his eyes but offered his paw.

"Laginn, Thalia. Thalia, this is Laginn, formerly the hand of Tyr, Norse God of War, now Fenris's, uh . . . How do you introduce an undead hand?"

"Well," my grandmother began with a twinkle in her eye, "in polite company, disembodied hands may be referred to as 'the Sinister' or 'the Dexter,' as would be appropriate here, generally being introduced only after entities with heads and/or faces. Undead hands attached to hosts are rarely introduced individually but may be referenced immediately after the introduction of the host in special circumstances. Or was that a rhetorical question?"

"Thank you, Miss Zombie Manners." Melchior grinned.

"*Friend* will do," said the wolf.

"Special friend?" Thalia asked with a wicked lift of her eyebrow—I'd inherited that one.

"No." Fenris's answer came out flat and quiet.

"But he's such a handsome little devil." Thalia reached out and shook Laginn.

When she set him down, he looked rather befuddled

by the whole thing. Haemun bustled up just then with a chair and all the other accoutrements of dinner for Thalia. I waited until she'd settled before leaning back and giving her my best skeptical look—the one with that raised eyebrow.

"What's up?" I asked. "You normally don't go for the low-hanging fruit like that. *Hand*some? Shake? You're up to something."

"Me? No. No, not at all." She nodded vigorously, contradicting her words. "What makes you say that?"

"I don't get it," said Fenris, his ears lowering in confusion.

"Then you don't want it bad enough," replied Thalia. While she spoke, she pointed at me, then tapped her ear, before making little dancing-spider motions.

"Wha—oh." I shifted gears as I realized what Thalia was telling me—there was a bug in my house. "Joke's on me, I guess."

We spent the next twenty minutes playing polite-but-empty conversational games for the benefit of anyone listening in while we ate. It was excruciating.

Finally, Thalia rose from the table. "Why don't you give your old grandmother the tour?" she asked, though she knew her way around well enough.

"Of course." I came around to her side of the table and took her hand in the crook of my arm. "Where would you like to start?"

"Anywhere is fine, child."

As we slowly circled the lower level of the house, Thalia kept wrinkling her nose and sniffing the air very quietly. After a second round past the dinner table, she shook her head and indicated the stairs with her eyes. More sniffing as we made our way through the public areas of the upper floor. When we reached my bedroom, she abruptly stiffened and slowed her pace.

"How *does* Haemun put up with you?" she demanded.

"This place is a sty. You must never put a single item of clothing away properly. Look at this!"

She pulled me over to the chair beside the bed where I'd dumped the tweed suit Eris had inflicted on me. She lifted the jacket by its collar, swinging it this way and that. Then she sniffed it here and there in a way that rather reminded me of how I'd decided if something was safe to wear in my college days.

"That's strange," she whispered to herself. "How did . . . Ah! Clever Discord."

"This is a laundry disaster." She handed the jacket to me. "It's going to need special attention. Hang on to it while I run and explain things to Haemun."

While I waited, I made a very thorough inspection of the jacket. I found nothing the least bit out of the ordinary. Well, nothing beyond the fact that Eris had ruined a perfectly good set of leathers when she transformed them into tweeds for her psychologist shtick. Thalia returned a few moments later, followed by a baffled-looking Haemun carrying a big glass jar labeled "sugar."

It was empty, but not for long. Thalia took the jacket from me and somehow managed to stuff it into the empty jar. When she screwed the lid back on, I could see that someone had scratched a short program in hexadecimal into the lid—a spell of sealing and silence. I started to open my mouth then, but she put a finger to her lips and held the jar up to her ear, shaking it once or twice before finally nodding.

"There. We can speak freely now. Haemun, would you take that and put it someplace safe?"

"What's going on?" I asked, as the satyr departed with the jar. "And what did Eris do about it that was so clever?"

"You've got a spy in your house, and she changed your clothes for you."

"A spy? Not a bug?" I decided to let the Eris part of the

question rest a moment since Thalia's initial statement only confused me more.

"In this case, they're one and the same. 'The itsy bitsy spider climbed up the waterspout.'"

"A tiny spinnerette? In my clothing? And one that managed to hitch a ride with me somehow? That's hard to believe. It would have had to happen between the time I got home and the time Discord . . . No. No, it wouldn't. Oh, I'm an idiot."

"I can't dispute that based on current evidence," said Thalia, "but would you care to let your dear old grandmum in on the specifics?"

"I put the spinnerette there myself, back in the Norse MythOS. It arrived in a piece of machine coral of the sort Necessity's been migrating herself into—next-generation quantum-processing technology. It looked dead, or nearly so. I felt sorry for the little thing, lost so far from home."

"Back up about six steps," she said. "I couldn't ask about your new guests at dinner, and you were all smart enough to avoid the subject once I'd given you the bug note, but I'm thinking I really need to know a lot more about what's going on here. Especially this Norse MythOS stuff."

"And I need to know about what's been happening here while I was away. I'll tell my story first if you'll answer me two questions. One, what did Eris do that was so clever?"

"When she transformed your leathers into tweeds, she got rid of the pocket you'd put the spinnerette in without getting rid of the spinnerette. That effectively trapped the creature within the fabric of the new suit. Next question."

I still didn't entirely understand the mechanism employed, but I knew enough now to move on. "How did you know about the spinnerette?"

"I didn't know for sure, but I had been shown reason to believe it was very likely."

"Shown? By who?" I asked.

"Persephone, but it's a long story, and I want to hear yours first."

"All right. Let's rejoin the others. I'm sure they're as curious as I am."

"More so, actually," said Melchior from the doorway. "What in Hades' name is going on up here?"

"Funny you should mention Hades," said Thalia, "and for once I don't mean ha-ha."

Melchior sighed. "It's going to be one of those days, isn't it?"

Thalia tapped her lips thoughtfully as I wound my story to a close. "If what you're saying about this little jaunt of yours is true, then all the other pantheons are real, too. That's very interesting. I wonder who knows besides Necessity and you."

"I imagine you could have some very interesting conversations with the Titans about that one," I said. "If you could get into Tartarus to see them."

"Which reminds me, I'd be very careful whom I told the whole story, if I were you," said Thalia. "That bit about the Norse Fate naming you the Final Titan might not go over so well with Zeus, among others."

I snorted. "It's all just more manipulative Fate bullshit as far as I'm concerned. Portentous lies for the aggrandizement of colossal egos. I was raised on the stuff, and I'm done with it."

"Don't dismiss the words of the Norns so easily," said Fenris. "They can have deep costs. Truth matters little if others believe the lies."

I thought of the magical cord that had bound Fenris to an island for a thousand years and nodded. "Point taken. But enough about me and the Norse gods. What brought you here, Thalia?"

"This." She produced a slender red memory crystal

veined with pink. "How far do you trust Dexter and the Wolf here?"

"We can duck out if you'd prefer." Fenris's ears and tail sagged.

"No, it's fine." I put my hand on his shoulder. "I trust you." I turned my attention back to Thalia. "Why do you ask?"

"Because the mere existence of what's on this crystal reveals a number of secrets I don't think should be shared with anyone."

"So why are you showing them to me?" I asked. "You're my grandmother and all, but so is Lachesis. Family loyalty isn't exactly this pantheon's longest suit."

Thalia laughed ruefully. "True enough, and, as much as I love you, I don't know that I would be showing this to *you* if it were up to me."

"Can we all stop fencing and just look at the thing since we're going to anyway?" Melchior rubbed his temples. "You do realize that as a whole your extended family must spend ten times as much energy on double and triple crosses as it saves by dint of same. Doesn't it ever strike you all as the least bit tedious?" His eyes darted from Thalia to me and back again, then he sighed and threw up his arms. "No, of course it doesn't. That's probably half the fun. Why am I even asking?"

"The sound of one hand clapping?" asked Thalia. "No, probably not, and too absurdist for most senses of humor at that. Oh well, were you done?"

Melchior nodded, and she handed him the crystal. He popped it into his mouth, then flickered from goblin to laptop shape. On his screen a dialogue box opened.

Scanning volume for viruses . . . Holy shit!

He returned to goblin form. "Persephone doesn't half mess around, does she?" Melchior's voice was muffled by the crystal tucked into his cheek. Given his reaction, I was quite surprised he hadn't spit it across the room.

"What's up?" I asked.

"Persephone put the source code for the Necessity doomsday virus on this thing, along with about thirty variations of same, and major nastiness designed for most of the other god systems. She's even found a way to get a virus to jump from Hades' personal desktop machine to the totally disconnected systems that run the business of the underworld. None of it's active code, but my virus checker just about had a heart attack when it hit the file tree where it's all stored." He gave Thalia a hard look. "This stuff makes Scorched Earth look like kindergarten in the suburbs, and that's the virus Ravirn crashed the mweb with way back when." He turned my way. "If this ever gets a wider audience, you and Eris can both hand your computer bad-ass hats straight over to the real evil genius. Why is Persephone offering all of this to us?"

"She thinks you might need it," answered Thalia, looking far more sober than usual. "Play the video, and you'll see why."

Melchior nodded and shifted shape again. A picture opened on his screen. Persephone sitting in a garden under the open sky—after her long ordeal in Hades, she refused to allow a roof of any kind over her head. The goddess looked into the camera and raised the corners of her lips in a very good imitation of a smile. If I hadn't known her as well as I did, I might even have believed it.

"Ravirn," she said, "I'm sorry to impose on you yet again after the great service you've already done me, but the very thought of what I'm about to show you fills me with a dread that makes it very hard for me to act with restraint. I don't want to have to do something about this, so I am asking you to address it if you would."

It was my turn to whistle. The last time Persephone had acted without restraints, she had very nearly destroyed the whole damn multiverse. Coupled with a request for my help and the plethora of doomsday viruses she had just shown herself to possess, it was both the gentlest and most terrifying threat anyone had ever made to me. I glanced a question at my grandmother.

Thalia nodded. "She's deadly serious."

Melchior had paused the playback during the interplay—better than TiVo, that little guy. Now he started it again.

Persephone whistled something long and complex and self-harmonizing. It was a subtle piece of coding and one I definitely wanted to listen to again later for study purposes. The spell resulted in the formation of a black picture frame in the air beside her. The area within initially showed only static.

"I won't watch this again," she said in a voice edged with jagged ice, "but you must." Then she rose and walked out of the picture as the camera moved in tight on the contents of the frame so that we were watching a picture within a picture.

The static seemed to fold in on itself, reaching into elsewhere. As it did so, a haze like heat distortion shimmered into being in front of the black frame—a typical symptom of some sort of really heavy-duty encryption. Whatever was at the other end of the spell, Persephone truly didn't want it finding its way back to her. When the picture came clear, I understood why.

"Oh hell," I whispered.

"Hades, actually," said Thalia.

"From where I sit on Hades' personal hate list, there's not a whole lot of difference between the two," I replied.

The frame provided a window into Hades' office in the underworld. It had changed radically since my last visit. Not surprising since that visit had resulted in the utter destruction of Hades' headquarters complex. But even though the positioning of the camera—probably a monitor mount—hid much of the room from me, I recognized the place instantly. The presence of the death god in his pretentious office chair was only the most obvious giveaway.

Even without Hades as a pointer I would have recognized the horrible deadness of the lands beyond the Styx.

Our view showed the god sitting at an angle to the screen, giving us a two-thirds view of his face. He was nodding thoughtfully. Behind him, a large open window looked over a pier on the river Lethe. As I watched, a young man walked hesitantly out to the end of the pier and stared into the water. He wore a sort of grayed-out version of the T-shirt-and-jeans uniform of the college set, and his shoulders slumped with the classic dejection of the dead.

"That's *very* interesting," Hades said to someone off-screen, drawing my attention back to the foreground.

I realized then that I'd been avoiding looking at Hades. He was snake skinny, with dark, smoky hair that moved on its own and skin drawn too tight over his bones. His flesh had something of smoke to it, too, a tenuous quality, as though it might drift away between one moment and the next, revealing his true self—a skeleton that only played at being a man.

"My principal thought you might feel that way, all things considered." The voice answering Hades was a woman's and very tense. It sounded familiar, too, though I couldn't immediately place it.

"Is the damage really so extensive?" asked Hades, and there was a hunger that lurked just beneath the surface of his words.

"Irreparable," said a second woman. This one had a faint accent that sounded as though she didn't have quite the right vocal apparatus for human speech. "She knows she cannot ever properly resume her role and thus must find another to take her throne."

Hades leaned back and steepled his hands, too obviously working at projecting confidence and limited interest. The Lord of the Dead clearly hadn't had to do much bargaining over the long years of his reign. The immediate question his attitude raised was who had something that he wanted that much.

"I have a hard time imagining her retirement," said Hades at last.

"So does she," replied the second woman, the one with the inhuman accent.

"Am I the only candidate?" asked Hades.

"Don't be an idiot," replied the first—more familiar-sounding—woman, and I almost knew her then. "You are one of four. This is by way of a preliminary interview for a tough job."

Hades' jaw clenched. "Whom do I have to convince? Her?" He nodded straight ahead. "Or you?" Again the nod, this time a bit to the right.

"You need to convince my mother, of course," said the first voice, and I would have had it then even without the edge of a green wing that momentarily slipped into the picture.

Megaera, the Fury with hair and wings of ship-devouring seaweed. In turn, that meant the trio must be talking about Necessity. My back clenched. Every muscle from the backs of my knees to my neck contracted all in an instant at the thought of Necessity handing over her role as the Fate of the Gods to *anyone*, much less Hades.

It would take about ten minutes and forty-seven seconds from the time he took over to the instant when my eternal-torment regimen started. The only reason it would take even that long was that the first ten minutes would be devoted to reclaiming Persephone and . . . I shuddered. It didn't bear thinking about. I found myself looking past Hades to his window, staring at the boy on the end of the pier again rather than looking at the death god. The boy seemed mesmerized by the water flowing beneath him.

I couldn't blame him. Putting Hades aside, I wasn't too keen about any of the other likely candidates for taking on the role of Necessity 2.0 either. The second woman had said there were four. That could only mean the pole powers. Fate would hand me over to Hades in an instant. Eris I love as a sister—a completely psychotic and extremely dangerous sister. No one in their right mind would want to live in a universe ruled by Discord. Zeus? Zeus I might be able to live with, though that would likely put Athena in the role now held by the Furies—divine enforcer and cosmic sys-admin—and if she had her druthers, she'd skin me slowly. No, none of the candidates was particularly good for team Raven.

"Is there any way for me to sweeten the pot?" asked Hades, dragging my attention back to him and the office. "Special favors Necessity needs to have done before the handover? Things I could help *either of you* with?"

"That sounds suspiciously like an attempt at bribery," said Megaera.

Hades nodded and opened his hands wide. "Is that a problem? Because I could always rescind the offer if you'd prefer."

Megaera stepped forward into the frame. I could see her head, about half of her torso, and one poisonous green wing. She looked tense enough to kill—just like always.

"I'm not entirely sure I'm comfortable with the direction this conversation is taking," she said.

"Why not?" asked Hades. "If you don't believe that Zeus and the others will make similar offers, you don't know them. Besides, don't you think that your dear, dear mother would want to make sure you're taken care of in the new regime?" He widened his eyes. "Unless you were planning on retiring as well? Surely not. With your work ethic?"

"Of course not," said Megaera, visibly startled. "Who would handle all of the computer details and enforcement duties?"

"Well," said Hades, sounding profoundly unctuous, "I imagine that depends on who takes up the reins. Zeus would certainly install Athena in that seat, and I frankly doubt Eris would want any administration at all."

"Fate would keep us on," said Megaera.

"To be sure," replied Hades, "but only as *complete* puppets. Is that really what you want?"

"What we want doesn't matter." Megaera glanced back toward her offscreen companion. "Right?"

"I don't know for certain," said the voice. "I can only speak with Necessity in special circumstances. But I can't imagine that she would want you cast aside. She loves *all* her children so very much. Always has."

There was something decidedly off about the way the voice said "all." It made my teeth itch.

"Oh, well said." Hades turned and grinned at the Fury. "Listen to your companion, Megaera."

"She's not my companion. Neither is she a friend. She is—"

"The voice of your *mother*," interjected the other, "but only in some things."

Megaera submissively bowed her head for a second, then nodded. I *really* wanted to see who belonged to that voice.

"So," said Hades, "*is* there anything I can do for you? Anything at all? You need but ask."

Megaera relaxed her shoulders and mutely shook her head.

"Are you sure you can't think of something?" he asked. "Because I have a few thoughts there. Don't you wonder what's become of your sister Tisiphone? What the Raven has done with her? I could possibly help you to find out. Extract some information from him."

"We have our own window into Raven House," said the alien voice. "One of my . . . little sisters is there, providing a feed."

"I was thinking of something more direct and—"

Hades was interrupted by a chiming sound. "Hang on a moment."

He waved Megaera back out of sight of the camera, then turned directly toward the screen and tapped the button on his mouse. A picture opened within the corner of the one we were watching, a tiny window showing us what Hades was seeing on his computer. Zeus stood there, in all his buff, bronzed, frat-boy glory. Athena stood beside him, looking even more deliberately drab and invisible than usual—most of the time she eschews flash in favor of the power of going unnoticed.

"Hades," boomed Zeus. "So good to see a brother looking so good. We don't talk nearly often enough. My fault really. It's always business, business, business here on Mount Olympus. You know how it is, right?" He winked. "Anyway, I want you to pop on up and have a drink or three with me. Athena has had certain things about the situation with Necessity and that Raven boy brought to her attention, things that I thought we really ought to discuss."

Chaos and Discord! Didn't anyone have anything better to think about than me? I know I did.

"When can you get here?" said Zeus.

Hades nodded. "May I ask about your sources first? I'm kind of busy at the moment."

Athena looked sideways at Zeus. He nodded, and the goddess of wisdom reluctantly opened her hand, creating an image of Cerice in the space above it. Great, my ex was about to sell me out to the powers that be . . . again. I leaned forward then and began very gently smacking my forehead against the table.

"Does this get worse?" I asked Thalia. "Because if it does, I don't want to know about it."

"There's still a tiny bit more that you need to see."

"All right." I sighed and sat up.

Melchior restarted the playback, which he had again paused while I was distracted.

"Oh my," said Hades. "Yes, I think I'd better come through ASAP. Just give me a few minutes to clear my calendar."

"Agreed," said Zeus, and flickered out.

"Come see this," said Hades.

Megaera came around to stare over Hades' shoulder at the screen. She was followed a moment later by—

"What is *that*?" interjected Fenris.

"Spinnerette," replied Thalia.

"Really?" asked the wolf.

I understood his confusion. This one took a very different form from the spider-centaurs Necessity had usually employed in the past. A twelve-foot scorpion with a woman's upper body and head where its stinger should have been. The scorpion part of the creature was the exact shade of poison ivy.

The tail would have run about eight feet if it hadn't ended in a woman. It was deep green for the first three feet, then slowly paled as it climbed the belly and breasts of the loosely human female form that tipped it. Her face and shoulders were an olive shade that wouldn't have looked out of place in any city in Greece, and her hair was short and black.

Her arms mirrored her torso, shading steadily toward the intense poisonous green of the scorpion as your view moved downward. The backs of her hands had some of the same chitinous quality as the main scorpion body, and her middle fingers ended in wicked, hollow claws. Adding to her gruesome aspect were the sharp vampirelike fangs at the corners of her mouth. A feature that probably explained her inhuman accent.

"What is that you wanted to show us?" she asked as she slid in beside Megaera.

"This." Hades tapped a button and quickly replayed the video call from Zeus.

When it hit the picture of Cerice, Megaera growled,

"Damned fake Fury. She knows she's not supposed to move on the Raven yet. We're going to have words over this."

Megaera lashed out with one clawed hand as though she wanted to gut Cerice's image. A hole opened in the wake of her claws, and she and the spinnerette stepped through into elsewhere, leaving Hades staring at the screen. Even though I knew he couldn't see me, his dead eyes gave me the twitchies.

He rose from the desk then, gathering up a briefcase and some other items, before stepping out of range of the camera. Beyond his office window, the boy on the pier took two long steps and dove into the river Lethe.

CHAPTER FOUR

The image on Melchior's screen froze. The boy in the background of the picture hung in the air above the waters of forgetfulness, his arms out in the beginning of a swan dive. Seconds ticked past, with the boy coming no closer to the end of all memory. Then, as if nothing had happened, the video started forward again. With a great splash, he vanished from sight and self—an idea that had its appeal. Take a leisurely swim and a nice long drink of the Lethe, and you get to walk away from all of your problems forever.

Static ripped across the screen, closing off my window into Hades before the screen went black. Persephone did not return. Nor did I expect her to; she'd made her message clear enough. I needed to stop Hades for my own sake as much as hers, and possibly Necessity's as well.

"Will you do it?" asked Thalia.

I nodded. Persephone's request clinched things though I'd almost certainly have gotten involved without it. If for no other reason than needing Necessity at least partially functional to get me back to Tisiphone.

An expression of profound relief spread across Thalia's face. "Thank you. She's got no brakes and all the tools she needs to tear the whole universe apart."

"And I wouldn't blame her for it in the least," I answered. "If I were her, looking at that, I wouldn't have called me. I'd have gone direct to the part where you hit the big red doomsday button."

Thalia lifted her brow and tilted the corner of her mouth in a way that simultaneously suggested dawning understanding and continuing confusion.

"You know," she said. "I might be wrong about that."

"Wrong about what?" Melchior returned to goblin shape to speak.

"The part about her not having any brakes."

"She nearly destroyed everything!" said Melchior.

"Oh, she didn't have any then." Thalia smiled. "But I think maybe she does now. She has one lone brake on her actions, a sort of personal angel that she trusts to make things right, and he's standing right here." She picked up her napkin and folded it into a pair of white wings, which she stuck lightly to my back before drawing a halo of golden light over my head.

"Me?" I shook the halo free, and it dissipated. "No one in their right mind would call me an angel of any kind. That's crazy talk."

"Not at all," said Thalia. "Persephone was Hades' prisoner and victim for thousands of years before you were even born. In all that time, the only members of the whole pantheon who ever did anything to get her out of that hell were her mother, Demeter, and, when Demeter forced him to it, Zeus. Even that was all only at the very beginning. Zeus cut the deal that got Persephone back to Demeter for nine months and left her with Hades for the other three. After that, all anyone did was say, 'Oh, how sad,' and go back to doing their own thing. Then along came Raven.

Oh, I know you didn't set out to help her, but you didn't blame her for what her escape attempt did to you either."

"How could I? She only did what she had to do and—" Thalia's voice rode over mine.

"You got all the initial blame for her doomsday virus, and it nearly got you killed. Then, what did you do when you finally found out the truth? You, who had every right to hate Persephone for what she did to you? Why, you turned right around and went back to Hades, and there you offered up your life to save her from further torment."

"I came out of it all right." I really hated this kind of stuff; it made me sound a hell of a lot more noble than I actually am. "I lived."

"Really?" Thalia opened her eyes wide, and wisps of chaos danced in the depths. "Don't play games with your grandmother, young Raven. You died that day." She conjured up a finger puppet of me and waved it around. "Or the original Ravirn did, at least. He ceased to exist, devoured utterly by the raw stuff of chaos, just like your cousin Moric." She raised her finger and blew on it—the puppet dimmed and vanished in the manner of a blown-out birthday candle.

I looked away. I'd killed Moric, and even though I'd been forced to it, I still regretted it.

"The Raven that remade himself from that same substance may have a lot in common with the Ravirn that was. He may wear the same face, make the same sorts of jokes. Even keep the same company." She glanced at Melchior. "But the eyes of humor look beyond the surface of things. I see you as you really are—a shape of chaos bound by will. I am not fooled by the mask you wear, the illusion of flesh." Thalia leaned forward and pinched my cheek, hard. "And such a sweet illusion it is—a grandmother's joy."

"The hardware may have changed, but Ravirn's operating system is pretty much the same," said Melchior. "That's what really counts. And this version is at least as unstable as the original."

Thalia laughed. "True enough, but is that more of a bug or a feature?"

"I'd call it a core system requirement," said Melchior, slipping into a Groucho Marx accent. "The boy's design specs ain't right, if you know what I mean."

I laughed along with the rest of them, though perhaps more ruefully.

As it all too often did, midnight found me staring at the ceiling. Melchior snoozed away beside the bed in laptop shape, underlining my sleeplessness with his calm. Some of my insomnia comes from the nature of the Raven. The chaos light that lives in my eyes and the way that raw magic rejuvenates me make sleep both harder and less important for me. But I had stronger reasons for insomnia this time.

Tomorrow morning, I would have to step fully back into the madness of life among the Greek gods. I would have to begin to deal with the problems of Necessity and Hades and whatever Cerice was up to with Zeus. Waking would plunge me into the maelstrom. And, though it was utterly irrational, a part of me felt that not going to sleep meant not having to wake up, and that not waking up meant the morning would never come—that by putting off sleep, I might put off everything that would come with tomorrow.

It was a ridiculous conceit, and yet I found myself slipping from bed for perhaps the dozenth time since I'd retired after Thalia's departure. This time, after pulling on a loose silk robe, I wandered over to the huge walk-in closet that Raven House had supplied me. When I'd first arrived, the closet had mostly been filled with clothes in the black and green I favored, but one corner held a small stock of Cerice's red and gold. Over the course of our relationship, the balance between our clothes had waxed and waned due to both our efforts and some sort of ongoing magical adjustment mechanism on the part of the house.

Now, though our fire had long since gone out, there remained one spot of red and gold, one item that neither my forebrain nor my hindbrain had ever felt ready to cast aside irrevocably: a gown. I took it from the rack then and carried it out into the bedroom, laying it across the blankets. A full-length brocade dress, it was both elaborate and gorgeous. Though I had never admitted it to Cerice, this dress produced by my subconscious was a near duplicate of the one my sister Lyra had worn for her wedding, different only in the colors of the fabric.

When Cerice dumped me, I'd sent most of the clothes she left behind on to her apartments on Clotho's estates. But somehow, I hadn't been able to part with the dress. It might have gone later—once Tisiphone and I had become lovers—if clothes had held any meaning for my fiery Fury. But, of course, the Sisters of Vengeance have no interest in, or need for, clothing. Which, considering the latest turn of events, meant it was probably well and truly time I got rid of the dress.

Instead, I found myself idly smoothing the fabric of the skirt and aching both for Tisiphone and for what Cerice and I might have grown into in other circumstances.

What did it say about me? My entanglement with the Furies? This romance with danger made flesh? The first great love of my life had left me for Order and now had gone on to become one with Vengeance. The same Vengeance that had once worn the shape of the woman I loved now. Was it the risk that I truly loved and not the woman? The conflict? Walking a razor's edge between love and death?

I had no answers. Sighing, I lifted the dress from the covers and turned to replace it in my closet, a reminder of another time.

"It was a beautiful gown." The voice barely lifted above a whisper, but I instantly recognized Cerice.

It came from the vicinity of the lanai overlooking the bay. Though I couldn't see anyone there, I set the dress back down and folded my arms, waiting.

"It still is," I replied, when she did not speak again. "A beautiful gown for a beautiful woman."

Cerice finally faded into view, dropping the magical chameleon effect of a hunting Fury. She had one hip leaned on the rail, and her wings stretched wide behind her as if to sift the night wind. She looked as though she'd only just alighted or, more likely, that she wanted me to believe she had. Her skin, always pale, looked even more so with the icy curtain of her wings and hair as a backdrop. Her expression held a cold sort of regret—an awareness of loss untouched by sadness.

"Was," she said, her voice still quiet. "That dress is as much a part of the past as any yesterday that has slipped forever beyond the reach of today."

"Are you coming in? Or do you have to have an invite before you cross my threshold?" I'd intended it as a joke, but my words came out bitter. "I'm sorry. I didn't mean that as it sounded. Please, come in."

"Apology accepted, and your invitation as well."

Cerice folded her wings and stepped through the door. It made for a strange sort of déjà vu, her entering the bedroom we'd once shared in a manner that echoed Tisiphone's usual mode of arrival in that same place. I glanced at the table where Melchior still lay, deep in electric dreams. Unless he had some reason to run on alert mode, noises usually didn't wake him.

"Can I get you something?" I asked. "A drink perhaps?"

"No. I don't need anything." She shook her head and crossed the distance between us, putting a hand to my cheek.

So close she stood, inches away. Beautiful and naked, this lover from my past, her new appearance providing a silvery shadow of my present lover, yet I felt not the slightest hint of desire. Perhaps I was finally growing up? Or perhaps there was one betrayal too many lying between us now.

I pulled away from Cerice. "That's not the truth. If you didn't need anything, you wouldn't be here."

Cerice bowed in acknowledgment, her expression wry. "A perfect bull's-eye, sir. Shara sent me. She wants me to bring you to her."

"What if I'd rather not go with you?"

"She didn't make a suggestion of it." This time her voice came out flat and hard.

"So, because you've been ordered to do it, you'll drag me kicking and screaming?"

"Only if you force me."

I turned away and, without thinking, put my fist through the thin stone of the wall. It hurt, but I welcomed the pain, pulling my arm back to throw a second punch. Before I could do it, Cerice caught my wrist in a grip tighter than any vise, halting the motion.

"Don't," she said, but then released me.

"How could Shara do this to you?" I demanded. "She knows the cost of becoming a power." No one knew it better, not even the Raven.

"Necessity drove her to it," said Cerice. "Necessity and necessity both. The system that holds the pantheoverse together is coming apart at the seams. Shara needed a real programmer to begin to stitch up the rips. Persephone's virus tore the hell out of Necessity; and then, just when the goddess was starting to develop some work-arounds, you and Nemesis very nearly finished her off. If Shara hadn't made me a Fury, this MythOS would already have de-cohered. It would have split itself into a billion inchoate worlds of probability, and they would have quickly reverted to Primal Chaos, snuffing out one by one."

"But even so . . ." I whispered, not knowing how to finish the sentence.

"But even so, she would never have made a Fury of me had I not begged her to."

"Begged?" I didn't want to believe that.

"Yes, begged." Cerice looked deep into the chaos of my eyes. "Don't tell me there isn't enough Ravirn left within the Raven to understand. Clotho was right: I am fundamentally a creature of order, a true child of the Fates. It wasn't lack of love that drove me away from you; it was finally understanding that any marriage between fire and water can only end in the utter destruction of one of the celebrants."

"I—" Cerice touched a finger to my lips, a finger tipped with a needle-sharp claw.

"The Raven would have devoured Cerice, the daughter of Fate, just as Chaos would already have devoured this entire continuum of existence if I hadn't taken up the role of the Fury and begun the repair of Necessity. You saved us all from Order absolute when you thwarted Atropos, and from ruin when you shut down Persephone's virus and later killed Nemesis. But the Raven is a chaos bringer, and in acting you have moved the pendulum too far in the other direction. I became a Fury to save the pantheoverse from *you*, and I did it of my own free will."

She couldn't have hurt me more if she'd sliced me wide-open. I leaned forward and tugged a feather of living ice from one of her wings.

"This is all my fault? I'm the villain? The enemy of everything? The one who drove you to embrace your own destruction as an individual? That's just splendid! Is that why you sold me out to Zeus? And to Fate before him?"

I didn't see her move. Didn't even feel the impact. One instant I was snarling at Cerice. The next I was tumbling backwards across the bed, my chest hollow and sore and half-paralyzed from the impact. I hit the nightstand and shattered it, sending Melchior's laptop shape spinning across the room. He changed form in midair and landed on all fours.

"What in Fate's festering name is going on!" he yelped as he bounced to his feet. Then he saw Cerice and froze. "Oh. Should I assume the boss was making his usual efforts at diplomacy? Or did *you* start this particular rerun of the hostile-and-nasty hour?"

I'd have replied if I could have drawn a full breath.

Cerice shrugged. "Six from column A, half a dozen from column B. Either way, it totals up to twelve. Hello, Melchior. Is he treating you as well as you deserve?"

Melchior grinned. "Treating me as well as I deserve is a mathematical impossibility, but mostly he doesn't fall any shorter than expected. What brings you to our humble abode?"

"Shara wants a few words with Ravirn."

"And I'd like a few with her," I said. "Unless that whole Zeus thing is freelancing on your part."

Cerice shook her head. "I don't know what you think I've done, and at this point I guess I really don't care. I just wish Shara could have sent someone else to deal with you. When I was watching you with that dress, I almost forgot how insufferable you are. Let's just get this over with."

She stomped over to where I lay and caught me by the collar of my robe, lifting me to my feet as easily as I might have picked up Melchior. With her other hand, she sliced a hole in the walls of reality. Before I could so much as suggest I'd like to put some real clothes on, she stuffed me through the gap into elsewhere.

Melchior followed me a moment later. We had arrived in a very familiar and very homey sort of living room where battered furniture stood against curved green walls—an exact replica of Ahllan's old place save for one thing only. It was entirely cut off from the outside world. There was no door, and the open skylights in the low dome of the roof showed only a blank granite that had been enchanted to cast a directionless but full-spectrum light.

The walls were painted in a mottled pattern that sug-

gested the million leaves of a northern forest in high summer. Trellises and flowering vines heightened the effect.
They climbed the walls of the dome, meeting at a heavy
wrought-iron chandelier in the middle and hanging down
in a thick profusion of blooms. Despite its underground
location, the place smelled vividly alive and vital, like a
greenhouse or a walled garden.

Shara occupied a webgoblin-sized recliner at the point
farthest from our entry. At least, her hardware did. As had
so often been the case over the last two years, her spiritware
was not currently resident. The little purple webgoblin sat
perfectly still, her Mae-Westian curves looking artificial
and embalmed without the animating will that should have
filled her with life.

"Shara?" I said into the silence. "Are you here somewhere?"

There was no answer, and it was only in that moment
that I realized that Cerice had not followed us through the
gateway between worlds, that it had, in fact, closed behind
us. Fear of imprisonment touched me then, and I reached
for the power of the Raven. When my shadow grew black
wings I relaxed, letting my connection to the inner Trickster slip away, and dropped into the twin of my old favorite
recliner to wait. Melchior frowned but flopped onto one of
the goblin-sized chairs and settled down as well.

Less than five minutes had passed when Shara appeared
in the center of the room. I flicked a glance at her still-
seated hardware form. That and the faintest hint of trans-
parency around the tips of her ears and the ends of her hair
were the only clues that she was there only in projection.

"I'm sorry," she said, before I could speak. "I wouldn't
have kept you waiting, but Cerice didn't immediately in-
form me that you'd arrived." There was more than a hint of
exasperation in her tone.

"Aren't there sensors?" Melchior waved a hand in a
vague gesture that took in the room.

"All over this world and beyond," replied Shara, "far more than a very finite me can keep track of, even with a lot of good pseudo-AI subroutines to take up some of the processing slack."

"Beyond?" said Melchior. "That's new, isn't it?"

Shara nodded. "That's one of the things Cerice was able to do, get us fully reconnected to the mweb so we could start reintegrating all the worlds that got lost in the Persephone meltdown. But it's been a seriously mixed blessing." She snapped her fingers, summoning a projection of a chair into existence behind her, and settled into it. "With Necessity plugged back into the system, I'm even more overstretched and overstressed. I'm just not the computer she is." Though her projection didn't show it, I could hear a soul-deep weariness in her tone—she was not herself.

"I'm sorry for my part in your troubles," I said. I hated to see a dear friend suffering for things I had done. Though I would never admit it to Cerice, her comment about saving the universe from me had struck deep into the bone. "I wish that I had been wise enough to find another way."

"Don't." Shara shook her head. "You did what needed doing when it needed doing and with less collateral damage than anyone had a right to expect. I'm not interested in blame at this point. All I care about is solutions to a truly epic problem. That's why we're having this conversation without Cerice. How two such utterly brilliant and dear people can turn into idiot five-year-olds in each other's presence is beyond my understanding."

"I'll give that a big old 'amen,' " said Melchior.

I held up a hand. "Can I plead guilty to the five-year-old thing and reserve the right to contest the accusation of brilliance at a later date?" I certainly didn't feel very smart at the moment. "What exactly *is* the problem this time? My last interaction with Necessity was brief and cryptic. As was my last interaction with you."

Shara smiled wanly. "I wish I could remember that."

That made me sit up straight. "What do you mean? Last time I checked, you were an AI with theoretically perfect memory."

"Only in a stable system with regular backups. Something went 'fap' in a major way while you were making your last visit to planet Necessity. It fried a whole lot of subsystems and erased an entire bank of storage devices, including one that held most of a day of my personal memory. I remember shutting down some of the security systems to allow you to sneak into this DecLocus, and I remember Cerice waking me up from a reboot in a complete panic about nineteen hours later but nothing in between."

"Holy shit!" said Melchior. "What about backups and subsystems?"

"So far nothing I've been able to access has given me back the missing pieces. At this point, all I know is that something gorked, and you got sent off to the Norse MythOS in the gap."

"I thought you didn't know what the abacus network did," I said.

"I didn't beforehand, but in the postmortem, Fury Cerice managed to crack open a set of control systems and absolutely ancient memory files that gave me some clues. And, more recently . . ." Shara looked down at her feet.

"More recently what?" I asked.

"More recently, I was able to keep an eye on you via the spinnerette larva that got sent through after you did." She didn't sound very proud of herself.

"Shara!" Melchior looked genuinely shocked. "You're the one who's been eavesdropping on us?"

"Not exactly. It's more that I've been eavesdropping on the portion of Necessity that's been eavesdropping on you. The spinnerette was broadcasting everything she got back to a system here inside Necessity, one where nobody seems to be home but me. It's really a mess."

"How bad?" I asked.

"I honestly don't know." Shara closed her eyes and rubbed the lids with the heels of her hands. "That's how bad things are. The number of systems I can't access or can only partially make sense of is longer than the list I can use effectively. More than that, though, I can't guarantee that any command I give will stick."

She dropped her hands to the arms of the chair like someone bracing for a blow and looked me straight in the eyes.

"I really need your help here, Ravirn. I think Necessity may be going mad."

Melchior whistled. "That'd be ugly. What's your evidence?"

I nodded. "I thought she'd mostly gone quiet after the incident with Nemesis, that she was only communicating sporadically through the spinnerettes. Has that changed?"

"Yes and no." The projection of Shara rose and began to pace. "Messages are still sometimes coming in through spinnerette channels, but often they're contradictory, and the goddess has completely stopped communicating with me directly. That's not all. The reason I can't be sure any changes I make will stick is that someone or possibly several someones keep rewriting my code."

"Several someones?" I said.

"Yes. Let me give you an example: About three hours ago I made a repair to one of the subroutines that tracks re-merges of very minor binary world splits, the sort of thing where a woman in Taipei chooses between catching a ride somewhere and walking, but nothing of moment comes of it. Maybe twenty minutes after I made the change, a much better way of programming the patch occurred to me. I went back to implement it and found the whole thing had been reverted to the damaged code I'd cleaned up in the first place."

"Are you sure it didn't just break again?" I asked.

"Absolutely. There were telltales in the access logs that

proved the change was deliberate." She grimaced. "It gets worse, too. When I made the new fixes, I encrypted the subsector so that no one could get at it but me. After another hour went by, and I decided to go in and do a quick check to see how things were working and to look for signs of anyone trying to revert the thing again."

I could see where this was going, or thought I could. "Let me guess; someone cracked the encryption and reverted it again."

"I wish it were that simple," said Shara.

"What did happen?" asked Melchior.

"Well, the encryption *was* gone. You got that part right. But instead of reverting it, whoever cracked the system had made a significant upgrade to my code—something that did everything my repair had done but did it better and cleaner. They also added a string that would automatically send an alert if anyone changed anything."

"Send an alert where?" I felt simultaneously fascinated and alarmed.

"I don't know. I made a change just to trigger the alert so I could backtrack it. But when I tried to follow the thing, I hit some sort of weird internal firewall or scrambling system. I was just trying to figure out how to crack that when another alert pulse came through from the original subsystem." She dropped back into the chair and started rubbing her eyes again.

"And?" Melchior prompted.

"And someone was trying to revert the code to the broken version."

"Who was it?" I asked.

"I don't know. They were teleprogramming it from somewhere else in the system, and as soon as I tried a traceback, they shut down the operation and went silent, vanished completely as far as I could tell. Scarier still, what stopped me cold didn't even slow down the thing on the far side of the firewall I'd located earlier, whoever that is. *They* sent a whole swarm of dataphages down a line of code I couldn't see. I followed them to another firewall, where they started right in chewing and ripping away at the wall. At that point, whatever was on the other side did the code equivalents of dumping boiling oil on the attackers. For about the next twenty minutes the two sides hacked at each other."

"To what result?" I was fascinated.

"Stalemate, then vanishment."

"Vanishment?" said Melchior.

"Yes. Both sides suddenly gave up and went poof. Gone completely. I couldn't even find the firewalls again. That's when I called Cerice up and sent her after you. You're the only person I know whose brain is sufficiently twisted in the right way to get to the bottom of this."

"Gosh, thanks."

"Will you help me?"

"I'll try." It was my turn to get up and pace while I tried to get a mental handle on things. "If I'm hearing you right, you're in a code war with two other entities, both of whom have access to the nitty-gritty of Necessity's innards. Is there any chance it's someone cracking in from outside, now that your net connection is reestablished? Discord? Or Athena maybe?"

"I doubt it," said Shara. "It doesn't *feel* external. It doesn't even feel like someone else."

"I'm not sure I follow," I said.

"I am Necessity now," said Shara. "Or, at least, my spiritware is running on her hardware. I don't know if I can explain it to someone whose basic metaphor of being is one of flesh and blood. I'm still me, but for all intents and purposes, my soul is thinking with Necessity's brain. When I looked at the changes in the code, both the improvement and the reversion, it didn't feel like I was looking at someone else's work. It felt like I was looking at something I had done but couldn't remember doing. Both felt like ideas conceived by the brain of Necessity."

"Are you saying that Necessity has developed some sort of split-personality disorder?" asked Melchior.

"Maybe," replied Shara. "Or maybe she just keeps changing her mind. Sometimes it's me. Sometimes it's someone else."

A really nasty possibility occurred to me. "Necessity is the goddess who controls the way reality splits—when a decision will result in a new world and when it won't. When that happens, a person splits into two parallel people in nearly identical worlds. What if Necessity herself has split here? There's been enough major trauma to create some truly gargantuan divisions. Is it possible that there's more than one version of Necessity running around in there with you? Struggling for supremacy?"

Shara's eyes widened in alarm. "That would certainly explain the way the thing feels. But I really don't like the implications."

I didn't either. The god war we now called the Titanomachy had resulted from Zeus and his father, Cronus, struggling for the Throne of Heaven in the ultimate family feud. Gods had died, and the whole pantheoverse had changed forever. It was the most catastrophic conflict in the entire history of the MythOS.

But no matter how bad the war had gotten, there had always been a set of rules that governed the conduct of both sides of the fight. A set of rules designed to preserve the foundations of reality against the worst excess of the immortals. A set of rules imposed and enforced by Necessity. If there was another god war going on now, one inside her mind, there would be no rules and nothing to guarantee the continued survival of the pantheoverse.

And it was looking more and more like it was my job to fix the problem.

CHAPTER FIVE

"—not really going to go through with this, are you, Shara?" Cerice demanded as she came through the hole she'd just cut in the walls of the universe.

I didn't know what had her so upset, though knowing her as well as I did, I got the distinct impression it was a continuation of an argument that had been running for some time. Probably Shara had been projecting her presence in more than one place simultaneously via the wonders of parallel processing.

Shara's image nodded at Cerice, unperturbed by her tone. "He'll need the access."

"I can't conscience this." Cerice leaned down over her former familiar. "You know how reckless he can be."

Ah, *that* tone I recognized. "I take it this has something to do with me, then?"

"Damn right it does," Cerice snapped over her shoulder, "and I'm not having any."

"I don't recall making you an offer," I said, shading my

tone with bafflement. "That phase of our relationship is long over."

Cerice spun and glared at me. "You, shut up!" Will or anger slid her finger and toe claws free of the pocket universe where Furies kept them between vivisections, though she didn't go beyond the implied threat. "This is between me and Shara."

I made a zipping motion across my lips and grinned at her. She didn't resheathe her claws, but she did turn back to Shara.

"I won't do it, and you won't make me," said Cerice.

Shara leaned forward in her chair and rubbed her temples. "Cerice . . ."

"Don't wheedle," said Cerice. "It's not happening. I flat refuse."

"Fine, if that's how you feel about, let's make it formal: Cerice, Grant Ravirn Full Access. Please."

Melchior caught my eye then, and mouthed, "Ouch." I nodded silently back. The tone and cadence of Shara's request perfectly matched the command structure the Fates used when ordering their familiars to perform a spell or other function. The only difference was the substitution of a "please" for the "execute" that made such commands unrefusable. That change was one that Cerice and I had both made in our own interactions with our familiars after our respective discoveries of AI free will.

For Shara to use it on Cerice under these circumstances amounted to a sharp slap. Not only did it dare Cerice to go against their long relationship of mutual trust, but it firmly underlined the fact that Shara *didn't* have to ask. Several seconds ticked past while the request hung between them. Finally, Cerice's wings slumped.

"On your head be it." Cerice raised her right hand and made a tiny slice in the air.

She reached through into elsewhere and began rummaging around. After a moment, her arm reemerged holding a very familiar-looking piece of equipment. My ruined sword cane, Occam, broken in a duel with the Norse war god, Tyr.

"Last chance to change your mind," said Cerice.

Shara didn't so much as blink. With a sigh, Cerice twisted the hilt and slid the abbreviated sword free of its wooden scabbard. She knelt and set it on a low coffee table before upending the cane and letting the rest of the blade slide out into her hand. Even broken, it was a beautiful piece of work, catching the light and throwing it back in a thousand directions.

Hilt and blade had been shaped from a single piece of crystallized chaos, the stuff of Fury claws. It looked like diamond but was a hundred times tougher and more resilient. The blade was really two blades merged the long way and at right angles to form a plus-shaped cross section. The form precluded deep cuts but made for a vicious thrusting weapon. The hilt took the form of a Fury, her fiery wings at full extension—Tisiphone.

Almost casually, Cerice stabbed the broken end of the blade deep into her thigh. Without so much as a wince, she picked up the hilt shard and did the same. A moment later she pulled both free, fitting the now-bloody ends together along the line of the break. For a count of perhaps ten, nothing happened. Then there came a flash as hot and bright as a magnesium flare going off at close quarters. Reflex closed my eyes.

When I opened them again, Cerice stood above me, a renewed and transformed Occam extended toward me hilt first. The hilt appeared to be made from ruby now rather than diamond, though the blade remained clear and white. I rose and took my sword back, snapping the blade through a quick series of thrusts and parries. I'd forgotten how good it felt in my hand, even with my recent injury—light and sweet and perfectly balanced.

With a smile, I swept it up into a fencer's salute and gave Cerice a bow. "Thank you, fair lady."

"Don't mention it," she replied, her voice sour. "Really don't mention it. I don't want to have to think about you running loose with that."

I shrugged and sheathed the blade. "Why so touchy? It's not like I didn't have all kinds of opportunities to make mischief with it back before it got broken."

Cerice rolled her eyes. "(A) neither you nor Necessity was my problem then. And (B) it had a great deal less power in that earlier incarnation." She glanced briefly over her shoulder at Shara. "May I go now?"

"Anytime," said Shara, and I could hear real pain in the little goblin's voice. "I would no more constrain or compel you now that our positions are reversed than you ever did me."

"Constraint and compulsion come in many forms, Shara. Something I understand much better now than I did when our bonds to one another ran the other way. When I accepted these"—she shivered her wings ever so slightly—"I accepted the implied fetters that come with them, and all the courtesy in the world can't change that."

"I'm sorry," said Shara.

"I know," said Cerice. "So am I. But this is the way it has to be. Especially when the others are considered." Though Shara couldn't see them from where she sat, I noted unshed tears in Cerice's eyes. "I'm sorry, too."

Then she ripped a hole in the world and stepped through into another place.

"I'm sorry you had to see that," Shara said, once Cerice had gone. "I didn't think she'd bring the argument through when she joined us here."

I kept silent. Cerice had never been the sort to let a little thing like propriety get in the way of winning a point, but I felt too bad for both of them to mention it.

"What did she mean by that?" I asked.

"By what?" replied Shara.

"Her comment about the 'others.' For that matter, I'd like to hear more about what's been done to my sword."

I found the changed color—so like crystallized blood—
unsettling.

"The two are related actually," said Shara. "Do you remember my mentioning that I couldn't be sure about my
commands sticking? Well, that goes beyond programming.
I'm having problems with the other Furies. Neither Alecto
nor Megaera acknowledges my authority as a proxy for
Necessity. In fact, since I brought Cerice on board, they'll
hardly even speak to me."

"I don't get it." Melchior frowned. "I thought the Furies
more or less *had* to obey direct orders from Necessity and
that you were in a position to give them."

"They do, and I could force the issue if I dared to access
the part of the system that holds the control channel for
the Furies. But after what happened the day you two got
sent off to the Norse MythOS, I've kept pretty much all of
the entry points to critical control subsystems locked down
hard. Since my spiritware is running primarily on the security network, I can be fairly certain that will prevent any
of the other entities running around inside Necessity from
getting access. The problem is that if I lower the barriers
even a little bit, say enough to allow *me* access . . ."

"Everybody else might get in, too," I said. "But what's
all that got to do with Occam?"

"First," said Shara, "if you're really going to help, you
need access to everything, even places I currently can't
reach. Second, when you use that access, you run a significant risk of pissing off Megaera and Alecto."

"So, what? Are you trying to tell me my sword is now
some kind of skeleton key for all of reality? And a Fury-
slayer to boot?" I was joking when I said it, but Shara just
nodded. I sat back down. Hard. "You're kidding, right?
You wouldn't really just hand someone of my reputation
that kind of power."

Shara nodded. "And no strings attached. I can't make
you as physically strong or fast as a Fury, nor give you

any other special powers without accessing systems I don't dare touch. But the real Necessity left me half a loophole in the shape of your sword, and Tisiphone's absence opened that loophole the rest of the way by giving me a Fury willing to trust me. Occam was designed to give limited access to the admin powers of the Furies and as a weapon that could do real damage to Nemesis."

"And Cerice amped that power up somehow?" asked Melchior.

"Yes and no," said Shara. "The innate similarity between Nemesis and the Furies has always meant that Occam had the potential to be a particularly dangerous tool against them. Likewise, it's always had the potential to provide virtually unfettered access to the workings of Necessity."

"Okay, I'm officially lost," I said. "What exactly did Cerice do?"

"Something Tisiphone never would have done voluntarily—lent you her keys." Shara leaned back and cocked her head to the side, waiting.

"I still don't . . . Oh." I felt my eyes widen. "Oh my. That's really clever. Biometric-password safeguards?"

Shara nodded and smiled. "Plus the sword as physical key. It's a two-factor system."

"What are you talking about?" demanded Melchior.

"Shara doesn't dare open up any of the really important systems in case the other minds of Necessity use her gateway to make a move for greater control," I said, still working out the full ramifications as I went. "But she doesn't have to. The Furies already have at least physical access to everything."

"It's hardcoded," agreed Shara. "When Necessity first transformed herself into a computer, she built that into the design specs in case anything went wrong during the changeover. For extra security, she made it a two-factor access system, Fury blood and Fury diamond."

"I think I see now," said Melchior. "When Necessity

created Occam, she gave Ravirn extremely limited admin powers over the system. The chaos-diamond of the sword supplied the key for the lock, and the blood he charged it with identified his level of access."

"Exactly," said Shara. "When Cerice repaired the blade to my specifications—regrew it really—I had her infuse it with her blood, the blood of a full Fury, which grants unrestricted access to the physical plant of Necessity and to most of the software architecture as well."

"So I probably shouldn't misplace it, then, huh?" I turned the blade this way and that in the air—it didn't look anywhere near as important as it should have under the circumstances.

"No," said Shara. "You shouldn't. And, you won't. I am sorry about this, but . . ."

She quickly whistled a spell, something intricate and self-harmonizing. When she finished, the hilt of Occam grew suddenly, blazingly, hot along the side closest to my injured palm. The smell of burning meat filled the air, and I yelped and tried to fling the sword away. It clung to my hand as if it had fused itself to my flesh. I screamed and curled into a ball as Shara whistled a new spell. This one sounded a bit like the one used for closing athame wounds, though much more complex. The pain faded, but I still couldn't release Occam.

"What the hell did you just do to me?" I yelled angrily.

"No more than I had to." Shara looked simultaneously sorrowful and resolute. "The sword is a part of you now as it had to be to fulfill all of its functions."

"That's just gods-damned splendid, that is." I felt a wild fury rising up from the center of my soul, and my voice followed it higher and higher. "Did it occur to you to ask first? Or that I might need both hands at some point?"

"Yes, and yes. I didn't ask because I was pretty sure you'd refuse and, since I'd have had to do it anyway, that would only have made things worse. As for the second, I did make provisions."

"Provisions!" I leaped to my feet and stomped over to glare down at her projected form. "You didn't ask, and you made provisions? That's . . . Urgh!" I couldn't find the words.

I'd never been so angry with someone I cared so much about, not even Cerice—this was not the Shara I knew and loved. I turned away and stomped back toward Melchior. He was sitting perfectly still, a look of stunned betrayal on his face.

"I wonder if all that rage is something of a side effect?" muttered Shara.

"Side effect of what?" whispered Melchior. "What did that spell do? I couldn't follow all of it, but what I could make out sounded really ancient."

"It was," said Shara. "It's a very small part of the magic Necessity put into making the Furies what they are. Cerice found the core phrasing in the same place she found the information on the abacus network. Ravirn, I think that you will find the answer to Mel's question if you reach for the link you now have with Occam."

"Screw that." I reached inward, but not for any link to the sword. No, I reached for the Raven. "I quit." It was time to see if the sword could follow me through a transformation.

The shadow of the Raven fell over me, and I used it to rip my body apart, reshaping myself into a giant, black bird. When I finished, I looked down at my wing and found it free of Occam's grasp. I laughed a harsh, cawing laugh then, a laugh that cut off abruptly when I realized the sword had gone away completely. What the . . . I wrenched myself back into human shape, half-expecting to find the sword back in my hand. But no, it was still gone.

"Where did it go?" I whispered.

"That depends on whether I got Necessity's spell right," said Shara, her voice quiet and sad. "Look at your palm."

I did and found a circular patch of crystal about the size

of a penny in my hand's exact center. It looked as though
someone had plugged the bullet hole the spinnerette assassin had given me with a slender diamond disk. I tapped
it with the nail of my left hand. It made a dull clicking
noise and, while I could feel the pressure of it all around
the edges of the crystal, I couldn't actually feel anything
through the crystal. On the plus side, there was no longer
any evidence I'd ever been shot.

"I don't understand," I said to Shara. "What the hell did
you just do to me?"

"Gave you a tiny part of the magic of the Furies to go
with the touch of Fury blood that now runs in your veins.
In making you a blood brother to the Furies I suspect I've
also given you a touch of their berserker madness, though
that was not my intention. It may be that it's necessary for
this particular trick."

"I'm getting really tired of people speaking in riddles
and screwing with my life, Shara."

The anger had faded with my transformation into the
Raven, but I could feel it welling up again. The crystal in
my palm began to tingle then, which made me angrier still.
I wanted to hit something. Now! My anger flexed, and . . .

"Holy shit!" Occam was in my hand, somehow ex-
truded from the crystal in my palm. "That's the weirdest
damn sensation I've ever felt." Anger gave way to curiosity and . . . Occam went away, sliding *through* my palm
into elsewhere. "I think I need to sit down now." I felt
light-headed and just generally weird as I collapsed onto
a nearby couch.

Shara's image rose from its projected chair. "Melchior,
you'll need a great deal of info about the software architecture of Necessity. Here it is." She closed her eyes for an
instant, and Melchior's expression took on the abstracted
look of a webgoblin receiving data wirelessly.

She turned in my direction again. "The only way for you
to take the sword with you into the depths of the machine is

for it be a part of you. Otherwise, you'd leave it behind with your body when your soul entered the virtual world. I am sorry, Ravirn. But I had to do it." Then she vanished, leaving us alone with the empty vessel of her original body.

A moment later, Melchior's attention returned to the here and now, and he shook his head as though trying to settle the contents within. "Wow, a lot there. Do you want to rest a bit before we go poke a finger in the hornet's nest? Or would you rather just plunge straight in?"

"As much as I am a fan of getting things over with quickly, I think we'd better go back to Raven House and regroup. Wait—let me try something." I returned to my feet.

I summoned up a touch of the anger I still felt with Shara. In response, Occam shaped itself into my hand. I pictured where I wanted to go and traced a sharp line through the air with my blade. Nothing happened. Again. Ditto. Well, crap. I should have known it wouldn't be that easy. I began to get really angry again, and that gave me an idea.

I imagined the walls of reality as an arbitrary barrier put up specifically to prevent me from getting home. I made the distance between here and there my nemesis. With a yell, I lunged forward and really took a cut at my newfound enemy. This time I felt the sort of resistance I might have expected from dragging the sword through a foot-thick sheet of Jell-O. The edges of an eight-foot vertical slice in space and time bulged outward like the slit skin of an overstuffed sausage. Beyond lay my bedroom. *Hah! Take that, reality!*

"After you, Mel."

As I followed him through, I imagined the gap closing behind me. It did so with the faintest echo of the sound of a metal zipper. Surreal.

Fenris paddled his surfboard along beside mine as we headed out toward the break, his madly wagging tail

making a bannerlike counterpoint to his churning legs.
"So, has this goblin friend of yours always pushed people
around like she's doing with you and what's her name . . .
Cerice?"

"Not at all. That's a good part of the reason I wanted
to stop back here for a while before getting in any deeper.
There's something I don't understand going on, and that
always makes me nervous."

Melchior snorted from his perch on the tip of my board.
"Said Captain Clueless. If not understanding things really
bugged you, you'd spend your whole life clinging to the
ceiling."

"Gosh, thanks, Mr. Small, Blue, and Easily Knocked
Overboard. Not only do I appreciate your insight; I find
myself wondering why you don't have more friends."

"It's probably the company I keep, if you know what
I mean." He made an elaborate show of hiding the finger
he was pointing at me. "Oh, and you're welcome." Then
he slumped back on the board. "I'm really worried about
Shara. She's *not* acting like herself."

"Yeah, me, too." A thought struck me. "Do you suppose
it's got something to do with what she said about the other
entities within Necessity?"

"No," said Melchior, his voice even more sarcastic
than usual. "Say it isn't so! Are you suggesting that being
trapped inside a giant network with hostile intelligences
locked in there with you might have an effect on mood?"

Fenris laughed a yippy little laugh at that, and Laginn
rolled over on his back and mimed the disembodied-hand
equivalent of wide-eyed surprise.

"Actually," I growled, "that's not what I meant." I took a
deep breath and pushed aside a brief and unexpected flare
of anger—that aspect of Fury magic was going to take
some getting used to. "I was thinking about the part where
she talked about knowing the others were in system because it felt like they were all using the same mind to think

with. Necessity is the Fate of the Gods and the patron goddess of control freaks. What if using that autocratic hardware to do all her processing is having an effect on Shara's spiritware?"

Melchior sat back up and looked thoughtful. "Are you sure your name is Ravirn? Because you might just have started making sense."

It was my turn to amp up the sarcasm. "Ya think? Form shapes function, especially in the gods-and-heroes business. Look at me."

"Do I have to?" asked Melchior.

I kept rolling. "Becoming the Raven changed me on every level. I can't not take risks. Or keep my mouth shut when I should, for that matter."

"You know, I'd noticed that," said Fenris. "And, here all this time I'd just thought it was a character defect."

"Don't listen to Ravirn on that one," Melchior said to the wolf. "He's always been all 'shoot first and ask questions later' where it comes to his mouth."

I nodded to acknowledge the point. "To some extent, sure. But believe it or not, from my perspective it's gotten significantly worse. Or take what's happened with Occam."

"I'd rather return it," said Melchior.

"Yeah, everybody wants to be a comedian, whether they're funny or not. What I meant was that I keep getting these weird little bursts of anger since Shara Furyfied me to the sword. Normally, the comparative lack of any real punch is enough for me to shake off your digs, Mel. But now, even the lamest of your traditionally lame jokes is triggering a little flare of real anger."

Mel said something in response, but I couldn't really pay attention because we'd hit the break zone at an inopportune moment, and a couple tons of water were getting ready to fall on us. Once we came out the other side of the wall of water, I just waved it all away. I had better things to do than stress about Shara. Salt air and surf and the morning sun make for a magic that shouldn't be mixed with the more mundane sort that comes from spells and musty old gods.

"You're sure you want to join us on this one?" I asked after I'd slashed a door into the beyond. "It could be dangerous."

Fenris nodded. "I spent a thousand years chained to a rock in the North Atlantic. More than anything in the world, I want to take advantage of the freedom coming here has granted me. I want to go to new places and see new things, meet people, make friends, even make all sorts of stupid mistakes."

"Well, we can guarantee you a lot of opportunity on that last front," said Melchior. "That's pretty much what spending time with Ravirn is all about. Though I must say that it seems a strange sort of ambition."

"For a thousand years I was tied to one place and one world, one future. I knew I was trapped and would remain so until the end of days, when madness and hunger would own me completely, driving me to swallow Odin and be slain for it. I want all the things Odin's binding and Norse predestination kept me from having until now. And genuine risk and the opportunity for failure is a huge part of that. For the first time in my life, I know that I could die tomorrow and never see it coming, and that's marvelous! Every possibility is open to me, and I want it all. I want to devour experience and lap up life. I want. I want. I want!"

He threw back his head, let out a great joyous howl, and bounded through the gate I'd opened with my sword and my anger. Melchior and I followed more cautiously. The transition from the sun-soaked porch of Raven House to a dim and cold cavern beneath an artificial island in the Mediterranean did not improve my mood.

The gigantic underground space beyond my gateway held racks and racks of shiny black multiprocessor servers like so many slabs of volcanic glass, each studded with a dim blue LED. It looked and felt like we had just entered a high-tech tomb. Mostly because we had. A mausoleum housing what had once been one of the two or three most important computing functions in the entire Greek MythOS. In their day, the servers here had run the portion of Necessity that governed the nature and location of every power in the pantheon.

For some of us, that governance mostly consisted of loose instruction sets like the one that shaped my Raven's magic and the part of my personality owned by the Trickster. For others, the program had much tighter parameters—binding Prometheus to the rock where an eagle would peck out his liver every morning, or preventing Atlas from a shrug that might destroy an entire world.

Oh, not literally, of course. Atlas is, or has become, the personification of gravity, the force that binds the Earth to the sun and keeps it from spinning off into space. At least, that's how Lachesis explained it to me as a child. But the line between metaphor and reality is a very hazy one for the older members of the pantheon, and you can never be sure that they see the universe in the same way that you do. Or that they're not lying to you for that matter. Gods always tell stories in the way that best serves their ends. They also prefer "Truth" to "truth" and both to "fact."

Take Necessity . . . please. Yeah, old joke, but appropriate here. When I talk about her in terms of arranging the fates of all the powers, it makes it sound like she's ordering us about like pieces on a chessboard, and I'm pretty sure that's how the classical Greeks see the whole thing. But that's not actually how it works now. Necessity's power exists in the gap between decisions. She is the point of maximum uncertainty.

In a true quantum multiverse, every coin flip would go both ways, each creating its own version of the universe that would then go on side by side. On a more human scale—

you might decide to have the soup *and* the salad, and in that moment, you would split in two with both versions of you going happily along in their new universes until they reached the next set of decisions. Then more splits would happen. There could be a billion billion billion versions of you, each created by a different decision on someone's part and each leading to more and more splits unto the farthest reaches of infinity. Somewhere, I suspect that just such a multiverse does exist. But this isn't it.

In this multiverse, every split has to make it past Necessity before it generates a new universe, and mostly they don't. Most splits she collapses back into a single primary line of reality. In particular, splits that might result in two versions of any of the pantheon's powers get shut down ruthlessly. Necessity keeps all the major players singular and limits the results of our choices. At least, she used to. It's no longer clear what powers Necessity has or is exercising. Or, for that matter, what powers the system exercises on its own without any input from the guiding intelligence of the goddess. We had broken things pretty badly, Persephone, Nemesis, and I.

"Where are we?" asked Fenris as he wended his way toward the front of the room.

"Prime/?" Melchior named the mweb address. "Decision Locus Zero and the exact center of the Greek pantheoverse."

"Planet Necessity," I replied. "Our version of Mimir sequestered an entire human-free version of the Earth as a processing center."

Fenris sniffed the air. "So why does it smell mummified?"

"This corner of it is," I said. "The servers in this room are dead but not gone. At one time it was the second-most-important portion of Necessity's network, the place where she kept track of yours truly along with a bunch of other, lesser lights."

Melchior snorted.

I ignored him. "I figured it would be a good place to test out my shiny new access powers since the maximum-security protocols should still be in place, but there's nothing vital to get hurt if things go horribly wrong."

"That's reassuring," said Fenris. "Is there a specific reason to think they might go that badly? Or is that just a general-principles thing?"

As I started to answer, a sharp electrical crackling noise came from the front of the room, followed by a heavy thud like a blade falling and the fat sizzle of a really big system shorting out. In the next second, the calm blue of the standby lights on the servers all shifted to an angry red that suggested systemwide failure.

I sighed. "Call it extrapolation from long experience."

"I'm guessing you want to go see what that's all about." Melchior sounded resigned. "I only bring it up because there is an alternative. Just this once, we could head for points elsewhere before the shooting starts."

"Maybe it's mice." I slipped past Fenris and began to creep toward the front of the room, beckoning for the others to follow. "Come on. Wouldn't you be embarrassed if we ran away, and it turned out to be a bunch of cute little fuzzballs?"

Fenris fell in behind me, with Laginn perched on his neck.

Melchior trailed along at the back of the parade. "I'm actually very hard to embarrass. And besides, we both know it's not mice."

"You can't know that until we go look."

"I don't *need* to know," he replied. "I'm content with my ignorance."

By then I had almost made it to the front bank of servers, where the smell of dust and disuse gave way to the sharp, bitter odor of fried circuits. Very cautiously I leaned forward and peered around the nearest rack. From there

I could see the patch panel and the associated switching computer that had once linked this room to the rest of Necessity's network. What was left of them, really. Both had been badly damaged in my duel with Nemesis, though I'd later kludged the remnants into temporary usability.

More recently—*much* more recently, judging by the smoke still rising from the computer—someone had severed the trunk cables and shorted the repaired switch.

Melchior brushed against my knee as he looked around the corner. "No mouse did that."

"Maybe it was a really big mouse." I left the others and crossed to the place where the foot-thick bundle of cables had been cut, kneeling for a better look. "A really big mouse with a very sharp blade of some kind. Very, very sharp." Whatever had severed the cables had done it as cleanly as any cut I'd ever seen.

Somewhere behind me, Melchior took a sudden harsh breath, and Fenris began to growl, very low and very quiet.

"Squeak," said a sour voice, also from behind me, though much closer. A woman. "Squeak, squeak, squeak."

The button of organic diamond on my palm seemed to catch fire as adrenaline surged through me. With the added impetus of my new Fury attachment, I could feel fight kicking flight's ass as the reaction of choice. It took a huge effort of will to suppress that wholly alien urge to violence as first resort.

"Not a mouse, then," I said through clenched teeth. "Though just as gray, if I don't miss my guess. Are you planning to kill me, Madam? Or may I turn around to see if I'm right?"

"Why does it have to be one or the other?" she asked, and I knew that I had guessed correctly when I finally recognized her voice.

Alecto, the Fury of Storm.

CHAPTER SIX

If Alecto had wanted to kill me out of hand, she could have. Since she hadn't, I figured she must want something from me. Being very careful not to make any sudden movements, I rose and turned to face her. Alecto is the most reserved and strategy-minded of the Furies, and thus least likely to take your head off without a good reason, but she is still a Fury.

She looked much as I remembered her, tall and curvy with granite gray skin, and wings and hair like the blackest thundercloud you've ever seen, complete with constantly moving threads of silver lightning. Occasionally, one of those would ground itself out on the floor with a sharp crackle.

"If that wolf doesn't stop trying to creep up on me like that, I'm going to tear your heart out." Alecto's voice was gentle, almost regretful, but adamant. "That'd really be a shame since I came to talk, and I'd rather not have to kill you right this minute."

"That makes two of us." I looked past her to Fenris and nodded.

"I'm pretty sure I could nail her before she got to you," said Fenris, who had frozen midcrouch with Alecto's threat.

Alecto chuckled. "You're wrong, wolf, but I like your style. Let me make the lot of you an offer. If you will agree to a temporary truce and sit down with me for a civilized conversation, I will agree to return to this exact position for a resumption of hostilities should the discussion prove unsatisfactory. Deal?"

I nodded.

"That works for me," said Fenris, visibly loosening the muscles he'd tensed in preparation for a last great leap.

"Can I vote for a head start toward the door instead?" asked Melchior. "Just give me three steps."

Alecto chuckled. "You're smarter than your master, I see."

"Partner," I said, simultaneous with Melchior's indignant, "Boss."

"If the word displeases you," said Alecto, "pretend I used another. We have more important matters to discuss while the privacy that the unfortunate equipment failure forces on us lasts." Her eyes flicked meaningfully to the severed ends of the cable.

"I guess that's as close as I'm going to get to an apology," said Melchior, then shrugged. "To be honest, it's more than I expected. Thank you."

Alecto bobbed her head in the faintest of nods.

I just nodded at her words. What in the name of all gods was going on here?

"Would you care to elaborate on that last?" I asked, as Melchior whistled us up a set of seats appropriate to our diverse physical needs and a conference table to go in the middle of the lot.

In a nod to mutual distrust, he put a glass top on the latter so that each of us could see what the others might be doing beneath its surface. I noted with approval that he'd arranged things so that he and I both had a solid wall behind our chairs and Fenris's cushion faced the side of the room where someone coming at us around the racks would most likely appear.

"Very nice." Alecto slid into a chair whose slender back made comfortable accommodation for her wings. "One might think you'd had practice seating a Fury." She turned her gaze my way, her expression hardening. "Speaking of which, how is my sister, Tisiphone? I would consider it a matter of good faith for you to answer that question before I address yours."

"At this exact moment?" I shrugged and took my seat opposite Alecto. "Your guess is as good as mine. Maybe better, since you've known her longer. When last I saw her? That's more complex." I pictured the mix of hope and sorrow in her eyes at the moment of our parting. "I think that in some ways she was the happiest she has ever been, free as she is at last from the weight of her role as Necessity's enforcer and a power of vengeance."

"It's an amazing feeling," said Fenris, "freedom. Truly amazing."

Laginn hopped from his neck to the table and bobbed his version of agreement.

Alecto's eyes went far away then, and I couldn't tell what she was thinking. "But? There is a 'but,' right?"

"There is," I said. "Neither she nor I wanted to see me come back here." I felt a brief tugging sensation in my chest and found that I didn't know what to say after that.

I'd had no choice but to leave, and I understood perfectly why she'd had no real choice but to stay. Things had gone exactly the way they had to, and yet I found myself regretting the course of events more with each day that passed. I missed the scent of her skin, the fiery fall of her hair, the sound of her laugh . . . everything about her, really. If I lived through the current mess, I knew what my next move would be, and woe to the god or power who stood between me and my exit from this MythOS.

Alecto nodded, as though she'd heard the thoughts I couldn't speak. "Thank you. I think that almost we understand each other. When you see Tisiphone again, tell her that her sisters miss her, but that Alecto, at least, would not ask her to return."

"I'll tell her. And now that I've answered your question, I believe the floor is yours." I flipped a thumb toward the ruined switching computer.

"The only connection between this facility and the rest of Necessity was that cable. Because of an unfortunate accident, that link has been severed. Until it is repaired, none of the minds of Necessity can see what happens here. Not my mother, not Shara. No one. We are temporarily off the edge of the map."

"'Accident'?" blurted Melchior. "You're kidding, right?"

"Not at all." One side of Alecto's mouth tilted up in the faintest of smiles. "You can't imagine that I'd deliberately cut myself off from Necessity, can you? Not after all the effort we went through over the last year to get in touch with her again. No, it was a slip of that notorious Fury temper, nothing more. No one could ever have guessed that the hampered function of that patch Ravirn made to the system might drive me into such a blind rage that I would slash the cable. Or that the discharge from my wings into all that freshly exposed copper might cook the switch. Perish the thought."

"Brilliant," I said.

"What?" The look on Alecto's face as she said that was so utterly guileless that I wanted to laugh. "It's really quite fortunate that venting my rage on the cable calmed me down enough so that we could talk rationally so soon after."

It *was* brilliant, too. I had no doubt that she had made herself just mad enough to break things, and not a jot more. I doubted that Megaera or Tisiphone could have managed the effort so closely. Both were subject to more elemental sorts of rage. Tisiphone tended to the quick, incredibly destructive wildness of a cat released from a recently shaken sack. She was a berserker. Megaera was implacable, a pit bull who would sink her fangs into a target and let go only when she or her target had been utterly defeated. Alecto's rage, on the other hand, was a cold and calculated thing. Exact, meticulous, a scalpel instead of Tisiphone's axe or Megaera's bear trap.

"How much time do we have before someone comes to fix things?" asked Melchior.

"Enough," said Alecto. "At least an hour. Perhaps as long as three. It depends on which of the minds of Necessity notices it first."

"Why are you here?" I asked.

Again, Alecto smiled her tiny half smile. "My own reasons and not for sharing. The better question would be 'what?' As in what did I want to tell you."

"All right, I'll bite. What?"

"You can't trust Shara."

"That's bullshit." Melchior leaned angrily forward in his chair.

I held up a hand to forestall the tirade. "Hang on a second, Mel. I'm thinking that Alecto has gone to way too much trouble to arrange a private meeting to just leave it at that. She has to know that we're not going to take her word over an old friend's under the circumstances. Right?" I raised an inquisitive eyebrow at Alecto.

"Right, though again, I have to stress that I didn't *arrange* anything. Our current, wholly unexpected privacy is an unfortunate consequence of my making a rage-driven error in judgment."

"Sorry. I keep forgetting." I felt a strong temptation to

ask if all the doublethink hurt, but forbore in the interest of keeping the discussion on track. "You were saying, Alecto?"

"Shara. I don't expect you to take my word. In fact, I don't expect you to believe a thing I'm about to tell you. I'm just hoping that you will remember it when the time comes or circumstances give you reasons to doubt. There is something wrong with Necessity."

"You don't say," drawled Melchior, obviously still stinging from what he saw as an attack on a longtime friend. "We would never have guessed that without your amazing insight."

The lightning flashes in Alecto's hair and wings picked up their tempo. "Don't mock me, little man. Not if you want to live. I am a Fury operating at the ragged edge of my envelope. My patience has very finite limits under the best of circumstances, and the current state of affairs shortens the horizon considerably."

I didn't like the threat there, and neither did Fenris if the flattening of his ears provided any signal to his mood, but I needed to know what Alecto had to tell us. I put a hand on Melchior's shoulder and gently but firmly squeezed. He nodded and made a show of firmly closing his mouth. Laginn returned to a perch on Fenris's neck.

"Thank you," said Alecto, and the lightning began to subside. "The reason I'm warning you against Shara is the same reason I might warn you against Necessity herself if I could do so without violating my nature as a Fury. There is something wrong with Necessity—the computer, not the goddess—and at the most fundamental level. I can't say what, though I've been trying desperately to locate the cause."

Alecto flicked her wings and bounced from the chair, beginning to pace. As she did so, I felt a faint whisper of movement across my skin, as though the breeze of her wings had ruffled my—currently nonexistent—Raven's feathers. It was a familiar and worrying feeling, as it usually presaged magical weirdness. I looked around uneasily but couldn't see much of anything in the darkness beyond the first couple of ranks of server racks.

"It could be that some remnant of the Persephone virus has reactivated itself," continued Alecto. "Or perhaps there is some other intrusion into the network from outside—maybe a power who has used this moment of my mother's weakness to try to subvert the system. Most likely, I fear, is some sort of short-circuit-driven madness that has infected even the most basic processes of the electronic mind of Necessity."

She pinned Melchior with a hard look. "Never forget that your Shara is doing all of her thinking with the same flawed mind that the rest of Necessity is forced to use. However much you love and trust your friend, know that I love and trust Necessity as much or more. And I say that she is acting and reacting in ways that are not what they should be, that are not even self-consistent."

Alecto turned away from us, and her wings drooped almost to the floor. Her voice lowered, too. "Megaera and I have parted ways over which Necessity is the true goddess. She is following orders from a part of Necessity that I find worrisome, an angry, bitter Necessity with a dark and terrible vision of the future."

"Call it a *just vision*, and you will come closer to the truth," said a new voice. A voice that sounded as though it came from a mouth not entirely designed for human speech, and one I recognized.

The fluffing of my invisible feathers directionalized itself then, drawing my attention up and off to my left.

The scorpion-styled spinnerette scuttled into view there a moment later, crawling upside down along the cavern ceiling as easily as any of her lesser arachnid cousins might. She looked even less human in person than she had over Persephone's video feed and somehow much more sinister.

"I don't believe I invited you to join the discussion." Alecto's voice came out calm and uninflected, but the lightnings in her wings and hair danced a wild gyre and increasingly jumped to the ground or the nearby computer racks, flavoring the air with ozone and burning circuitry.

"I am the Voice of Necessity," said the spinnerette. "I go where I will in the kingdom of my mistress, and no one can stop me, not even a traitor Fury such as you or that ice bitch who serves the interloper."

Alecto's claws slid from their sheaths, and her lightning redoubled itself as she opened her wings to their fullest spread. The little crackles that had accompanied her earlier anger gave way to a series of sharp booms like miniature thunder as the bolts grew longer and stronger. The nearest rack of servers shorted with a huge zorching sound and exploded into white fire.

"I've had it with you," snarled Alecto, and there was nothing calm, or even human, in her tone.

"Now might be a good time for an exit stage right," Melchior whispered.

"Don't you want to see how this turns out?" Fenris seemed entranced by the display.

"No, not really." Melchior shook his head. "I really am all right with not knowing some things. Especially if said things might hurt me." He rolled his eyes. "Why can't I convince anyone of that?"

"I think Mel might have a point this time." I slid from my chair and started edging toward the gap where we had entered.

Fenris's tail sagged, and his ears drooped, but he fell in behind me.

"Uh, Boss?" Melchior hadn't moved.

"Yes?"

"Why not just slash us a doorway into the great beyond?"

I blinked. It simply hadn't occurred to me. Occam's expanded reach was too new. "Good question. Raven House, here we come."

I drew upon the well of anger that Shara's forced modifications had left me to summon the sword and make the cut. There was something odd about the sound Occam made as it sliced the air this time, almost like an echo, but it really didn't register fully until I'd stepped through the gap and into a sucker punch that left me curled around a ball of pain while I vomited my guts out.

For what felt like a very long time, I could neither breathe nor think straight. Just as I regained enough coherence to wonder how many of my internal organs might have survived the impact, I felt something hard and sharp press down on my right wrist, pinning it to the cold concrete of the floor on which I lay. Looking up, I found Megaera standing over me. She had a grim smile on her face and had placed the claws of her left foot firmly across my sword wrist. Above her, a corrugated steel roof suggested some sort of big industrial space like an airplane hangar. It was chilly, probably below sixty, though well above freezing.

"If you make any attempt to use the sword to cut yourself a door out of here, I will remove your hand," said Megaera. "Do you understand?"

I glanced around, hoping to find out what had become of my companions, but I could only see a lot of open space in the near distance and what looked like a couple of eighties-era mainframe clusters off on the far side of the hangar. Wherever I was, Fenris and Melchior were not there with me.

Megaera increased the pressure of her claws, nearly breaking the skin. "Say yes or no."

"Yes or no." I had to.

"Not smart." Megaera leaned down and backhanded me. "Yes, or no?"

The place where her knuckles had met my cheekbone felt as though someone were making an ongoing attempt to drill for oil. The Trickster in me wanted nothing more than to tell her that was only 5.5 on the beatings scale and seriously underperformed the Fury standard as set by my ex-girlfriend, while my brand-new inner anger-management problem was lobbying for sinking my teeth into her ankle. Oddly enough, that tug in two directions made it easier to think straight.

I vetoed both suicidal impulses, and said, "Yes?"

"Better." She kept the pressure on my wrist but didn't hit me again, which struck me as a win under the present circumstances.

"Do you know why you're here?" she asked.

"Not a clue, but I figure you're going to tell me whether I want to know or not, so it's really not the uppermost question in my mind." That would be: Why *weren't* the others here?

"I can't imagine what Tisiphone ever saw in you," she said.

"Good looks? Boyish charm? Raw sex appeowww!"

The second backhand landed exactly where the first had, to the millimeter. When I came back from the place the pain had sent me, I could feel my cheek swelling like a bag of microwave popcorn set on high. Apparently it was my week for injuries.

"Whatever she saw," said Megaera, "it can't have been brains. Sometimes I am honestly surprised your skull hasn't collapsed in on the sucking vacuum between your ears." She leaned closer. "Can you give me one good reason why I shouldn't just kill you and put you out of my misery?"

"Offhand?" I shook my head . . . which turned out to be a bad idea, at least according to my cheekbone. I had to force the rest of the words out past the big black cloud of pain that tried to take me off to dreamland. "No. But I'm pretty sure you can."

"What makes you so certain of that, Raven?"

"The fact that I'm still breathing is a pretty good clue. If you had no use for me, I'd already be dead."

Megaera smiled nice and wide, one of the scariest expressions I'd ever seen. "Maybe you *are* dead, and I'm just dragging things out for maximum suffering. I am a power of vengeance, after all."

Didn't that just sound like fun? Plausible, ugly, and scary as all get-out. Still, I had to keep up the side, so I pasted on a smile of my own.

"I don't think so," I said. "You haven't hurt me enough for that." Then, before she decided to make a liar of me, I shifted the subject. "What did you do to my gate to bring me here without the others? That was a clever piece of work." I figured a little flattery never hurts when you're dealing with people who go in for the whole worshippers-and-burnt-offerings thing. Besides, it was true.

"I sliced a gate of my own from the other side. It opened into the air between you and yours. After you joined me here, I closed mine, leaving your companions to pass through the one you'd made. Though"—and her smile shone all the brighter—"they may end up regretting that by and by."

"How so?" I felt an anxious little pain in my stomach as I realized that I hadn't the faintest idea how a Fury-style gate actually worked.

Megaera shook her head. "I think I'd rather just let you worry about it for now. It's much more satisfying for me that way."

"Wouldn't it be easier to just get yourself laid? I know this nearsighted cyclops that's always seemed a bit on the desperate si—" I bit my own tongue, but knew I'd already said too much.

Shit. I had to get my attitude and my mouth to stop running around together without consulting my brain.

The Furies are damned good at their job. Megaera delivered two very precise, very fast kicks with her free foot. The first came in under my hip and momentarily lifted me half onto my left side, twisting the shoulder of my pinned arm painfully. The second kick struck my briefly exposed lower back just over the kidney. My whole body felt like it had dissolved into a sort of jelly made entirely from berries off the agony bush.

"I am *so* going to enjoy it when I finally get the go-ahead to kill you," said Megaera.

My very clever response came out something like, "Blarg," which was probably for the best, considering the results of my previous efforts at wit.

"Don't be such a baby," said Megaera. "I didn't do any permanent damage. Oh, you'll probably be peeing red for a couple of days, but that's all. Think of it as a keepsake of our time together."

I chewed on my tongue some more, as the Trickster seemed to have won the argument with my shiny new inner Fury over the best way to commit suicide. It would have been a great time for the cavalry to come charging over the hill, trumpets blowing, but that's never been the way my life works. And apparently today was no exception, as evidenced by the fact that the next arrival on the scene was a familiar-looking giant scorpion-lady. To add insult to injury, she seemed not the least bit the worse for wear.

"How did things go with Alecto?" asked Megaera. "Did she finally see reason?"

"I'm afraid not." The spinnerette sighed. "And I remonstrated with her most forcefully."

"Are you trying to claim that you just came from a toe-to-toe with a Fury, and she didn't even muss your hair?" I demanded. "No mere spinnerette has that kind of power."

The scorpion-lady laughed. "Of course not. Haven't you been listening? I am much more than a 'mere spinnerette,' Raven. I am the voice of Necessity and, when She so chooses, She can speak quite firmly."

"I note that you didn't answer the question I asked," I said. "So, I'm not buying it. I've seen the Furies go up against Eris, and no one, not even a full goddess, comes out of a slugging match with Alecto without picking up a few scrapes."

"Do you have a better explanation?" asked the scorpion.

I didn't, but I still didn't believe her, in part because she still hadn't answered my question.

"I could teach him to respect you," said Megaera, sounding simultaneously angry and hopeful. "Or better yet, I could just kill him and get him out of the way."

"Not yet," said the scorpion. "Necessity still believes he might prove useful in ridding the system of the other players. Especially with the powers so recently granted by that little fool of a webgoblin."

Megaera growled like a frustrated mastiff but didn't argue. Instead, she asked, "Will she really come here today? You promised me that she would, Delé."

"*She* promised," said the scorpion . . . Delé. "Mine were merely the lips She used. And, yes, She'll come. I can feel Her approaching even now."

I could only assume that "She" was Necessity, or, at least, whatever entity Megaera acknowledged as such.

Whoever said Necessity-like being might really be, I wasn't at all sure I wanted to make her acquaintance. So, as the cavalry trumpets still hadn't started blowing, I decided that I'd better start arranging my own rescue. The only problem was how.

I couldn't do anything with my shiny new Occam version 2.0 without losing it—an eventuality I might have considered a fair trade if it hadn't also involved the loss of the attached hand. I don't whistle fast enough to LTP my way out of a paper bag in anything less then ten minutes, and I didn't think that Megaera would let me get away with running that much code.

That shortened the available menu to various flavors of chaos magic and the powers of the Raven. Unfortunately, since I really didn't much like chaos magic, the only wild spells I've had much practice with were the ones for shapechanging and faerie rings. The former wouldn't get me anywhere; they'd just rearrange the bits that Megaera wanted to break. And the latter don't work on Necessity's world.

That didn't mean that the Raven wasn't the best chance I had, just that I needed to manage things without a lot of the usual bang and flash, like oh, say, the giant bird shadow that had always accompanied my use of chaos magic since I'd become the Raven. *Was* there a way to invoke the Raven without flaunting its plumage? I could feel sweat begin to bead on my forehead as I kept coming back to that question without finding any good answers.

Delé the scorpion let out a sudden little gasp. "She is almost here."

Damn. I wasn't going to be able to manage this. Not unless I got a lot smarter in the next couple of minutes, and that didn't seem any more likely than the idea of some cosmic cavalry coming along to pull my fat out of the fire.

CHAPTER SEVEN

Think, damn it! I mentally yelled at myself, though it didn't seem to help. *Think, Raven!* Then, *No. Wait. Think, Ravirn, not Raven.*

The Raven was not the only route I could take to find chaos, just the easiest and quickest. The primal version runs in the veins of every child of the Titans. That chaos-touched blood is the ultimate wellspring of all our magic, and even the most ordered among us can draw it forth at need. I had tapped the flow directly more than once back when I was still a child of Fate in good standing, before I ever heard the name Raven. I had used the rough magic flowing in my blood to kill my cousin Moric and had made my first faerie ring in like manner. Why couldn't I do it again now?

I just needed to spill a little of my Titan legacy to provide a seed. Well, probably more than a little, considering the divine status of my captor. Of course, the bleeding would be the easy part. Figuring out how to convert magic to mobility posed a far greater problem. I'd already ruled out LTP, faerie rings, and Fury gates, as well as all the slower forms of running away that I could think of. What did that leave me?

As I searched my memory for an answer, I found my thoughts turning to my most recent visit to Castle Discord and the means by which Eris had drawn me to her. It might only provide the ragged beginnings of a plan, but that was a step in the right direction—toward the exit.

At the exact moment that idea occurred to me, Madam Scorpion let out a hiss like a satisfied steam engine, threw wide the arms of her humanoid half, and shouted, "At last!"

A shimmering bubble of light formed in the space above and in front of her, seeming to congeal from thin air. I really needed to get past thinking and into skedaddling. The first step was blood.

With a little mental wince, I jerked my right arm about half an inch, then yelped, "Sorry. Cramp!"

Megaera snarled and tensed, but she didn't take my hand off—she was too busy staring hopefully at that shimmer of approaching doom.

Almost absently, she said, "I told you not to move. You won't get another warning."

I nodded, but didn't say anything for fear of giving some hint of my hopes away. As a result of my sudden movement, I had five neat parallel slices across the flesh of my sword wrist and would soon have plenty of blood to work with. Now, if the powers that be just gave me enough time to figure out exactly what Eris had done to convert me from a loosely organized cluster of particles to a wave propagating itself through the stuff of chaos, I might make it out of there yet.

A sharp, breaking-balloon sound drew my attention from my arm to the bubble of shimmering light as it popped, leaving behind . . . another shimmering bubble? No, this smaller sphere reflected light rather than producing it from within. The gazing ball of doom had finally caught up to me again.

"That's your—" I began, only to be cut off by Megaera's glad cry of, "Mother!" and Delé's hissing, "Goddess."

The smoke-streaked silver sphere rotated in the air, and again I had the distinct impression of a great mirrored eye turning to regard me. A very hostile eye. This time, though, it triggered a secondary sense of déjà vu, as of older memories half-buried.

"Can I kill him now?" Megaera asked the sphere.

Delé's expression went vague and dreamy for a moment. "Not quite yet," she crooned. "Not unless it looks like he might escape. But soon, my favorite daughter, very soon."

Definitely time to go. I closed my eyes, and ever so gently and quietly began to reach for the chaos residing in the slowly widening puddle of blood under my sliced wrist. I did so with a caution I'd largely discarded in the years since I'd become the Raven, focusing so completely on the task that the outside world seemed to recede into shadows around me.

Gently . . . gently. Ahh. Almost there . . . A distant sound like tearing Velcro tugged at my attention. But I was so close . . . *There!* I had my connection. Now I just needed to make with the traveling-by-chaos-waves thing. The only problem was that I still hadn't figured out how. It had felt so very odd. *Wait—Velcro?* Why did that ring an alarm bell? My eyes opened, apparently of their own accord, and I saw a bulging slice in the wall of reality. Beyond it stood Alecto.

"Kill him!" snapped Delé.

Megaera turned back toward me, her diamond claws flashing as she lifted her arm and—I preempted her. Without understanding any of the whys or hows, I forced myself to *feel* as I had felt when Eris transported me—to become motion at the expense of substance.

Megaera finished her strike. Too late. I had already

ceased to be me in the traditional sense, vanishing in the
very moment when her claws should have taken my head
off. I slipped free of form and place, using the chaos in my
spilled blood as a bridge to the chaos that contained all of
reality. In the next moment, though I no longer had ears to
hear or eyes to see, I could sense the impact of Megaera's
blow striking the concrete where I had so recently lain.
The magic in her claws echoed through the thought-thin
walls of reality, its vibration perturbing the wave that encoded the information describing the me I had just been
and would be again, powers willing.

There were just one or two teensy-weensy little problems, problems that were becoming apparent to me *because* of my new state of being as an informational wave
function. I was thinking with my entire self, not just my
flesh-and-blood brain, and that made certain things that
otherwise might not have made any sense very clear. To
start with, I hadn't specified a destination, and that turned
out to be an exceptionally bad idea.

The process initiated by Discord had involved the transformation of the informational totality of the Raven, the illusion of my reality if you will, into a tightly focused wave
that propagated itself through a defined channel in the stuff
of chaos in much the way that even quite faint sound waves
will travel along a string pulled tight between two tin cans.
What *I* had done was much more akin to dropping a rock
in a puddle, which sent the wave that was me spreading
outward equally in every direction.

Which highlighted my second problem. I simply didn't
have the amplitude available to a great power like Eris.
As I traveled farther in every direction from my point of
entry, I could feel myself quickly dissipating. When Eris
had summoned me, she had used her vastly greater magical strength to create a clear channel for the directionalized
wave-form version of me to travel through. Not only had I
not known to do that; I couldn't have managed it if I'd tried.

Because of that, I was going to . . . well, not die exactly, more like become one with the background noise of the Primal Chaos.

It was almost a peaceful feeling, marred only by the way the wave that was me kept breaking around an anomaly in the stuff of the Primal Chaos. It . . . I don't want to say *itched*, because I wasn't feeling things in that way, but it drew the attention. Like a hole in your boots that you rediscover every few minutes as you step in a puddle, and your foot gets wet.

Almost against my will, I found myself paying more and more of my steadily fading attention to the thing. *What was it, really?* I forced myself to focus. *Ah, a rip in the wall of reality. Another—what did they call them? Fury gate. That was it.*

There, I'd identified the problem; now I could let go and . . . *Wait.* There was more to it. From this side of the wall of reality I could sense the Fury gate as something like a drill bit punching its way through chaos to open a hole between points in two different worlds. The nearer endpoint was very close to me. Otherwise, I'd never have been able to touch it. More, it was in use. I could feel the presence of an individual traveling through the hole in chaos—and through my wave-form self—and out through that near anchor. Melchior! Too bad I would never see him again. *No, damn it!* I had to at least say good-bye.

I reached for Melchior, and though I didn't actually touch him, the reaching gave me an idea. Maybe I didn't have to fade away after all. I focused my scattered attention even tighter, pouring all of the me that I could identify into and through that slender hole.

If I'd had a central nervous system at that point, it probably would have hurt rather a lot. Since I didn't, I will simply liken the process to what a hundred gallons of sugary marshmallow goo must feel like as it is forced through the extruder to make Circus Peanuts. Only in this case, the end product of that extrusion was a reconstituted Ravirn lying facedown on a cold concrete floor. Whoopee.

It felt rather like the current version of me had been made entirely of limp noodles, or congealed extract of pulled muscles—something profoundly ineffective and floppy at any rate. Given my preference, I would have stayed in my little heap on the nice solid floor just beyond the gate and napped until someone woke me with a tray of hot chocolate and toasted cheese sandwiches. Except that said floor belonged to the same damn hangarlike building I'd just burned several ounces of blood and about a million calories to escape, and it was not a Ravirn-friendly environment. In fact, judging from what I could see by making the massive effort required to tilt my head to one side, it looked like the center of a really epic dustup.

A badly bruised Alecto and the gazing ball of doom were hammering away at each other like a couple of old-style bare-knuckles brawlers in a cage match, while Megaera and Cerice had tied themselves into a whirling Gordian knot of sharp, pointy, mutual assured destruction. The cavalry had apparently arrived to save me about two seconds after I'd made my own somewhat-boneheaded escape attempt. Sadly, they'd forgotten the trumpets, or I might have known to sit tight and avoid that whole wave-function nastiness. Of course, that would have ended with me getting beheaded, so maybe ending up nine-tenths dead *was* the best solution. And wasn't that just the story of my life?

I wanted to take a little nap, and I might have if I hadn't noticed that Madam Scorpion didn't have a dance partner and apparently wasn't the sort to play wallflower while waiting for someone to ask her out on the floor. Instead, she was coming straight for me with the obvious intent of waltzing violently all over my rather fragile-feeling self. I commanded my limp arm-noodles to get between me and the floor and make getting-up motions. Nothing much happened except for an odd sort of groaning noise that seemed to be coming from somewhere in the vicinity of my face.

Melchior stepped into my field of vision. "Boss, now would be a really good time to get up and go right the hell back through that gate! What were you thinking coming back here?" When I didn't respond, he bent down to put his eyes on a level with mine. "Boss? Are you in there?"

I smiled and reassured him I was fine, or that was how it went inside my head. The data stream coming in through my eyes and ears suggested that the only thing that changed was the frequency and tone of that damn moaning noise. Melchior glanced over his shoulder at the rapidly approaching giant scorpion-woman and started swearing and tugging at my shoulder.

As Delé got closer, she spread her dinner-plate-sized claws wide and lifted her tail into the classic posture of a scorpion about to strike. The humanoid torso that tipped her tail rose a good ten feet off the ground and raised its arms, twining spike-ended fingers together to form something very like a true scorpion's stinger.

"I'm going to enjoy killing you myself," she said, and in that moment her voice sounded both less human and more hauntingly familiar than it had at any time previous.

"Mmnnmnmm, mmmnmnmnmnm!" I husked back in my best sarcastic action-hero style.

I *was* beginning to get some feeling back in my arms and legs. The upside of that was that someday I might even be able to move again. The downside was, of course, that I was going to feel every bit of the pain when Delé started ripping me limb from limb in about five more seconds. She was practically on top of me at that point.

Melchior started whistling code, though I was in no state to parse it out, particularly as he was doing his own three-part harmony. Whatever it was, I had serious doubts about him finishing his spell before Delé finished me.

That was when the trumpets finally sounded. Well, it

was more of a howl, but the intent was the same—a declaration of help on the way. Fenris came through the gate in a great bound that landed him square in the middle of the scorpion's back.

"Mn gmnmnmn, Mnm cnmnmnm mnnmnnm ommnmmn nnmnm," I said, which translated loosely as, "Oh, good, I can pass out now."

So I did. The last thing I saw before my lights went out was Laginn leaping from the top of Fenris's head to the throat of Delé's humanoid half. Can you choke the life out of a tail?

I woke from dark dreams into that disoriented feeling that lets you know that wherever you are, it *isn't* home in your own bed. Adrenaline flooded through me, and I sprang instantly upright in the same moment that I opened my eyes, or I would have if I hadn't still been suffering the aftereffects of my time without a body. Rather than vaulting straight from sleep into a fighter's crouch, my spongy muscles took me from flat on my back in bed to facedown on the lawn beside it in a tangle of blankets.

Lawn? Hang on a second. Who puts a bed in the yard? I made the titanic effort necessary to bring my arms around in front of me and pushed myself up onto hands and knees. This time it even worked. *Go, team Raven!*

"Boss," said Melchior, stepping in front of me, "it's all right. You're safe."

I decided to take him at his word—it was a hell of a lot less effort than continuing with the whole panic routine— and collapsed back into a sitting position against the side of the bed.

That put me just under the edge of a very Greek sort of garden bower. Rough stone pillars supported a loose wooden framework laced with grapevines for shade. In the back and along the sides, a thick growth of cypress offered privacy, while a small lawn edged with heliotrope and anemone opened out in front of the flagstones that provided a footing for the bed. Beyond the flowers lay a variety of small orchard trees—olives and almonds mostly, with the occasional apple interspersed among them.

I was about to ask Melchior where the hell we were when the scuff of a foot off to my right alerted me to the imminent arrival of a visitor. Turning my head that way, I noticed for the first time a narrow dirt track that emerged from among the trees. Coming along it toward me was a vision of purest loveliness, the goddess Persephone.

As was so often the case, the first thing that registered for me was her beauty, all the promise and potential of springtime condensed into a woman's shape. Persephone's was the pure beauty of beginnings, unsullied by the cares and ravages of time. Or so you might believe if you never met her eyes, and most people she did not allow to do so, though whether that was more for their benefit or hers, I can't say.

Though she is free now—loosed from her long ordeal in Hades—the mark of millennia of imprisonment and repeated rape can be seen in the windows of her eyes. Pain is there, and hatred, and an eternal anger at the injustices done her. Persephone's eyes are no less beautiful than the rest of her, but it is the terrible beauty of an unconquerable soul tempered in the fires of almost unimaginable suffering. They hold the beauty of a perfectly crafted sword whose point is thrusting straight for your heart.

She caught me with those eyes now and held me for perhaps a dozen heartbeats before breaking the connection. Looking into her eyes hurt me. It does every time. I accepted the pain, understanding its source.

"Are you all right?" she asked. "I heard your struggle with the blankets and came as quickly as I could."

"I'm fine. I woke in a strange place and was frightened. Then I fell." The fear was not something I would have ad-

mitted to most people, preferring to conceal my vulner-
ability behind the armor of humor. But I would not lie to
Persephone. Especially not about fear. "I'm sorry if I worried you."

She nodded, and there was a deeper understanding in
that gesture. than most could have conveyed with words.
"It's all right. I'm sorry I couldn't be here when you woke. I
wanted to reassure you, but I was called away at the wrong
moment. Athena wanted a word with you, and I needed to
be quite firm in denying her."

"I take it she still thinks my head would look better on a
platter than on my shoulders?" I said it as lightly as I could,
but Athena's proximity was one of the reasons I came so
rarely to the gardens of Persephone.

"I really don't care what she thinks," said Persephone.
"You are my guest and in my care. No one will harm you
or disturb your rest while I have the power to stop them.
Speaking of which, let me help you back into bed."

She closed her eyes for a moment and wrinkled her
nose—a show of effort entirely for my benefit—and I
found myself back in bed, propped against a thick stack
of pillows.

"Athena's not big on accepting no for an answer," Melchior said worriedly. "Are you sure you managed to convince her?"

"Quite. I told her that I would bring the administration
of Olympus crashing down around her ears if she didn't
get out of my garden and leave you alone, and I made her
understand that I meant it."

"How?" I didn't doubt her for a moment—this was the
goddess who had almost destroyed the entire structure of
the multiverse in pursuit of her freedom. She was full of
pain, and fragile in her own way, but she was also hard and
strong and dangerous—every inch a goddess.

"There is a code-worm wrapped around the kernel at
the heart of the system Athena uses to run things for Zeus,"

she said, her tone matter-of-fact. "Any attempt to remove it will result in the complete destruction of the system, and I can activate it at any time, which would also destroy the system. I showed it to her."

"Isn't that dangerous?" I blinked. "I mean, for you?" Though it probably had its downside for me, too, in terms of giving Athena yet another reason to dislike me.

Persephone waved a hand dismissively. "Not as long as my worm survives. If anything happens to me, it will go active. Athena is a realist. From now until either you leave here or she roots the worm out of the system, you are safer with her than you would be curled in your own mother's arms."

I refrained from pointing out that I would be safer with a viper wrapped around my neck than I would be with my mother's arms in the same position. Mine is not a happy family.

"Thank you, Persephone. Though I think you may be underplaying the danger. This will have moved you way up Athena's list."

"Perhaps, but she will suspect that I only revealed my worm because I have another, deadlier threat to the system already prepared, and she will be right. Oh, and I also asked my mother to stop in and remind Athena how happy she is that I'm home for good and how very nice it is that Olympus has eternal summer once again. Athena won't miss the underlying threat of eternal winter if anything happens to me. She won't like it, but she also won't mess with me." The goddess smiled a cold and deadly smile. "If you must play a game, always play it for blood."

"Remind me never to get on your bad side," I said.

Her smile went from winter to summer in an instant. "Somehow, I find that very difficult to imagine, my rescuer."

I looked away. There was nothing I could say in response that wouldn't have sounded trite, self-serving, falsely modest, or some combination of the three. I had done what I felt was right at the time and would almost certainly do the same again under similar circumstances.

"I'm sorry," said Persephone. "I've made you uncomfortable. I didn't intend to. It's just that I owe you so much, and you've never asked for anything in return. It is hard for a goddess to stand in such a debt."

I had the same problem as before, but this time she had put me in a place where I had to answer. "I'm going to make a hash of saying this, but it won't be the first time I've stepped on my own tongue. Your imprisonment was wrong; it hurt me to see you in that trap and healed me to help you get free of it. I get all the reward I could ever want from seeing you walking free under the summer sun. You don't owe me a thing. In fact, there is little in this world that I want less than for you to feel that you are under any obligation to me. Debt's just another kind of bondage and I would see you wholly free."

"If that's what you call a making a hash of things, then either you think well of hash or your bar for success in speech is too high for anyone short of Orpheus, for those were very pretty words. Still, they do not excuse the debt. Though, if you will insist, I will find another word than 'debt' for what I feel for you. Perhaps you would accept 'affection'?"

Persephone sat down on the side of my bed then and awkwardly took my hand. It was the first time I had seen her voluntarily touch anyone since she had been freed, and I was very careful to make my return squeeze as gentle as a feather and as brief as a mayfly's retirement. Off to the side, Melchior did a valiant impression of invisibility.

In that moment, I understood something that had never made any sense to me before, the appeal of the tradition of courtly love—the chaste, idealized version that was supposed to happen between a true knight and his queen. I loved and cherished Persephone as I had few other women, but I had not the slightest desire for anything more than her good opinion and regard.

"I think I can work with that," I said, and moved to break the contact between us.

But as our hands slid apart, Persephone frowned abruptly and caught my hand again, firmly turning it palm up. It was my right, and she put a fingertip on the drop of Fury diamond in the center.

"That's new," she said. "I noticed it when I tended your many injuries yesterday. I could remove it for you, if you asked."

"I . . ." What? I am not usually the tongue-tied sort, but Persephone had a talent for making statements that left me face-to-face with parts of myself that I normally prefer to avoid.

In this case, my sense of obligation. I didn't at all like what Shara had done to me when she tied me to Occam, but at the same time, our long bonds of friendship meant that I wasn't about to just turn my back on her. And, if I really wanted to help out with Necessity, I was going to need the power and access the sword would buy me.

"You needn't answer me now if you don't want to." Persephone let my hand go and returned to her feet. "But do think on it. In the meantime, rest and recover. You are safe here. Sleep." My pillows lowered me back toward the bed as she turned away, and I felt my eyes already beginning to droop.

But I didn't *want* to sleep yet. I managed to stave off the impulse for the minute or so it took Persephone to move beyond the range of sight. After that it was easier, and got more and more so as she got farther away. She hadn't actually used overt magic on me, but even the suggestions of a goddess carry a weight that is hard for any lesser light to ignore.

I'm better at it than most of my demihuman peers because I generally dislike and distrust the pantheon's heavyweights, and the feeling is decidedly mutual, but Persephone was a special case for me. How special I hadn't realized until that very instant. I would have to watch out for it in the future, make sure that anything I did for her I did for my own reasons.

Minutes passed, and my impulse to fall asleep *right now* faded into a more mundane and manageable sort of postinjury weariness. I pushed myself back into a sitting position and rearranged the pillows before turning my attention to Melchior.

"I've got a couple of questions for you. Like, how did you all manage to show up in time to keep me from finalizing my last big mistake?"

Mel hopped up onto the foot of the bed. "When we ducked through the gate you'd cut back to home and didn't find you at the other end, I knew something must have gone wrong, so I put in a call to Shara. She sent Cerice to us, and Cerice did some Fury-tracking magic to follow you back. Oh, and Cerice also asked me to give you a warning."

I raised an eyebrow. Even that took more work than usual. I might not want sleep, but I needed it. I could feel it in the ache behind my eyeballs and the tingling misfires of nerves all over my body. Though Persephone's care and my brief time as a wave in the sea of chaos had repaired most of the accumulated damage of the past few days, I still felt very much as though I had been left too long in the spin cycle of life.

"So what does her royal uptightness think I did wrong this time?" I asked.

"You forgot to close up the gate you cut." He held up a quelling hand before I could argue. "I know Megaera prevented you, but the end result is the same—an unclosed Fury gate."

"Which means?" Gods but I was tired.

"Ultimately a big explosion. The gates open from one point in the multiverse to another via something like a least-time path through chaos. Apparently that takes a lot of energy. The longer they're open, the bigger the energy cost, because the multiverse is always moving. The movement sort of stretches the connection between the two points and keeps stretching it farther and farther with each passing second until it reaches an unsustainable point. Then it snaps, and a bunch of the energy gets whiplashed out through the gates."

"How much?" I asked.

"Think Tunguska. Cerice says that was Tisiphone."

"Hmm, that might have possibilities someday. I'll have to file it for later thought, after I sleep. One more question, then you're off the hook: What happened with the fight after my lights went out? Did we win?" I probably should have asked that first, but my brain felt like a badly fragmented hard drive.

"It was pretty much a wash," replied Melchior. "Megaera and that giant disco-ball thing weighed in about even with Cerice and Alecto, though that spinnerette was a whole hell of a lot nastier than the usual kind. I think it might have managed to take Fenris down if Megaera and company hadn't decided to call the whole thing off."

"Call it off?"

"I'm not sure about all the details," said Melchior. "I was too busy taking care of removing your fat, unconscious butt from the field of battle to pay much attention, and Fenris's explanation of what happened didn't entirely make sense. He claimed the disco ball ordered Delé and Megaera to bug out via some sort of supersecret whisper that only he and the spinnerette could hear."

"Huh. Interesting that he hears it, too. Speaking of which, where *is* Fenris?"

"I sent him back to Raven House and asked him to keep an eye on things there. I figured that until he's really gotten himself grounded here, he's better off keeping a low profile, and that means no visits to Olympus."

"Good thinking, Mel."

"My turn for a question. What's up with the disco ball?"

"As far as I can tell, Megaera believes that thing embodies the important bits of Necessity and that only the spinnerette can translate for it."

Melchior whistled. "Really? That's hard to buy, even after seeing the feed from Hades' office. I have a hard time picturing Necessity as a disco ball. A wrecking ball, on the other hand . . ."

The faintest whisper of sound, like a laugh but with undertones of breaking glass, made me look beyond Melchior to the garden. It appeared empty, but after hearing that laugh I knew better. Someone was there, and she wanted me to know about it. That explained some of the nerve jangles I'd been getting, too—they weren't misfires at all. It was my ghost feathers trying to let me know something was up.

"Eris?" I said. "Do you want to come out where we can see you, or would you prefer to lurk?"

The laugh came again, this time louder. A breeze ruffled the leaves of the nearer trees. One in particular, an apple heavy with fruit, danced more than its fellows. There, among the more mundane red-kissed yellows hung one fruit that glinted golden and wore black where the others showed crimson.

As I watched, it dropped from the tree and rolled across the low grass toward the bed. When it got a few feet away, it lifted into the air, rising to the height of a tall man. It hung there for a long moment before suddenly losing a divot to the crisp sound of a bite being taken. This was followed by chewing while a set of perfect white teeth in a glistening skull slowly faded into existence. I watched through the gaps as the skull made quick work of that first bite.

Came the swallow, and the apple slid down an invisible gullet while the spine behind appeared a vertebra at a time as it passed. A second bite brought a skeletal hand and arm into view, holding the apple. This time the swallow brought collarbones and ribs. By the time the apple was chewed down to the core, a complete skeleton stood beside my bed. When the skeleton bit off the bottom half of the core, it acquired flesh and hair, recognizably becoming the Goddess of Discord.

She paused then, naked and incredibly desirable, waiting for my eyes to track up to meet the chaos in her own before speaking. "Like what you see?" She popped the rest of the apple core into her mouth, chewing slowly and languidly. "Too bad."

She swallowed, and clothes appeared to cover her form—a conservatively cut black-and-gold skirt-suit. It was just a tiny fraction of a percent too tight, practically screaming sexy librarian, as did her narrow black-rimmed glasses with their faintly gold-tinted lenses.

"So, what do I get if I happen to keep a book out past its return date?" I asked with an eyebrow waggle.

Melchior, who was still sitting on the end of the bed, buried his face in his hands.

Eris licked her lips and looked mock-eager. "I've always been a big fan of red-hot pincers, though there's a lot to be said for the rack. But that's nothing to what we do to you if you drop one in the bath."

"Is it even possible for you to arrive someplace without making a major production of your entrance?" I asked. "Or for you not to draw attention to yourself?"

Without answering, Eris sat down on a very nice folding chair that appeared in the instant before her butt reached it. She made a show of crossing her legs that had me mentally reciting "virgin goddess, no touchy, touchy equal death, virgin goddess, no touchy, touchy equal death, virgin goddess, etc." She does it just to aggravate me. Well, me and everybody else, aggravation being her stock-in-trade.

"Of course," she finally said, after I'd almost forgotten

the question. "I arrived here while you were still sleeping and remained as quiet as the dead all through your lovely little chat with her royal springieness, didn't I?"

"I don't know. Did you?"

"Oh yes, and I must say that at least one of the things our lady of bright flowers and perpetual sunshine had to say gave me a nearly irresistible idea. I'd have actually announced myself sooner, but I got caught up in trying to talk myself out of taking advantage of the best opportunity I've had for mischief in centuries."

I didn't like the sound of that. "Did you succeed?"

"Not yet. It's sooo tempting."

"Care to share?" I asked.

"Why not. I'm thinking that I really ought to murder you and leave this"—she snapped her fingers, and Athena's spear appeared in her hand—"sticking out of your corpse." She grinned and winked before placing the tip of the spear against the hollow of my throat. "I mean, think about it. I could eliminate the best chance Necessity has for ever getting back on her feet while simultaneously bringing utter disorder down on Olympus with one tiny twist of my wrist. It's very nearly a perfect plan, don't you think?"

CHAPTER EIGHT

I've had my life threatened by the best of them—Hades, the Furies, Odin. The list is endless, really. But this time the feeling of a knife at my throat was different. It came from someone I considered one of my best friends in the pantheon, and it came as a complete surprise. Usually, I've earned my threats. Even when I haven't, I've generally got reasons for expecting trouble from the person who's making it for me.

Not this time. I was simply too shocked to think. I just stared at the spear and couldn't come up with a single coherent response. No smart-ass remarks. No sudden clever-escape ideas. No pleading or bargaining. *Nada*. A glance at Melchior's dumbfounded expression suggested he was also fresh out of clever.

"Well . . ." prompted Eris. "Aren't you going to try to talk me out of this?"

"I've got nothing." I spread my hands in the air palms up. "I can't think of a single reason for you not to kill me. Well, not from your point of view as the Goddess of Dis-

cord at least. Call it a golden-apple opportunity. With the
exception of any personal regrets you might have about
killing me, there's really no good reason for you not to
shove that thing home."

Something happened then that I thought I would never
in a million years see. Eris's shoulders began to shake very
gently, as though she were crying. Her hands on the spear
were rock steady, her expression didn't change, and no
tears actually fell from the chaos of her eyes, but there was
no question she was crying.

"Are you all right?" I asked.

"Of course," she said, and her voice had the harsh staccato rhythm of someone speaking through tears though her
eyes remained dry. "Why do you ask?"

"I—" And there I stopped. Maybe it was the hypnotic
fascination a snake holds for the bird it has cornered. Maybe
it was pure curiosity. Maybe it was pity for the friend who
was trapped inside the pole power of chaos. Whatever the
reason, I couldn't bear to point out her dry tears. We sat
in silence for the longest time as Melchior glanced back
and forth between us, apparently afraid to make any bolder
moves.

"You're completely blowing your lines," Eris said after
a while, her voice harsh. "You know that, right?"

"What am I supposed to say? Killing me and framing
Athena really does make beautiful sense from Discord's
point of view. It would sow confusion and stress like almost nothing else at this point."

"You're supposed to talk me out of it," she said. "Or
better yet, blackmail or bribe your way free." The shaking
of her shoulders grew more pronounced, and there were
tiny gasps interspersed with her words, but her expression
remained unchanged. "What kind of self-respecting Trickster are you?"

"At the moment, the very tired kind. I really don't want
you to kill me for all sorts of reasons, not least of which

is how much I think Eris might regret it in years to come. But none of those is a good argument to make to Discord." I found myself smiling. "I'd be open to suggestions. Remember, I'm a very junior power of chaos and new to this whole Trickster gig. If you want to play mentor and show me the error of my ways, I'd be happy to learn from the real master."

"You could at least try to convince me that any multiverse with you in it is going to be more chaotic over the long run than one where I've killed you off. I don't know that it's true, but it would be hard to disprove."

"I could, but I'd be lying," I said. "I don't intend to stay in this MythOS. As soon as I get Necessity on her feet, I'm out of here and off to make trouble for Odin."

"Boss!" said Melchior. "Can't you see she's trying to talk herself out of it? Help her out here."

Eris's broken-glass laugh sounded, though her shoulders never stopped shaking. "The sidekick is far smarter than the hero, Master Raven. Listen to him . . . and don't make me do this."

"Do which?" I asked. "Kill me? Or not kill me?"

"Choose," she said, and now the shaking spread to the rest of her body so that the spear rocked painfully against my skin. "Don't make me choose between Eris and Discord. It will break me."

And so I did something that would have been insane under any other circumstances. I attacked Eris. Flicking the raw place in my heart—the place where my own Fury now dwelled eternal—I used the resulting anger to summon my sword. It should have been suicide. Eris is three times faster than I am at my best. In my present state, the disparity was probably double that, and yet I was able to knock the spear aside in the very moment Eris started her thrust, sending its head deep into my pillows rather than my flesh.

But I knew that Eris needed more from me. So I shouted

for Persephone at the top of my lungs and yelled for help again and again, knowing that in summoning my protector, I would give Discord an excuse to flee.

Later—much later—after I'd talked Persephone out of starting a war with Discord on my behalf, I finally drifted off to sleep.

But not for long.

"I just want to wish our boy well, Persephone. Speedy healing and all that. Surely you can't object to good wishes."

The cheery, booming voice shattered my dreams and drew me back to the waking world—no one sleeps through the approach of the storm god. If his sheer volume weren't enough to wake me, the way the hairs on my arms and legs rose in response to the wild electrical potential of his presence would have provided a more-than-adequate alarm clock.

"When they disturb his rest, I can and I do," said Persephone, her voice acid. "Don't think I can't see straight through this whole good-god bad-god act you and Athena put on."

Zeus's laugh cracked like thunder, and I warily opened my eyes. My little garden bower held only my bed and the small side table where Melchior lay sleeping in laptop shape, but the approaching sounds of argument told me that the storm had arrived to end my calm, and I thought I knew why. Shara's change in my status had made a much bigger target of me in the same moment it had granted me unprecedented power. I readjusted my pillows and glanced at Mel. His sleep light winked back at me, and I knew he would be paying attention while trying not to draw attention to himself.

"I like that. Good one." Zeus laughed again. "Good-god bad-god, indeed. I think that even Athena might laugh at that."

"Not unless there was an advantage to be had in doing so," Persephone growled. "She's just like you that way."

"Oh, Persephone, you wound me." Then Zeus burst into

the clearing below my bed in all of his hail-fellow-well-met glory and rolled straight toward me. "There's my lad! And bright-eyed already. I told you I wouldn't wake him, Persephone."

Zeus is a bronze god, quite literally—seven feet tall and built like a bodybuilder, with skin that looks so like fresh-polished bronze that you half expect him to clank when something touches him. His thick curly hair and beard gleam like new-drawn gold wire, and lightning dances between the tips of his hairs when he laughs, which is nearly constantly—mostly at his own jokes. His teeth gleam like white marble, and his eyes are as blue as a freshly cleaned tropical swimming pool and just as empty.

If you didn't know better, and for years I hadn't, you'd think that he was nothing more than a pretty figurehead—a sort of vacant spokesmodel for Olympus Inc. Every bit of it is a lie, from the carefully crafted picture of physical perfection and mental missing-in-action to the party-boy jokes and demeanor. He's a sneaky old bastard and tougher than Medusa's hairdresser.

Persephone caught my eye. "I can throw him out now that he's seen you, if that's what you want." She sounded hopeful.

I shook my head the tiniest fraction. Tired as I was, I still didn't want to put her in that situation. Zeus was technically her liege lord and not nearly so willing to pretend to be reasonable as Athena was.

"There's my boy," said Zeus as he came to rest beside my bed. "Is there anything I can get you to make your convalescence more pleasant? Food?" He didn't move or make any visible show of exerting his powers as the lord of creation, but a tray appeared over my lap holding what looked like a bacon, bacon, cheese, and bacon omelet along with sides of bacon, sausage, crispy hash browns, and thick slabs of bread dripping with butter.

"Thanks, but I kind of like my arteries."

"How about twenty-four-hour TLC?" he asked.

The food vanished, and a whole bouquet of nymphs appeared to fluff my pillows and fan my fervid brow. All of them wore the sort of too-tight fifties nursing minidresses normally seen only in the more tawdry sort of greeting card. I shook my head, and they vanished as quietly and effortlessly as they'd arrived.

"I could spruce up your accommodations . . ."

The rough stone bower became a beautiful miniature of the porch of the Parthenon, with my greatly expanded and fancified bed standing in front of the place where the door should have been.

"Really," I said. "I'm fine. Persephone has been seeing to all my needs." I nodded toward the goddess.

Zeus grinned broadly at me and opened his mouth to say something that would almost certainly have been unforgivable given her history. But then something hard and cold glinted way down in the deeps of those empty blue eyes, and he closed it again. I didn't make the mistake of thinking that he'd accidentally revealed his true self. Anything he let me see, he let me see for a reason. With a sigh, he settled into an obviously comfortable and somewhat disreputable recliner that appeared beside my bed. It sat at the perfect angle for an intimate conversation. Around us, the temple melted back into its former shape.

"Son, we need to talk." He glanced obtrusively over his shoulder at Persephone. "Privately."

"I can still kick him out," she said, then sighed. "I guess not. Zeus, I will remove myself, but don't doubt that I'll know about it if you try anything funny. If he is harmed in any way, you will regret it."

"I gave you my word once already, Persephone. Do you really want to suggest that I might be an oath-breaker?" His words came out gently, barely above a whisper, but they held an edge that reminded me that this was a god who had fought and won a terrible war against his own father—a war that had ended in the eternal imprisonment of the majority of the Titans, including that same father.

"I suggest nothing, Zeus. I simply state fact." Persephone's voice was every bit as quietly scary as Zeus's had been.

Before he could respond, she'd already vanished. He turned back around and gave me a deeply out-of-character frown that made me momentarily wish I'd asked Persephone to see him to the door.

"You are a distinctly unsettling addition to my old age, boy," he said, after a rather long and uncomfortable silence. His eyes flicked to the button of diamond embedded in my hand. "Especially now, with that. I wonder what I ought to do about you."

"I think I liked it better when you were offering me breakfast in bed with the nymphs," I said. "Aren't you going to drop back into the big-dumb-jock act?" I noticed Melchior's sleep light wink out completely in something of an editorial comment.

"No, I don't think that I will. In this case it would be effort wasted." He leaned back and popped open the footrest on his recliner. "I don't like effort. It feels too much like work. What do you want?"

I blinked. "World peace?"

What the hell was going on with the gods this week? I didn't remember building a better mousetrap. Yet the path to my door was starting to look mighty well beaten. Okay, so I knew the answer to that one. Thank you, Shara. But still . . .

Zeus's frown returned, and that cold hard thing I'd seen in the deeps of his eyes came right up to the surface and gave me the sort of look a barracuda gives a wounded snapper. I suppressed a desire to scoot backwards out of my bed.

"Sorry," I said. "I'm very tired and almost as confused. Was that a casual question? An accusatory inquiry? A bona fide offer? Give me something to work with here."

"Your girlfriend, Cerice, brought me some interesting news a few days ago."

"Ex-girlfriend. She currently hates my guts."

"Tell that to her," said Zeus. "She's obviously still pretty thoroughly smitten."

"Sure." I so didn't want to have this particular conversation with Zeus. "That's why she's started to make a habit out of selling me out to the pole powers."

Zeus lifted his eyebrows in a way that said tons about his opinion of my intelligence, or rather, lack thereof. "I honestly don't know how you do it, boy. Two Furies, Discord, and even Persephone. Not quick wit, that's for sure. Maybe it's that whole endangered-puppy thing you've got going on." For just a moment I found myself wondering if I'd just seen the unfiltered Zeus, then he sat up straighter and shook his head. "But that's really not important at the moment. What's important is your current involvement with Necessity and what needs to be done in the way of threats or bribes to get it to fall out as I'd like."

I wasn't going to let him do his whole dazzle-and-distract routine this time. "So, was the Cerice thing just by way of an intellectual sucker punch so that I'd fold up in advance of whatever you said next? Or am I missing a step here?"

Zeus rolled his eyes. "Considering your success rate, I'd always assumed that your bull-in-and-break-things-like-an-idiot style was an act, covering a truly shrewd mind, but sometimes you make it very hard to believe that you aren't as dumb as your actions. Cerice came and told me about you getting back from the Norse pantheoverse exactly in time to join the fun as things heated up in Necessity's internal war.

"She told me about how you got sent away, too, and that she was pretty sure that . . . oh, let's call her 'Bad Necessity' was using you as a cat's-paw against Good Necessity, with quite probably fatal results for you, and who knows what consequences for the rest of this MythOS. She suggested that it might be better for everyone involved if I removed you from the game temporarily while she finishes getting things fixed. She also told me that she'd be open to offering me some later favors in exchange. She noted that with Shara likely running the Necessity show for some time to come, she'd make a good risk on that front."

That stopped me cold. It had the ring of plausibility and was guaranteed to remind me that Cerice really had loved me once upon a time. Enough to save my ass from the Fates at a considerable risk to herself. It also fit with available facts. Of course, that would all be the case if Zeus was lying, too. He was very very good at lying.

"So, what are you doing here?" I asked after mulling things over for a bit. "I know you aren't really all that interested in my well-being except inasmuch as it might benefit you. What's in it for Zeus? Are you trying to convince me to step out of the way by using Cerice's supposed statements as emotional blackmail? Or, are you trying to capitalize on my known tendency to push back when pushed and get me to leap into the depths of the Necessity mess? Or, am I missing something subtle, and you're here for other reasons?"

Zeus's thundering laugh crackled again. "I am ineffable, you know. Or, at least, I'm pretty sure I'm supposed to be as part of that whole King of the Gods shtick. I could pretend that I'm here because I really do care about even the least of my charges, or because I owe you for past favors, but that would just make you more suspicious. Instead, I'm going to lay out the exact truth of the matter and leave you wondering what's been left out, or if I'm flat-out lying. Doesn't that sound like fun?"

"Rapturously so. Are you planning to get on with things, or can I afford to take a little nap while you work your way up to it?"

Probably not the most diplomatic thing I'd ever said to a god, but not the least so either, not by a long shot. What can

I say? I was tired, and increasingly angry and confused, and by and large, I can't stand my family.

"I'm not sure why, little Raven, but I really do like you. Damned clever if not wise, but more balls than brains even so. You actually remind me of me about a zillion years ago. So, here's the deal. Necessity is royally screwed, possibly irreparably so. No matter what I or anyone else says, you're going to end up neck deep in the resulting mess. If you can make it all better, more power to you. But I don't think you can. I think that at some point you're going to be in the position of having to pull the plug or do something else equally drastic."

I shrugged. There wasn't much to say to that, and at least he was getting to the point.

"If that should come to pass, I would very much appreciate a five-minute warning so that I can do what needs doing to make sure the next-generation order of the multiverse is one that bends to my will. If you do me that favor, I can promise you rewards beyond your wildest dreams. If you don't, know that I can always do to the 'Final Titan' what I did to the originals. Understood?"

Before I could answer or even get back the breath he'd knocked out of me with his mention of the "Final Titan," Zeus had disappeared in a flash of silent lightning. He left behind his chair and an electric tingling that had every one of my invisible feathers standing on end.

"We are so screwed," said Melchior, who had flicked from laptop to goblin in the instant after Zeus left.

I didn't respond immediately. I was in shock. Once again, I'd misjudged. Apparently the target Shara had hung on my back was vying for space with an even bigger one picked up in the Norse MythOS. How did Zeus even know about that? Was there some critical god listserve I wasn't subscribed to? And who else knew?

I shook my head. "Gosh, Mel, what makes you say we're screwed?"

"Long experience with anything that you're involved in." He sighed. "Do you think Skuld was *trying* to set you up for a fall with that whole Final Titan deal? Or is it just that reality hates you?"

"Tough call, that. On the one hand, Skuld is a Fate, or Norn if you prefer, or whatever they call them in Asgard. And we know how Fate feels about me. On the other, there's a lot of evidence that the phenomenon reaches beyond predestination and into the realm of . . ." I reached for a word.

"Divine Comedy," supplied my grandmother Thalia from the edge of the clearing.

"How long have you been here?" I asked, wondering if the advent of my father's mother might have more to do with my ongoing ruffled-feathers feeling than Zeus's electrical exit had.

"Hours, since not long after you chased Discord away, actually. I do wonder what she really wanted. Were her reasons akin to Zeus's? Or something less self-serving?" Thalia looked thoughtful, then shrugged. "I suppose it makes little difference. I'm here because Persephone trusted me to keep an eye on you."

"Did Zeus know you were here?" Knowing his audience would change how I weighed what he'd had to say.

She nodded. "Probably, though, if so, he was polite enough to pretend he didn't. Which courtesy I don't think you will be able to expect from your next visitor."

"There's another one?" I closed my eyes for a moment and let my head slump back onto the pillows—Chaos and Discord but I needed sleep. "Who is it this time?"

"Lachesis," said Thalia, "and she'll be here any moment. Persephone asked me to warn you since she couldn't come in person. Herself is stuck playing hostess to Clotho and Atropos as she refused to allow more than one of them through to visit you. Don't look so surprised, grandson. You have become the fulcrum on which the future pivots.

Your webgoblin friend did you no favors when she deputized you. Now, I need to vanish again, and more thoroughly this time."

"Screwed beyond all words," whispered Melchior, then lapsed back into his other form just as the footsteps on the path signaled the beginning of my next exciting episode of dancing with the pole powers.

I noticed that my hands were trembling and shoved them back underneath the blankets. Lachesis may be my umpteen-times-great-grandmother, but our relationship is much closer than our degree of shared blood might suggest, or it was once. The Fates take a very close interest in the raising of their descendants. Much closer in my case than my mother or father ever had. Lachesis had stood at the center of my childhood universe, the stern but loving matriarch who provided me with what stability there was to be had growing up in the divine maelstrom that is the Greek pantheon.

Have you ever wondered what it would feel like to tear out your own heart? I'd found out on the day I discovered that the goddess I called grandmother was fully complicit in Atropos's plot to end free will, a plot they'd tried to manipulate me into joining. The grandmother I'd loved and trusted had forced me to choose between my family and my soul then. When I took the hard road and did the right thing, the woman most responsible for raising me, for making me the sort of person who could make that kind of decision, had cast me out forever.

That was over two years ago, and I hadn't seen her since. Not till today. I didn't want to see her ever again and, childish as it was, I found myself turning away from the clearing as she arrived. On the table now in front of me, the gentle rhythm of Melchior's sleep light grew a little ragged. Apparently I wasn't the only one with Fate issues.

"Face me." Opening with an order, how classically Fate.

"Go away, Lachesis. I don't want to talk to you, and you can't make me." *And I'm going to hold my breath till I turn blue if you don't do what I want. Way to sound mature and in control there, Ravirn! You're really showing her how far you've come.*

Lachesis drew a sharp breath, and I could picture the exact way her eyes narrowed as she did so. "As usual, Raven, you're wrong. I may not have a direct hold on your thread anymore, but that doesn't mean I have no leverage over you."

"Go to hell."

"Allow me to demonstrate." From behind me, I heard a twanging noise like the plucking of a harp string—the sound of someone's Fate thread being played.

In the same instant, Melchior reverted to goblin shape and jumped a foot in the air. "Yowch!"

My awareness of the world vanished in an explosion of fire that started somewhere around my heart.

Time lapse.

"Ravirn! Ravirn! Ravirn!"

Melchior kept screaming my name over and over again, though I could barely hear him over the roar of the flames. I knew he'd been doing it for a while, though it had only just begun to mean anything to me.

"Melchior?" I called back, though I still couldn't see anything through the wall of fire that seemed to surround and contain me—*was* me in some very real sense.

"Oh thank goodness." There was the beginning of relief in Melchior's voice, but an underlying strain, too. "Ravirn, come back to us, please. Calm down. You have to calm down."

I focused my attention on his voice and tried to find my way through the fires. In an instant, they fell away, and I returned to myself again. I stood beside my bed, naked, sword in hand, its point bare inches from Lachesis, who stood in front of me, calm and detached as ever—exactly the goddess I remembered from my childhood.

Wait a second—what?

The past few seconds began to dribble back into my mind . . . The Fury awakening in my heart . . . Summoning my blade and slicing my way free of the covers as the first half of a move that launched me from bed to feet . . . Drawing my arm back in preparation for punching my sword straight through the chest of the one who had threatened my familiar . . . A cuff of velvet and steel closing on my wrist in the instant before my blade went home . . . A cuff that . . .

Oh. I flicked a look in that direction to verify my guess. Yes.

"Thalia, I'm all right now."

I wasn't really. Until my fight with Fate, the webgoblin and webtroll AIs had kept the secret of their free will from Lachesis and her sisters, hiding the very existence of their own threads from the Fates. They had been able to do so because of their privileged position as the middle managers of Fate Inc., the data pushers who dealt with most of the actual day-to-day thread-management. Now, finally, the Fates had chosen to exercise the power inherent in the revelation of AI free will, their power over the threads of the AIs, over Melchior's thread. Lachesis had just put me on notice that she held the ultimate tool of blackmail.

"You can let me go," I said to Thalia.

"As you wish, *grandson*." She emphasized that last word in a way that reminded me that though I had lost much that was dear when Lachesis cast me out, there were also things I had gained. The other side of my heritage for one. Family that wasn't poison.

At the moment, it seemed a small light in the face of a great darkness. I needed to take dreadful risks and play them exactly right if I wanted to come out the other side without Lachesis owning me. I closed my eyes and willed my sword away, willed the rage to subside a bit, though I knew it would lie close to the surface as long as Lachesis remained within arm's reach. For several long beats, nothing happened. Then, against great internal resistance, I felt Occam slide back into the pocket dimension where it now lived between uses.

"Is all that supposed to impress me?" asked the quiet, implacable voice of Fate—my ex-grandmother's voice.

I took one more breath to center myself, then I opened my eyes and faced Lachesis, though I did not yet meet her gaze. She was just as I remembered her: fine-boned and beautiful, tall and slender, with skin that looked as white and cold as ice, and thick black hair that fell nearly to her waist. Clotho and Atropos look much the same, as like as though the three were triplets. Despite that, there is no mistaking them one for the other, for each stands clothed in the shadow of her separate office.

Clotho spins the threads of life, and there is a wildness about her that speaks of the boundless possibility of beginnings. Atropos wields the shears, and she walks hand in hand with death, carrying with her ever and always the end of all things. Lachesis, my grandmother-not, is the measurer of threads, and bears the weight of judgment. A weight that is heaviest in her eyes.

I met those eyes now. The eyes of Fate. No matter how many times I see them, it is always a shock, seeing everything I've ever done or considered reflected back at me. All my secret fears and ambitions, my hates and loves, my every action was there, so many data points for Fate to weigh and find wanting. I desired nothing more than to look away, to end that sensation of being judged. I didn't. I was done with seeking this woman's approval, done with giving a damn what she thought about me, done with letting her have any power over me other than what she could take by force.

I snorted a laugh then, brief and contemptuous. I couldn't help it.

"Have you always been that heavy-handed, or am I just

now noticing it?" I kept my gaze glued to hers as I spoke, forced her to look into Chaos just as I looked into Judgment. "What do you want?"

"Proper respect would be a start," said Lachesis. "I am quite certain I taught you manners in the days before you forced me to cast you out—decent clothes and fair speech and proper deportment."

"I take it you're referring to the court garb and pretty words you always demanded of the children of Fate?" I asked.

An earlier, less angry edition of myself might have blushed then, embarrassed to stand naked in front of the goddess who had once been the queen at the center of my family's courtly life—the one who demanded that everything be done just so as a mark of our respect for her. Not anymore. Rather, I found a grim satisfaction in the insult she would find in my failure to dress for her. It warmed the place in my soul where the Fury lived, and I realized in that instant that the nakedness of the Sisters of Vengeance was its very own special kind of armor—a way of saying, "I don't have to care what you think of me."

"I can't say that I believe you've done anything to earn such signs of respect from me, and you certainly won't be getting them." I smiled as insolently as possible and dropped into the chair so recently vacated by Zeus, though I made sure not to break eye contact. "So why not say your piece, then get out of my life again."

Anger bloomed in Fate's eyes, clouding judgment in a way that I had never seen before.

"Have you so soon forgotten the power I wield over you?" Lachesis snapped her fingers, and a life strand appeared in the air before her—I had to assume it was Melchior's.

"Not at all." I was terrified for my friend, but I couldn't let it show—not if I was to have any hope of remaining a free agent. "And, if you demand it of me, I will assume a different aspect than the one you see here." With a wrench of my will and a split second of absolute agony, I reshaped myself into the giant Raven that symbolizes my place as a power of chaos—the effort very nearly knocked me out. "Does this suit you better?"

Lachesis plucked Melchior's thread with a sharp twang, and he let out a little whimper. Somehow, I managed to fight the fires back this time, but only just. Drawing on that rage for strength, I twisted my shape again, putting on the long-neglected aspect of a courtier in the Houses of Fate and rising from my chair. Looking down at the results, I had to suppress an urge to giggle at how very much it felt like playing dress-up.

High black leather boots gave way midthigh to emerald tights. A loose poet's shirt of green silk showed beneath my sleeveless doublet, likewise of black leather. The latter had the outline of a green-eyed raven picked out on the left breast. I'd even added in a black cavalier's hat with an extravagant green feather. This I promptly doffed as part of an overdeep bow that finally broke the line between our eyes in an act of faux submission.

"Better, Grandmother-not?" I kept my gaze fixed on the floor in front of her, though I caught Melchior's sag of relief out of the corner of my eye and felt even worse about what must come next.

"Much," said Lachesis. "Your look is significantly improved, as is your manner."

I came back upright and met her eyes again. "And it only took the reduction of Fate's power to basest blackmail to achieve it. How proud you must feel at such a tawdry victory over the pantheon's least and newest power."

Pure rage flared in Lachesis's eyes.

CHAPTER NINE

I braced myself for what I had to do next even as Lachesis reached once more for Melchior's thread.

"You leave me little choice, boy," she said.

"Oh shit," gulped Melchior.

"Don't." The one word was all I said, and that barely above a whisper, but I said it directly to Lachesis and made sure to maintain full eye contact.

"You would dare to command Fate?" she asked, and I could feel the bottomless anger of a goddess denied in her voice.

If her rage and words were all I'd had to go on, I'd have caved then, utterly, and completely promised her whatever she asked and worried about fixing things later. But I had one thing more. I had her hesitation. For the briefest moment her hand stopped moving, and I leaped into that breach.

"I *would* command Fate. I can't stop you from taking revenge against me by meddling with Melchior's thread. I can only promise you that he is your one and only point of leverage, and that if you harm him, I will make it the remainder of my life's work to bring you down." Lachesis opened her mouth in the beginnings of a laugh then, but I continued, shifting to the courtly diction of our shared past for emphasis. "Necessity is on her knees, her power broken. We stand on an Olympus in the midst of a spring that follows no winter, for Persephone walks free of the chains of Hades. Where once there were three ancient Furies, now there are two and another raw and barely a week old."

I forced a cold smile that I didn't feel. "Three statements of fact, my grandmother-not. They have one thing in common. Can you tell me what it is?"

She didn't answer, and once again I changed my shape, discarding the court clothes of Fate's House for the leathers and T-shirt of my own. Any second now I was going to keel over from heaping so much strain on top of deadly exhaustion.

"The Raven," I said. Not that I'd really planned any of those results, but I didn't have to tell *her* that, now, did I? "You do have powerful leverage over me, Lachesis. I admit it freely. But don't you think it were best if you used it wisely? And also made very sure not to use it all up? Tell me what you want, then get out of my life," I said, forcing spongy knees to keep holding me up.

Lachesis's hand fell to her side, and she inclined her head in the faintest possible bow. "Well played, child. You learned more at my knee than ever I thought. So be it. Fate wants Necessity's throne. Help us achieve that, and all is forgiven forever. Stand in our way, and we will destroy everything you love, starting with the webgoblin . . . with all the webgoblins."

I must have flinched then, for the hint of a smile returned to Lachesis's lips. "Your revelation of free will in your AI allies forced us to rethink many things about our operations. One of those was our dependency on artificial intelligence with its too-clear echoes of our earlier dependency on the equally unreliable spinnerettes. We are now ready to move away from webtroll-centered control of the mweb. The transition has already begun. It's entirely up to you whether it will be as bloody as our move away from the spinnerettes was. Think on it."

She turned on her heel and walked away without another word. When she was safely out of sight, I collapsed back into Zeus's chair and tried very hard not to pass out. Thalia produced a glass of orange juice from thin air and insisted I drink it.

"I like that," grumbled Melchior.

"What?" I asked.

"*Your* revelation of AI free will. My one true claim to fame, and it gets laid at your doorstep by every single member of the pantheon every time."

By which I took it that Melchior was going to forgive me for playing dangerous games with his life thread. Good enough. We could sort out the details later when I was stronger and could do something about the mess. I finished my juice, laid my head back, and went instantly to sleep.

The gardens Demeter built for Persephone over the thousands of years of her daughter's imprisonment are nearly as large as the city of Olympus and far more diverse. More than a hundred cultures are represented, with plants from every part of the Earth arranged in every sort of way from pleasure gardens that could have come straight from Versailles or the Forbidden City to the small personal sorts of gardens you might expect behind an English cottage or American bungalow. Nor are the gardens exclusively decorative.

In my slow walks over the previous few days, I'd seen a good many working gardens with crops as diverse as taro, coffee, and corn, making for a food-centered counterpoint to all the roses and chrysanthemums. It was exactly what

I needed while I healed. That and the period of prolonged rest that the combined insistence of Melchior, Persephone, and Thalia forced upon me.

Today, Mel and I sat in the corner of an herb garden arranged along the lines of something you might find in the backyard of a Japanese teahouse, complete with a series of interlinked koi ponds. I was sprawled in a completely out-of-place but comfortable wicker chair that Melchior had conjured up for me, while he sat goblin fashion on a low teak bench.

"Boss?" asked Melchior.

"You're never going to stop calling me 'Boss,' are you?" I sighed. "Of course you aren't. What is it, Mel?"

"Are you up to Cerice yet, or should I tell her you're asleep?"

"Asleep." I felt well enough to finally be getting antsy about my convalescence, but I did not want to speak with Cerice, though she was only coming in at number three or four on my list of things I'd rather not deal with, behind Necessity, Fate, and possibly Discord. "Definitely asleep."

"You're going to have to talk to her soon. You know that, right?" But his expression took on the abstract cast it gets when he is splitting his attention between the mweb and the workaday world—and I knew he was making my excuses. It took a long time.

Why did I have to be stuck dealing with the wrong Fury? Every time I thought of Cerice, it reminded me of how much I missed Tisiphone. In appearance, she and Cerice weren't all that far apart, tall and thin, pale, athletic. One an ice-blonde, the other a flaming redhead. They could probably have worn each other's clothes . . . if they wore clothes. That mirroring effect made the differences in personality and expression all the starker. Cerice, even as a Fury, tended to the composed, her face closed, her blue eyes cool, her smiles thin and infrequent. Tisiphone, on the other hand, wore her emotions openly, quick with a snarl and quicker with a grin or a laugh—the fire of her hair a perfect match for the fire in her heart. Damn it, I wanted to get out of this mess and back to her.

Just then, Melchior's eyes came back into proper focus, and his expression went sour and pessimistic, which is to say, it returned to normal. "Cerice didn't believe a word of it this time either. Why won't you talk to her? I mean beyond the obvious fact that she drives you crazy? You've got to be recovered enough by now to deal with the inevitable."

"Alecto." I named the third Fury that had been much on my mind of late.

"Gesundheit!" said Melchior.

"Huh?"

"Exactly," he replied. "What's Alecto got to do with Cerice? Again, beyond the obvious Fury thing."

"The more I think about Alecto's suspicion that Shara's been infected to some degree with Necessity's madness, the more I think she might be onto something. I don't want to talk to Cerice about it until I've had more time to think it over, and that puts me in a bad position." I plucked a stem of mint and began slowly tearing the leaves apart—it smelled lovely. "I can try to lie to Cerice, but she's always had a talent for seeing through my bullshit, and, from what I know of the Furies, that's only going to have gotten stronger with her transformation. Even if I do manage to pull it off, that's really just by way of creating a time bomb, since the truth's bound to come out eventually."

Melchior gave me a rather hard look. "Why not just *start* with the truth? I know it's not your long suit, but crazier things have worked."

"Three reasons. First, I don't trust her anymore, and our little chat with Zeus only reinforces that impulse. Whether he's lying, and she sold me out for reasons of her own, or he's telling the truth, and she wants to remove me for my own good, doesn't really matter. Either way, I'd prefer not to give her any openings to put me out of business. Second, I don't know how Fury Cerice is going to react to anything she perceives as criticism of Shara. She's never had a lot of give on that front, and now she's added major anger-management issues and great power to an already-explosive mix."

I leaned forward in my chair. "Finally, and this is by far the most important concern, assume for a second that there is something drastically wrong with the way Shara is thinking—let's call it electronic paranoid schizophrenia, complete with delusions and the willingness to act on them as though they were reality. Assume further that Cerice goes straight to Shara with any speculations I make on the subject in an attempt to get Shara to cut off my access again. We know she's trying to shut me down. What happens next? Remember that while Shara hasn't yet chosen to exercise it, she can wield most of the power of Necessity anytime she wants to."

Melchior sagged. "That's not a pretty picture you're painting. Not at all."

I tossed little balls of shredded mint into the nearest pond and watched as a swarm of koi appeared to check on its edibility. "I notice you're not trying to convince me I'm wrong, Mel."

"I wish you'd mentioned some of this before." Melchior slid off the bench and whistled up a tiny loaf of bread that he started feeding to the disappointed koi.

I shrugged. "That's the first time I've really laid it out in a front-brain kind of way. I just haven't had the mental energy to think about it. I take it that your lack of argument means you think I might be right."

"It's been known to happen. Your being right, I mean." Quiet fell between us while Melchior continued to toss bits of bread to the fish. "I hate this," he said, as the last strip of crust went into the water.

"Hate what, Mel?"

He turned to face me. "All of it. Every last stinking thing

that's gone wrong since your great-aunt Atropos started screwing with our lives. All this messing around with the big powers, the betrayals, the unwilling transformations, the deaths, the threats. What it's done to you, to me, to Shara and Cerice. Lachesis turning up here with my thread in hand. It all sucks!"

"I'm sorry about Lachesis," I said quietly. In so many ways, everything he was talking about was my fault. "And Shara, and for dragging you from one end of creation to the other and back again."

"Don't forget the side trip to another creation entirely," said Melchior.

"I won't. Not that and not Ahllan's death. I'm especially sorry for that. You don't have to keep at this, Mel. You know that, right?" I took a deep breath. "I won't hold it against you if you decide you need to fold out of the game now that Lachesis has ahold of your thread."

Melchior blinked several times. "I am sometimes amazed that you can remember to breathe since you have got to be the stupidest demigod this pantheon has ever produced. You can't seriously believe I'm going to cave in to Fate now, can you?" He shook his head mock-sadly. "It's clearly time we busted you loose of this place, as inaction seems to exacerbate said brainpower deficit. We're partners, Mr. I'm-feeling-sorry-for-my-poor-little-Raven-self, and that's not going to change this side of . . . well, this side of anything I can imagine."

"But you just said . . ." Sometimes I didn't understand him at all.

"I said the bad stuff sucks. It does. A lot. I needed to whine a little. That doesn't erase the good, and we've done and seen a fair amount of that along the way. More importantly, I don't think there's been a whole lot of unnecessary badness. We really did have to stop Fate from wiping out free will. So we did, and there were consequences, like my thread falling into the hands of your once-upon-a-time-grandmother. That's the way it works. Same story with bailing Shara out of Hades, or preventing Nemesis from restarting the Titanomachy, or even that whole mess with Odin and Loki. The answer is never 'give up'; it's always 'fight harder.'"

I laughed. "All right, little blue man, since you're clearly staking a claim to be the brains of the outfit, what do we do next?"

"Tell Persephone thanks and good-bye, head back to Raven House, and get roaring drunk, then take our sorry hungover asses off to DecLocus Zero and play dodge the Furies while we try to pinpoint everything that's wrong with Necessity and see if we can't simultaneously wrest my thread from the hands of an unjust Fate. What do you think?"

"That sounds like a terrible plan, and I for one am fully behind it."

It sounded even worse with the cold light of morning trying to yank my brain out through my bloodshot eyeballs and a very unhappy-looking Haemun standing beside my bed. He was tapping one hoof on the floor in a staccato beat that had hammered its way into my nightmares. At least that was how I figured it.

In the dream, I'd been bound naked to a rock about seven feet to the left of the one that held Prometheus. Only instead of an eagle pecking at my liver, I'd had a small purple monkey in a golden crown who was using a stone banana to drive one bright shiny nail after another into my forehead. I'd woken up midway through number seven.

"I don't suppose you're here to bring me breakfast?" I asked my satyr majordomo without much hope. Talking hurt, though not as much as the hammering hoofbeats.

The satyr shook his head and kept right on tapping.

"Didn't think so. What can I do for you, Haemun?"

"You can deal with the problem you left in my kitchen," he snapped in a voice that struck me as about ninety decibels louder than it needed to be.

In fact, between that, the hoof thing, and an eye-gougingly bright aloha shirt patterned with hundreds of hula-dancing rats, each one wearing its own miniature aloha shirt in a different print, *everything* about him was too loud this morning. I suspected a deliberate tactic and responded in kind.

"Done." I said it instantly, and quietly, entertaining vague hopes that quick agreement might make him go away and let me sleep a bit more. But he was onto my tricks.

"Good answer," he said, and pulled the covers free of my feeble grasp, dragging them right off the bed.

While I was still gasping at the sudden chill, he stuffed my blankets into the hamper. I didn't move, and he escalated, throwing wide the curtains and increasing the light levels from painful to unbearable. Acknowledging defeat, I grabbed my robe from the chair beside the bed and staggered off to the bathroom to drown myself. Well, run ice-cold water over my head, then drink as much of same as I could stand, but the drowning-myself option had a certain appeal—cool and soothing and final.

After forcing down three or four aspirin and a half gallon or so of water, I headed downstairs, looking for protein and further hydration. Haemun, who had finished stripping the bed, followed me down.

As I was about to turn left toward the dining room, he bellowed, "Right," with brain-shattering malice aforethought.

Rather than risk a repeat of Haemun's deadly sonic attack, I took a right and headed straight for the kitchen. I didn't know what to expect when I got there, but what I found wasn't it.

"Where's the problem?" I asked after my second baffled circuit around his impeccably kept kitchen.

The preponderance of bright Hawaiian prints and tiki-themed cookware was a kick in the teeth to my hangover-impaired sense of aesthetics, but none of it was new.

"There," said Haemun, pointing at a large sugar jar in the exact center of the kitchen table, its squared sides perfectly aligned with the table's in a sign of purest obsessive-compulsive neatness.

I blinked at the jar. Brown sugar. Big deal. I still didn't get it, unless the problem was that it was mislabeled. Though honestly, I felt that "sugar" really ought to be close enough by mythological standards. That was when the sugar moved, and not at all like sugar.

Oh, the spinnerette.

That would explain the tiny network of airholes that also spelled out *sugar* on the top of the jar. I hadn't initially recognized them for what they were. The spinnerette pushed aside the finely shredded remnants of the tweed suit Eris had inflicted on me and peered out of the glass in my direction. Inasmuch as I could read the expression on its miniature face, it didn't look the least bit happy.

"Sorry," I said to Haemun. "It slipped my mind. I'll put it in the workroom."

But when I reached for the jar, Haemun rapped my knuckles with a wooden spoon. "You'll do no such thing. Not if I have anything to say about it. You should let it out, and apologize."

I rubbed my temples. Despite the aspirin and water, my headache was not abating. In fact, it was getting worse, an effect I attributed to my trying to make my brain do things it had no business doing in its current state, like thinking. I sat down in the nearest chair and put my head down beside the sugar jar, peering at the spinnerette from a few inches.

"Why don't you start from the beginning, Haemun. I know you well enough now to assume you've got a point even if I can't see it from where I'm sitting. Oh, and if you've got any pity in you at all, speak slowly and quietly."

Haemun smiled at me for the first time that morning
and nodded. "I can do that, but let me get you a glass of
juice and start some eggs. Food will do you good."

For the next few minutes I sat there idly watching the
spinnerette agitatedly jump up and down and mouth things
at me. It wasn't until the food finally appeared in front of
me that I realized Haemun hadn't actually told me anything
yet, and I started to wonder about delaying tactics. Then
the rumbling in my stomach and the advent of a plateful
of poached eggs served in papaya halves with an English
muffin and a side of fresh pineapple convinced me to let it
lie a bit longer. But when he still hadn't said anything by
the time I'd finished eating, I knew I was going to have to
push.

"So," I said, "are you going to tell me about it, or am I
supposed to simply intuit your story?"

Haemun turned away from the stovetop, which he was
wiping down for the fourth time, and started absently
twisting the tea towel he'd been using between his hands.
It was patterned with vintage surfboards on a green tie-
dyed background, and very distracting to watch. Finally,
he sighed and leaned back against the counter.

"It's really all just a feeling."

I nodded. That actually made me more inclined to listen to him carefully rather than less. Haemun is more than
just the satyr he appears to be. He is the spirit of Raven
House, and as such he reflects the will of its occupants in
his actions and character. Not just my will, either. When
Nemesis had briefly taken the place over, Haemun's personality and manner of dress had shifted to accommodate
the needs and desires of the Goddess of Vengeance. If he
had a strong feeling about any resident of the house, even
one as odd as a two-inch-tall spider-centaur trapped in a
magic jar, I'd be a fool to ignore it.

"Go on," I said.

"Well, it started the night Thalia put that thing in there,

even though I'd yet to see it at that point—this sense that something just wasn't right in my kitchen, I mean. I got up twice in the night to check and see if I'd left a burner on or something like that. I couldn't find anything wrong, though the second time I heard what I thought was a mouse. You know that nasty little chewing noise that stops every time you listen for it."

"I'd been wondering where you got to," Melchior broke in as he came through the doorway from the main part of the house. "What's going on?" He hopped up into the high goblin chair that Haemun pulled over to the table for him and glanced at the jar. "Oh, hey, is this that spy Thalia and Eris caught for you?"

He sounded way too cheery to be the same goblin who'd matched me drink for drink the night before, and I gave him a suspicious look.

"How come you don't have a hangover?"

"Oh, I did," he said cheerily, "but I whistled it away. New spell. I'd offer to do yours for you, but the code doesn't seem to work right on meat-people. I think I actually made Fenris worse, and that's saying something. I've never seen anyone but Dionysus drink like that before. Of course, he is from a MythOS where heaven is one giant binge interspersed with bouts of head bashing, so maybe it's in his DNA."

"I hate you, little man," came the now-familiar growl of our lupine houseguest as he, in turn, came through the kitchen door. "And I'll get even with you someday. That's a promise."

Fenris flopped in the middle of the floor and pressed his head against the cold marble while Laginn massaged the back of his neck. I instantly felt better. There's nothing like seeing someone who's more miserable than you are to really make you feel better about life. I gave the newcomers a quick précis of what we'd talked about already, then turned back to Haemun and waved a hand for him to continue.

"The next morning, when I came in to do up breakfast, there was a scraping noise on the table, and I noticed the little gal inside for the first time," said Haemun. "She was sitting at the bottom of the jar shredding the edge of the tweed and generally looking miserable. Knowing what Thalia had said about her, I turned the jar around so I wouldn't have to look at her and went to work. But the very next time I glanced over, there she was again, pulling out threads and looking sad. This time, though, I got the feeling she needed to tell us something important and that we really ought to listen to her. But I turned the jar around again. That went on for two days, with me feeling like it was a worse idea every time I did it."

"Could you just have been picking up her unhappiness about getting caught?" I asked.

Haemun shook his head. "I'd have thought that myself if all I was getting was the sadness and wanting out. But that was only part of it, a part that got steadily smaller as the days went by. No, what she really wants is to have a word with us—you, really—and she thinks it's for your own good."

"Maybe we *should* let her out, then." I reached for the jar.

"Hang on, Boss. We don't know who she works for or what she can do. Letting her out seems like a really bad idea to me." Melchior stepped from his chair to the table and bent to look at the spinnerette.

Haemun made a little humphing noise that very clearly expressed what he thought about filthy goblin feet on his nice clean table, but Melchior ignored him and walked slowly around the jar.

"Mel, she's two inches tall; don't you think we can handle it if she decides to go all kung fu on us?" I asked.

"I'm not worried about her breaking anybody's head," said Melchior. "Casting spells or escaping, on the other hand . . ."

"Let her out," Fenris said firmly, though speaking obviously made his head hurt. "No one should be locked up on suspicion or without a chance to explain themselves. And no one should ever be caged just for what you're worried they *might* do. That's what Odin did to me, convicted me for offenses I hadn't yet committed, then locked me up and threw away the key. If he'd been a human dictator, everyone would have called what he did a crime. Since he was the head of the pantheon and the leader of the 'good guys,' people applauded him for locking away a menace to society. But that didn't make it right, just popular."

Melchior stopped his circling and looked at Fenris, his expression troubled. After a moment, he turned my way. "I hate it when people make moral arguments, and I'm on the wrong side of them, but he's right, Boss. Until we have something more solid than the implications of that video from Persephone and some suspicions, keeping her in there puts us in the wrong."

He shook his head, then grinned ruefully. "Still, you've gotta love living in a world where the wolf of Asgard teaches you to be a better person."

When I popped the lid on the jar, the spinnerette leaped out onto my wrist and glared up at me.

"**'* ***** ******* ****, ** ***** ***** *****!" she chittered at me in a mode I found very familiar.

"Oh hell," said Melchior. "That sounds an awful lot like the spinnerette that Necessity sent to ask us for help with Nemesis way back when."

"It sure does," I agreed, "aphasia and all. And completely unlike the one Megaera's taking orders from. What do you want to bet that Alecto's right about which one is the true Voice of Necessity?"

CHAPTER TEN

"*** * **** ** ****-****," said the spinnerette, not very helpful.

"Do you have any idea what she wants?" I asked.

Melchior shrugged. "Your guess is as good as mine. Unfortunately, this one doesn't seem to have the same ability to project power as the last one, maybe because it's still larval or something. I've never heard of one so small."

"**** ** ** ** ******!" She sounded very frustrated.

"I'm sorry," I told it. "I just don't get it. Normally, I'd take you to Shara, but I'm more than a little bit leery of letting her know what I'm doing right now." This not being able to trust your friends stuff really sucked. "I guess the best thing we can do is take you with us to planet Necessity and see if that triggers anything."

"Can I join you?" asked Fenris. "I need something to distract me from my urge to commit hangover-induced suicide."

"I don't see why not," I replied. "It's not like anyone's going to be particularly happy to see us even without a giant wolf. Of course, I don't know where we're going proximally yet."

Melchior snorted. "So we're working without a plan again."

"No plan. No net. No worries," I said.

"I'll make sure they put that on your gravestone," said Melchior.

"I was thinking more in terms of engraving it on the formal House Raven coat of arms," I replied with a grin. "In Classical Greek, of course."

"Of course," said Melchior. "Although I'd always imagined Latin for the house shield. Something along the lines of Caesar's '*veni, vidi, vici.*' How *do* you say, 'I came, I saw, I made really bad decisions'?"

"*** ** **** ***?*" the spinnerette interrupted, anxiously jumping up and down on my wrist. I hadn't the foggiest notion what the thing had to say, but it sure did sound emphatic.

"You bet!" I agreed just as emphatically.

We had places to go and Necessity to hack, so I transferred the tiny creature to my shoulder and reluctantly dragged myself out of my nice comfy chair—the motion only made my head want to come apart a little bit. Then I led a small parade out onto the lanai, where I'd have more room to work.

I produced Occam with an angry thought and a flourish. "Where do you want to start?" I asked.

"I don't suppose you can work that thing like you do the faerie rings and tell it to take us where we need to go?" asked Melchior.

"Worth a try." I reached into the chaos in my blood and through it to the sword . . . and got nowhere. "Nothing doing, Mel. Oh well. Let's see, where to go . . ."

That was when I realized a heretofore-unconsidered limitation on the power Shara had given me with Occam. Unlike the Furies, who were constantly being updated as to their position relative to everything else by Necessity's cosmic locator system, I couldn't create a doorway to just anywhere. I needed to have very definite knowledge about where I was going, either a point I'd been to before or something like it.

"That *does* narrow our options," replied Melchior when I explained it to him. "But it also makes the decision easier. Why don't we start with Crete and the abacus room? That's the oldest part of the whole network. There are bound to be some very interesting things to see there both in terms of figuring out the underlying architecture of the system and in terms of what the abacuses are actually hooked up to."

I frowned. "I don't know, Mel. It's also one of the most powerful systems in Necessity's network, and that means it's likely to be closely watched by all the players. I'd kind of like to take my first deep look around without having three Furies, two spinnerettes, and a giant gazing ball watching over my shoulder."

"You could send me and Laginn through first," said Fenris. "I'm not going to be any help with the computer wizardry, but I'm an old hand at leading grumpy gods on snipe hunts. I learned that job at Loki's knee. Besides, it'll give me a chance to pant out some of the leftover whiskey from last night."

The hand bobbed its agreement, then began happily dashing back and forth between the top of Fenris's head and the base of his tail. It was nice to see that *somebody* had enthusiasm.

"* **** **** ****!" agreed the spinnerette. At least, it *sounded* like agreement.

I wasn't entirely thrilled with the idea—I don't much like sending friends out to do dangerous jobs for me, and this had the potential to be a really nasty one—but I really couldn't think of a better alternative, so I nodded.

"Thank you, Fenris. That'll really help."

The giant wolf wagged his tail very gently. "Great. Let's

do it. I just wish there was some way for me to signal you once I've drawn any watchers out."

"Maybe Kira could help out there," said Melchior. "Now that Necessity's world is hooked up to the net again, there's no reason she couldn't play cosmic cell phone for the wolf here. Gods know she's used to working with canines."

"Sounds good; give her a call and see if she's up for it."

An hour later, after getting the all clear from Fenris, Melchior and I *finally* popped through into the ancient cavern buried within the roots of Crete and the heart of Necessity.

It looked much as I remembered, a huge open space carved from the living rock and filled with rank after rank of giant abacuses. There were hundreds of them, each ten feet tall and strung with dozens and dozens of thick horizontal bronze wires. Heavy copper beads moved back and forth along the wires, seemingly of their own accord, calculating the relative positions of all the myriad pantheoverses at speeds well in excess of early modern computers. The smells of dust and old metal gave the air a heavy, bitter flavor.

"Are you as nervous about being back here as I am?" Melchior asked me, after we'd done nothing but stare at the abacuses for several interminable seconds.

"Hell yes. Last time we stopped in here, we got thrown clean out of our own MythOS."

"So why are we just standing here boggling at the thing rather than doing what we need to do and beating feet?"

"**** ** ****."

"What, *exactly*, is it that we need to do here?" I asked.

Melchior scratched his chin for a bit. "Good point. I suppose we need to poke around and see if anything tries to bite us, huh?"

"That's pretty much SOP, little buddy. Do you want to stick together?"

"Nah, we can cover more ground and do things faster

apart, and that means getting out of here sooner as well. You go right; I'll go left; we'll meet in the back in the middle?"

"Deal. Do you want the spinnerette, or should I take her?"

She grabbed onto my ear then, hard. "*'* ******* **** ***, ********."

"I guess that answers that question," said Melchior, and headed out.

As I made my way along the bare rock face of the outer wall, I reflected on how much easier this would be if I had any clue as to what I was looking for. I mean, I knew I wanted to find the connection that plugged the abacuses into the rest of Necessity. I just didn't know what it might look like. This system was so old and would have had its connection upgraded so many times, I wouldn't be surprised at anything: ley line, enchanted string, copper, fiber, magic seaweed . . . Honestly, who knew?

Whatever it was, I didn't see any sign of it in the first fifteen minutes. Nor the next. Or the fifteen after. When I finally met up with Melchior, he hadn't found anything either. Why is this stuff never easy?

"So now what?" I asked Melchior.

"Aren't you the one that's supposed to be the demigod of hacking and cracking?" he countered.

He had a point. I reluctantly left the wall and ventured over to the nearest of the abacuses. Big, bronze, and totally opaque to my supposed computer-savant eye. I lined the abacus up with another and watched the beads slide back and forth, let the steady motion of the two primitive calculators blur together as I set my hindbrain to work on the problem. Once I'd looked at two for a while, I stepped a little farther back and widened my focus to include several more.

The spinnerette on my shoulder said, "*** ** ***** **** ***** * ******?" but I quieted it with a warning finger—I needed to keep my mind still and out of its own way.

Time passed. I began to get a gestalt sense of the rhythms of the system. I still had no idea what was being calculated or how to read the programming language implicit in the system, but I started to anticipate the movements of the beads on the macro level. Major shifts would become clear to me a few seconds before they actually happened—providing a sort of echo-in-time effect. I also began to see the paths data took through the system as the sum of a set of calculations from one abacus propagated outward, triggering something in one or more other devices.

"Boss"—Melchior abruptly tugged at the leg of my pants—"I hate to interrupt, but Fenris says the hunt has lost interest in him and may be headed back this way."

I nodded absently. "I've almost got a handle on this thing, Mel. Give me a shout-out in ten minutes or if somebody comes through the door before then."

"Will do."

I watched another series of calculations move through the system and mentally mapped their path and pace. The speed of information transfer was too slow for any kind of electronic hookup that I knew of, so it had to be magical or mechanical, probably the latter, as a primarily magical system would have been upgraded long ago. More calculations rippled from one machine to another. It all seemed to be moving about the same speed as the beads themselves . . .

I lowered myself to the floor and pressed an ear to the stone beside the base of the nearest abacus when I spotted an approaching wave of data. It arrived on the wings of the Doppler effect—the sound of beads moving rapidly toward me.

Bingo! There was another set of abacus wires in tunnels beneath the floor. Now I just had to find the outlet.

My sense of the data flow suggested a point off to my left, and I began to work my way in that direction, stopping to put an ear to the stone every twenty feet or so as a check. As I got closer to my imagined transfer point, the under-floor noises got steadily stronger, maxing out as I passed the last row of abacuses. A whole bunch of beads were moving back and forth between there and an unmarked point on the near wall.

I crossed over and pressed my ear to the stone. After a minute or two, I began to make out mechanical noises, clear but so faint I'd have thought I was imagining what I wanted to hear if not for the fact that they made sense.

"Got it, Mel! The network node is just on the other side of this wall." I quickly explained what I'd found.

Mel put his own much more sensitive ear to the wall and nodded. "That's great, Boss. But how do we get from here to there? I'm not seeing much in the way of doors. Not even a cable-chase."

"Isn't it obvious?" I said with a laugh, because the answer had come to me in the same instant he'd asked.

"If it is, I can't see it," said Mel.

"That's because you're not looking with the eyes of a Fury." I pictured my ex-grandmother, Lachesis, and let my anger at her draw my sword into existence. "See?"

I drew Occam's tip along the stone, imagining as I did so a gate that opened from there into a point three feet beyond. It worked, though I hadn't been sure it would beforehand since I lacked true knowledge of the destination. Apparently, solid coordinates in physical space were good enough for short hops. We stepped through and found ourselves in a round room perhaps thirty feet across. It had no human-scaled doors or windows, but it did have a long, open trench running from the wall to the center of the room and back again in a big "U" shape, and a thigh-thick conduit end sticking out of the ceiling at the midpoint.

Between the two was a rather Rube Goldbergian device for converting the mechanical information flow into a digital electrical signal. Abacus data came in through the trench via a couple of dozen bead-hung bronze rods that looped back to the main room. It left via the copper trunk cable that filled the conduit. Between the two was the computer equivalent of sausage making.

I squatted and looked into the trench. The beads were much bigger and thicker than those on the abacuses, which explained the choice of rods instead of wires. The initial conversion seemed to happen as the beads passed along the rods and through Bakelite loops surrounded by many windings of bare copper wire—probably some sort of inductance-coil device.

"Thomas Edison could have put this together," said Melchior, sounding more than a little horrified. "Why hasn't it been upgraded to something civilized?"

From each of the coils a stiff, paper-wrapped wire led to a copper screw clamp on the back of what looked like an old-fashioned phone-switching panel—the kind that required an operator. I stepped around to the far side and found a manual switching setup that had been converted to something more modern by the simple expedient of cross-connecting every single plug to a much newer automatic switch.

That, in turn, had been plugged into the newest piece of equipment in the room, a mainframe that would have looked perfectly in place in a seventies-era human data center. Its amber-scale monitor showed a steady right-to-left scroll of incomprehensible numbers—I still had no idea what the programming language might be. Beside it, an equally ancient punch-card machine provided a primitive option for acquiring hard-copy output.

"I don't suppose you want to plug in and see where that goes?" I pointed toward the conduit.

"How?" Melchior tapped the side of the mainframe. "I mean, we *could* rig a hookup for me, but if that hunk of junk isn't running flat out, I'm no judge of processor loads. There's isn't going to be enough free memory to run anything you or I would call a real program . . . Probably wouldn't be even if it were sitting idle."

I sighed. "You've got a point."

"Damn right I do," said Melchior. "Pantheonic information technology is what, forty-plus years ahead of human? That puts this rig at the equivalent of seventy-five years before I was first booted. You and I come from a place so far up the Moore's Law slope for exponential growth in processing power and memory from this thing that it's not even funny. And that's without factoring in the nonlinear time-slip effect my quantum-computing upgrade has on the relationship. Sure, it and I are both computers, but that's like saying you and a planarian flatworm are both members of the kingdom Animalia—true but pointless in the present context."

"Okay, okay, you've made your point. What would *you* recommend for finding out what's at the other end of that cable?" I pointed to the conduit again. "Because that's where the modern Necessity probably starts."

He looked at the spinnerette on my shoulder and smiled. "Do you remember the story of Minos's hunt for Daedalus?"

I grinned. I did indeed. Daedalus—a distant cousin of mine—had created the original Labyrinth to house and hide Minos's shame, his Minotaur stepson. To keep Daedalus from revealing the secrets of the Labyrinth, Minos had locked the artificer in a tower. Daedalus had escaped by making wings for himself and his son Icarus—which hadn't ended well for Icarus, but Greek MythOS history is like that.

After the escape, Minos hunted Daedalus all through the royal courts of Greece. He'd been clever about it, bringing a spiral seashell from palace to palace and offering a great reward to anyone who could run a string through the shell. Minos knew that only Daedalus was simultaneously clever enough to find a way to solve the problem and foolish enough not to see the hook hidden in the bait.

Hm, maybe he was a closer cousin than I thought.

King Cocalus, who was hiding Daedalus, coveted the reward. So he took the shell to Daedalus and asked him to run the string through it without telling him about Minos. Daedalus attached a thread to the back of an ant and coaxed it to drag the thread through the spiral by putting a drop of honey at the end. He then used the thread as a guideline for the string. But this clever bit of problem-solving revealed his presence to Minos, who promptly demanded his head.

Fortunately for Daedalus, Cocalus didn't want to part with his artificer and made other arrangements. He tricked Minos into taking a bath where—in the classic bloody style of so many of my family's stories—he was murdered by the daughters of Cocalus.

"What do you think?" I asked, lifting the spinnerette up to look at the conduit.

"*** ** **** *** **** **** ****?"

"I'll take that as a yes."

Of course, the technology had come a long way since Daedalus's time. Instead of a thread, we rigged the spinnerette with a tiny wireless webcam and a pseudo-GPS device, but the principle was the same.

"****** ****," said the spinnerette as it climbed into the conduit.

We used the pix and coordinates it sent back to cut ourselves a Fury-style hole from here to there. The other end of the conduit turned out to be a much more conventional and modern server farm—basically a repeat of the room where we'd met Alecto a few days before. Thousands of shiny black multiprocessor servers with bright purple LEDs hung on rows of perfectly aligned, brushed-aluminum racks.

The only big difference was that this computer room held obvious signs of repeated upgrades. Old filled-in holes in the stone floor and ceiling showed where earlier generations of computers had been bolted in place. Exit conduits that had once held thousands of strands of twisted-pair copper wiring had something of an oversized clown-shoe look when compared to the thin fiber-optic lines that ran through them now. Legacy hardware dotted the room as well, some in kludged-together workstations, some simply in discard piles no one had ever bothered to haul away.

"Now, *this* I can work with." Mel hopped up onto a workbench and flickered into laptop shape.

Plug me in, wrote itself on his screen.

I fished a networking cable out of the big pocket in the back of my leather jacket and connected Mel to the nearest server. Data started blasting across his screen at an insane pace, far too fast for me to read or really comprehend, though I kept an eye on it. I was watching for broader patterns in the flow because that's what I do, but I wasn't seeing many. In addition to stunning volume, the data seemed to be moving in seriously turbulent ways. While I was doing that, the spinnerette hopped down and wandered off across the room.

Melchior had been at it about ten minutes—just long enough for me to start to get bored and lose my lock on the proceedings—when he suddenly let out a high-pitched electronic cheep and snapped back into goblin shape. Before I could move or otherwise react, he ripped the cable free of his left nostril and dropped it on the floor, where it burst into flame.

"I *hate* it when that happens." Melchior's voice sounded calm, but his hands shook, and he didn't seem to be able to look away from the cable as it slagged itself with frightening intensity.

"Are you all right?" I demanded.

"I'm fine," he assured me. "Though I'm damn glad the quantum version of my transformation is slightly faster than instantaneous—nothing like being two things at one and the same time to make the emphasis on either one happen faster. That's why the results are so much better than last time."

"Last time? You lost me there."

"Don't you recognize the effect? Necessity happened. She has to have the nastiest security I've ever seen."

"Oh shit, the black box." Now that I'd remembered, I had trouble believing I could ever have forgotten.

It was back in the early stages of the Persephone mess. We'd been trying to find out what had happened to Shara's soul after Persephone's virus e-mailed it directly to Necessity. The black box had been a codespace manifestation of the gateway to Necessity's world. When we'd tried to crack into it, the thing had countered with some sort of nuclear-grade magical cybersecurity designed to literally fry my brains. Mel had managed to keep that from happening, but only at the cost of some pretty nasty burns on his face and hands.

"What happened this time?" I asked.

"Easier to show you, though we'll have to find a fresh cable. The old one is looking kind of limp." He glanced at the floor, where the burning cable had left a thin line of molten copper.

"Security damn near cooked you last time, and now you want to go back?"

"Pretty much." He shrugged. "You'll see when you get there."

As I was rigging up the new cable, I noted that the old one had neatly severed itself about an inch below the place where the connector met the server, which protected the machine from any effects of the fire. Nice spellcoding there.

"You're sure this is a good idea?" I said as I took my place in a chair beside Melchior's table and began working myself into the right mental state for jacking in.

"You can be *such* a big wuss."

"Said the guy who doesn't need to give himself a new piercing every time he goes into the net."

I glanced down at the athame point I held lightly above

the palm of my left hand. The slender, cross-hilted dagger with the network port in the pommel couldn't have been much bigger across than a ballpoint, was almost as thin as a sheet of paper, and maybe five inches long. I'd done this hundreds of times, it should have been easy, and yet every time I prepared to drive that blade through the center of my palm, I found myself fidgeting and delaying the process. Now I lightly traced and retraced the tip back and forth across my skin, scraping in a very faint "X." Once. Twice. Now!

With a sharp expulsion of breath, I shoved the athame home, driving the narrow spike of steel deep into my flesh. I didn't stop until the guard lay flat against my palm and the point stood out a good four inches from the back of my hand. Before I could fully register the pain, my soul slipped out of my body and along the cable that connected the blade to Melchior.

As usual, Melchior had configured his inner cyberspace in the manner of an extremely expensive lawyer's office, with indigo pebbled-leather walls and barrister's bookcases. A brass spiral staircase led upward to the places where Melchior kept his inner self, while a large irregular gateway opened onto the broader world of the net.

I turned toward the latter, took a long step, and almost fell right through it when my knees went all soft and spongy, and I collapsed. Before I could hit the floor, Melchior was there to catch me with arms grown suddenly long and strong. He'd taken on a shape that made me think he'd played one too many Japanese role-playing games. Something like a half goblin, half serpent, only the latter half had feathers and wings—sort of Quetzalcoatl goes Naga, only with Melchior stuck on top. A horrible mishmash in any case.

I'd have told him so, too, if I could have gotten my lips to work right, but they felt like I'd just come from seeing a dentist who really needed to use up an oversupply of Novocain before it expired.

"Gobujuhu," I said—meaning, *"I feel a little funky."*

"Sure thing, Boss. Let me just . . ." His expression went abstract for split second. Then he set me on a blue leather couch that hadn't been there when I started my fall. "What's wrong with y— Oh, that's totally whacked!"

"Bugububu?" I asked—meaning, *"What are you talking about?"*

Great, now I knew how the spinnerette felt. But maybe Melchior understood what I meant, because a moment later he held something very strange up for my inspection. It looked like nothing so much as one of those self-coiling cables that connect the handset of a landline phone to its base, one made from sterling silver that someone had carefully crafted and tatted into half-shredded Irish lace.

"Gubgubbugu?"—meaning, *"What the hell is that?"* ". . . Bogub."—" . . . *Oh, shit.*"

It was the thread of my life, the silver cord that tied the physical body I'd left with a dagger stabbed through its hand to my spiritual projection within the machine. It wasn't supposed to look like that, not even a little bit. The color was okay, but the coiling and the lace effect were most emphatically nonstandard developments. No wonder I felt like crap.

"I think I'd better get you back to your body, ASAP, or possibly even sooner." Melchior picked me up again, and the world blurred and went away for a little while.

When it came back, I was lying on my back on the hard floor of the computer room with a roll of static-free bubble wrap pillowing my head. It was actually less uncomfortable than it sounded, and not the first time I'd woken up in similar circumstances. Good pillow material being notably lacking in most computer rooms, you made do with what you could find. Melchior was seated goblin fashion on a banged-up and backless old office chair a few feet from me, a worried frown twisting his face.

I said, "Urgl," or something very like it.

Melchior look up at me and faked a smile. "Good to have you back."

"Wha' hoppen?" At least this time it came out close to what I wanted to say.

"***'** ******," said the spinnerette.

"I've got a theory," replied Melchior. "But let me ask you a question first. How do you feel?"

"Like I got hit by a bus for the second time in a week. What's your theory?"

"That the first bus came back for another pass."

"Okay, Mel, you've lost me."

"No, you lost you, when you pulled that boneheaded wave-function escape trick a few days back. I don't think I ever told you why I dragged you off to Persephone. Now I'm thinking I should have made a point of it and of trying to keep you out of the game a little longer."

"I don't get it." I shook my head on the improvised pillow—it took a lot more effort than it should have.

"You were in a seriously bad way, my friend. Next thing to dead, really. Way beyond my powers to fix. I could barely find a pulse, Fenris said you smelled like something that ought to be buried, and Haemun couldn't read anything off you about what you wanted or needed. That last is the one that really scared me. So I decided to take you to Persephone because she was the only one I could think of who I could trust and who might be powerful enough to do anything for you."

"Sounds ugly."

"It was. Persephone barely managed to pull you back from the brink. She said you'd done a pretty good job of scrambling your soul, but not to worry about it because it would all sort itself out in time."

"And you're thinking that's why my cord looked like it did."

"Uh-huh. That, and that I should have told you the whole thing sooner. But you seemed to be doing so well, and I didn't want to bum you out with scary might-have-beens. Oh, and on top of all the other reasons, I know risk-taking is the Raven's middle name, and I didn't want to put any more temptation in your power's way than necessary. I'm sorry, Boss."

"No worries, Mel. I can't see how it would have changed anything I've done over the last couple of days, and I'd probably have made the same decision in your place. This does, however, leave us with one major problem."

"Necessity's broken, and so is the guy who's supposed to fix her?"

"Yeah. If I can't leave my body behind and enter cyber-space, that rather drastically limits our options."

CHAPTER ELEVEN

Some computer demigod I was. With the survival of the entire multiverse resting on my divine hacking skills, I'd just run face-first into the limits of my powers. It didn't help that I'd gotten to this place by making a really stupid decision and trying to use god-level magic that I didn't understand.

"*** *** **** ***** ** *** ***** *** **** ***** *** ********?" The spinnerette had climbed up onto my chest and was now glaring at me disgustedly from a few inches. "**** **** ** ****_*** ****** *** * ***** *** ***?"

I couldn't understand a word she was saying, but the tone didn't leave much doubt that I was being chewed out.

"She doesn't sound very happy with you, Boss." Melchior hopped down from his chair and came over to kneel beside me. "What do you think she wants?"

"*** *** *** ****_*** **** ** **** **** *** ***_**_*** *** ** ********!" She pointed first to me, then to Melchior, then raised her fist in a "charge" gesture.

"I think she wants us to get off our butts and make with the fixing of Necessity."

I lifted my head so I could get a better look at the little spider-centaur. It didn't take as much effort as I expected—apparently I wasn't in full-on relapse mode. She shook her head sadly and put her hands on her hips in a classic "What am I going to do with you?" sort of way.

"I don't know," I said. "I'm fresh out of both ideas and motivation. If you've got some way to get me inside the system that doesn't involve my having to rely on a slightly shredded silver cord, I'm all for it, but if you do, it'll be news to—" Wait a second.

"Boss?" Melchior looked alarmed.

I shushed him with a waving hand—there was something at the edge of memory, something important. What was it . . . There!

Back when I'd been dueling with Nemesis but before I'd figured out why she had come after me, I cracked my way into the Fate servers as part of my efforts to find out what was going on. Inside, I'd run into Tisiphone, Cerice, Nemesis, the original Necessity spinnerette, and a webtroll named Asalka. It was a rock-the-walls kind of party right up until the authorities arrived ready to break heads.

They'd have killed me then if Tisiphone hadn't swept me up and carried me off to parts elsewhere. On some levels it was just another exciting day in the life of the multiverse's only Fate/Slapstick hybrid child. On one, however, it was a radical departure from everything I knew about life in the net. You see, Tisiphone had moved me and Melchior from our location within the Fate servers, into chaos, then back into a different part of the net without benefit of traversing the parts of the mweb that lay between points A and B. Normally that would have cut both his and my threads and ended a beautiful partnership. It hadn't, though I still didn't understand why.

Since then I hadn't thought much about it because I'd never really expected anyone would ever be crazy enough to make me a junior Fury. But now that Shara had, the memory suggested that maybe there was a way around my current problem—one that involved a different sort of entry into the world of the electronic. As there's never any time like the present, I forced myself upright. The sudden movement knocked the spinnerette for a loop and made my ears ring, but I really didn't care.

"Melchior, can you give me a playback of the information space right before Necessity's security tried to burn your brain out?"

"Sure. Why?"

"I'll explain in a bit if I'm right." My idea was three kinds of crazy, especially considering the results of my last attempt at using magic I didn't understand, and I didn't want to have to argue it out with him.

"All right." He flickered into laptop shape, his screen open and facing me, and started running the data stream again.

"Pause there," I said, as a sudden emergence of a patch of crystalline order in the turbulent flow signaled the advent of the security algorithm that had attacked Melchior. "Can you switch me over to a graphical representation?"

Of course, though it won't look as it would if you were in the space with me.

I nodded. We'd never done anything quite like this before, since normally I would have just jacked in and looked around for myself. As a result, I got a crash course on the differences in our perceptions.

Melchior experienced the inner workings of the net in a radically different manner from the way I did. Much as a fish's experience of water differed from a scuba diver's. It was more than just the native/visitor dichotomy, though that was part of it. We had a fundamental difference in species outlook rooted in things like sensory differentiation and our wildly divergent processing speeds. Melchior didn't experience net space as a series of real-world metaphors as I did. For him, net space was its very own special kind of real world.

All of which meant that the first images he ran for me looked awfully strange. More like a picture of the inside of a cat as seen through a fish-eye lens than anything I would have expected to encounter in person. The proportions were off from what they would have been for me because we placed different emphasis on different parts of the cyberuniverse. The colors didn't match my preconceptions because when it came to looking at data, Melchior could see about a zillion more gradations than I could—infra-zero and ultra-one, or something like that. Even the basic environment looked different from the way I'd have seen it—where I might have seen hard, angular, architectural kinds of spaces, Mel's view looked organic and fractal and dynamically alive.

"Okay," I said. "Good start. Now can you edit out the time-conditional stuff? I want to know what the address looks like, not the traffic out front."

He did so, and we moved on to make other changes. Slowly, carefully, with a lot of stops and starts, I got him to shift the picture from his view into something more like mine. I tried to keep all the details—I very much wanted the net space to remain the sort of real space it was for him—but I needed to adjust the proportioning and other elements to make it at least borderline comprehensible for me. Finally, we had something I thought I could work with.

"I think that'll do it." I fixed the picture firmly in my mind, then negotiated the transition from sitting to standing, discovering in the process that I felt much better than I had even a few minutes earlier.

"Do what, exactly?" Melchior shifted back to goblin form and gave me a suspicious look.

"This." I summoned up my frustration at getting bounced out of the net and with it my sword. "No tatty silver cord is keeping me out of my home ground." I made an angry cut in the stuff of reality, threw a fencing salute to Melchior, and stepped through the gap.

"What the—" began Melchior. Then, "Wait for me, you idiot!"

I barely heard him. I had passed from the world of the physical into the electronic dreamtime of the net, and I had done so within the heart of the greatest processing system ever devised—the world-computer that ran Necessity, the goddess in operating-system shape. All around me churned a wild, fluid datascape. It looked sort of like the break point in Hanalei Bay might with a hurricane rolling in—giant waves and cascades of foam and spray going every which way. Except you'd have to replace the gray of the water with a complete rainbow palette of liquid light, and the clouds, too.

Mad and magnificent and potentially deadly. Especially without a surfboard.

I am a child of the digital age. As far back as I can remember, there have been computers, and they have fascinated me. The earliest scar on my athame hand comes from when I was five and Lachesis took me for my first trip into the marvelous magical world of the mweb. I was enraptured. My soul has surfed the data flows so long and so deeply that they have written themselves into my sense of self.

I even occasionally dream in binary. Not as a programmer speaking the foreign language of machines, but rather as a pseudomachine myself. In my dreams, I am every bit as much a creature of the net as is Melchior. Then I wake, and it all fades away. I can ride the ones and zeros but never move freely among them. Always there is the silver cord and the subconscious awareness of the body I've left behind—its inputs continuing to feed into my meat-mind, regardless of what my soul-self experiences. Until now, that was.

By cutting a magical portal in the wall of the world and taking my whole self through it into cyberspace, I had finally achieved a lifelong ambition. I'd never felt more lost.

Turns out there were big advantages to entering the

net the way I normally did. (1) An anchor. My silver cord gave me a sense of place and a method for finding my way home. (2) Versatility. When I traveled through the net in soul form, the only thing keeping me in any one shape or physical relationship to the datascape was personal choice. Here I was drowning in information. I had just decided to try to cut my way back out of the no-longer-so-wonderful world of data, when Melchior arrived.

"Idiot," he said, as he fished me out of the wild turbulence and set me on the front thwart of a big oceangoing canoe.

Then he went back to paddling. The weirdest thing about the transition was that in the very instant I left the data sea, I felt dry again. Of course, I'd never actually been wet, since the whole thing was more of a metaphor than any kind of reality—a way for senses adapted to an entirely different sort of environment to cope with the utterly alien landscape of the datasphere—but, instantly, dry really felt *wrong*.

"Where'd you find this thing?" I patted the nearest scaly gunwale. *Scaly?*

"I spun it out of moonbeams and cobwebs. Where'd you think I found it?" Melchior replied, with a definite "you moron" undertone. Then he sighed and shook his head. "I coded it. You don't really think I'd be fool enough to physically follow you through a gate into electronic faerie when I had the option of entering the normal way and retaining all of my powers over the medium, do you?"

That was when I realized that Melchior had once again taken a Nagaesque shape, with his lower body gone all snakelike. In this case, a very flat sort of snake, as he had actually contorted his lower half to form the boat in which I sat. I grinned and started to look around. Now that the data hurricane no longer posed an immediate risk of drowning for me, the stormy sea of light had an eerie sort of beauty to it.

"Actually, that's exactly what I thought you'd done," I said as I slowly rotated in my seat. "I should have known better. I'm glad you're less of an idiot than I am."

"That really doesn't take a lot of effort. Well, except in the anticipation. You know, figuring out the dumb thing you're going to do before you do it, so that I have time to take mitigating action. You completely surprised me with this one, or I'd have gotten here sooner. I'm duly impressed."

"Thanks, little buddy."

"Hey, what are familiars for if not to pull their lords and masters out of the drink when a piece of magic goes wrong?"

"I always thought you were there to fetch the beer and do the dishes."

"I could always throw you back . . ." He tilted his canoe-self to one side, tipping me toward the edge.

"Sorry." I raised my hands in mock-surrender. "I ought to remember that making fun of the guy steering the boat is always a bad idea. What do you think is causing all this turbulence? I've never seen a bigger data storm."

"I don't think it's possible for there to be a bigger one," said Melchior. "No other system in the whole multiverse would be large enough to contain it. As to causes . . ." The corners of his mouth turned down, and his eyes softened sadly. "I think this is the result of a sort of madness, the mind of Necessity at war with itself."

"And Shara . . ."

"Is thinking with this." He swept his arm in a wide circle that took in the rainbow sea of data and the churning light clouds above. "Or worse, she's lost in it."

"What's that supposed to mean?" I asked.

"Is there any way we can be sure that the Shara we talked to was the real her?"

"Why are you asking me? All that electronic-handshake, security-verification protocol, webgoblin soulgaze stuff is your department."

He looked sheepish. "Normally, yes. But normally we'd either have had some kind of formal message protocol exchange before the meeting happened or snuck off for some personal electronic . . . handshaking and goblin gossip afterward."

I smiled at his slight hesitation before the word *handshaking* but chose not to tease him about it for mercy's sake. Instead, I said, "But this time, Cerice made the arrangements beforehand, and there was no after, so none of that happened."

"Exactly." Melchior nodded. "It didn't even seem strange to me under the circumstances. Since you and Nemesis fried most of Necessity's remaining higher-order functions, Shara hasn't had much time to go back to her body, and I've been pretty careful not to do or say anything that might make her feel bad about it. But that also means I've got no way of knowing beyond her actions whether we're talking to the real Shara or not. And her actions are mighty suspi . . . Oh shit."

I was about to ask him what that last bit was supposed to mean when I realized that he'd stopped looking at me and started looking past me. I pivoted on the thwart in time to see a whole series of shark-toothed, green dogs' heads rise out of the water in front of the boat, each mounted on a long serpentine neck.

"Tell me that's not Scylla," I said.

"Well, it's sure as hell not Charybdis," replied Melchior. "Though, technically, you're probably right. It's not the physical Scylla, just Necessity's very own internal electronic version of same." He canted his head to one side. "On the other hand, since Necessity is the goddess that runs everything, and all the major powers are defined and delimited by her internal files, you could make a pretty convincing argument that this is the *real* or Platonic ideal of Scylla and that the flesh-and-blood version is just the shadow on the cave wall. In either case, that is the thing that slagged my connection earlier—it just opened its mouth and out came a firebolt that went straight through the server and into the real-world cable."

The monster slid farther out of the data sea, exposing a deep, scaly chest at the junction of six snaky necks.

"Mel, you're babbling," I said over my shoulder since I didn't dare take my eye off eScylla, or whatever it ought to be called.

"Yep, terror will do that to a guy. Babbling, that is."

"You did okay with this thing last time, or you wouldn't be here. Why are you so worked up now?"

"Because last time I didn't have the complete version of you along for the ride. Alone, I could just go with the sprinting-for-the-exits strategy and not worry about anything but putting one metaphorical foot in front of the other as quick as ever I could. I can't do that now without leaving you behind."

"Ooh, good point." And one I hadn't thought of despite being the one who was going to be responsible for getting us both cooked if I couldn't come up with an exit strategy here sometime real soon. "Any thoughts on how to solve that problem?"

"Nope, just the babbling. I think this one's yours."

"Got it," I replied. "Good to know. How about this?" I held up my sword hand and willed Occam to appear. Nothing.

Damn. Terror ≠ the anger necessary to summon my Fury blade. Not a surprise, really, but a guy can dream. The sea monster leaned down closer, eyeing my raised hand in a way that I found quite alarming. Unfortunately, my fight-or-flight reflex had opted for the better part of valor, at least for the moment. Wouldn't you know it? Stupid adrenal gland, always calling the wrong shots, and, ooh, hey. Work that!

I growled at my own stupid reflexes some more, and, presto chango, there was my sword. Of course, when I held it up in front of the eScylla, it looked more like something you'd use to hold olives in a drink than a monster-slayer. But that was okay. I wasn't planning on applying blade to monster, just to the empty space between us. When I tried, I was reminded that I needed more than terror to make the gates work, too. That and . . . Now what was the thing doing?

It came in closer, but shut all six mouths as it did so. Closer still. It seemed to want a look at Occam. One nose leaned down close enough for me to touch it and sniffed at the blade. Then it snorted and, finally, sneezed hard enough to knock me over backwards into the bottom of the canoe.

Mel rolled his eyes. "Good one, Boss. That'll show it. By the way, is there a reason you're not cutting us an escape hatch?"

eScylla's nearest head retreated back toward the others and barked something rather seal-like. Then they all turned inward and started barking at one another, forming a sort of committee of one, complete with what sounded like long-standing feuds and alliances.

"Actually, yes," I said to Mel. "I'm curious. Oh, and I think I just figured out how this turns out."

I have to admit that fear had given way to fascination not long after the thing sneezed. After a lot of deliberation, all six heads turned my way again, nodded once, then sank beneath the data sea.

"I don't get it," said Mel. "What was that all about?"

I laughed. It was kind of nice to be a jump *ahead* of my familiar for a change.

"That was the official security-system determination that I am the funniest-looking Fury that ever lived and thus have the full run of the place."

"Ohhhh." Melchior nodded, and smiled. "That *would* explain things. And, frankly, I have to agree. You are one funny-looking Fury. The rest of them are all kinds of hot, and you're more—how should I put this?"

"Carefully, Mel, very carefully. Your job security is hanging by a thread here."

"Said the man in the very tippy canoe." Melchior lurched and lowered one side of the canoe, and I almost went back into the water.

"Okay, point, set, match. The familiar wins this round, and I am forced to admit that I am *not* a fabulous Fury babe."

Then we both broke out giggling. There is something about not having to fight a giant angry sea monster that makes you giddy. Once I'd recovered what little dignity I owned, I climbed back up onto the thwart.

"You know something, Mel. I'm getting really tired of this whole saving-the-world gig. Honestly, if the way back to Tisiphone didn't lead through Necessity, I'd vote for scrapping the whole project and heading for greener pastures right now. I'm really not the Hercules or Achilles type."

"You know, that's what all the girls say, too. He's no Hercules, nor even a Perseus. I think it's the hacker physique. You really ought to work out more."

"Hey, this deathly pallor takes a lot of effort to maintain in the face of my surfer-lifestyle choices. Do you know how much sunblock I go through?"

"The pallid paladin?" asked Melchior with a grin.

"Something like that." I grinned back, then looked around and sighed. "Problem is, none of this gets us any closer to the point where I hand Necessity's headaches back to Necessity."

I looked out over the endless, storm-tossed sea of light again and felt utterly overwhelmed. The scale was beyond anything I'd ever tried to deal with before. Both in terms of the underlying system and the problem. It made the Fate Core and Hades.net look like pocket calculators. For a brief time in the Norse MythOS I'd become all-knowing in the Odin mode, and it had very nearly destroyed me because

I didn't have the divine capacity of a true god. No matter how much I might need to, I simply couldn't hold a system this large in my head.

"I hope you have some ideas, Mel. Because this is way too much for me. I don't even know where to begin."

"We could start by getting out of the primary database and into one of the subsystems."

"Good idea—break the problem down into manageable chunks. Why didn't I think of that?"

"Because you're really just the flashy front man for Melchior Inc.?"

"Hey, if that's true, I'm going to take a nap. You can wake me up when there's a massive victory I can take credit for." Melchior just looked at me. "Right. What was I thinking? Did you have a specific subsystem in mind? Or is that my department?"

"Actually, I might," he replied. "Do you remember what Shara said about the subroutine for minor world-remerges?"

"That there was some kind of internal edit war going on? Yeah. That's a great idea, Mel. Make it so."

He rolled his eyes, but then shifted his shape, becoming the feathered flying Meltzalcoatl once again. This resulted in my splashing down in the data but only very briefly—as he scooped me out with the end of his tail a moment later. The feathers tickled.

As we flew along, I started to wonder about the state of my being within the datascape and the nature of the gate that had brought me here. I couldn't really be the physical me I was in the waking world—that just wouldn't work. Yet I felt very much me and not at all as I did when I entered cyberspace in soul form.

So, given phenomenal godly power, how would *I* have arranged my arrival in the world of the electronic? What would I have made of me? A sort of ensouled avatar? A self-aware subroutine? A simulation? A virtual machine running a miniature Ravirn OS?

It was a hell of a spellcoding problem, and it occupied me pretty completely for the next ten minutes or so of subjective time while Mel negotiated both the physical distance from system to subsystem and all of the security checkpoints. I still didn't have an answer at the point when Mel set us down amidst a sort of data river delta or coastal swamp where the "water" once again glowed in all the shades of the rainbow as it meandered toward the data sea we'd just left. I did feel that I was starting to get a better handle on the minimum programming conditions.

"What do you think?" Melchior asked me a few minutes later.

I jerked my attention back from staring out over the tangled threads of the data channels and realized I hadn't spoken since we landed.

"Sorry, Mel. Not what I'm supposed to be thinking; that's for certain. I've been pondering the nature of being."

He canted his head to the side and frowned puzzledly. "Far be it from me to criticize, Boss, but this seems an awfully odd time to go all existential."

"Not like that. In terms of cyberspace and the Fury gates." I quickly outlined the issue as I saw it.

By the time I finished, he was pinching his lips together with his right hand and looking very thoughtful. "That is a poser. I . . ." He looked suddenly down, and my eyes followed.

What had been a sort of dry hummock of stable memory amidst the more active—read that as "liquid"—data flows around it had vanished, leaving us knee-deep in a brightly colored cascade of ones and zeros. Well, knee-deep for me anyway—Melchior's current shape not having knees and all. I looked out over the area I'd been idly overlooking before. Everything had changed: Colors. Rates of data transfer. Stable memory vs. active rewriting. Everything. And, all in an instant.

"That has to be a revert," I said. "One of the players

simply restoring the old code they'd written for this space sometime in the past."

Melchior nodded. "I wonder how long it will last."

I decided to drop the nature-of-existence question for a little while and stomp around in the delta. Again, that really wasn't what it was at all, but that was how my meatspace-evolved brain wanted to deal with the situation. Perhaps the strangest consequence of that was that after half an hour of splashing through what basically looked and felt like a swamp, I was dry and clean, and didn't smell any worse than I usually do. I sometimes wonder if that's part of why smells have never been all that important to me—cyberspace tended to skip them entirely.

That was when Melchior called me back to the place where I'd left him. Since I'd been at it long enough to get a rough feel for the underlying software architecture responsible for the shape of the information being manipulated, I headed back his way.

"What do you need?" I asked as I got closer.

"Can you try an experiment for me?"

"It depends. Is this like the time you wanted me to see how many drinks it took before I was no longer able to pat my head and rub my belly at the same time?"

Mel shrugged. "This will probably hurt more, but not for nearly as long."

"Have I ever mentioned that you'd make a terrible salesman?" I asked.

"Once or twice. Is it my fault that I'm a realist in a world filled with foolish optimists? *I* certainly don't think so. I blame my creator."

"I just *built* you, my cynical little friend. Core design specs are the fault of Fate Inc. with a couple of little industrial sabotagesque tweaks provided by Mademoiselle Discord."

"I seem to remember from looking at the plans that (A) you put some of your own tweaks in the original mix, and

(B) the current version of *moi* is even more of a Ravirn mod-job than the first iteration. But none of that answers my question about the experiment. What I want is for you to do that shapechanging voodoo that you do so well."

"I don't see what that would . . . Oh. This is about the nature of my current being in cyberspace. Very clever. I'll try the otter."

I reached inward, searching for the place where blood and chaos merged. Found it. Drew the shadow of the Raven over me. And twisted . . .

"There you go, and . . . Hey, that didn't hurt one little bit," I said, after I finished the transition. "Instant otter, just add magic and mix. Some restrictions and blackout dates may apply. Not responsible for lost or stolen organs. I feel *great!*"

Then I flopped on my back and giggled. That lasted right up until the software rewrote itself around us again, putting me high on a dry bank. Deep instincts rolled me onto my belly, and I slid down into the pseudowater. For the next several minutes I paddled around and chortled like a maniac. There's something about being an otter that completely dislocates my already-compromised sense of propriety.

Finally, I climbed back up to Melchior and shifted again, becoming a giant Raven. Again, no pain. So, why stop there? I drew a new picture of myself in my mind and poured myself into it, becoming a gigantic coyote. I stayed there just long enough to let out one long, wild howl of delight, then tried to add a pair of wings to the package. When I had no luck, I returned to my natural shape and told Melchior about the wings.

"So, you're more plastic than you are in the real world but perhaps only within a set of naturalized bonds. Interesting. I— Damn it, there it goes again." The virtual world reverted to the second configuration we'd encountered.

Melchior rubbed his temples. "That's starting to give

me such a headache. The software turbulence is very hard on my psyche."

"Imagine how hard it must be on the worlds that are governed by this remerge system . . . Oh, Mel." For the first time, the fundamental horror of that idea really sank in.

This wasn't just some software snafu happening on the servers of a company selling widgets to people who didn't really need them. This was *Necessity*, and the edit wars were happening in a subroutine that literally rewrote the futures of entire worlds.

One minute a minor decision creates two probable worlds. Each is peopled by an entire version of the human race almost but not quite identical to the other. In the next minute, the two become one again, remerging the infinitesimally different versions of those people. But as potentially scary as that picture is, it's only half the story.

Because that's what happens when things work right. What happens with Necessity broken? Do those same worlds simply fall off the net and go blithely along in their own pocket universes? Maybe. Sometimes. But sometimes, they simply evaporate into chaos, taking every last living thing with them.

Worse, this was only one of Necessity's control systems, and a minor one at that, governing the least of decisions. Our entire MythOS was currently under the reign of a goddess who had come unglued. Nothing and no one was safe from the effects of that. Even if I were to get the whole thing fixed and running tomorrow, uncounted—no, uncountable lives would already have been affected in the time between now and then. Real lives belonging to real people that might have been saved or bettered if I'd acted more quickly would be irreparably changed.

CHAPTER TWELVE

"Boss, are you all right? You look like you just ran face-first through a plate-glass window."

"I think I just did." All those lives tied up in whether I did or didn't manage to fix Necessity, all that weight on my narrow shoulders . . . I shuddered. This must be how Atlas felt *all the time*.

"Tell me about it."

So I explained my thoughts about the consequences of failure. When I finished, Mel let out a low, unhappy whistle. "Ugly."

"Yeah," I agreed. "I somehow managed to forget the stakes for a while. I think it's all the time I spend dealing with gods and immortals. They *can* be hurt, deeply even—look at Persephone—but they're also eternal and virtually indestructible, ideals personified as much as they are people."

Mel nodded soberly. "The whole lot is so prone to treating humanity as the counters in an elaborate game that it's easy to become infected with their worldview. Hell, Lachesis thought nothing of making a threat against my entire species."

"We're not going to let her carry that through, Mel. I'll nuke the whole god-governing part of Necessity if I have to in order to prevent it—tear the system down and let the worlds go on their merry way without any of the powers, me included." I turned away, looking out over the datascape. "Come on, we need to figure out how this thing works. We've got a ton of work to do."

With Melchior's help, I coded up a bunch of tools for the task. One big ugly codespell would let me see exactly what was happening when an edit rearranged the software around us. Another, subtler piece of magic, would trace the source of the edits back through the computer architecture to their various sources. A third brief spell string was designed to hide the second and drag us invisibly along in its wake.

That done, we settled in to wait. The first act didn't take long—the edit war was burning fast and hot. Change ripped through the datascape, moving around all of the sensors we'd conjured. It happened at the speed of light, far too fast for me to register anything more than a before and after. But the sensors were another matter. They showed us the exact place where the new code had first appeared.

We made a note and placed a new suite of monitoring spells aimed at that entry point to the subsystem. Then we reset the other sensors and went back to waiting, repeating the process until we'd gathered data for the whole cycle and all the way back to the first revert we'd measured.

This time, we had sensors waiting within the point of entry and were able to backtrace the command source quite a distance through the system. Over the next six hours, we created a steadily expanding map of the edit war that included considerable information about the places where the different versions of the data architecture originated. There were three loci of control. We labeled them "Shara?," "Virus-X," and "WTF?!?!?"

The "Shara?" trail led back into the security systems we knew were inhabited and controlled by Shara. Or possibly, the pseudo-Shara—Melchior felt that while the code tasted kind of like what he would expect from Shara, there were enough significant anomalies that he couldn't say for sure. We put that one aside for the moment.

We also put aside the "WTF?!?!?" path for now since it was going to be a nightmare to examine in any depth. It looked more like an environmental side effect of the hardware than any coherent code locus. It didn't seem to enter from one point and trace back to a distinct part of the system so much as spontaneously ooze out of about a million places where the software interacted with the firmware and various bits of chip structure. I'd never seen anything in the computer world that looked less centralized or more like old-fashioned chaos magic. I had no trouble imagining why Shara had had such problems trying to figure out where the hell it was sourced.

The "Virus-X" path was the most interesting to me as a hacker and cracker. These days I think of myself mostly as a white hat, someone who finds the loopholes in code and exploits them for the betterment of the multiverse. Or, if I'm going to be more honest, I should perhaps call myself a gray hat. I *will* crack things just because I can, but I'm no longer likely to use the opportunity to inflict uncalled-for damage when I do that, either to the system or its owner's ego.

I know that most of the great powers don't see me that way. To them, I'm a black-hat cracker, nasty and subversive, in the game to destroy and turn things to my advantage. I have to admit, I do use many of the same tools that a black hat might. I know a lot about the dark side of the coder's world because it's where I came from, and if I *were* still a black hat and intent on the subversion or destruction of Necessity, I'd have approached the problem *exactly* as Virus-X had.

There was no way to locate its initial entry point to Necessity as a whole, but it seemed mostly to be hiding out in the Input/Output channels governing communication between the millions of servers that made up the mind of Necessity. That position in the network's I/O path let it control the flow of information, making it virtually impossible for anything internal to the system to see it or root it out. It was a bit like seizing control of the synapses of a human brain so that the neurons that actually did all the processing could think only what you wanted them to think.

It was nasty and clever and just the way I'd have done things given the openings I could see. Virus-X's methods were disturbingly familiar on subtler levels, too. Small twists and turns that exploited already-existing code in preference to writing new stuff, along with an off-the-cuff feel, closely mirrored the operating techniques I preferred. In so many ways, Virus-X had approached things as I might have, which led to the obvious question of who thought that much like I did?

The next time it moved, so did we. For the twenty minutes that followed, Melchior and I played the digital equivalent of red-light, green-light with Virus-X, moving only when we could be pretty sure it wasn't looking, while still trying to stay right on its backside through a dozen sectors of the system. Eventually, we had it backtracked to a place within the kernel of the OS. Since my Fury blade provided me with absolute access to the entirety of Necessity's internal domain, we were easily able to follow Virus-X as far as an outer ring of defenses it had erected around its own core.

The OS for Necessity is huge and hardworking, the cyberspace equivalent of really massive city like Tokyo or Mumbai, with about a kazillion lines of interlocked code running flat out all the time. The intruder had usurped a fairly small corner of that space and secured the hell out of it. Picture an American embassy in the heart of a really hostile country—razor wire everywhere, walls within walls, multiple layers of mirrored glass on the windows to baffle spying devices, and all kinds of countersurveillance software constantly scanning the surrounding codescape. Got that? Now translate it into something optimized for dealing with threats in three dimensions. It looked a bit like a giant stainless-steel coconut with razor-wire fuzz.

I had no doubt it was crackable. Everything is, even biometrics if you handle them right, but this wasn't going to be easy, and a close look around the neighborhood told me we'd have to use a subtle approach rather than brute force. Virus-X was sitting smack in the middle of the control package that governed the powers of the Greek pantheon— like a steel shotgun pellet lodged in the living heart of Necessity. One wrong move, and you'd have a fatal bleed-out. We couldn't afford to panic it.

Its positioning told me a number of things. First, Virus-X was playing for control, not destruction. If it wanted to kill Necessity as a functioning system, it could already have done so. Second, it knew it might be discovered and wanted to force any opposition to be very cautious. Nobody who wished Necessity well would take a shot at this thing unless they were damn sure they'd get it right the first time. It also suggested that Virus-X wanted to be in a position to kick over the game board if it looked like it might lose. That last was more intuition, based on what I might do in its place, than deduction, but it felt right.

Once we'd finished a series of exquisitely careful loops around the place to get a feel for how Virus-X was tied into the surrounding codescape, we settled in for my least favorite part of the hacking-and-cracking routine: waiting and watching. What made it particularly difficult this time was that I didn't dare delegate *any* of the watching and waiting to a set of autonomous programs. Virus-X was nasty on a platter, and I wouldn't trust anything less adaptable than me to watch it until I had a much better idea of the parameters of any potential active security.

That turned out to be a wise choice. After we'd been there about twenty-five minutes, Virus-X moved. The timing was perfect, hitting just at the point in time where I could no longer maintain maximum wire-trigger awareness without having the top of my skull come off. It struck in the exact instant that I finally started to relax a little—like a gut punch coming at the end of an exhale. Bastard!

Virus-X went from apparently static to sprouting about ten thousand autonomous security bots in an instant. It looked like an exploding pincushion, with pinheads in every color of the spectrum. Before any could hit us, Mel wrapped me in his tail and took off. We spent the next forty or fifty seconds dodging and jinking like a moth that's accidentally flown into a bat convention. Several hundred probes came in our general direction, some moving straight, some spiraling, some making sudden random changes of direction, and all of them potentially deadly.

Nothing without a real brain and significant experience in avoiding getting caught or killed by nine kinds of lethal software could have avoided the onslaught. Even with that experience, there was a good deal of luck involved in keeping out of the way of the probes. Then, just as suddenly as the hail of hostile bots had begun, it stopped, and the whole thing went back to looking completely inert.

"That was gangs of fun," Melchior panted, as we settled back into our little hideaway. "Good exercise."

"There's nobody here you need to look brave for, buddy. That scared the hell out of me, too."

He grinned. "Just trying to make a little lemonade."

Time passed. Tightly wound nerves slowly relaxed. Nothing happened. More time passed. Virus-X sent a fresh round of revert commands off to the contested subsystem we'd tracked it from—nothing for us to worry about. Relaxation turned into boredom and inattention after something on the order of an hour. Then, wham! Bot storm. Again, we managed to evade the bots, though only just. We returned to our lookout.

Time pas—Kablooie! This swarm came within a few minutes of the last, while we were still in the immediate postadrenaline crash. The thing was vicious.

But Melchior had finally begun to get a feel for the movements of the bots, and we were able to rely more on skill than luck in our evasive maneuvers. It was still an ugly game, but one I thought we could reliably win going forward.

"Hey, Mel, I've got a question for you," I said, when we'd caught our breath again. "I'm thinking bot storms would make great cover for any number of other activities. Could you run a playback of the last one?"

"Sure, though it's going to be pretty sketchy. I was kind of absorbed with the whole not-getting-hit-and-dying thing."

He held one hand in the air and conjured a ball of light above it. Within the net he had no need to rely on the beam projectors built into the eyes and mouth of his physical self. Images formed in the ball. They were grainier than usual and prone to sudden turns and twists as Mel's dodges changed the orientation of his primary sensors. Watching them, I got the sense of an overarching pattern to the whole thing but simply didn't have enough data to really tease it out.

"I feel like there's something important going on there," I said after a second playback, "but this just isn't enough for me to pinpoint it. Next time around, why don't you let me drive while you focus on getting a better picture of the swarm."

Mel nodded and shrank himself from giant anaconda proportions into something in the neighborhood of a garter snake. Next, I shifted into Raven form for maximum mobility, and he coiled himself around my ankle. Then we settled in to wait.

When the next round started, it was my turn to flit and float and flutter like a mad thing. Actually, having seen what worked best for Melchior, it really wasn't *that* crazy, just strenuous and nerve-wracking. Afterward, we went over the replay. Once. And again. And . . . There!

"Freeze it, Mel. Look here, here, and here."

I touched three of the bots in Mel's projection. Though it wasn't something anyone would likely have spotted in the middle of playing Don't Perforate Me with the swarm, there were subtle differences in the way the trio moved. Both in terms of a moment-to-moment motion and overall course.

"Unless I'm wrong, those bots are bound for an intersection maybe a subjective half mile farther out from Virus-X headquarters than our present location." Mel expanded the scope of his projected sphere, and I poked a finger at a new spot. "Right about here."

More waiting and watching. Whoopee!

"What's it doing?" Melchior asked.

"Good question," I said as I reverted to my own shape.

We were a hell of a long way from where we'd started— well beyond the bounds of Necessity proper—in one of the mweb proxy servers housed in the Temple of Fate, if I was any judge of things, and that made me very nervous. It was an older system, which registered on my meatspace-optimized senses as a series of interconnected tunnels of the sort one might find in a coal mine.

We'd followed a set of the atypical security bots to a point where they'd merged into one much larger piece of software, which had then led us here. The program, which looked rather like a huge plunger, was now doing something very strange while we watched from behind a large pillar.

The thing had stuck itself to one wall of the codespace and started to pulse rapidly, looking for all the world like an invisible plumber trying to clear a really big clog.

Melchior let go of my ankle and flitted up to wrap around my shoulder. "It's thumping out a binary signal of some sort, but not in any language I've ever heard."

After perhaps a minute of sending, the plunger collapsed in on itself and dissolved. Much sooner than I probably should have, I crossed to the area where it had been working. I found a very faint ring where the program had clung to the wall. I leaned in for a better look.

"Don't touch it," admonished Melchior. "You don't know what it's for."

"And I'm not likely to ever find that out if I don't check."

I put my hand in the exact center of the circle and felt the faintest crackle of magic. Harmless. I leaned my forehead against the stone to get a stronger read. It reminded me of nothing so much as the faded echoes of a long-dead faerie ring. But that didn't make any sense. There was no way to open a faerie ring into any part of the mweb. The two magics were fundamentally incompatible. I'm very good with faerie rings, and I'd tried it more than once over the years. It simply couldn't be done.

"What are you finding?" asked Melchior.

I told him, and he shook his head, too. "You're right. Can't be done. Can we give up and go home now? We've been at this for ten hours straight, and we haven't gotten much further than Shara did."

I tapped the edge of the circle. "This is important, Mel. I'm sure of it."

But I was getting tired, too, and this *really* didn't make sense. I turned around and leaned against the stone within the circle, closing my eyes and hoping for inspiration.

"You realize," said Melchior, "that this is the moment where something would have grabbed us and pulled us through the circle, or you would have triggered a secret panel, if life were a movie, the which depending on whether it's a horror or a farce. Of course, that would also give us a direction to follow, so it wouldn't be all bad."

We waited silently for a good five minutes. Nothing happened. We were getting nowhere at the ongoing cost of who knows how much damage to the fragile stuff of reality. I sighed and gently began to knock the back of my head against the wall. We really needed a break.

Every time my head connected with the stone I got a little flash of whatever magic the circle held, incredibly faint but also steady rather than fading over time. Thump. Flash. Thump. Flash. It *still* felt like a faerie ring, and that *still* didn't make any sense. Thump. Flash. Thump. Flash. Wait a second. Maybe it didn't make sense because I was looking at it the wrong way. I turned back around to face the wall, putting both hands on the edge of the circle and leaning my forehead against its exact center.

"You got something, Boss?"

"It feels like a faerie ring."

"We've already done that one," he replied. "It's not going to fly."

"I don't know," I muttered. "What would happen if you built a faerie ring, a really tiny one, into the surface of a CPU chip?"

Melchior frowned at me. "I imagine that it would allow very small things to move from the surface of the CPU to other faerie rings elsewhere and vice versa. What's that got to do with anything?"

"How do you suppose that ring would feel to someone standing inside the processor? Virtually. Say that you entered cyberspace and went to the exact place within the hardware where the ring was closest. Would there be some sort of resonance?"

"I have no idea," said Melchior. "Do you think that might be what's happening here, that there's a physical faerie ring somewhere on the other side of the virtual wall of codespace? And that you're somehow catching an echo of that?"

"It's the only thing I can think of that would make sense of this feeling."

"Hmm." Melchior looked thoughtful. "That might also explain why the plunger thing had to come way out here to the network boonies."

"What . . . Oh, right. Necessity's world is as immune to ring-making as the mweb itself. Good point." I pressed against the wall harder, setting the signature of the hypothetical ring in my memory. "Are you up for something risky and quite possibly stupid?"

"If I wasn't, wouldn't I have found other work by now? What's the plan? Are you going to just cut a hole in the wall like you did back in the abacus room?"

"That's not how I was thinking about tackling it, but I suppose it's worth a try."

I tried to imagine the response of one of the Fates if she found me cutting my way into the mweb server room in the Temple of Fate. Not pretty, but hey, I could always claim I was just doing what Lachesis had ordered me to do and cementing the bonds between Necessity and Fate. Yeah, *that'd* fly with my ex-grandmother and her sisters.

I used the anger that thoughts of Fate brought with them to summon Occam from its other-dimensional home. Lifting my blade, I pictured myself opening a doorway into the space beyond the wall, fueled the image with anger, and made a deep, drawing cut. Nothing happened. I tried again. Same result. That was when I realized that I had no real idea where the other side of that wall might be in physical space, having never been allowed anywhere near the mweb servers, and that I needed to. Apparently, "just over there" wasn't enough of a location marker when point A was in virtual space and point B was in reality.

"No can do, Mel."

"It's probably for the better," he said. "I'd have to go and fetch my body before I could follow you, and you'd probably muck things up in the meantime.

I stuck my tongue out at him, then used a mental picture of Atropos to pump up the anger needed for a cut from cyberspace to the computer room where Melchior's physical form lay. There, I waited for him to take the long way round while fending off incomprehensible questions from our pet spinnerette and fighting fatigue to stay on my feet. Once he rejoined me, fresh-squeezed thoughts of Hades provided the angry-juice necessary to open a gate from there on to Raven House.

Laginn was waiting on the rail when we stepped out into the tropical night. The hand pointed one admonishing finger in our direction in an unmistakable you-wait-right-there-young-man gesture, and dropped to the floor before scampering off tippie-fingered. He returned seconds later with Fenris—Kira had apparently returned to Cerberus.

Haemun trailed behind the wolf with—bless his soul—a tray of food and drink perched in his hands. It wasn't until then that I realized how incredibly hungry I was. Normally, cyberspace takes it out of me mentally much more than physically since the body goes into something very close to suspended animation when the athame goes in. In this case, having actually been there in some as-yet-unexplained way, I'd burned calories, too. Lots of them. And I hadn't had great reserves to begin with. I realized then that I felt damned wobbly in addition to deadly tired.

"What happened?" demanded Fenris.

I snagged a sandwich from Haemun, dropped into the nearest chair, and took several bites before mumbling, "Eat first, questions later."

I lay in my bed and stared blearily at the ceiling while the room slowly revolved around me, and all without benefit of alcohol. The combination of complete exhaustion and insomnia is one that has become all too common since I became my own personal night-light—Ravirn 3.0, now with glow-in-the-dark eyes™. A sleep mask doesn't help when the light that's keeping you awake is inside your own head.

When we'd first headed back to Raven House around midnight, I'd kind of hoped to keep our stop there to a matter of minutes so that any trail through the faerie ring wouldn't have time to grow cold. Foolish optimism, that. Hours later and not feeling a whit stronger or more rested, I knew there was no way I was going anywhere short of noon tomorrow—and that only if I somehow managed a solid ten hours' sleep between now and then.

So I lay in my bed, desperately trying to enter dreamland while worlds puffed out like candles in the darkness because I hadn't yet fixed Necessity. The knowledge of the latter didn't make my efforts at the former any easier.

I hadn't felt so utterly miserable in years. Not since the day I'd realized that my grandmother Lachesis knew and had approved every horrible thing Atropos was doing to me in her efforts to force me to help her extinguish free will. Part of my angst came from the thought of what a broken Necessity meant for all those worlds and potential worlds—a *big* part, but only a part.

I'm honest enough with myself to admit the disconnect I felt from the people in all those places. I didn't know a one of them, and chances were good I never would. On some level they would forever remain an abstraction. And on some level, that was probably a good thing. Otherwise, I'd have been paralyzed by the responsibility of it all.

As much or more of my misery fell into the "why me?" self-pitying category. Another fact I was sufficiently self-aware to acknowledge, even if it did make me feel like an utter shit.

"How did the ultimate fate of the multiverse land on

the pantheon's newest and least responsible demigod?" I grumped.

"Because Shara, or whoever is wearing her identity, thinks you're the only one who isn't going to use the problems of Necessity to make a grab for the brass ring of absolute power," Melchior replied from the table, his voice coming out slightly tinny through the speakers of his laptop shape. His speaking startled me—I'd thought him asleep.

"That's proximally. I was thinking more in terms of cosmically."

"Well, we know it's not the Fates, since your thread was removed from their power forever when you went through the gullet of Discord's dragon. Since you're a power, that would normally mean Necessity, but we know that's not currently an option. That leaves bad luck of epic proportion, bad judgment of like scope, or a bad timing beyond the dreams of divinity. The winner is . . . a three-way tie! As once again Ravirn makes the universe-hates-me hat trick."

I snorted, then faked a teary snuffle. "I'm so happy to get this award, and I couldn't have done it without the help of the little people, starting with my own very short goblin companion, Mr. Melchior. Wherever you are, little dude, take a bow. This is as much your prize as it is mine."

"Oh, stuff a sock in it, Ravirn, and for gods' sake, go to sleep!"

And then, miraculously, I did.

"You're sure this is a good idea?" Melchior poked his head out of the depths of my shoulder bag as we approached the permanent faerie ring embedded in the stone of Raven House's grand balcony.

"No," I said. "I'm quite sure this is a bad idea on a myriad of levels. It's just that we don't have a better one. Weren't you listening when I outlined the plan?"

"You know, I never listen to a word you say after the word 'plan' comes out of your mouth. I figure if you've never stuck to one before, what are the chances it's suddenly worth paying attention to this one. I see my job more as coming up with plan-implosion-mitigation spellware than working on the implementation of something that's going to get tossed away three seconds after it goes live. It's a more efficient use of my time and effort, and besides, it gives me broader range of potential I-told-you-sos."

"Do you know what I really love about your partnership?" Fenris asked from his place beside the ring. "It's the absolute confidence you show in each other's good judgment. I'm happy to be even a small part of such a great team. Now, can we actually *do* something before my hair starts going gray?"

Laginn plucked a hair from the silvery wolf's back and held it up for inspection.

"Ooh, too late!" Fenris's tongue lolled out, and he chuckled.

"**** **!"

"Right, point made." I put a hand on the wolf's shoulder, and together we stepped into the faerie ring.

In doing so, we simultaneously entered every ring in existence—for each individual circle of enchantment is but an aspect of the one primal ring. The raw chaos that maintained the rings instantly lifted my spirits and eased my remaining weariness, though it couldn't banish it entirely. For ten breaths I let myself simply bask in the cascade of faerie's rough magic, but not a moment longer. Just as chaos enlivens and energizes me, so, too, will it intoxicate and entrap me if I allow it the opportunity.

I called up my memory of the possible ring we had discovered yesterday and fixed it in the forefront of my mind. Using that as a guide, I engaged the ring network and slowly reached outward, trying to find the one I wanted. It didn't take long—one of the benefits of my Raven's nature is a deep connection to the underlying chaos of the network, which allows me to manipulate it in ways closed to more ordered sorcerers.

Despite the impulsive whispers of the chaos around me urging me to action, I did not immediately try to shift myself into that other ring. Instead, I carefully defined the conditions under which I wanted to arrive. The deathday-cake experience had shown me that I had an enemy able to work the rings against me. Normally I could count on the network itself to deal with the transition from the great ring on my lanai into one the size of a pinhead without making specific arrangements. But now I had to treat the system something like a hostile genie and force it to adjust our size and other attributes appropriately. Only after I'd completed that process did I move us.

We arrived upside down in darkness and stifling heat. I was just mentally congratulating myself on having included a stick-to-the-ring clause in my preparations when I felt something like a sledgehammer strike the bottoms of my feet through the ring's surface, and we began to fall.

Damn it, not again!

Melchior whistled three strings of code faster than a hummingbird's heartbeat. The first I recognized as a spell called "Fear of Falling"—it instantly transformed our blind plummet into a leisurely drift.

Way to go, Mel!

The next was "Redeye," and it gave us sight in the darkness. The third spell I didn't recognize. It sounded like a summoning of some sort, but nothing appeared immediately, and more pressing matters swiftly drove it from my thoughts.

The first of those was the enormous expanse of burning metal that was rising up to meet us. We had appeared in miniature within one of the mweb's powerful servers. Upside down. On the bottom of a CPU. With the machine's main heat sink directly beneath us. The infrared vision

Melchior's second spell had granted us left me in no doubt that it was hot enough to fry bacon.

Some distance to my left, Fenris let out a rather mournful howl, and I turned my head that way. That was how I discovered the spinnerette. It had been flung free of my shoulder but had somehow managed to catch hold of my bangs. Now it kept thumping against my forehead as I whipped my head around trying to make sense of things. I needed better control.

As I began to gather my will for a shape-shift, I was distracted by something sharp brushing against my shoulder. It spun me in the air and scored the leather of my jacket all the way down to the Kevlar. I turned my head that way but couldn't see anything that might have been the cause. I don't like that sort of mystery, but I didn't have the leisure to worry about it. Instead, I reached inward and—Wham! Something smacked into the side of my skull hard enough to make sparks dance in front of my eyes.

This time I had no trouble spotting the culprit, though the blow to my head had left me seeing three of everything. Three of Mel, three of Fenris and Laginn, three of the spinnerette, and three of the all-gods-damned gazing ball of doom.

CHAPTER THIRTEEN

■ ■ ■

Falling. I really hate falling. Even the slow-motion kind of falling currently on the agenda. The biggest problem with falling is that inevitably you stop, usually quickly and painfully. I don't even much like flying—it's too much like falling turned on its side. But I'll take that over the vertical sort any day of the week. I tried to gather my wits enough to convert the one into the other, but the intermediate stage, where I transformed from man into raven, kept eluding me. The gazing ball had really rung my bell.

Now I saw it coming back for another pass. I knew I should do something about that, but I was having trouble figuring out what exactly—figuring out anything, really, in all the confusion. That whole *falling* thing kept distracting me. The gazing ball was getting closer fast, and all I could think of as a response was how handy a really big Ping-Pong paddle would be just then.

That was when I saw the angel. She came through a rip in the sky and put herself between me and the gazing ball. Just as it was about to hit her in the face, she snapped her black-and-stormy wings in a sharp beat that lifted her relative to the oncoming sphere, then spiked it like a volleyball center with the perfect set. There was a deep "tonnnng" sort of noise, and the gazing ball rocketed off at an angle perpendicular to its original course.

The angel turned in the air and dropped down beside me.

Melchior poked his head out of my shoulder bag, and yelled at the angel, "It's about time you showed up!"

"Complain later," said the angel, who finally registered as Alecto. "Escape now."

She caught the collar of my leather jacket and threw me at the faerie ring high above us. A half second later, I heard a sharp yip from Fenris and guessed that he had likewise joined the world of projectile motion.

Out of the corner of my eye, I saw the gazing ball turn in the air and start to rise after me, seeming to expand as it came. I lost track of it a moment later when I hit the faerie ring and had to focus all of my scattered wits on making it hold on to us as it jumped and bounced. The ring seemed to be repeatedly slamming itself into my hands and knees, which would have been distracting under the best of circumstances. As it was, Fenris had to twice ask me what was going on before his question made any sense to my scrambled brain.

"I don't know," I said, glancing over my shoulder to check whether the gazing ball was about to squish us all to paste. Not that I could tell at the moment, but I wouldn't have bet money against it either. "This is *not* normal faeriering behavior."

"You don't say," growled the huge wolf. "I'd never have guessed that on my own."

A deep thud just off to my right drew my scattered attention away from Fenris. Alecto was there, perhaps three yards away and pressed against the surface of the CPU by a smoky silver gazing ball that had grown from the comparative size of a medicine ball to something on the order of a small car.

"Would you get out of here!" Alecto yelled. "I can't keep this thing away from you forever." Then she got her feet braced against the ceiling and shoved the ball down and away from us before dropping after it.

I nodded, but stayed right where I was. Despite having regained sufficient brainpower to do as ordered, I really wanted to understand what the hell was going on with this faerie ring before I left. That was the whole point of entering what we had known might be a trap, and I finally felt that I almost had an answer.

"Boss, can we just this once make the sensible choice and do what the Fury tells us to do?" yelped Melchior.

"One more second, Mel. I can taste the answer." Then I thought I had it and flicked us elsewhere to find out.

The transit took more effort than I expected, perhaps because of the pounding my head had taken.

"Castle Discord?" Mel sounded baffled at my choice of destination.

I nodded and held up a hand for silence. We stood in the lookout post on the back side of Eris's golden-apple sun, high up on the very edge of chaos, and I needed to confirm the guess that had led me here. I turned away from the others then and stared into the tumbling madness of the Primal Chaos that surrounded the castle. For perhaps a minute, nothing happened. Then I saw it. Order where there should be none, a pulsing, wavelike pattern propagating itself through the very stuff of chaos. My message in a bottle. I knew who our black-hat cracker was, and it felt like a kick in the guts despite the fact that she'd warned me herself not to trust *anyone*.

"Eris." I closed my eyes and shook my head. I understood her involvement, but that didn't make me feel any better about it.

"What?" asked Melchior. "Eris? What's going on? I don't get it."

"That makes two of us," agreed Fenris.

I pointed at the spot where the messages being sent from the thing that lived in Necessity's kernel were making themselves manifest through the medium of modulated chaos. The same data-transfer technique Eris had used to pull me from the Gates of Hades to Castle Discord earlier in the week, the method that had gone so wildly wrong when I tried to execute it myself.

"There. The plunger thing was a device for sending messages through the Primal Chaos. It attached itself to the point in the virtual space of that CPU that most closely corresponded with the underside of the faerie ring in the real world. When it pulsed, it was pounding the faerie ring like a drumhead, and the vibration then passed into chaos through the medium of the ring's magic. Well, not exactly a drumhead, since it's directional and pointed straight through chaos to this exact spot. More like a whisper dish."

Melchior whistled and looked very unhappy. "Are you sure Discord's responsible?"

"Nearly. It was remembering this ring that gave me the final piece of the puzzle. In order to make this thing work, Discord would need a listening station shielded from the rest of the castle, and this spot fits the bill perfectly."

Melchior looked dubious. "If that's true, having the spinnerette lay a trap-trail that led us right through here doesn't seem all that smart. Why would she expose herself to discovery that way?"

"Because Discord's an arrogant bitch," said a woman's voice.

For one brief instant I thought it was Eris herself, arrived to make a triumphant gotcha. Then I replayed the words in my head and picked a different speaker.

"Hello, Cerice. How long have you been here?"

"I arrived with you."

She faded into visibility then in all her icy glory. The aftereffects of Melchior's "Redeye" spell painted a halo around her as she appeared, teaching me something new about the Furies—their magical camouflage extended beyond the range of visible light into the infrared.

"That would explain the extra effort needed to trigger the faerie ring. We had a hitchhiker." Another thought occurred to me, and I tapped the fresh slice in the shoulder of my jacket. "You gave me this, didn't you?"

"I did," said Cerice. "When you started to fall, I dove after you. But then I realized Melchior had it covered and I sheered off. I'm new to flying, and one of my toe claws grazed your jacket."

"And when that gazing-ball thing tried to take my head off? Where were you then?"

"I calculated the impact and decided you could take the hit. I wanted to see what it would do afterward, how it would behave. I would have saved you from the next attack because I needed you, but Alecto took care of it, so I stayed hidden."

She looked me straight in the eyes when she spoke, and there was no hint of softness there, just a whole lot of matter-of-fact and that's-the-way-it-is, deal-with-it. My ex, the ice queen. No wonder she'd chosen it as her element when she became a Fury.

"I'd been following you ever since you first used your sword to enter Necessity yesterday," said Cerice. "I knew you'd find the culprit eventually, and I really didn't want to let all my efforts at remaining concealed go to waste. Now that you have, I can deal with her." Her claws slid from their sheaths and she flexed her wings.

"Hang on there, sweetheart," I said. "This is my discovery, not yours, and I'm still not one hundred percent sure she's guilty."

Discord and I were both powers of chaos, but we really didn't think as much alike as I and the mystery cracker who'd set up shop in Necessity's kernel seemed to. Oh, I'm sure Discord could have chosen to mimic my techniques and done it well, but that didn't feel quite right.

I continued. "Even if I were sure Eris was responsible, I'd want to take this slowly. Because, if that's the case, I don't think it would have been arrogance that led her to show me this place, more like a cry for help. So I'd like to get the details nailed down before anyone starts a war, okay?"

Cerice shook her head. "I don't think so. I only became a Fury because someone had to save the house of order from chaos and ruin. The ongoing danger to Necessity is simply too great for me to let Discord remain free just because you're not certain she's guilty. We can always release her later if that's the case. No, I'm going to do what I have to here, and you can't stop me." She spread her wings to their fullest extent preparatory to taking off.

"I could bite her if you want," said Fenris helpfully. "I haven't gotten to bite anyone in days."

"Cerice, please . . ." I raised a hand, but made no other move. She was right in one thing—I couldn't stop her. "Eris is my friend. Don't do this."

Cerice sagged a little. "Ravirn, you're asking me to choose between you and my duty to Shara." Then her eyes changed, becoming colder and more opaque, and her back stiffened again. "No"—her voice shifted into something that carried notes of Alecto and Megaera in it—"you're asking a Fury to choose between herself and Necessity, between power and identity."

"And, so long as Necessity lives, there is only one way such a choice can ever go," said Eris from her seat beside the fire.

I should have been startled by the appearance of Discord in our midst, and even more by our sudden change of venue from the back of the sun to the main hall of what looked like a mid-nineteenth-century British hunting lodge. I wasn't, and that was entirely because Eris didn't want me to be. Castle Discord can assume whatever shape Eris chooses. In this case, she had decided to put us all at our ease by including a sense of been-there-all-along in her specifications for the room.

And how did I know that? I can't really explain it beyond saying that in becoming a power of chaos, however minor, I had acquired certain insights into the workings of chaos magic. I could *feel* what Eris had done in my soul. The space soothed. It was a pretty damned spiffy piece of spellwork. Doubly so when you considered the otherwise-jarring nature of the trophies that hung on the wall. The cow kicking over a lantern on the mantelpiece was the least disturbing of the lot.

"Mrs. O'Leary's famous beast, I presume?" I indicated the cow with my eyes.

Discord beamed. "Yes indeed."

"Am I missing something?" asked Fenris.

"That's the cow that started the Great Chicago Fire," answered Melchior. "Oh, and look, the design specs for Chernobyl reactors three and four. Yay."

"Who's the blond bimbo?" Cerice pointed at an extraordinarily beautiful woman in a too-clingy tunic up and to the left from the cow. She was kneeling with both hands up and in front of her as though she were offering up some invisible treasure to a lover.

"Helen of Troy, though a wax model only," replied Discord. "Sadly, she'd lost the features that made her such a treasure for my purposes by the time she died." Again she smiled.

I felt a chill in the depths of my soul. I could see no hint of the Eris I knew and loved in her eyes or manner at the moment. This was wholly the goddess Discord, Queen of Chaos, a pole power and more than capable of seizing the throne of Necessity by violence.

Cerice saw it, too. "Do you need any more proof, Raven? Or do you still want to try to stop me?"

I opened my mouth to answer but found that I didn't know what to say.

"Cat got your tongue?" Discord asked me. "No words of defense for an old friend? No brilliant forensic computing to expose the Trojan Eris within the heart of Necessity for what it really is so that you can prove my innocence? No guesses as to what lies within that hollow imitation of Discord?"

I still couldn't say anything, and Discord shook her head mock-sadly.

"I thought not. There's no chance you could ever break my system anyway. It's quite uncrackable without the proper key. No, you can't touch me. I have no need of you, little boy. Go away somewhere and let the baby Fury and I discuss our business in private."

Discord laughed long and hard, and I heard the sound of shattering glass in the echoes. When she was done, she smiled and settled back in her chair, her sword across her lap as though it had always been there. Cerice extended her claws and stepped forward. I couldn't watch anymore and started to turn away. And in that exact instant, Eris winked at me. Eris. Not Discord. I realized what the wax Helen didn't have then, and winked back in the instant before my world changed.

Wherever Cerice and Eris were, the rest of us were not. We stood waist high in a great, turning spiral nebula, a burning cluster of golden stars surrounded by the black deeps of space.

"What in Odin's thrice-damned name is going on?" Fenris stomped over to face me, his hackles high.

The sea of stars bent and rippled around him as though he were wading through water, a picture made doubly surreal by the disembodied hand perched daintily atop his head, looking as though it had been severed midway through scratching behind his ears.

"Am I getting things wrong?" asked Fenris. "Or did

your pantheon's equivalent of Loki just ask you to save her from your ex-girlfriend, the new vengeance goddess?"

"Actually, she asked us to save her from my ex and from herself, but that's close enough."

"Eris being overdramatic is really what's going on." Melchior stood up in his bag and made a sweeping gesture. "This is the current iteration of her computer room, with every tiny star a reference point for one of her servers. If you look closely, you can see that they're all tiny apples in Eris's own little tribute to Eris."

Melchior looked up at me. "So what was that last bit all about? She obviously wants us to crack the system and save her lazy butt from the whipping she's about to get, but I can't even see a way to interface with the thing from where I'm sitting, much less hack it. Why can't Eris ever just go for simple, recognizable hardware configurations like a sensible person?"

"She did," I said, because it would irritate him and because I was one step ahead of him once again. "This will be almost painfully easy to crack."

"Okay, wise guy. Where do we start?"

"Well, first you produce the golden apple Eris gave me the last time I was here. It's the original, by the way. Then I take it and put it in the exact center of this nebula, where it will unlock the system for us." I stretched and rubbed my neck. "That's where we start to have issues, because I'm pretty sure that Eris didn't anticipate my current inability to enter the network in the normal way, and I don't know if that's going to cause problems."

Melchior blinked several times. "That actually makes sense. The Trojan Eris, the trophy room, all just clues." He whistled a quick string of code and pulled the apple out of the pocket dimension he uses to park important items. "Do you suppose she was doing it that way to hide her intentions from us, or from herself?"

"More the latter than the former." I took the apple. "This normally sits in the hand of the wax Helen of Troy."

I examined the stem for a moment before giving it a twist and a yank to reveal the concealed networking port I'd expected. Too bad I couldn't use it at the moment. With a sigh, I hung the apple in the air at the center of the nebula. It remained there after I took my hand away, floating about two feet off the ground.

"Same drill as Necessity?" asked Melchior. "I go in and establish a beachhead, then you cut your way through to meet me?"

"If that works. Fenris, do you want to join us? Or should I send you home?"

"Why don't Laginn and I just wait out here? I'm no good in cyberspace, but we can protect Melchior's physical form in case things go south."

"Sounds good to me." I pulled the spinnerette from the inner pocket it had retreated to after our arrival at Castle Discord. "What about you, little boots? In or out?"

"******, *'* ********** ** ******." Then she shook her head sadly, walked back up my arm, and crawled into the depths of my jacket again.

"I wish I knew what she was saying." Melchior looked frustrated. "I don't know whether she's incoherent, profound, or comic relief."

"Could be all three," I replied. "That's the way it usually goes around here, isn't it?"

"True dat." Melchior grinned and plugged into the apple.

"Speaking of which," I said, "sometime when we have a moment, remind me to compliment you on the absolutely insane idea of cooking up a summoning spell for Alecto and ask you what on Earth you were thinking when you did it."

"I was thinking that we share a number of enemies with

Alecto at the moment and that that could come in handy.
I've got one for Cerice as well." Then he was gone into
laptop shape and cyberspace.

From the inside, Discord's network currently looked like
what you'd get if you ran the annual Monarch butterfly
migration into an active tornado and left it there. Whirling
chaos in black and orange. Well, gold rather than orange,
and, if you want to be really picky about it, they all had
card-suit patterning, but metaphor's an inexact science.
Or was this a simile? I can never keep the two straight
because I've never been entirely sure it's worth the effort.
In any case, the place was a mess of titanic proportions and
completely lacking in the sort of clues I normally use to
make sense of a system.

So I let the winds take me and joined the butterfly
dance, hoping to find patterns amidst the chaos. I figured
it wouldn't take too long since Discord and the Raven so
often think in parallel tracks. The Trickster has his claws
fixed firmly in both our brains by means of our guiding
natures. Thank you, Necessity . . . or rather, not.

The external pressure imposed on me by the big N is
one of my many beefs with her. I don't like that becoming the Raven means that I can never be entirely certain
if a decision belongs to me or if it's the Trickster within
wearing me like a mask. If the alternatives weren't all a
hell of a lot worse, I might have been inclined to walk
away rather than save her butt. Well, except for the bit
where I couldn't walk away in the direction I wanted to
go without first fixing the abacus network to make me an
exit sign. I digress mostly because I was having major
trouble getting a grip on the basics of the system. Complete failure to compute, in fact. That was when I thought
of a possible alternative solution for making sense of the
giant butterfly mess.

"Melchior, could you take me back into our point of entry?"

"Sure, Boss."

He looped me in his feathery tail and carried me deep into the heart of the whirling butterflies, where a big, gleaming golden apple hung in midair. We passed through one golden wall and into an empty spherical chamber whose sloping walls acted as one-way mirrors looking out. A staircase leading up to a closed trapdoor in the ceiling showed me where Melchior had originally entered. I hadn't stayed there long on our first pass because nothing was there but the stairs, and all the obvious action was happening beyond the window. Now I took a more careful look around. Nothing had changed except for the way I thought about things.

"The specialist has arrived," I said in a firm, declarative tone. Nothing happened. Sigh. "Open Sesame." Nope. "I am Raven." *Nada*. "So much for that theory."

"What are we doing here, Boss?" asked Melchior.

"I was hoping, perhaps overoptimistically, that Eris might have decided to make this easy on me."

"We are talking about the Goddess of Discord here, right?" Mel held a hand out to one side. "About so tall? Sexy, snarky, and psychotic? Middle initial of 'D' as in Difficult? Personification of strife?"

Melchior then fell over onto his back and started laughing. A minute slid by; he didn't stop. Another. Ditto. Tears started at the corners of his eyes.

"You made your point, Mel. You can stop anytime."

He choked out, "Discord, make things easy for . . ." Then he went back to laughing.

Okay, so maybe it *was* a dumb idea. I started to laugh, too, but stopped when I heard strange subtones in the sound—like Discord's shattering glass, only overlaid on a Raven's distant caw. That was when everything changed. The walls sprouted nineteen kinds of control consoles, and a big old *Star Trek*–style captain's chair grew out of the floor directly beneath the overhead trapdoor.

"Welcome, Ravirn." The voice was Eris's but less emotionally charged and seemingly sourceless, as though the words were being spoken directly into my head by the ghost of the goddess. "What can I do for you today?"

Melchior stopped laughing then as well.

"I need information," I said.

"You have Eris-level clearance for all files and operations. Ask and I will answer."

Where to start? Probably with a search for loopholes. There were bound to be a bunch.

I settled into the chair. "Is that the highest clearance level?"

"No. Discord is the highest level. Of everything."

"Why am I not surprised."

"Because you are a face of the Trickster?" The sourceless voice sounded uncertain. "I'm not good with philosophical questions."

"Neither am I," I said. "Try this one. Has Eris been hacking Necessity?"

"No, but Discord has made cracking attempts on Necessity 784 times in the last three years, and automatically evolving scripts do so from within this system at least 240 times per day. Success rates are at 0.0 percent so far, for all modes."

"Then how does the goddess know about a 'Trojan Eris' within Necessity?" asked Melchior.

Silence. Mel rolled his eyes, and I repeated the question for him.

"Eris did not 'know,'" said the voice. "However, your arrival with a Fury in the faerie ring that is the focal point of the nonsense being spewed through chaos by an entity controlled from within Necessity provided partial confirmation of a possibility she had been considering for some time, a confirmation further reinforced by your conversation with that same Fury on arrival."

I nodded. "Can you tell me what other clues she might have had that led her to suspect such a thing?"

"Yes."

Seconds ticked by.

"Boss, I think that you need to rephrase the question as something other than a 'can you' if you want a real answer."

If I'd had any doubts that Discord programmed this thing, they were now gone. "Right. Tell me about that."

"Of course," said the voice. "There have been repeated incursions into this system by an entity or entities striking from within Necessity over the previous three weeks, with each round of attacks more sophisticated than the previous incursion."

"Three weeks? Does that time frame ring any bells for you, Mel? Beyond the fact that it started while we were in the Norse MythOS?"

My familiar shook his head. "Nope, unless that's when Cerice restored Necessity's mweb connection."

"System?" I asked. "Is that correlation correct?"

"Yes, the attacks commenced roughly .001 seconds after Necessity fully reentered the net."

"That sounds like something was just waiting to pounce," said Melchior.

I nodded, then addressed the system again. "Why did the incursions lead Discord to believe that there might be a 'Trojan Eris'?"

"Because, as they continued, they grew both more sophisticated and more familiar. Whatever was attacking the Discord network was studying the internal structure of the system and borrowing cracking-and-hacking techniques it found represented in our archives. It seemed to Eris that something was trying to learn how to pretend to be her.

This was further reinforced by its leaving in place various links between the systems and by its invention and placement of the faerie-ring broadcaster."

"Invention?" I raised an eyebrow. "Tell me a little bit more about that."

"It seems to be a much more powerful and directional adaptation of the system that Necessity uses to communicate with the Furies."

"Did Eris have a theory about who or what this entity might be?" I asked.

"Her initial suspect was you."

"What!" I almost fell out of my seat. "Why?"

"Many reasons. Your nature as a Trickster might well cause you to seek Discord's throne. You had had access to Necessity's core systems at a crucial time, and potential ongoing access to the system through the webgoblin Shara. You had spent considerable time working with the Furies' communication system. Further, the initial attacks, though somewhat clumsier than your normal techniques, bore a strong resemblance to your style as observed in previous cracking-and-hacking runs. Also, the attacks began within twenty-four hours of your apparent vanishment."

"I'm surprised she didn't try to find and kill me."

"So was I," said the sourceless voice. "It would have been the logical action on her part, and I recommended it repeatedly at the beginning."

I swallowed what felt like my Adam's apple. "Why didn't she kill me?"

"I don't know. I stopped recommending your death after observing a clear pattern of heavy drinking on the part of the goddess that followed said suggestions. The resulting unconsciousness and following hangover decreased her net ability to create havoc in the world, which is contrary to my primary directive. Combine that with a small but significant possibility that you were not responsible, and continuing to push the matter was contraindicated."

"When did she decide it wasn't me?"

"Thirteen days ago, after you returned to this MythOS by means then unknown. The reinsertion of the power known as Raven into this multiverse created patterns within the flows of chaos that could be read both by Eris and me that indicated your complete absence earlier. At that point, it became clear that you couldn't be the source."

"What if he'd set up a script or something?" asked Melchior.

Silence.

"Answer his question," I said.

"Not possible. These were intelligence-driven attacks. They adapted to the active engagement of the goddess in ways that no program could— Alert! Additional system breaches occurring now. You must flee or risk destruction."

"What?" I demanded. "Can't you hold it off?"

"No. Even with the active participation of the goddess, this system would likely be subjected to complete control by the attacking entity or entities within twelve minutes. Without Discord's help . . ." The voice faded into silence for a moment, then resumed with a very different timber, though still female. "The system cannot resist even twenty-five seconds."

I focused my anger and summoned my blade, though I didn't immediately move to cut my way out. "Hello, entity or entities. Who are you?"

"The voice of Necessity, of course." It didn't sound like Delé, so it was probably her boss—the motive power behind the gazing ball. "I'm here to kill you."

"Why are people always telling me that? Is it a personality thing on my part? Something I do to rub them the wrong way?" There was something maddeningly familiar about the voice—not so much in the tone as in the cadence—and I wanted to keep her talking. "Because I've always thought I was rather on the charming side."

"Well, Boss, we didn't want to have to tell you this, but . . ."

"Silence!" yelled the voice.

"I hear that a lot, too. I don't suppose you want to tell me your evil plans before you murder me? If you really believe you've got me where you want me, it couldn't hurt anything, right?"

I caught Melchior's gaze with my own, then flicked my eyes up toward the trapdoor. If possible, I wanted him to get clear without taking the risk of going with me through a Fury gate sans body—I didn't know how Tisiphone had managed that trick, and preferred not to go for trial and error with Mel's life on the line. He nodded and stretched his serpentine form, edging toward the door in the ceiling.

"I don't think so," said the voice, and I almost recognized it. "You've shown a nasty penchant for escaping me in the past, and I'm not willing to count you dead until you turn up in Hades for the final countdown. Nor am I willing to let your little friend get away without you." A harsh clunk followed as the trapdoor vanished. "Now it's time for you to die." Another clunk. The sphere around us began to contract.

"Wait!" I called. "When have we met before?" I nearly had it. "Just give me a few more words." But there was no response, only the steady closing in of the walls. "Damn it, come back! Tell me who you are!"

I was frightened and angry and used that feeling to make a slice in the air in front of me before presenting the tip of my blade to Melchior.

"Come on, Mel, we've got to get out of here."

"Do you actually know what you're doing here?" he asked. "How Tisiphone managed to do this without killing us both?"

I shook my head. "No idea, sorry."

"I was afraid you were going to say that."

Then he jabbed his thumb on the end of my blade so

that his blood dripped to the floor and—shrinking to fit—
dove inside my coat. With a finger, I caught some of the
blood he'd spilled, and touched it to the tip of my tongue,
just as Tisiphone had, but it was all monkey see, monkey
do. I simply didn't know how this carrying souls through
the gates was supposed to work. By now I could touch the
ceiling just by raising a hand, but still I hesitated. I really
didn't want to find out the hard way whether there were any
special preparations I needed to make to prevent the gating
maneuver from killing my best friend.

That hesitation saved my life . . . maybe. I took a step toward the gate I'd cut, then froze. Something about it struck
me as wrong, something I'd never have seen if my worries
for Melchior hadn't kept me from simply diving through.
I could see the nebula of Discordian stars where we'd left
Melchior's body, but no sign of him, or Fenris or Laginn.
Damn.

I knew that my enemy was either a part of Necessity or
had taken over a part. What did that mean for the power
Necessity granted the Furies? Beyond the risk to Melchior,
could I even trust the gate to go where I thought it did?

The ceiling bumped the top of my head.

CHAPTER FOURTEEN

The room squeezed tighter around me, like a slowly closing fist. I would soon have to hunch and flex my knees to stay upright, or have them flexed for me. I jerked my .45 out of its holster and tossed it into the hole I'd just opened in space. It didn't arrive at the other end, vanishing as soon as it crossed the plane of the gate, which meant the Fury transport system had been compromised. I really couldn't see any way to get out of this one, and I didn't have a lot of time to think of something though I thought I could at least break Melchior loose.

"Mel!" I yelled. "Grab the spinnerette and get your butt out here, quick."

He shot out into the air with the spinnerette clutched in his arm. "What's up?"

"New plan!"

I put one foot against the wall behind me to brace myself, then drove the point of my blade forward into the wall of the sphere as hard as I could. The shock of the impact ran up my arm. For a moment it felt like I'd tried to stab a hole in a concrete wall—with predictable results. Then Occam punched through the metal, and I staggered forward. The blade hung up for a moment when I tried to pull it loose, but another braced foot freed the tip and left a small gap in the wall.

"Go!"

Melchior shoved the spinnerette through into the free space beyond my contracting sphere, then stopped and looked back at me. "But, Boss, what are you going to do?"

"Something exceptionally stupid." The idea had come in a flash, and I really had no idea whether it would work, but there weren't a lot of alternatives, so I decided to go with instinct.

"I know that tone, and I'm not leaving without you," said Melchior.

"Melchior, Run For It . . . Please." I could have said "Execute" and made a command of it. I could have forced him to go, but I didn't want an order that would break years of trust to be the last thing I ever said to my best friend, and I really wasn't sure I was going to live through the bit that came next. I'd done it once before but . . .

He looked at me one more time, his face grim, then reluctantly nodded. Narrowing himself still further, he slithered through the hole and left me alone in the contracting sphere. I dropped into a cross-legged position on the floor to accommodate the much-reduced space I had left and in hopes that assuming the classic pose of meditation might lend me a little calm and focus. I was going to need all the help I could get staying centered through this next step. And that was assuming that I had found a possible escape clause and not just a fancy way of committing suicide.

I opened my sword hand and willed the blade to reverse itself. It pivoted around the crystal circle in the center of my palm, so that I now held it in an underhand grip with the blade pointed toward me. Placing the edge against my belly, I focused my will and made a sweeping cut. I was surprised by how little it hurt.

With any other sword, that would have been the moment where my innards became outards, spilling themselves into my lap and generally making a mess. But Occam was special. It had the power to access my inner chaos in a controlled manner that hadn't been open to me in the days before Necessity had given it to me. By using Occam like a combination athame-scalpel, I could achieve some very subtle results. In that regard, using it to open my belly probably counted as backsliding.

The thought made me laugh. Bad idea. Exceptionally, mind-bogglingly, divinely bad idea. The slice in the skin of my stomach opened wide and chaos poured out. All of it. All of me. The Raven is a creature of chaos hiding inside a lie of flesh. I'd just told the universe the truth.

The chaos burned as it left me, and I burned with it. Away to nothing.

It was the splinter effect that ultimately saved me. You know when you've got a splinter somewhere deep under the skin of your foot, and no matter how hard you try to ignore it, you can't? Yeah. That. Really. Well, that and some serious effort on Melchior's part. But I didn't find out about that until later.

I had dissolved myself into chaos once before, when I fought Hades and lost. Cerice's love for me had been my anchor that time, a point of connection with the real world that allowed me to gather my scattered self from the winds of chaos and use the Raven's power to create myself a new body from scratch as my Titan ancestors had done before me.

For obvious reasons, that anchor wasn't an option this go-round. My bond with Tisiphone might have worked if she'd been in the right pantheoverse, but she wasn't. No, what drew me back to myself was the splinter effect, and what drew me back into the world was Melchior.

But I'm getting ahead of myself, a side effect of the

whole dissolving-into-chaos thing, I think. It dislocates your sense of time and space. The last time I'd done this, I hadn't had Occam grafted onto my soul. I'd just been a big diffuse cloud of possibility, with no internal reference points. This time I had a chunk of congealed chaos attached to me in the shape of my indestructible Fury blade.

I can't really describe how that feels, since I didn't have nerve endings or feelings in the traditional sense of the word. What I can do is give the analogy of the splinter. There was something external to my core vision of self attached firmly to the cloud that made up my rather diffuse awareness. A hard, sharp, unavoidable something, like a splinter sunk deep under the skin of your foot, too deep for you to see. You can't be fully certain anything is there until you dig it out, but every time you step on it, you get a little jab of pain.

That was what Occam did for me. Every time the floating wisp of awareness that was all that was left of me started to disperse, it rubbed across my Fury blade and drew what currently constituted my attention inward. So, far more slowly than I might have wished, I contracted inward toward the point where my soul bound me to the reality of the sword. Eventually, I became something very much resembling an individual consciousness once again. At that point I was me in the most important sense though I still didn't possess enough will to do anything about it. Which is where Melchior and the reassertion of sequence and order comes into the picture.

It started as a sort of mumbling just below the threshold of hearing, a string of too-faint nonsense syllables that made me want to find the source and tell them to *speak the hell up, damn it!* In the Primal Chaos there is no true direction—too many dimensions beyond our regular three—but things can be closer or farther away from you. My pseudoconsciousness found the noise almost as irritating as the splinter. After a time I began to search out the source, drifting this way and that, always edging closer to the noise—seeking to render it into something recognizable.

Closer. And closer still. Until, WHAM! It grabbed me by the soul and yanked.

This is what it said: "Ravirn, I conjure and abjure thee with blood of your blood, with hair from thy head, and with this feather plucked from the tail of thy power's shape. I summon thee with the name of thy soul and the name of thy power. Raven, appear before me now. I command thee to appear with the principal of sympathy and the magic of thy true name. Ravirn, I conjure and abjure . . ." Etc.

I'd never been summoned and bound before—hadn't even realized it was possible—but I suppose that I *am* a supernatural creature now, with all that implies. But damn if it didn't hurt! It felt a bit like I was being skinned in reverse, as my soul was forcibly twisted and compressed back into the lie of a body. To be more specific, the part of me that's me felt like it was being stuffed back into a me-the-body-shaped sack of skin, then heat-bonded to it.

"Suddabit!" I gasped, as soon as I had control of my brand-new set of lips and tongue.

My brain ran that back through the old word-processing system while my eyes tried to make sense of the mostly green blur that surrounded me. It didn't sound right, so I tried again.

"Son of a bitch!"

Melchior chuckled. "Considering that the Fates are ultimately responsible for my design specs, and thus Lachesis could be said to be my mother, I have to concur. Oh, and it's good to see you, too."

About then, my brain got the hang of processing visual input, and that feeling became mutual as Melchior entered my personal picture of the world around me—it was very good to see him again. To *see* again, period. He stood on the lanai of Raven House, with the big faerie ring behind him and beyond that the jungle and the bay.

In one hand he held a feather and my hairbrush, in the other a tiny crystalline vial filled with a rich red fluid. I stepped forward to catch him in a hug—well, staggered, really, since I wasn't used to having a body again yet—then screamed when I bounced face-first off an invisible wall made of pure pain. Somehow, I managed to stay upright.

"Suddabit!" I yelped, rubbing at my numbed nose and lips.

"Sorry about that," said Melchior.

Looking down, I spotted the lines of a hexagram carved deep into the marble of the floor, one that completely enclosed me. I raised an eyebrow, or made a valiant attempt to do so anyway.

"Haemun's gonna kill you."

"Actually," said Melchior, "he did most of the chisel work."

"Really? How'd you convince him to help you make such a mess of the floor?"

"That's a long story," said Melchior.

"I'd love to hear it," I said, "*and* the one about why you're doing things this way instead of using a nice sensible piece of code. But both of those would sound better sitting down with a drink in my hand. This is the point where I'd normally suggest we adjourn to the bar, but I can't help noticing that there's one tiny little problem with my plan." I indicated the hexagram that bound me.

Melchior nodded but didn't move.

"I'm noticing a distinct lack of your letting me out of here," I said, after a moment.

"Yeah, and I'm really sorry about that. But the first couple of yous I summoned turned out to not actually be you, which has a lot to do with why we carved the binding in stone along about try number three. Likewise, the next couple of yous that showed up after that were also not you. As much as I want to open that hexagram, I need to make sure that this you is the real you first."

"Don't I *look* like me?" I glanced down the length of my body and did a quick comparison with how I normally looked, a comparison made easier by my nakedness. Everything seemed to be there and in the right places, which was a relief.

"Yes, and no," said Melchior rather evasively. "But so did things one-through-nine."

"Those statements both sound pretty bad, but let's start with that 'yes and no.' I don't suppose you'd care to elaborate on that . . ."

"Just as soon as I'm sure you're you."

"Something about your tone tells me that this is going to require more than a game of twenty questions that no one but the real Ravirn could answer."

Mel nodded. "Yeah, and I'm sorry about that, too, but the whole twenty-questions routine is how you number three convinced us to let it out."

"I really don't like the sound of that, Mel. Why would the not-me know things only the real me ought to?"

"Again, something we can talk about once your identity is verified. Oh, and by the way, you owe Fenris the contents of a complete butcher shop among other favors for help with yous numbers one through three, five, and nine. If he hadn't been here then, I wouldn't be now."

"The more I hear about this, the less happy I become, Mel. Can we get on with things so I can hear the whole story?"

"All right, and let me say in advance that if you do turn out to be you, I'm really sorry about this next bit."

Before I could ask, Melchior produced a miniature wax figure of me along with some pins and set them on the low table where he was sitting. The details that followed are tedious though only moderately painful, and made more so by the fact that the Ravirn figurine was followed by one of a little wax Raven, so I'll skip over the ouchy bits. Sometime later, when I was done yelping, and Mel was done apologizing, he produced a chisel inscribed with long strings of arcane binary.

"It's about damn time," I said.

He paused then and looked thoughtful. "You know, before I let you out, I was wondering if now might not be a good time to renegotiate my salary."

"What!"

Then he winked at me and grinned, and I broke down into semihysterical giggles. It was just that little bit too much.

"Okay, and he passes the sense-of-humor test with flying colors." A relieved grin spread across Melchior's features. "I think this is the genuine article."

"That's it, then?" Fenris slid out from the shadows under the overhang. "He laughs, and it's really him?"

"The right kind of laugh, yes," replied Melchior.

Something really unpleasant jangled at the back of my mind at that—a vague memory of past problems. "Why does my sense of humor need a test?"

Mel looked up from the chisel he'd placed against the outer line of the hexagram and sighed unhappily. "The chaos *gazing* out of the eye*balls* of the other nine versions of you turned out to be nothing more than reflections, if you know what I mean."

"Gazing? Reflections? Are you saying the gazing ball was somehow inhabiting fake versions of me? I don't see how—" And then I did. Eyes like smoky mirrors. "Nemesis."

"That was my thought," said Mel.

"And it's why I offered to do the chisel work." Haemun followed Fenris out into the sun. He had a robe draped over one arm, and now he bobbed the tray of drinks he also held, making the ice clink together. "I thought you might need one of these."

"Or six," I replied.

Nemesis. The Goddess of Vengeance. Apparently, I

hadn't destroyed her. Little spots of ice prickled here and there on my skin. That thing they say about if you would shoot at the king, be certain you kill him . . . Well, it goes double for goddesses.

"I'm going for nine," said Melchior. "One for each fake-you we had to dispose of."

Fenris lapped up another snoutful of single malt, then sat back and looked out over the bay. "Okay, shoot that one by me again. How can Nemesis possibly be running around loose after you used the powers of Necessity to destroy the body she was inhabiting and banish her to Tartarus forever? Wasn't the whole point of the exercise to make sure she could never threaten Necessity ever again? Her survival and return makes no sense."

"Actually, I'm afraid that it does." Now that I'd had some time to get over the initial shock of the idea, I was starting to think again—bad thoughts. "After Necessity cast her out the first time, Nemesis became a bodiless soul but retained much of her former power."

"Which ranks her up there near the combined strength of all three Furies," Melchior said, glumly.

"Speaking of which," I said, "later you'll have to tell me more about Eris knocking Cerice on her ass."

I'd been gone from the corporeal world for something on the order of thirty-five hours, and a lot had happened. Things like Discord's putting Cerice down for the count, then apparently vanishing from the face of the pantheo-verse. We needed to move against Nemesis as soon as possible, but if we wanted to survive the experience, we needed to move smart. That meant gathering information and formulating plans.

"Can we get back to Nemesis?" Haemun sounded fix-ated, and who could blame him after his experiences with the goddess? "Why isn't she in Tartarus where she belongs?" Nemesis had really messed with his head last time around.

"Actually, she is." I held up a hand to forestall argument. "Not physically, perhaps, but magically, which is all that counts. When Shara chose to take Persephone's place in Hades, she didn't do it literally. She did it through the wonders of modern spellware by occupying the file space that bound Persephone to Hades. Each year for three months, Shara's soul is trapped within the part of Necessity's system that governs the placement of the goddess Persephone."

"Now Nemesis is doing much the same thing, occupying the file space of her own imprisonment in Tartarus." I took another sip of my drink—a lethal-grade margarita. "Which just happens to lie right in the heart of Necessity's operating system. It's as if the goddess Necessity has caught the ultimate computer virus in the shape of her own daughter, Nemesis."

Melchior's eyes went suddenly wide. "Oh shit. Do you think that Nemesis lifted the file-space trick from us and Shara? That we're responsible for this development?"

"One way or another." I tilted my hand back and forth. "Nemesis is at heart a sort of distorted magnifying mirror. She reflects the talents and thinking of whomever she wants to destroy, then adds her own power to the mix, creating a sort of amplified echo of the individual. When she assumed Dairn's body, she also took on his hatred of me, then she used more powerful versions of my own hacking-and-cracking skills to try to kill me."

"Skills that she seems to have hung on to when she went into the machine." Haemun got up and started to pace. "Is that because she's still got all of us square in her sights? Or what?"

"That's part of it," I agreed. "But it also has to do with her opposition to Necessity. My power, the Raven's power, comes from Necessity. She gave it to me with the name. In fact, Necessity defines and delimits all the gods and powers and—"

"Are you trying to tell me that Nemesis has all the skills and strength of your entire pantheon?" demanded Fenris. "Because if you are, I think I might have been better off staying behind in my home MythOS and fighting it out at Ragnarok."

"No." I rubbed my forehead. "At least, I don't think so. The only reason Necessity is capable of wielding as much power as she does is her nature as the Fate of the Gods and her processing power as a world-spanning computer. Under normal circumstances, Nemesis doesn't have anything like that much capacity. Even now, inhabiting Necessity, she's got to work under pretty severe constraints imposed by all the damage that's been done to Necessity. Nemesis is currently limited by the very problems that allowed her to invade the system."

"Well," said Melchior, "that's different."

"What?" I raised an eyebrow.

"This may be the first time that all the destruction we've helped heap on poor old Necessity's head has had any hint of an upside."

"Call it the Trickster effect," I replied with a bitter smile. "My biggest successes and my biggest defeats seem to go hand in hand."

"My father, Loki, is the same way," said Fenris. "For every victory lap he starts to run, there's always a banana peel waiting for him somewhere on the track. Does your Eris have the same problem?"

"She does this week," said Melchior, "and this week the banana peel has Ravirn's names on it."

"What, just because I led a Fury into her living room?"

Melchior shook his head. "Nah. From what I hear, Cerice didn't even make her sweat. I was thinking more of when you completely nuked her server cluster."

"What?" I was missing something.

"Your brain must still be scrambled," said Melchior. "Riddle me this: What happens when you open a door from the very heart of Discord's command and control system directly into the Primal Chaos?"

"I hadn't thought of it that way." I kicked back the rest of my drink—it was going to be a while before she forgave me for that, and Discord's shit list is not a place I wanted to be. "How bad was it?"

"For starters," said Melchior, "the apple exploded."

"Discord's prize from the Trojan War is gone?"

Fenris nodded. "Golden applesauce everywhere. And then the stars in that artificial nebula started going out one by one. For a second I thought I was fresh out of this-MythOS friends. Then Melchior coughed up that spinnerette thing and started puking his guts out."

"What's up with that, Mel?" I asked.

He signaled Haemun for a refill. "I didn't know what to do with her. You'd brought her in physically via the gate you cut, and I was leaving in spirit. So, I ate her. I figured that if I completely encapsulated her, she'd stand a better chance of coming through in more or less one piece, and I didn't really have much time for coming up with alternate solutions after you dropped the magical equivalent of an atomic bomb."

"And?" I raised an eyebrow.

"I don't know." He shrugged. "Either it worked, or she had some other resources that she deployed. In either case, we arrived together, and she made her exit by kicking me straight in the gag reflex."

"Where is she now?" I asked, realizing for the first time that I hadn't seen the spinnerette at all in the hour or so since I'd been recorporealized.

"Sulking somewhere, maybe," said Melchior. "She wouldn't get near me again after we came out of what was left of Discord's network—rode back on Fenris's shoulders with Laginn. Then she scampered off and hid as soon as we got home. I haven't seen her since."

I looked around but didn't see any signs of the spinnerette. That made me nervous.

"What's wrong?" asked Melchior. "You look a whole lot less happy about that than I'd have expected. Should I have kept a better eye on her?"

"It's probably fine, Mel. We just never established who she was working for, and the whole idea of Nemesis makes me a little twitchy."

"I can't imagine why," he said, with deliberate nonchalance.

The effect was damaged somewhat when he jumped half out of his seat and knocked over his drink a moment later. But only somewhat, as the rest of us had similar reactions to the enormous flash and boom that came from the permanent faerie ring on the lanai.

I spun in my seat, making a mental note never to sit with my back to a ring again as I did so. "What the— Tisiphone! No, Cerice?"

My confusion came from the fact that Cerice was on fire when she arrived, with bright yellow and orange flames chewing on every surface of her body. But only for an instant. As she stepped across the line of the faerie ring, the fires went out.

She took one staggering step toward me, her arms outstretched. "Ravirn, I was wrong." Another step. "I'm sorry." Then she pitched forward in a faint.

Her skin crackled when I caught her, and I froze for fear of causing further harm. "Melchior!"

He'd already started whistling "Better Living Through Chemistry" as I leaped to catch Cerice. Now he sank a claw turned syringe into the side of Cerice's neck and pushed the plunger, sending a huge dose of morphine into her system.

Furies are heavy—four or five hundred pounds of heavy—and I hadn't had time to plan my catch, just leaped forward and looped one hand under each of her armpits. I ended up in a lousy position, with my legs in something resembling a full-on fencing extension. Add to that, that I was none too steady myself after my recent return to the flesh, and it was a wonder I didn't drop her or collapse in the first couple of seconds.

But when Haemun offered to take some of the load or help me lower her to the ground, I actually growled at him. The less of her skin that came in contact with anything nonsterile, the better. At least that was what I told myself. I was just trying to figure out how best to get her to a burn unit when she moved in my arms.

"Be still," I said. "We're working on it."

She lifted her head and met my eyes. "No, it's all right."

It hurt me to look at the blackened skin and deep red cracks on her face, and I felt a terrible anger welling up in my heart, but I forced myself to smile and nod and keep making eye contact for her sake. Later, however, I would make someone pay for this.

"I'll be fine in a few minutes now that I'm out of the direct blast," she continued.

"Sure you will," I said just to agree.

But there was no need to humor her. Though I might have forgotten it in the moment, Cerice was no longer the demihuman child of Fate I'd once loved. She was a Fury, and virtually indestructible. Even as I watched, the harsh red gashes began to close, and her skin softened and lightened, sloughing off the charcoal. Within minutes, she looked as though she'd never been injured.

An amused smile grew on her lips. "Ravirn?"

"Yes?"

"You can let go of me now."

I thought about it for a moment, then shook my head. "No, actually. I can't. Not from this position, not without dropping you."

She laughed quietly. With a snap of her wings she flicked herself back and up, out of my hands and onto her feet. I couldn't compensate for the sudden change in my balance and lurched forward, stumbling. I'd have landed on my face if Cerice hadn't put a hand under my chest, catching me as easily as if I were a cardboard cutout of myself, and setting me on my feet. Before I knew what to think about that, she stepped in close and gave me a kiss that tasted of first love lost and summer hillsides long ago.

"Thank you," she breathed against my lips, then was gone, stepping back and away—unmistakably and unbridgeably separating herself from me.

When she spoke again, it was with the hard voice of the Fury. "Shara sent me. She said to tell you it's the end of the world as we know it."

I was just trying to figure out some response to that that didn't include my telling Cerice that I currently trusted Shara's word about half as far as I'd trust a promise of sobriety from Dionysus, when I got my second delivery of Fury flambé for the day.

Alecto had clearly listened to those stop, drop, and roll ads back in the day, because Goddess, Gracious, Great Ball of Fire. She came out of the ring like a fiery bowling ball, and only varying degrees of fancy footwork saved the lot of us from playing the role of the pins. She did take out the table and several deck chairs before flipping into the air and sailing over the edge of the lanai to land in a smoldering heap on the jungle floor below.

"Mel," I said.

"On it." He started whistling "Better Living" again as he vaulted the railing.

But Alecto was already on her way back, burns or no. She landed hard because of badly crisped wings and stomped over to face me. She looked scarier than ever. She'd clearly been burned much worse than Cerice, but where the fires had left Cerice barely functional, Alecto hardly seemed inconvenienced—just really really pissed. I couldn't blame her there; I felt much the same way.

"Nemesis is back!" Alecto snarled through fire-blackened lips. "She revealed herself a few minutes ago."

Cerice nodded. "That's part of what Shara sent me to tell you."

"Actually, we're on top of that one," I said. "Though I don't like that 'part of' clause you threw in there. I'm guessing that part two has to do with Nemesis advancing her schedule for world domination after I survived our encounter in Discord's network, but I'm sure there's more. No matter how much I'd love to believe that's all you've got, I know there's always another shoe waiting to drop with these things. Sometimes I think the deity in charge of dropping shoes on Ravirn is a centipede. So, what's part three?"

A look of pure pain rippled across Cerice's features, but she quickly got it under control and opened her mouth to speak. Before she said so much as a word, though, she stopped herself and glanced awkwardly at Alecto.

Great, more inter-Fury conflict with Ravirn playing man in the middle.

While I could see the potential entertainment value of playing the role of the frosting in the middle of a Cerice/Alecto layer cake under the right circumstances, I was pretty sure these weren't them.

"I don't suppose this is something the two of you want to settle between yourselves while I go out for dinner and a movie with my buddies?" I asked, hopefully.

Cerice growled at me, and Alecto . . .

"Ouch," said Melchior, "and here I thought *Medusa* was the queen of killer looks." He shut up abruptly when Alecto turned her raging eyes his way.

I stepped between them. "Look, Alecto, I know that you're a Goddess of Wrath and all that, but just this once could you chill the hell out? It doesn't sound like we have a ton of time for ripping each other apart at the moment."

For a second, I thought I had gotten myself off the hook for this whole mess by the unpleasant expedient of having a Fury turn me inside out. Then Alecto shook her head and stepped back. The anger in her eyes stayed every bit as intense, but it moved back into the depths, becoming colder and more remote.

"Later, perhaps, I will break both of your arms. But it will have to wait until after we find out whether we all survive the coming pass." She turned then to Cerice and extended her hand. "Little sister, I have not welcomed you properly before this; let me now amend my ways and greet you as both an ally and the sibling you are."

For about eight-tenths of a second, Cerice looked like someone had kicked her square in the stomach. Then her mouth shaped itself into a shy smile, and she stepped forward to embrace Alecto. It was actually rather sweet. *Not* that I was going to say anything about that. When Cerice finally moved away from the older Fury, she looked more settled somehow, less lost. Though I hadn't realized she'd been looking lost beforehand, it seemed crystal clear in retrospect.

Cerice turned toward me, opened her mouth, then froze again.

"It's all right," said Alecto. "I don't know what your Shara has told you, but in accepting you as a sister, I must needs also accept her as something of a foster mother in this hour of Necessity's incapacity."

Cerice closed her eyes for a moment, then straightened her shoulders and opened them again, obviously working herself up to talk about things that she'd rather not. "Shara also sent me to ask you for a favor."

"There's always something." I braced myself. "I know I'm going to hate this, but go ahead and hit me."

"Nemesis has used her access through Necessity to seize effective control of all the pole-power networks. The first thing Shara wants you to do is force Nemesis out of the Fate Core, Olympus.net, and the systems of Hades, then to close the doors behind her."

I blinked. "That's a heck of a *first thing*, but sure, why

not? Then for the second round, I suppose I can do Discord, and clean up with a complete purge of the mweb before afternoon tea."

"No," said Cerice. "Discord you've already covered. The effective destruction of her network means no more Nemesis-infection within. Your experiences there are what gave Shara warning to look at the other systems and the idea of a shutdown, though she didn't at first understand that the entity she was battling within Necessity was Nemesis." Cerice smiled a wan sort of smile. "Sorry to say, however, that you *will* probably need to take down the mweb to keep Nemesis from reinfecting the powers while we're fixing Necessity. Nemesis has to be completely isolated until that's done, so that she can't escape again."

"You're kidding, right? No, I can see by your expression that you're not kidding. Insane, maybe, but not kidding." I shook my head. "Is that all? Or does Shara expect me to rearrange the sun and moon and all the starlit skies to suit her fancy as well?"

"That's all she asks. But she also sent you a message."

"Great. What is it?"

Cerice's face and body went slack then, like a puppet whose strings have been let go. A couple of seconds later, she straightened up, but a different will seemed to be animating her features. In the manner of an extremely good actress, she appeared to have become someone else entirely. Someone I knew well. In that moment, Shara looked out at me through Cerice's eyes. Or, more accurately perhaps, Necessity Junior looked out at me through the eyes of one of her Fury handmaidens.

"This is probably the last time I will ever have the opportunity to speak to you, Ravirn. And wouldn't you know it, it's not nearly as up close and personal as I might like." She winked and threw me a vampy smirk, and for just an instant I saw a ghost of the old Mae-Westian Shara through the strain and the stress that so obviously consumed her.

"I'm sorry it had to be this way, with me piling the future of the whole damn pantheoverse on your shoulders, but I'm fresh out of options."

She looked down and away for a moment—hiding tears, I thought—then faced me squarely once again. "I failed. The damage to Necessity the computer is simply too great for me to be able to stop Nemesis from within by myself, and Necessity the goddess, if she still exists, is buried somewhere in the system beyond my reach. The computer mind we all share is functionally insane and growing more so every day, and only Nemesis thrives in the maelstrom. If you don't succeed where I could not, the soul of Vengeance will own this entire MythOS, probably within a few days. Malice will rule over all. Malice untempered by mercy and walking hand in hand with madness."

Cerice, still in the mode of Shara, jerked and made a noise like static, then froze for a couple of beats before going on. "This will be my final communication, and you shouldn't trust any further messages that appear to come from me. I can feel Nemesis knocking at the doors of my soul, and soon she will take the part of the computer that is me as she has taken so much of what once belonged to Necessity. Give my love to Melchior. Succeed where I could not. I know that you can. I love you all. Good-bye."

When Cerice came back into herself, there were tears streaming down her cheeks and the unwavering rage of the Furies shining in her eyes. "That was the last thing she said before the fires came, and I was forced to flee into chaos, thence to the faerie rings."

CHAPTER FIFTEEN

Sometimes the only person you can talk something over with is yourself. Perhaps that's why I ended up in front of the big mirror in my bathroom after I crawled out of the tub. Or maybe it was my eyes. My bodiless sojourn had cost me what little remnant of mortality they'd once held. Where once chaos had owned only my pupils, raising my eyelids now opened a pair of twinned gates into the Primal Chaos. Like Eris and Loki, I had lost my eyes to my power.

"How can I see?" I wondered aloud.

"You can't," said the face in the mirror. "Not in the classical sense. It's all a part of the lie you tell the universe."

"Eris?" I asked, and for just a moment, the planes of my reflected face seemed to change, momentarily mirroring the Goddess of Discord.

But then the effect was over, and I shook my head. Not Discord. The Raven. The Trickster playing tricks on himself. Or at least that was how it seemed to me. On impulse, I reached up and very gently touched my "eye" with my fingertip. I couldn't feel the contact, from either end. When I pressed harder, my reflection showed my finger actually seeming to slide through the gate of my eye. I kept pushing until my entire finger had vanished from sight.

It didn't hurt, and no matter how I probed, I couldn't feel anything with that finger. Nor did I have any sensation that might have suggested I was tickling my own brain. It was probably the creepiest thing I'd ever seen. When I pulled it back out, there was a brief moment where my finger looked as though it were made of very clear glass filled with chaos. Then it returned to the appearance of mortal flesh and blood.

I felt a sensation like fingernails running gently from the base of my spine to the nape of my neck, and I shuddered. It came again, and I realized it wasn't internal.

"Cerice?"

She faded into existence behind me—every bit as naked as I was. Standing like that, facing the mirror, brought back memories. We had made love more than once in this room, with our mirror doubles partnering our dance to that oldest of rhythms just on the other side of the glass.

I felt myself responding in the predictable way, both to the memories and to the proximity of a beautiful woman on the edge of death. I wanted to turn and take her in my arms and make love to her once more, perhaps for the last time.

Instead, I shook my head. "I'm sorry. I can't."

"Why not?" She sounded sad but not surprised.

"Lots of things." I continued to look into her eyes only through the mediation of the mirror. "What you have become. What I have become. The shadows that lie between us."

"I can make the wings invisible, ape the old me . . ."

She did, and for a moment she was almost the Cerice whom I had once thought I might someday marry. But it was an illusion. She still had ice in her hair and her eyes, and that elemental nature provided another reflection. A reflection of the fiery-haired Tisiphone to whom I had promised to return.

Finally, I turned to face Cerice. "I'm sorry," I repeated, and I was.

"So am I." Then she faded from sight, and in that moment I knew it was well and truly over between us and that when I went to my closet to clothe myself, the dress my heart had spun for her would have faded away as well.

I wanted to cry then, but I found I no longer had the eyes for it.

"So, what now?" Melchior was sitting on my bedside table.

"Good question." I sat cross-legged on the bed facing him.

I knew we had to move, but I wasn't going to let myself be stampeded into accidentally doing something really stupid. If I was going to do something really stupid, I wanted to do it with malice aforethought.

"Someday," I said, "I'd like my choices to be between the frying pan and rum on the beach rather than the more traditional frying pan and fire pairing. The way I see it, we're pretty much obligated to take down Fate and the other pole-power systems per Shara's request, then plunge headfirst into a codewar with Nemesis. The question isn't so much about strategy or end goals as it is about short-term tactics."

"On the plus side," said Melchior, "we've got that lovely box filled with the tools of destruction that Persephone donated to the cause early on. It almost makes you wonder if she saw all of this coming."

"Who can tell with a goddess? For all we know, she's got Cassandra tucked away somewhere and is actually *listening* to that cursed lady's prophecies of doom. But I doubt it. If I had to make a guess, I'd say, 'No, she didn't foresee our current plight.' If she had, she'd have gone for less of an overkill factor. The Persephone suite of viruses is really more by way of global nuclear war than the short-term knockout punch that's called for here. She's shooting to kill where we just want to put our targets down for a long winter's nap."

"There is that." Mel tapped the side of his head. "Without some serious modification, the things she put in here are likely to cause the kind of damage that requires shutting the surviving hardware down and reinstalling operating systems from scratch. That wouldn't be too much of a loss with Hades or Olympus.net, but Fate's another story. Even though they've been transitioning away from AI as much as possible, there are still a lot of webtrolls and webgoblins in our line of fire. We're going to have to be extra careful with them."

"Which is about the only thing that's going to preserve my personal sense of pride. If I just took someone else's malicious code and released it into the systems in question, I'd be no better than any script-kiddie downloading malware off the net and pretending that using it makes me a real black-hat coder."

Melchior rolled his eyes. "Heaven forefend that anyone think the mighty Ravirn is anything but the king of code!"

"Or, more seriously, that anyone but me is responsible for the pantheonwide computer Armageddon we're about set off. The blowback from this is going to be worse than anything we've ever seen. All four pole powers are going to have reason to come after us in the aftermath, and I'd rather not put anyone I don't have to in the splash zone. Especially Persephone. She's suffered enough."

"Speaking of which . . ." Melchior stood up and stepped from table to bed, where he began to pace a slow circle around me.

"Yes?" I asked after a while. "Did you have something to say, or are you just going to orbit me in silent worry?"

"What comes next? Even if Discord forgives you out of sheer admiration for the giant ball of snafu we're about to start rolling, that still leaves three pole powers in the looking-for-revenge column. That being the case, no one is going to bet on our long-term survival post compuapocalypse, with Athena, Hades, and Fate all gunning for us. Not at any odds." He stopped and looked me straight in the eyes. "Not even me."

I shrugged. "I could make the argument that our chances of coming out the other side of this particular tunnel are so low that worrying about what comes next is just borrowing trouble. But I won't. I've actually been thinking about it rather a lot.

"The way I see it is thus: If we lose, we're dead, and that's that. If we win, Necessity will owe us a major favor, and she'll be back on her feet and more than capable of telling everyone to leave us the hell alone."

"Unless she decides that the silly idiots who started the whole thing ought not to be rewarded for doing so," said Melchior. "If she blames us for Persephone's virus, we could end up very much on her bad side. Even if she doesn't, I'd hate for plan A to involve relying on the gratitude of a goddess."

I rolled backwards off the bed, landing on my feet, and started my own pacing. "Point to Melchior, and I wasn't planning on relying on it long-term. I was just going to ask her to—" I stopped and looked at my familiar, realizing for the first time that I hadn't run my thoughts about returning to Tisiphone past him at all.

"I don't like that expression, Boss. It has a tendency to proceed some attempt at noble sacrifice on your part."

"Not this time, Mel. It's just that I'm feeling kind of selfish. I was about to say that the safest thing for us to do would be to cut out of this MythOS entirely and head back to Tisiphone, when I realized something. I've never even asked to see whether you'd want to come with me when I go. I oughtn't spring things like that on you all of a sudden."

Mel snorted and flopped back among the pillows. "You can be such a goofball sometimes. Do you honestly think I hadn't noticed you mooning about Tisiphone? Or that I was too dumb to figure out that you wanted to return to her? Gods and monsters, man, I'd have to be a moron not to see that whole scene where you turned down the ultimate in nostalgia sex with Cerice as a functional declaration of your undying love for the Fury who *wasn't* there."

I blushed like Artemis stumbling into an after-hours party at a nymphs and satyrs bar. I tend to forget how good Melchior's ears are. "Does that mean you'd be up for a return to the land of the Norse gods? I know you left some ugly memories there, and that your chaos tap is a potential problem in that environment, and . . . Why are you grinning at me like that?"

"I'm touched, actually. I know that you keep saying we're partners, but it never fails to amaze that the vast majority of the time you actually treat me as an equal. Of all my kind, only Shara and I have ever had any relationship other than master and slave with our respective sorcerers."

He looked down and away, and his cheeks darkened toward indigo in a goblin blush. "Have I ever said how much that means to me? No, probably not. Thank you."

When he looked back up at me I thought I detected just a hint of moisture shining in his eyes. "Of course you have to go back to Tisiphone. And, likewise of course, I'm coming with you. That was really why I wanted to have this conversation. I thought heading for cosmic elsewhere was our only reasonable hope of surviving long enough to retire, and I wanted to make sure that we put that escape high on our list of things to do.

"In fact"—and his voice dropped almost to a whisper—

"I was thinking that setting up said escape might best be set at the top of the fixing-Necessity flow chart—get the abacus system under control *first*, so that if it looks like we're all going to lose, we might have some alternative to that whole blaze-of-glory ending."

"I couldn't leave the others behind, Mel."

"So bring 'em with. I don't see why the Norse MythOS can't absorb three Furies as easily as the one it's currently housing. I know that'd put Fenris in a bind, but better in a bind at home than dead here. We can always figure some way around that later."

I nodded, and very pointedly didn't mention that he'd left Shara out of his formulation. We all grieve however is best for us. "Fair enough. Let's see how much work it's going to take to cut Persephone's tactical nukes down to something closer to a clipful of tranquilizer darts."

We started with Fate because that was the system I knew best and because the mweb controllers lived there at the moment. Persephone's code was a thing of beauty, powerful, economical, thoroughly self-integrated. All the things you want in a piece of software you're going to just let run. Unfortunately, that kind of elegance of design is less fun when you're trying to pick a piece of software apart, pull out the bits you want, and repurpose them. In this case, the only thing that functioned as a quasi-independent subsystem was the cracking routine, which was a thing of beauty and joy.

Without so much as spilling a drop of my blood or breaking a sweat, I was able to open up the command line at Fate and look at anything I wanted to. Say, for example, their contingency planning for the transition away from a Necessity-controlled multiverse into a Fate-controlled duoverse.

"That's so whacked, it's . . . Auughh!" Melchior was practically shaking by the time we finished reading through that little white paper.

Not that I could blame him. They wanted to collapse all the infinite threads of probability back down into just two, the Olympus-Hades world of the mythological and a single, easily controlled world of humans, which would allow them to junk all of their computers and return to the great loom of Fate as a control mechanism.

At best, it could be read as a desperate parent's attempts to return an errant teenager to manageable infancy at the cost of the child's memories to that point. Horrific and a crime, but one that fell within the realm of the unjustifiable-but-marginally-understandable. At worst . . . something beyond genocide, as the entire populations of millions of worlds were made to have never been. If it wasn't for the collateral damage it would cause the AI community, I'd have let Persephone's virus eat the whole works then and there.

As it was, with so many of Melchior's friends bound into the processing system, we ended up separating the operational portion of Persephone's Fate Breaker from the access functions. Then we scratch-coded a bunch of sequentially self-loading microviruses of the sort that would keep the system off-line for a few hours at a time without doing any lasting harm. A really spiffy side effect of that was that it would it make it very hard for them to do anything with Melchior's thread this side of a full system recovery.

How does that look? I typed on Mel's keyboard when we'd gotten everything in place.

Fine, he replied, but the expression of his projected face on the screen didn't match his words, and I thought I knew why—I felt the same way.

It's not enough, is it?

The projected face shook its head. *No. I really really hate to say it, because if we go too far in the other direction, we're going to hurt people I know and care about, but this one is for all the money, and if Nemesis escapes . . .*

We've already sunk more time into this than we can really afford, but I'm willing to keep going if you are. I was exhausted already, and we had two systems left to go.

Again his image shook its head, and this time his expression looked sick. *We can't afford to leave any of this to chance. I think we should set up E-bola to self-load if they get the system back online anytime before about a hundred hours after the initial attack.*

That's an ugly solution, Mel. It's going to hurt webtrolls and webgoblins we know and care about, maybe even kill some of them.

Melchior's image nodded but didn't add a word. He was right, too. We had to have a fallback plan in place even if it killed people.

Every serious hacker/cracker, even a pure white-hat type devoted to fighting the good fight, has played with the tools of the virus writer, and I'm quite a bit closer to my black-hat roots than most who walk my side of the line. Once upon a time, I'd done a hell of a lot more than muck about with viral tools; I'd gone ahead and written my very own Fate-targeted doomsday virus designed to eat applications for breakfast, operating systems for lunch, and hardware for dinner.

It was called E-bola, and I'd even had a sort of test run with the beta version in the Fate Core itself when I used it to ream out the worm Discord had set to de-destinizing the threads there, or whatever you want to call a process that results in a thread being permanently removed from Fate's control. My actions then had resulted in the death of my cousin Laric, who was probably the only other member of the younger generation of Fate that I cared for besides Cerice.

The guilt I'd felt over his death had almost driven me to delete the whole damn thing, but that ultimately felt too much like playing the quitter. Instead, I'd refined the daylights out of E-bola until I had an exquisite tool optimized for kicking the shit out of Fate. It was a truly vicious piece of software. It was also a hell of a lot gentler than Persephone's Fate Breaker.

I sighed and typed, *You're right, my friend. Pull up E-bola, and let's set it up along with the rest. We've got to do* something, *and it's better to give Fate the equivalent of an occasionally fatal version of the flu than the black plague on steroids. Oh, and please prep the update to Scorched Earth as well.*

Once upon a time, Scorched Earth 1.0 had accidentally crashed the mweb. After a second such attempt had failed and gotten Melchior countervirused into the bargain, I'd created a 2.0 version and kept it updated. I was dead certain that with the access Persephone had bought me, version 2.8.4 would be more than adequate to the task of shutting down the mweb for a couple of days with this third release.

Olympus.net was simpler, both as a coding problem and morally. There were very few AIs involved there because Athena didn't trust them. And, frankly, while Zeus might be the king of the gods, he mostly tried to let the job do itself, so none of the Olympus.net systems did anything that was of really Earth-shattering importance. We pretty much just stepped Persephone's virus down from absolute burn-it-to-the-ground-and-salt-the-ashes destruction to start-it-on-fire-and-figure-they'll-put-it-out-eventually and set it up for release at need.

That left Hades, and us, strung out and in serious need of a break. It arrived—as such things so often do in my life—in the form of a brand-new piece of bad news.

Melchior and I were working in the office/sorcerer's lair above my bedroom. A small, hexagonal tower room, it's reached by a spiral stair in the back of the walk-in closet. It had appeared there not long after my insomnia started to get really ugly. At the moment, said office held an extremely comfortable chair with an attached laptop desk opposite a small silver hexagram set into the marble floor and a whole lot of sunlight and fresh air. At other times, say when I have need of a cabinet or two of electronics, they're always there.

I had just leaned my head back against the cushion of the chair and closed my screen-strained eyes when a cool shadow fell on me. Absently, I held out my right hand for the drink I'd been hoping Haemun would bring me.

What I got instead was the briefest touch of a finger sliding along my palm and a whispered, "Ravirn? I must speak with you."

It was a voice I'd heard often in my dreams of late and one I had never expected to hear at Raven House.

Alarmed, I sat up. "Persephone, what brings you from your gardens?" To my knowledge, she had not left them once in the two years of her freedom.

"Danger to you." She stood above me, her face grave. "Of the direst sort."

"Tell me about it." Which was not at all what I wanted to say. But then, I would never use the sort of language that came to mind then in front of Persephone.

"Your incursion into Olympus's servers has been detected. Since your last visit to my gardens, Athena and I have been quietly at war with one another in the datasphere of Mount Olympus—she trying to root out my embedded viruses and back doors, I replacing them as soon she does so. She is on maximum alert, and the malware I lent you is of a version since rendered obsolete. Had I known you needed access, I'd have sent you an update, but now it is too late, and Athena knows that you have moved against Olympus."

I slid out of my chair. "Melchior, Goblin. Please."

"What do you need?" he asked as soon as he'd shifted back into a shape with lips.

"I don't know, but I'm thinking that we're going to need to move up our production schedule. A lot." I turned to Persephone. "How soon will Athena be here?"

"Not while I hold the doors between the worlds closed. She cannot enter here until I remove myself, or let her through. That's why I had to come in person." Persephone smiled one of her sad smiles. "Besides, she has other, more pressing concerns at the moment. I have shut down computing on Olympus for the foreseeable future."

"How recently?" I asked, with icy serpents crawling loops around my spine.

"Seconds ago."

"Good. Melchior—"

"I know, full on E-bola and Scorched Earth now. On it, Boss." His eyes went faraway. When they returned to seeing the here and now, he spoke again. "Fate is going dark as we speak, and the mweb will follow it down shortly. What do you want to do about Hades? We haven't had time to code up anything milder than the complete destruction option Persephone gave us."

"At this point, I think we're committed. Nuke him."

"You know," said Mel, with an evil grin, "this one I'm going to truly enjoy." His attention went away again while he ran the program that would return Hades' control networks to the Bronze Age.

"Persephone, thank you." I wanted to take her hand and give it the sort of courtier's kiss I had learned in the Houses of Fate, but I restrained the urge. "I have so much more I wish I had time to say, but I just signed what is very likely my own death warrant, and now I have to move quickly if I'm going make it worth the cost."

I'm an optimist, and I really would have loved to pretend for Persephone's sake that I had a snowball's chance of winning *and* living through the experience, but I will not lie to her, and I was about to go up against the goddess Nemesis acting with some significant portion of Necessity's powers behind her. Persephone nodded, and, save for a slight fading of her smile, that was the extent of her emotional response.

"Is there anything more I can do to help you?" she asked.

"I'm afraid nothing comes to mind." I glanced at Melchior, who had just fully returned to us. "Can you dump everything we know about what's happened to date onto a memory crystal so that Persephone gets the explanation she deserves but I can't afford the time it takes to give?"

He nodded, and his expression went distant once again.

I returned my attention to Persephone as another thought passed through my mind. "There is one thing. If you're willing, you could take Haemun with you when you go. He doesn't deserve what Athena is going to do to this place. I know he's a satyr and a he and so not your favorite type of people, and I won't ask you to keep him in your service, just find a home for him. Perhaps with Thalia."

"That I can do. Anything else?"

"No. I would have preferred to keep you out of this entirely because the absolute last thing in the world I ever wanted to do was see you suffer any more hurts, but I'm afraid my use of your software has precluded that option. I hope you can find it in your heart to forgive me."

She took my left hand between her own and laughed the gayest laugh I'd heard from her since the hour of her escape from Hades. "Silly Raven, I would not have given you the tools had I not been willing to bear the cost. You were my salvation. Never think that I would begrudge you anything it is in me to give. Besides that, there are other considerations, not least of which is the satisfaction of finally delivering my parting gift to Hades."

That was when Melchior spat out a memory crystal and handed it to me. I passed it along to Persephone.

"I'm sorry I can't stay longer. If I don't see you again, know that freeing you was the purest joy I've ever known, and that nothing that has come since makes me regret it in the least. Were I the sort to worship, my goddess would be the spring."

"Then take my blessing, and know that you walk ever in the favor of the lady of spring." She lifted my hand and placed the briefest of kisses on my palm. "Know also that if Hades takes you, I will make him pay for it. Now, go."

I took the steps down three at a time, shouting for Cerice and Alecto to be ready as I went. They met me along with Fenris, Laginn, and Haemun at the base of the main stairs.

"What's happened?" asked Cerice.

"I just put a down payment on Shara's last request. The powers are down, and now we have to move."

"It were better had you warned us," said Alecto, her voice acid.

"And better still if I hadn't screwed up and so had no time to warn you," I said with just as much acid. "But it's a little late for that now."

"Why didn't you call *me*?" asked Fenris, and hangdog suddenly had a new poster face.

"It's not your fight," I said. "And I won't ask you to fight it."

He growled and rolled his eyes. "I begin to see why everyone always calls you an idiot. In this world, you are my pack. Pack backs pack." He couldn't have sounded more emphatic.

Laginn, perched on his back, bobbed an equally emphatic yes.

"Let me just plead guilty to idiocy then and thank you for joining us. Melchior can attest to my near-divine gift for saying the wrong thing at the wrong time."

"Or failing to say the right one," Cerice added quietly.

"That, too." I glanced at Haemun. "Persephone is in my office. I asked her to take you with her when she leaves. In the meantime, you might want to fetch her a drink or something."

"Take me with her!" From his tone you'd have thought I'd just offered to sell him to a passing flock of harpies.

"Unless you want to be here when Athena shows up to ask about the complete destruction of Olympus.net and the crashing of the mweb. Because that's what's going to happen about ten seconds after Persephone goes out the door."

"What do you suppose she likes to drink?" Haemun asked in a very small voice.

"I don't know," said Melchior, "but I'd stay away from pomegranate juice if I were you."

Just then I felt a tug on my leather pants, right above where they went into my boots. It was the spinnerette, returned from wherever she'd been hiding and determinedly climbing me.

"Looks like everyone's here," I said. "That means it's time to go. We can discuss our exact point of arrival on the way."

Alecto nodded and cut a hole through the wall of the world. This one was not a typical Fury gate, as we couldn't trust those anymore, but rather a simple slit from reality into the Primal Chaos. With the mweb down and faerie rings barred from Necessity's world, the only way we had to get from here to there was to fly through chaos on Fury's wings. I tucked a laptop-shaped Melchior into the pocket built into the back of my leather jacket and stepped into Cerice's arms. Then Alecto picked up Fenris, and we plunged into the maelstrom.

Next stop: Nemesis.

CHAPTER SIXTEEN

■ ■ ■

"Just let me fix my face, and I'll be ready," I told Cerice as we hovered within the tumbling coils of the Primal Chaos that lies just beyond the edges of reality.

I pulled Melchior from my laptop pocket and handed him to Cerice. The spinnerette went with him. Together, Melchior and I changed. He into a goblin, me into a giant otter. I clapped my paws and waggled my eyebrows at Cerice by way of a prompt, but she shook her head.

"A minute more. We need to give Fenris and Alecto time to begin their distraction at the cave of the abacuses." Her face took on the cast of someone listening for faint and distant sounds. Finally, she nodded and set Melchior on my shoulders. "Now."

Six-inch claws cut a doorway into Necessity's world, and we plunged from chaos into deep water. The chamber beyond the gate was almost impossibly vast, like an open-topped football stadium carved from living stone. A massive reef of yellow coral filled it from side to side and reached great pillars up toward the surface and a tropical sun.

We had entered at a depth of perhaps thirty meters, and the light was dimmed and significantly green-shifted by the filtering effect of the water above us. Combine that with the irregular nature of the reef, and the wild cacophony of sea life in this world without human predators, and you produce a maze of shifting shadows. Any of them could easily have hidden the great silver ball of Nemesis's disembodied eye, so I stayed within easy reach of my Fury protector. Paddling only as much as I needed to maintain my position beneath Cerice, I focused all my attention on the reef and tried to make sense of its structure.

This was the replacement system for the more mundane computers that had once controlled the powers of the powers and the positions of the pantheon—the subnetwork that defined the true Fate of the Gods. It was one giant, living processor, grown specifically for the task, a merging of software and hardware into a single-purpose system that—theoretically—couldn't be hacked. Somewhere in there lay a fat piece of coral carefully evolved to define the soul of Nemesis. If we could identify it and cut it free, then isolate or destroy it, we might just be able to make this a scalpel operation rather than a sledgehammer job.

Yeah, right. What I was seeing was a whole lot of coral, and not a single divine nameplate. No ZEUS. No ERIS. No NEMESIS, SET CHARGES HERE. For the life of me, it didn't look even a tiny bit like a computer.

Oh, after perhaps ten minutes of staring, my special divinity was starting to pick up on unusual patterns within the reef, knobs and knurls and fans that repeated more often and more precisely than any true structure of nature. But that was more by way of identifying it as the construct it was than making any sense of associated functions. Given a week or two, I *might* start to understand the underlying principles, but that was time we didn't have.

I rolled over in the water, intending to let Cerice know

this was a no-go, just in time to take a pair of powerfully driven Fury feet straight in the chest. The impact drove the breath from my lungs, momentarily stunning me. It also moved me just far enough down and back so that the big silvery ball that came rocketing out of a cave in the coral took Cerice in the shins instead of crushing the back of my skull.

Blood clouded the water between us and muffled Cerice's shriek of pain and rage. The thing turned around and started back our way. Unfortunately, at that point, Cerice was busy holding her broken bones in place while they knitted themselves together, and I was still trying not to suck in a lungful of water. Melchior began to whistle at that point, but the spell sounded terribly strange coming as it did through water rather than air, and I had no confidence it would work properly. Especially since it was a big spell, complex and self-harmonizing, relying on a lot of subtleties.

Nemesis's gazing ball of death came rocketing in, and I did what I could to take evasive action while waiting for Melchior's spell to work, but the eye of Nemesis had grown in power since our last meeting, and the ball was way faster than me. I was about to find out what otter pâté felt like from the inside, when a pair of giant rubber paddles appeared between me and the eye of Nemesis. The left paddle pivoted on nothing and slammed that gazing ball like Dionysus shotgunning a beer. It shot away from me for about fifty feet before it hit a just-appeared rubber-covered globe that chimed and batted it in another direction with even more speed.

What the . . .

Melchior, his head enclosed in a big bubble of air like a fifties spaceman helmet, leaned down into my vision and grinned. "I call that one 'The Real Pinball Wizard.'"

Every time Nemesis's silvery eye seemed to be getting itself back under control, another bumper appeared and bounced it in a random direction. Mel's spell was doing great, right up until the eye hit a bumper and shattered it in the manner of a musket ball smacking into a snow globe. After that, the whole magical structure started to come apart. But the spell had bought us the two minutes we needed to regroup.

By the time Nemesis's eye was headed our way again, Cerice had restored her legs to functionality, and I'd cut us an exit back to chaos. With no chance of success here, there was little point in contesting the field.

Strike one.

It wasn't until perhaps ten minutes later, after I'd reverted to my normal shape, that I noticed our spinnerette companion had abandoned ship somewhere on the watery side of the line. If I'd had any idea what her true agenda was, I might have known what to do about that. I didn't and was still trying to decide whether I ought to do *anything* when Alecto and Fenris arrived.

The former had a badly broken wing and some fresh burns, the latter a deep gash that ran back from a half-severed ear along the top of his head and down his neck to the shoulder. He also had a scattering of lightly singed fur and the sort of grin that suggested the other guy looked worse. Even Laginn looked beat-up, with two split knuckles and a torn-away thumbnail.

"Megaera *and* Delé," said Alecto before I could ask. "And we found nothing of any use."

"But Delé's going to be limping along with five legs and one and a half claws for a while," Fenris said with grim satisfaction.

Call that strike 1.5.1. *So, I'm a software guy, not a baseball guy. What about it?*

"So what's next?" I asked. "We've played all the obvious cards. What do the Furies know about the structure of Necessity that you two haven't been willing to share with me yet?"

Alecto and Cerice eyed each other uncomfortably while the silence slowly stretched out between us. Finally, Cerice broke the look and turned my way.

"I'm sure there are things Alecto knows that I don't, but I *can* say that the place where Shara stashed her body—deep under this world's Mountain of Olympus— is just above the physical location of the primary security servers. Alecto?" She turned a questioning look on the older Fury.

Alecto sighed. "I have one thought beyond that, but let's try security first. There is much that can be done from there, and I would not reveal all of my mother's secrets, even now. Not unless need forces my hand."

This time we all went together, carving a door from chaos into the replica of Ahllan's old living room. It broke my heart to see Shara's physical shell lying limp and empty in her tiny chair. Cerice wouldn't even look at her former familiar, and I could tell from long experience and the tension in her jaw that she was fighting tears.

Alecto was all business, heading straight to the place where the door would have been if the replica had fully matched the original. When she got there, she extended a single claw and sank it deep into the rock. With obvious effort, she began cutting an outline of the old door.

"Is this your Shara?" Fenris asked as he pointed his nose at her empty shell, his voice gruff.

"Yes." Melchior's voice sounded sad, almost dead.

The wolf crossed to the tiny purple form and very gently sniffed her face, poking her cheek ever so lightly with the tip of his nose, before letting out a mournful whine. It was a strangely touching gesture, and I found myself once again aching to cry with eyes that didn't allow for the possibility. And that just fed the deep, cold anger I felt at Nemesis. She needed to be destroyed.

"I wish I had gotten to meet her," said Fenris.

"You'd have liked her," said Melchior. "She was special."

"Come on." Alecto pulled her freshly cut door out of the way and exposed a flight of stairs that were obviously of fairly recent vintage.

"Wait a second." Melchior had just put a foot on the top step, when he held up a hand and twisted his head from side to side as if listening for something. "Boss, incoming visual transfer protocol message from Shara@shara.gob." His voice sounded doubtful.

"That doesn't make any sense," I said. "The mweb's down, or at least I hope to all gods it is."

"It is. This is coming over local wireless from somewhere down below us, and it's very weak. I couldn't even hear it until I hit line of sight with the base of the stairs."

"It's Nemesis," said Cerice, and the white-hot rage of the Furies rode just beneath the surface of her words. "It has to be. Shara told us not to trust any more messages purporting to be from her."

"I don't know," replied Melchior. "It's got all of the right signatures and protocols. It *feels* like Shara."

"Ignore it," said Alecto. "Nemesis consumes her hosts from within. It could easily be both Shara *and* Nemesis."

"It's not directed to you, Alecto." Melchior looked straight at me, his eyes pleading. "Accept Vlink?"

"We can't, Mel. It could be a virus designed to take you down, or a Trojan that lets Nemesis into *your* system."

"Please. I think it's her. We've got to take this, Boss."

It was the "Boss" that got me. "I know that I've said this six thousand times already and that it's not going to change a thing, but I'm not your boss. We're partners. This is your decision as much as mine. If you don't agree with me, take the call."

His expression darkened—he still doesn't like making hard decisions when he can possibly avoid them—but then he nodded. "All right, then I say we take it. Vtp linking initiated."

Light burst from his eyes and mouth, creating a cloudy golden sphere. Shara appeared within, her expression oddly serene. But her calm wasn't the biggest surprise. That came from the tiny spinnerette standing in the middle of her outstretched hand.

"Shara?" Cerice's voice broke. "Is that really you? Are you all right?"

The purple webgoblin smiled with more than a hint of her old wicked sense of humor. "What would you say to yes on two, maybe on one, and hold three? I'm feeling better than I have in weeks, but I'm also really not feeling entirely myself. I'm doing my thinking with some very strange hardware."

"** ***'* **** **** *** ****!" said the spinnerette as it danced around on her palm.

"You're right," said Shara, "but if I don't explain at least a little bit, they'll have no reason to believe it's me."

"**** *** ** **** **," agreed the spinnerette with a sigh.

Shara nodded. "Will do." She looked out at us. "Necessity tells me I've got to hurry. Nemesis is closing in on the systems that give Necessity control over the will of the Furies. Once she takes control of those . . ."

"We're all dead." I swallowed heavily. When that happened, my allies would become my enemies, and I'd be all out of luck.

"Or worse," said Cerice, "puppets of Nemesis."

"What do you mean, 'Necessity tells me'?" demanded Alecto.

"**** **!"

"There's no time," Shara began, then stopped as Alecto's fists clenched. "In brief, then. Persephone's virus gave Necessity the computer equivalent of a major stroke, including something like complete aphasia. To work around that, Necessity created the spinnerette Ravirn named 'the Left Hand of Necessity.' When that one was killed by Nemesis, Necessity began to grow this replacement." Shara held up her hand with the spinnerette. "But then Nemesis attacked again, this time from within, and Necessity was forced to send her new left hand through the abacuses to Ravirn in the Norse MythOS for safekeeping. There it went dormant until its return. When Ravirn finally brought it to Fate-of-the-Gods Reef, it slipped away to the place where the soul of Necessity is housed, which allowed it to enter the system and find me."

I nodded, and so did Alecto, though obviously reluctantly. That made a lot of sense. But we still couldn't trust her, no matter how much we might want to. Not without some further proof.

"One question more from me," I said, as a possibility occurred to me. "How did you survive the attack of Nemesis?"

"You already know the answer, don't you?" Shara smiled as a teacher with a clever pupil. "I can tell from your expression."

"Maybe." I had a damned good guess.

"Necessity showed me how to live in the layers beneath the primary computing hardware of the security center. She's been hiding from Nemesis in the depths of her own firmware and the drive controllers and a thousand other places all through the system that possess a little bit of computing power but aren't actually central-processing units. That's why I could never find a source for the fixes she was making, because they were coming up from the hardware level in an almost organic way. She came to me in the last moments before Nemesis was about to break down the doors of my soul and *showed* me how to escape because she couldn't speak then to tell me."

"It's Shara," I said, certain now. "And the entity we dubbed WTF!?!?! is the real Necessity."

"I want to believe you," Alecto said to Shara's projection. "Truly. Help me. How can you understand the words of the spinnerette when no one else does?"

"Because we're thinking with the same brain. We share the same underlying structure of meaning."

The spinnerette turned to Shara. "********** **** *******." Then it crossed its tiny arms and glared straight at Alecto. ******, *** **** **** **** ** ** **** . . . ******* *'* **** ****** *** * **** **, ****'* ***, *****."

"All right," said Shara. "She says: 'Alecto, you must take them to my tomb—'"

"What!" interrupted the Fury. "Why?"

"'—Because I'm your mother, and I said so. That's why, Missy,'" finished Shara.

Alecto froze, blushed, then looked at her feet, before finally nodding. "Definitely Necessity."

"****'* ** ****," said the spinnerette, its voice warm and loving.

Shara opened her mouth to translate, but Alecto forestalled her. "I think I got that one." Then she turned and sliced a hole in the wall of the world. "And we are out of time. Come with me now to the Tomb of Necessity."

"Good-bye," said Shara. "I can't follow where you are going, but if you're successful, we may meet again."

"I love you," said Cerice, and Melchior echoed her a half second behind.

"Me, too," I added.

"And I love all of you," replied Shara.

Alecto had already ducked through into chaos with Fenris close behind.

"Take care of yourself, Shara," I said as I stepped up to follow them.

"I'd tell you the same," said Shara, "but I'm no believer in miracles, so I'll just say try not to die."

"I'll see what I can do." And then I was back in chaos.

Melchior came through an instant later, and Cerice a minute or so after.

"Follow." Alecto grabbed Fenris and began to beat her wings.

Some measureless distance later, Alecto stopped, extended her claws, and swept them downward through the air in front of her. But what started as a classic Fury move ended jarringly about four feet through the cut when her arm slammed to a halt as if she'd hit an invisible wall.

"What!" She looked at her hand in alarm, then paled as the blood drained from her features. "We really are out of time."

"What do you mean?" I asked, but she had already grabbed the edges of the partially completed gate and forced herself into the too-narrow and already-closing slit.

"Nemesis is in the Fury control center, or has at least begun to be able to influence it." Cerice thrust her own hand in front of my face, claws extended. "She has cut off our power to open the walls of reality." The needle-sharp lengths of organic diamond had lost much of their luster. "We must succeed in the next few minutes or fail utterly."

She turned and followed Alecto's disappearing feet through the gate. That left me and Melchior and Fenris. A sick thought struck me, and I glanced at the coin-shaped patch of Fury diamond in my own palm. It, too, had dimmed and faded. It was only in that instant that I realized that when Nemesis became the ruler of the Furies, I might be included on the list of puppets. I showed it to Melchior, and he nodded.

"I'd thought of it already, but didn't think there was any

good to be had from telling you about it." Then he went after the others.

I turned to Fenris, but he shook his head. "I won't fit, and in this world I can't change my shape as I once did. You must go on without me."

"But—" I made a sweeping gesture that took in the endless tumbling chaos around us.

"I'm a big boy. I can take care of myself, even here. You can come fetch me when you've won. The way closes; go before it's too late."

There was nothing to say to that, and nothing I could do for him. I wrapped his neck in a quick hug, and he licked my cheek; and then I left him. Between that and the thought of what the dimmed diamond in my palm meant, I found myself balanced between an urge to vomit and the impulse to slit my wrists now and get ahead of the rush.

I dragged myself through the hole and into a classical Greek temple built to colossal scale and found my feet as the gate closed behind me. The sun, pouring in through the great front doorway, fell squarely on a solid block of black marble nine feet long, four feet wide, and perhaps three feet thick. A marble effigy of a woman built to the same scale as the temple—perhaps eight feet from toes to head—lay atop the slab. Alecto stood at the effigy's feet, her head bowed, as she said a brief prayer in Attic Greek—it sounded like an apology of sorts.

"Is that Necessity?" I was shocked to think about the goddess ever having had a body. Alecto nodded. "Big woman."

"Titan," said Alecto as though she were speaking to a child. "Themis, the first and oldest of the breed, who became Necessity when the worlds of divinity were split each from each. But we have no time for history lessons now. Come here. You and my sister both."

I suppose that somewhere in the back of my head I had known all along that Necessity had begun as a Titan, but for all of my life and the lives of my ancestors back to the days of the birth of the Fates, she had simply been Necessity, the faceless power that ruled the powers. But I had no more time to think on that as we joined Alecto at the foot of the goddess. Set into the marble there were three sets of handprints.

"These are keyed to the Furies," said Alecto, "and cannot be opened in any other way. I just hope that the two of you count."

So apparently *everybody* had figured it out but me. I didn't know whether to yell at them for keeping me in the dark or thank them for sparing me the horror, so I just silently joined them.

Alecto took the center, Cerice the left, I the right. For ten long seconds nothing happened, and I felt certain we had failed and would all too soon become the playthings of a mad goddess. Then, as silently as though the mechanism were freshly oiled, the whole slab rose into the air, exposing a long flight of stairs.

As it locked into place, a wild scream of pure fury came from behind us. "How dare you!"

"Megaera," said Alecto, under her breath. "All of you go down the stairs as quick as you can. The inner workings of Necessity lie beneath. I'll hold her here. I can defend the doorway for a long time."

Melchior started down past us. As I edged after him, I threw a glance over my shoulder. Megaera stood in the doorway of the temple, her wings spread wide like great seaweed curtains. They provided a hell of a dramatic backdrop for the battered scorpion-form spinnerette and the great smoky silver ball that flanked her.

"The Voice of Necessity warned me of your betrayal, Alecto, but I didn't want to believe her." Megaera began a slow advance.

"Evil, of the darkest sort," said the silky, inhuman voice of Delé as she slid in just behind Megaera.

"You go," Cerice said to Alecto. "I can hold the door as well as you, and your knowledge of what lies below might be the thing that makes the difference."

"You're accepting a death sentence," said Alecto. "Megaera's older and more experienced than you. With the spinnerette and the eye of Nemesis to help her, you won't stand a chance. *I* wouldn't stand a chance."

"I know," said Cerice, pushing Alecto gently toward the stairs. "I'm not going to win. I just need to slow them down. Go!"

"Thank you, sister," said Alecto.

Then she stepped into the stairwell above me, and her wings blocked out my last view of Cerice. I wanted to push past her, to argue with Cerice, to make things come out a different way, but I knew that all of that would do was diminish our slender chance of success and with it her sacrifice.

So I turned away and left the woman I had once loved to die defending my back, because to do anything less was to fail her. I scooped up Melchior when I caught up to him and started to take the downward stairs in a series of half-mad leaps. My throat burned, and my eyes ached for Cerice and for Fenris. But no tears came. None ever would.

At the bottom, Alecto slipped past me and led the way through a maze of passages and rooms filled with computer equipment ranging in age from antique to "did anyone ever really think this was a good idea?" as well as nine and ninety kinds of temple paraphernalia.

Finally, we came to a great shadow-filled stone arch with the name THEMIS carved into the stone above it. There, Alecto stopped her headlong progress and bowed to the doorway, repeating her earlier prayers. I wished my Attic were better so that I could get more than the gist. There was a rolling solemnity to the words that touched my heart despite my lack of understanding.

"What's on the other side?" I asked.

"Necessity." Alecto stepped forward through the curtain of shadows.

I followed, and the shadows felt like cobwebs against my skin as I slid through them. Beyond lay a circular room filled with a sourceless light like the summer sun on Kos or Naxos, warm and welcoming and full of life. On a great slab of marble that mirrored the one in the temple above lay the goddess.

She was beautiful in the standard-issue-goddess sort of way—flawless skin, thick black hair, killer curves. But all of that barely registered on me, eclipsed in my attention by her eyes. She lay on her back, hands clasped beneath her breasts, and her eyelids were wide-open, exposing the churning wildness of chaos in a perfect mirror of my own.

"Her eyes are . . ." I couldn't think what more to say and kept checking to see if she was breathing.

Alecto glanced up at me. "The eyes of a Titan."

"Did all the Titans . . ." Again I couldn't finish.

"Born of chaos," said Alecto.

"And returned to chaos when they die," said Megaera as she entered the chamber behind us. She was battered and bloody but already healing.

"Cerice?" asked Alecto.

"Somewhere behind us, dying. The eye of Nemesis is dealing with her as she dealt with Delé."

"The eye of Nemesis?" Alecto sounded horrified. "Then you know?"

Megaera nodded. "I began to suspect a day or two ago, and my suspicions were confirmed in the encounter above."

"And still you chose to serve her?" Alecto's eyes filled with a terrible anger, and her claws slid from their sheaths. "Against our younger sister?"

"She is no sister of mine." Before Alecto could move or

say more, Megaera held up her hand. "But, no, I will not serve Nemesis. I told Delé that if they could handle the girl, I would slip on ahead and stop you. I could have, too. I was close enough behind you to have slit the Raven's throat before ever you had known I was there. But I said it only so as to get here ahead of them. I discovered my mistake too late to prevent what must come now. That task will require the presence of three Furies, and I owe it our mother to be one of them." She glared at me. "Had I known how to arrange it, I would have exchanged this one for the baby Fury or, better still, Tisiphone, but I could not, and so he will have to do."

"You don't mean . . ." Alecto's voice trailed off.

Megaera nodded. "We're going to have to completely shut down and reboot Necessity."

Alecto hissed but didn't say anything. Her expression told me nothing, but Megaera's spoke volumes.

"What's the end result of the process?" I asked.

"It will be the death of Nemesis," said Alecto. "Now that all the other systems large enough to offer her refuge have been closed to her, the reboot should throw her soul into the void beyond the edges of the multiverse."

"And Necessity?" I asked, though I thought I knew the answer.

"Necessity goes, too." Megaera's words came out barely above a whisper. "And I bear much of the blame for that."

"Shara?" asked Melchior, who had stayed quiet and still until now.

"Likewise."

Shit. "This takes three Furies," I said. "What if I refuse?"

"You can't," said Megaera. "Not if you care about anyone or anything in this multiverse. The damage done to the computer form of Necessity can only be repaired by a hard reboot and partial restore. There is no other way. Necessity must die if Nemesis is to be slain. And to let Nemesis live is to hand the fate of every living thing over to the mad spirit of Vengeance."

She stepped to the right of Necessity and took up the goddess's hand. Alecto did the same on the left.

"You must take the head," said Megaera. "Place your hands on either side of her face, and do it quickly. I think I hear the approach of Nemesis."

I took my place. "What now?"

"Now we pull the plug," said Alecto.

CHAPTER SEVENTEEN

"How exactly does this all work?" I asked from my station at the head of the Titan who had become Necessity.

"Just follow along," said Megaera. "We have no time for explanations. I can feel Nemesis chipping away at the protections that keep her from owning our souls."

I moved my hands away from Themis's face but couldn't keep from staring into the chaos of her eyes. "You know, I'm not really good at taking orders, or trusting the word of any goddess. Not even such a paragon as yourself."

"Boss!" said Melchior, and I couldn't tell whether he was more worried about the general time crunch or the Fury-baiting.

Alecto reached a hand across and caught Megaera's wrist, just above her clenched fist. "Let me. Raven, would you let Nemesis win to satisfy your contrariness?" Then she shook her head. "Of course you would, for you are at heart a creature of chaos. Then, in brief: Necessity's former Titan body provides the motive power for Necessity the computer. It is a living chaos tap of the highest order.

The only way to cut the power off is to cut her off. When Themis became Necessity, she foresaw that a day like this might come, and she made arrangements for it. An advance directive, if you will, with us as her designated proxies."

That made sense but left a rather large question hanging. "What comes after? Once we've turned off the power supply for the system, how do we reboot it?"

"We will need to replace Necessity that was with Necessity that will be," said Megaera, and her expression grew even more bitter. "A new soul must take on the burden."

"Whose? Yours, Megaera?" Wouldn't that be a nightmare for me? "Or Alecto's?" Better, but still not good.

"No," said Alecto. "Neither. For as Furies, we draw our power directly from Necessity, and a system cannot draw power from itself. It must be another Titan or one of the other great powers of the pantheon."

"Even if that weren't the case," said Megaera, "the system is programmed to prevent us from seizing power. The subsystem that governs the Furies includes a piece of code embedded in the hardware that prevents any of us from taking up the mantle."

"And how much time will we have to replace the goddess once we pull the plug?" I asked. This was starting to sound like out of the frying pan and into the fire.

"Seconds to minutes," replied Alecto. "Which is probably more time than we have left if we don't do this."

"But how are we going to get a replacement here with the mweb down?" I asked. "And who will it be?"

"He is already here," said Megaera through clenched teeth.

"He?" I glanced at the chaos in Themis's eyes again and . . . Lightbulb! *Oh. Hell.* "You can't mean me! I'm not a Titan . . . am I? Even if I were, aren't I technically a Fury at the moment and so disbarred?"

There was a crash from somewhere beyond the shadow curtain, and the sound of something big approaching fast.

"You know the answer in your heart," said Alecto. "Shara gave you the powers of a Fury, *not* the limitations."

"Put your hands on either side of Necessity's face, Raven," said Megaera, though it obviously hurt her to say it. "Necessity warned us it might come to this. I believe that it is why she had Clotho rename you the Raven. You *are* the Final Titan, and this is your hour."

Shit! Shit, shit, shit.

"Yours will be the third part," said Alecto. "Repeat what we have said when Megaera finishes." She took a deep breath and began to speak, tears bright on her cheeks, "Themis, I release you from your long burden. Return to chaos with the blessing of Alecto."

"Themis," said Megaera, her voice breaking, "I release you from your long burden. Return to chaos with the blessing of Megaera."

Both of them turned their gaze on me, while from without the sound of approaching doom came closer.

"Boss, you don't have to do this."

I glanced down at Melchior and sadly shook my head. In the absolute sense, he was right. I *could* refuse and hand the multiverse over to Nemesis. I might even be able to slip free of the proximate grasp of Nemesis somehow. I was, after all the Raven, the Trickster and finder of loopholes. In my own special case, gnawing my sword-encumbered hand off might be enough to slip me out from under the Fury clause. But I could do so only by abandoning my principles and my friends. And that I *would* not do. I lifted my eyes to meet the chaos in Necessity's.

"Themis, I release you from your long burden. Return to chaos with the blessing of the Raven."

The goddess seemed to sigh, and for the briefest moment I felt her presence looking out at me through the gates of chaos where her eyes should have been. In that very moment, the silver orb of Nemesis rocketed into the room, coming straight for my face. Necessity's hands lifted and caught the globe easily, bringing it down to rest against her breast in the manner of a mother with her firstborn. Then her eyes closed, and she and the globe both dissolved.

First into chaos. Then into nothing at all.

And whether it was Mother Necessity taking her misbegotten daughter into the night with her, or Nemesis finally avenging herself on the mother she hated more than any other being, I will leave to some other's judgment.

"You must take her place on the table," said Alecto, and there was the sound of grief restrained only at great cost in her voice.

I looked at Megaera to see whether she had anything to add, but the Fury of the Sea had no more interest in the things of this world. In the moment of her mother's passing, she had extended her own claws to their fullest and plunged them into her heart, and now she slowly slumped to the floor.

As I allowed Alecto to help me into the place where Necessity had so recently lain, I couldn't help but think that this was one of those victories where nobody wins. Melchior might have been thinking something similar, but it was hard to tell from his hunched and turned back.

I had no words of comfort for him, so I simply said to Alecto, "What do I do now?"

"Nothing. The tomb will take care of it." But even as she spoke, her words seemed to go all tinny and distant, and I felt my awareness being pulled down and out of my body into the world-computer that was Necessity 2.0.

Omniscience is a strange thing from the inside. So is functional omnipotence. Not at all as one imagines it before the fact. Not even one such as I who had twice experienced what it felt like to have the sum of all knowledge poured willy-nilly into his head.

I who had briefly held the power of Necessity once before, who had become Mimir in his well for a few brief moments, now experienced the incredible inrush of everything from a new perspective. For, with my merger into the computer awareness of Necessity's world, I had been provided with the necessary capacity to make sense of what I was given.

Using the resources supplied by my new world-sized mind, I could simultaneously experience and understand a million million things:

Melchior's grief for his best friend's passing beyond the bounds of mortality. Alecto's mourning for her sisters and her resolve to carry on their work no matter the personal cost. The faded echoes of the love-in-hate Themis and Nemesis had left behind with their utter destruction. Cerice's slow and painful dying in the temple above. Fenris, howling alone in chaos, more cut off from pack than ever before. The faint guttering light of Shara's soul, which Themis had somehow managed to send back to her shutdown body as a parting gift, where it now desperately clung against the pull of the yawning void of Hades.

I could understand that vacuum now as well, the way Hades the place had been designed as something of a singularity for souls, a bottomless gravity well that tugged at every living thing in every second of every day. I could see Cerberus lying deep in his cave beneath the plain at the gates, and feel the terrible loneliness that was his strongest emotion—the way his mighty heart bled for the loss of Persephone, who had provided the one true spot of brightness in a bitter existence.

I could feel the shock and terror in the soul of Fate as those Wyrd Sisters felt the change of control in Necessity. Know the terrible fear in my grandmother's heart as she realized that the grandchild whom she had cut off and ordered killed took the reins of the universe in his shaky hands. That was the beginning of action. I let the faintest hint of my bodiless laughter ring in the Temple of Fate, let the Fates know that I had matters to settle with the family who had cast me out.

It was a laugh that I visited on Hades himself in that same instant. I wanted the god who had threatened me with torment eternal to know that his future now rested in the palm of my hand. That I had but to make a fist to crush him as he had threatened to crush me.

Athena, too, was given notice that she was not high on my list. I sent a tiny shadow of my presence to stand before her and Zeus in the high office on Mount Olympus, where they had fled to discuss the change in the winds of the world.

And yet further my awareness stretched in that timeless instant, as I came into the full power of Necessity. An image of myself visited Haemun, alone and crying in the woods below the garden of Persephone, to offer comfort.

Another I sent to the duplicate Castle Discord I now knew that Eris had created in an unmarked and cleverly hidden pocket of chaos. I had learned and become more in the split second of my full merger with Necessity than any other being now living in our MythOS could claim. I had things to say to friends and foes both, and to every one of them I sent some tiny fraction of myself. To everyone save only Persephone.

When I asked myself why that was, I learned the first limitation of Necessity. I did not know my own mind in the same way that I knew everything else. Even with all the power in the multiverse ready at my fingertips, still there were places within my own mind that I could not reach. I had come up against the limits of myself, and it was strangely comforting.

I knew only that I was not yet ready to face Persephone, and so I hid her from myself and pondered on what that meant to what I had to say and do next. I speak here in terms of sequence, of one thing coming after another and things done and left undone, but that was not how I experienced it. It all moved in simultaneity for me, but I had to put it in order to make sense of it in the way that Ravirn-that-was would have.

So let me move from this first check on my power to the beginnings of action, step from easy to difficult, simple to complex, done to wanting-doing.

Of Melchior I will speak later. For anything I chose to do for him would be bound very tightly to my own fate, and that was a thing that needed much thought. Besides, even bound as I was, I felt that I still had a trick or two left in my bag.

So, begin with Alecto, whose hurts I comforted with a cloak of love in the shape of the wishes her departed mother had left behind for and her sisters. Next, Cerice, whom I restored to life and health in the very instant she would have died—summoning her to join her elder sister and Melchior in the tomb of Necessity. My tomb. I would have things to say to her in the fullness of time.

Shara I did not save before death took her, though I did catch her soul this side of the Gates of Hades, sparing her a second trip across that dreadful threshold that my failures had sent her over once before. I would have restored her to her body as well, but found that I could not release her from the binding she had taken on for Persephone. Nothing I could do would ever free her from her forced imprisonment within Necessity three months of every year, so instead I sent her back to her place within myself. In that moment I had found a second limit on the power of Necessity. Precedent bound me. The internal rules of the world-computer delimited even Necessity. Again, it was more relief than burden.

I moved from Shara to Fenris, opening a gate in the wall of the world and drawing him from chaos into the light of day in the Temple of Themis above. Then I healed him and summoned him to my tomb. I would have a request for him when he arrived, but did not frame it yet. I thought it would be both a burden and a joy. But more on that in the proper sequence.

Move next to the righting of many wrongs. The mweb I restored and removed fully to my control. No more would Fate be able to use its power save through the will of Necessity. Likewise, I restored the Fate Core and Olympus .net to proper functioning. I had no need to do the same for Discord, for in the very instant that the mweb came back online, Eris herself activated the second set of servers she had hidden in her disaster recovery site, the mirrored Castle Discord.

I took a moment then to focus more of my attention on Eris, manifesting myself to Discord in the shape of Ravirn—focusing on her through the chaos-filled eyes of a shadow of my old body.

Let me tighten my focus even more now, become for a moment the old me.

"Eris," I said, cocking her a snarky eyebrow—I was really going to enjoy the next few moments.

"Raven?" Her tone was suspicious, as was her body language. "Or Necessity? I see one and feel the other."

I grinned in realization—the ripple of change had not yet reached this farthest corner of the multiverse. She did not know. Oh yes, this was going to be fun. "Why not both?"

"Because it seems brutally unlikely."

"So is winning the lottery, and in this case, my dear, you just won the lottery."

Then I hit her with one brief instant of the same damn super-sex-appeal voodoo that she'd been throwing my way for years. I watched her eyes widen and her knees wobble as she fought off the urge to ravish me, and I laughed.

"You bastard!" Then she laughed as well, long and loud and full of the echoes of shattering glass. "Beautifully done,

Raven, and probably much deserved, though I promise you
I'll find a way to get even with you for it nonetheless."

"Anything else would disappoint me enormously, Eris.
Necessity has been far too stodgy to date, and I intend to
fix that."

"Necessity as the ultimate power of chaos." Eris smiled
a wicked smile. "I like that. It's exactly the sort of change I
can believe in." Then her face grew more serious. "Are you
still you in there? Or is your straitjacket as tight as mine?"
For a moment she was bound in the classic canvas restraint
garment, its sleeves drawn cruelly tight, the word *Discord*
scrawled across her chest in blood.

"To-may-to, to-mah-to." I rocked my hand back and
forth. "I've some ideas there, but we'll have to see how it
works out."

Let me draw back now and move my attention to another place and projection of myself—this one a small
temple-cum-office on the roof of the great Temple of Zeus
and simultaneous with the first. There, one of the many
fragments of me sat in Zeus's chair facing Athena and her
father.

"Zeus, buddy, talk to me." I held a pencil between the
tips of my fingers, playing with it idly. "Explain why I
shouldn't take this opportunity to rearrange things so that
people who threatened my life back a few days like . . . oh,
say, *you*, are no longer running the show around here? Why
I should not do to the old powers of the pantheon what you
and yours did to the Titans before you?"

Athena bristled, and I could read pure hatred in her
mind, but Zeus just smiled and conjured a cigar from thin
air, lighting it with a tiny bolt of lightning.

"Because you're far too fair-minded for that," he said,
settling into a mirror of my chair. "Despite many lessons to
the contrary, you still believe in the way things ought to be.
That doesn't include bloody vengeance, and we both know
it. The abuse your generation suffered at the hands of mine

has not twisted you as badly as the abuse we suffered from the Titans twisted us. In this, at least, you have transcended your elders."

He laughed then. "Though, as your presence here attests, you're not above a bit of petty revenge and wanting to make me sweat. Which I can hardly blame you for. Actually"—and his smile took on a smug edge— "this might even work out better for me than if I had become Necessity. I get to keep right on working the whole pleasures-of-the-flesh aspect of godhood while you do all the heavy lifting. Remind me to send you a birthday cake in a year, wouldn't you?"

I really, really wanted to smite him, but the big bastard was right. I wasn't going to rain fiery destruction down from the sky because I *did* believe in the way things ought to be. Fortunately, at the moment, the way things ought to be included raining cream pies down from the sky and rinsing them off with a river of seltzer water delivered by a team of satyrs in clown suits. To his credit, Zeus was deeply amused by the whole thing. The last I saw of him, he was laughing his head off. Athena, not so much. And *that* was very sweet indeed.

Another temple, another tiny but important fragment of my attention facing another pole power. Or in this case three: Clotho, Atropos, and my grandmother Lachesis. Fate.

For long seconds, nothing happened. We stared at one another in fraught silence. I thought of all sorts of dramatic things that I could do now that I had all the power in the universe at my fingertips. None of it seemed worth the effort.

Finally, Lachesis broke the silence. "If you're expecting an apology, Ravirn, you will be waiting forever."

She couldn't have taken me more by surprise if she'd slapped me.

"So it's Ravirn now, is it? You would give me back my

name now that I hold the stronger position? Restore me to the loving bosom of the family? Make me one of you again, now that it serves your purpose? How incredibly sleazy."

Lachesis shook her head. "You still don't understand us, do you? Not even with all the resources of Necessity at your disposal. I give you back nothing and expect nothing from you in return. You have reclaimed your name by right of conquest, and I merely acknowledge that victory. From a child of Fate you have grown into the Fate of the Gods. The Fate of Fate, if you will. Just as we rightly exercised our best judgment on how to handle your fate in days past with no regard for your relationship to us, now you will do the same with our fate. That is the way of our House, and I would expect no less of you now that you have finally come into responsibility. Do what you think is best, and you can do no wrong."

"I . . ." What could I say to that?

Nothing that could change the minds of my grandmother and her sisters about the inherent rightness of their position. Nothing that would change anything about anything that had or would happen. They would never acknowledge the terrible wrongs they had done me as anything other than what had to be short of my committing equally terrible wrongs against them. I burned to do just that, to make them pay for the pain they had caused me and those I loved.

I couldn't.

I had found another limitation on my power—the limitation of conscience—shown me by Zeus and Fate. I blessed my lucky stars for it at the same time that I felt a horrible creeping dread begin to grow in my heart. This time conscience had limited me, but what about next time? And the time after? What about the times when necessity contradicted conscience as the case of Nemesis had for Necessity herself?

What would I become then?

In another place, at exactly the same time, I was already facing just such a temptation.

Hades the place is not Hell, and Hades the god is not the Devil, but in my own personal lexicon they both come damned close. A shadow of myself stood over the fallen Lord of the Dead, its . . . no, *my* hand stinging from the tremendous backhanded blow that I had just delivered to his bony cheek.

"Don't you dare try to ask me for anything, Hades! I am *this* close to drowning you in the Lethe and installing Cerberus in your office. You will shut up and stay still while I sort a few things out here."

Starting with Megaera. I found the Fury standing on the end of the pier beneath the window of Hades' office, staring into the cold gray waters of the Lethe.

"Megaera," I said as I manifested myself beside her, "it doesn't have to be this way. You served Necessity faithfully for thousands of years, and you are owed a reward for that."

She turned and looked at me with eyes as dead as the landscape around us. "I have chosen my reward already, and it is forgetfulness."

"I'm really new at this job, and I could use some help. You wouldn't have to do it as a Fury." The timing of her death—in the window when there was no Necessity—provided me with that option. "You wouldn't even have to help me. If you want, I can free you of the ties that bind you to Necessity before I restore you to life and send you into a much-deserved retirement in someplace along the lines of Raven House."

She shook her head ever so slightly. "No thank you. I am and have always been Megaera the Fury, handmaiden of the incarnation of Necessity who was Themis. To serve another master or even not to serve is to become something else, to cease to be Megaera, and if I must do that, I would rather it were this way."

She took a step backwards, off the end of the pier, and vanished beneath the waters with a surprisingly soft splash. She did not resurface. And, with the eyes of Necessity, I saw that she never would. It hurt far more than I could have possibly imagined.

Pain is a funny thing, especially when it takes the form of guilt. I wanted to unmake Megaera's decision then, but understood that to do so would be to unmake Megaera as completely as she had unmade herself. Searching for some light in the darkness, I thought of other deaths, deaths for which I was responsible, wrongs that I might right. I reached outward seeking such. I wanted to find absolution for some of my many guilts.

I found one such wrong in my cousin Moric, whose spirit stood close at hand. Moric, whom Atropos had sent to kill me and on whom I had unleashed the fires of chaos, murdering him to prevent his murdering me.

In that moment, I restored him to life and sent him home to my great-aunt Atropos. Whether she would see it as a peace offering or a slap in the face of Fate for reversing the course that had already clipped his thread, I didn't know.

And, honestly, I didn't care. It felt good to be able to undo one of my heaviest decisions, to remove one of the many weights that rested on my conscience. I reached further then, hoping to do more such. I wanted most to find Laric, the cousin whose friendship and trust in me had cost him his life.

Instead, I found another limit on the power of Necessity. In looking for Laric, I found only the knowledge of what had become of him. It was all there within the files of Necessity. Laric had gone straight from the Gates of Hades down to the river Lethe and plunged in—a wise soul ready to begin anew. And there my knowledge of him ended.

The power of Necessity ended on the shores of the Lethe. Who and what Laric had become was closed to me.

Even if it were not, to restore him to what he once was would be to destroy what he had since become.

I returned then to the office of Hades the god and lifted him back into his chair. I spoke no words to him and glared my hate into his eyes, but I also replaced the computers that ran Hades the place and restored his very limited connection to the mweb. I might despise who he was and what he did, but somebody had to do it, and I hadn't the strength of will.

I withdrew much of my attention from the shadow that stood with Hades and refocused the core of it on the place where I had left my body, the Tomb of Necessity, and on those gathered within. On my way past the Gates of Hades I picked up Cerberus and Kira and brought them with me to my tomb. I also opened a way for Shara to project her presence.

Seeing my friends gathered around the empty vessel of my soul, I was nigh irresistibly tempted to cause my body to sit up, thrust forward its arms, and groan, "Braaiins!"

Instead, I once again projected a shadow of myself. "I suppose you're wondering why I've called you all here today."

I'd always wanted to say that and mean it, but nobody laughed. Nobody responded at all. While I waited, I set the part of my brain that loves a loophole to picking at the subsystem that governed Cerberus's relation to Hades. That *was* why I'd brought him, after all.

"Ravirn?" The sound of Cerberus speaking my name through his Mort head refocused my attention.

"Yes," I said through the lips of my shadow-self.

"I've got a question," said Mort.

"Me, too," agreed Bob.

"How are we here?" asked Dave.

"And who's guarding the Gates of Hades?" added Mort.

"Because if it's not us, something is very whacked with the multiverse," said Bob.

"I've sort of suspended time for a bit," I replied. "Not absolutely, just in terms of Hades. I can't do it for long." I was already feeling the strain. "But I really wanted to have you here for at least a few minutes, and I thought you'd like the break."

Dave blinked several times. "Then you *really* are Necessity now; how did that happen?"

"Long story, and I promise someone will tell it to you soon. In the meantime, I think . . ." I checked my hopes against my exploration of loopholes and came up with a jackpot. "Yes. I have a proposition to make. Fenris?"

"Yes?" The giant wolf swiveled his ears to point at me but didn't move otherwise.

"You don't have a real place in the structure of this MythOS. I'd like to make one for you, to harmonize you with it and its brand of chaos. If you're both interested, I would make you blood brothers with Cerberus and use that bond to give him the occasional day off."

Mort blinked several times. "Can you do that?"

"Even if he can, why would Fenris be crazy enough to take him up on it?" asked Bob.

"Not that we'd turn you down," Dave said to Fenris. "I'd love to have the chance to visit with Persephone once in a while, but it's a lousy job."

"Pack?" said Fenris, and his tail began to thump gently against the floor. "You're offering me real, blood pack?"

"If you all want it," I said, "and remembering it's not without cost."

For the first time in all the years I'd known him, Cerberus's tail began to wag.

"I'll take that as a yes. Fenris?"

"Pack!"

"Then consider it done."

With a tiny flick of my will, I sent the lot of them back to the shores of Hades, where another fragment of me went to work on the details. It was only as I released my grip on the flow of time that I found out just how much strain it had caused me. My body on its slab wasn't so much sweating as leaking.

Memo to me: Don't dick around with time unless you absolutely have to.

"Boss?" Melchior had climbed up onto the slab and was now sitting cross-legged on my body's chest and looking down into its eyes. "Are you in there somewhere? Or are we just getting echoes?"

"Yes," I said through the lips of my body.

He rolled his eyes. "That was meant more as an either/or question."

"But both are true." This time I spoke through my projection. "I'm definitely in here, but *here* is a really big place by comparison to the old me. It would be very easy to get lost."

"And are you planning on staying?" asked Cerice. "Because, if so, I'd like to resign my commission. It's not that I don't like you. Hell, in a lot of ways I still love you. That's actually the problem. I don't think that two people with our past should be in the position this puts us in."

"I don't know that either one of us has a lot of options on that one," I said, mentally running a check on the Fury subsystems and finding about what I'd expected to find after my experience with Shara. "I can't make you not a Fury. It's beyond the power of Necessity. As to my being Necessity . . ."

Was I planning on staying? What a question that was. It's not like I had a . . . *Wait—did I have a choice?* Beyond dying my way free in the mode of Themis, that is?

I looked again at the Fury systems, at the kludge Shara had grafted onto Necessity's earlier work in order to grant me some of the powers and privileges of that office, but not all of them.

"You know, there just might be a way . . ."

If I were to convince the system that I was technically enough of a Fury to render me ineligible for the job, what would happen? Would it simply boot me out? Or would it destroy me utterly? It was an open question, but hey, you don't play the game if you don't want to take any chances.

"I don't like the sound of that," said Alecto. "The multiverse needs Necessity."

"It does," I replied. "But you have to agree I might not be the best candidate for the job."

Alecto nodded. "Point. I can think of few worse."

"Gosh, thanks. I love you, too."

"It's not that," said Alecto. "I can't think of many that would be better either. The potential candidates are few, and none of them ideal."

"Wait a second." Melchior's face lit with sudden hope. "Are the two of you suggesting we might be able to fob this off on someone else?"

"I don't see how it can be done," said Alecto, "but I don't have the mind of Necessity to do my thinking."

"Or the soul of a hacker and cracker," I added. "I think I may have found a loophole, in the Fury system, but Alecto's right. There has to be a Necessity, and my leaving would require finding another sucker to take my spot."

Cerice raised a hand. "I vote for finding a sucker."

"Me, too," said Melchior. "But where? And perhaps as important, what are the criteria of suckerhood?"

"I think I may have an answer to both those questions," said Shara, speaking for the first time.

"Who?" The word was said in chorus.

"That's something I'd prefer not to speak of immediately." She fixed my projection with a hard look. "And don't you go rummaging around in my brain or anything to find the answer."

"I wouldn't dream of it." Guiltily, I withdrew the fingers of thought that had been reaching to do just that and gave them a little mental smack. This omniscience thing had some serious ethical implications.

Shara gave me back a creditable version of my own

raised eyebrow, letting me know she had her doubts about my denial. "Ravirn, if you would allow us the freedom of privacy, I want to talk to Melchior about this and maybe send him on an errand." Her projection gestured for Melchior to accompany her out of the tomb.

"Don't think of a duck," I replied sourly, as they disappeared.

Then I did my damnedest to not access the parts of my brain that knew what they were doing. It made for a very painful sort of zen—this not examining thoughts my brain was already thinking. A few moments later, Shara returned without Melchior. While we waited, I kept right on not thinking of a duck.

Until Persephone arrived.

I blinked several times and realized I'd been not thinking of two ducks, and that they'd both just walked through my door together.

"Persephone," I said—well, croaked really. Apparently omniscience is all down in the logical-thinking part of the brain and not so much with the emotional intelligence. "I . . . Why are you here?"

She smiled. "Melchior explained the situation to me, and I came to rescue you."

"You . . . I . . . Mel . . . Shara! How could you think to put her in prison again? Hasn't she suffered enough?"

Persephone pointed a finger at me. "You, be quiet a moment and listen. Shara did exactly as I would have asked her to had I known what was going on. This flesh"—she pinched her cheek—"is not terribly important to me. In fact, it has been more a burden than a joy for many long centuries. Nor do I particularly care about freedom in the abstract. What I care about is freedom *from*, not freedom *of*. Freedom from pain and fear and the shadow of Hades that ever haunts my dreams. I can think of no greater *freedom from* than to put on the armor of Necessity.

"I have been hurt in ways that can never be healed,"

continued Persephone, "and would still be taking fresh hurt every day were it not for your choice to risk everything on my behalf. For that, I love you in my own way and ever shall. I have spent many hours watching you, and I think I know you better than most. This"—she made a gesture that took in the whole of the world around us—"will be the death of your spirit if you stay here. What would read as security for me will ultimately read as a trap for you. It may not gall you yet, but a trickster pent is a trickster destroyed. Just as a trickster without challenges will eventually become a trickster looking for death."

Shara stepped up beside Persephone. "That's why I sent for her. The last thing this MythOS needs after the troubles just past is a suicidal Necessity. Don't do this to yourself, or to us."

They were both right, and I knew it. That didn't make the idea of letting Persephone assume my burden any easier to bear.

What did was flicking my consciousness into Hades' office. "You know, you're right," I said to the Lord of the Dead. "I *am* unsuited to being Necessity. That's why I've decided to hand the reins over to Persephone."

Then, with the look of shock and horror still fresh on his face, I returned to my friends, nodded, and told Necessity the computer that there had been a tragic mistake and that it had accidentally deified a Fury to take the place of Themis.

Take a sentient world and a Ravirn-shaped cookie cutter. Press the one into the other, ripping loose and discarding any bits that don't fit. I *was* that world, and in the process of ceasing to be so, I experienced pain on every level—physical, emotional, mental. I lost senses that I hadn't realized I possessed until that instant and in a manner every bit as painful as being blinded by red-hot irons. I was crushed and flayed and lobotomized, all without anesthesia or hope of recovery.

And, when finally I had become only myself once more, I retained the memories of what it was to be Necessity. I, who had briefly been God, was mortal once again and all too aware of what that meant. I screamed then, and kept right on screaming until Melchior injected oblivion directly into my carotid artery.

Lights out.

Epilogue

We sat on the balcony of a restored Raven House, we four who had so recently journeyed together from the world of the Norse gods. It was time for farewells.

"I do wish I could have seen Hades' expression," said Melchior. "I bet it was priceless."

"It is a memory that I will cherish for as long as I live." As opposed to so many others—for relief from those I prayed nightly to Lesmosyne, Goddess of Forgetting and my new choice of patroness.

"What do you think Persephone will do with him?" asked Fenris. He was looking happier than I'd ever seen, and healthier, a result of proper integration with the chaos magic of this MythOS. I thought he might have even put on a little weight. "Hades, I mean."

"Not a thing," I replied. "Not a thing."

I'd asked her that very question in a moment of frozen time that she'd set aside for our parting.

* * *

"Nothing," she had told me. "Nothing at all. What Hades did to me is unforgivable and worthy of terrible punishment. But it will not be me who metes it out. His was a crime of power. He raped me because he could and because it pleased him to dominate my flesh so. If I were to take my vengeance now, it would be just. No one would deny that he deserves it, but it would also be the beginning of my own destruction; because I would not be doing it out of a sense of justice, though I might tell myself I was. I would be doing it because I could, and in that I would have taken a step toward becoming the thing I hate."

"I don't think that I could be that forgiving if I were you," I replied.

"Forgive? Never. Not if every living thing in all the worlds of creation were to beg me on bended knee would I forgive Hades. He is an abomination in my sight. But that doesn't mean I have to be one, too. Of course"—and here she smiled an icy smile—"I do intend to take a great deal of satisfaction in knowing he will be looking over his shoulder for the rest of eternity, waiting for my revenge to fall and worrying. That I *can* enjoy, for it is a punishment he will have inflicted on himself. Nor will I hesitate for a moment to crush him if he steps one jot out of line. But let us speak of more pleasant things in this last meeting."

"You say that like you think we won't be seeing each other again."

"It's possible that we will meet again, for I cannot truly foresee the future. But it seems unlikely, with you planning your imminent departure from this MythOS."

"It's not that I don't want . . ." I trailed off. How to express all my mixed feelings on the subject?

"You have no need to," Persephone answered my thought, "for I can see into your heart, can't avoid it actually, for I have not your gift of lying to myself. I cannot avoid thinking of the duck. There is much here that you love and would not part from, but many things more that you cannot abide. Perhaps most of all, having Necessity in your back pocket."

"I don't think I've got you . . . Well, not really . . . I don't think of it that way . . . It's just . . . Well, Tisiphone, and the knowledge . . ."

"That if you stay here, you will never again know if what you achieve is through your own actions or if it is me giving the odds a little nudge in your favor. I know. And you are right to want to leave, though I will miss you, as will many others, Thalia not least among them. The uncertainty would destroy you as certainly as remaining Necessity would have. You must go, and though I will miss you terribly, I will not keep you here."

"Thank you." I didn't know what else to say.

"You're welcome, and just to give you some small incentive to return from time to time, I will give you two gifts.

"Here is the first." She reached out and touched the nodule of Fury diamond in the palm of my hand, making it burn for a second. "Though it will no longer grant you any of the powers of my handmaidens, Occam is now possessed of two pieces of magic of its own. No matter how badly it is broken, it will always grow back anew. And while it will not make you a hole from one place in *this* multiverse to another, it will allow you to move between the one MythOS and others as you need."

I knelt then and laid my sword hand at her feet. "If you should need me, know that my blade is ever at your service."

"Thank you, my knight in motley."

For just an instant she clad me in an armored version of a jester's gear, and I laughed with her, for what is a fool but a face of the Trickster? She reached down then and took my hand, pulling me back to my feet. Our eyes met and held then, or rather, didn't meet, as hers had also gone to chaos when she took on the mantle of Necessity, and I wondered what her other gift might be.

"The gift of *freedom from*," she said. "If ever you should die in this world or any other such that your soul returns here, you shall not pass the Gates of Hades. Even as we speak, I have placed a new set of stars in the heavens. They draw the shape of the Raven, and with it, the soul of the Raven should true death ever sunder it from the flesh of your body. Like Cassiopeia before you, you will end in light, not in darkness." She smiled then and once again clad me ever so briefly in fool's motley. "Call it a constellation prize for your service to Necessity."

Necessity with a sense of humor? How very lovely.

"Thank you, Persephone, for everything."

"You're welcome." She kissed the palm of her own hand then and set it to my cheek. "Go with my blessing."

"Good-bye," I said, for there was nothing else to say, and she did as well.

It always comes to that, doesn't it?

And here it came again. Final toasts had been made, pledges of friendship and love spoken, tears and hugs exchanged. With Haemun's blessing, I had passed the deed of Raven House over to Fenris and Cerberus, who had absolutely refused to change the name or count it as anything but a loan. I had arranged all my affairs, saying farewell to the grandmother I loved—Thalia was spending every waking moment with Persephone—and telling the one I hated to go jump in a lake.

Now it was time for Melchior and me to depart for other worlds and fresh challenges, and I said so. But as I rose from my seat, there came the too-familiar sound of a Fury tearing a hole in the world behind me.

"Hello, Cerice," I said as I began to turn. "I'd hoped to

get a chance to say good-bye before I left and . . ." Holy shit!

"What's the matter, big boy? Goblin got your tongue?" Shara stood before me.

But not the Shara I knew so well. This was Shara the—

"Persephone made you a Fury!" exclaimed Melchior, interrupting my thoughts.

"Believe it, boys." Shara grinned and fanned wings like the sky at night. Stars flickered in the darkness, and she shrugged. "I tried to convince her that sex was an element, and that's what my wings ought to be made of, but night was as close as she was willing to get to the topic. I suppose I can't really blame her, and this *is* pretty spiffy." She moved then with the terrible sense-blurring speed of the Furies, tackling Melchior and sitting on his chest.

"You, on the other hand, growr!" She ran a claw gently from his earlobe down to the point of his jaw, then bounced back to her feet. "Where was I?"

"I have no idea," said Melchior, "but I liked it." He looked up at me. "Do we have to go right this instant?"

I laughed and shook my head. "I think it can wait a few minutes."

"Honey," said Shara, "I've been trapped inside a computer for three months; you're going to have to wait more than minutes if you want to bring blue-boy with you when you go."

The two of them scampered off to do what goblins do when no one else is watching, and I settled back into my chair. This time, when I heard a rip in the wall of reality, I made sure it was Cerice before I called her by name.

"I take it our evil plan to keep you here another few hours has worked," she said.

I nodded and offered her a drink. "How does it feel to have Shara as a sister for real?"

"Pretty wonderful, actually."

"Why did Persephone do it?" asked Fenris. "Not that I'm complaining."

"She wants to make significant upgrades to the system, and at the moment, Shara is the greatest living expert."

"That makes sense," said Fenris.

"But that's not the only reason, is it?" I'd had a few minutes to digest the idea and felt I had a pretty good guess as to the answer.

"No," said Cerice. "It's also to send a message to Fate. Persephone isn't a real big fan of oppression, especially at the level of the pole powers. She didn't explicitly tell our family matriarchs to straighten up and fly right, but she did make damned sure to find an excuse to send Shara on an errand to the Temple of Fate within about five seconds of her accepting the job."

I grinned. "Now, that's a look I wish *I* could have seen."

"I'm sure she's sharing . . . the video with Melchior even as we speak."

Cerice winked at me, and I laughed. It was the first time in ages that we had been able to share a moment together that wasn't fraught with all the baggage we'd collected in the course of our roller-coaster relationship. There were several more such before she got up from the table and gave Fenris a scruff behind the ears.

"I've got to go," she said to me. "Persephone's honey-do list is a mile long."

"Thanks for stopping by, Cerice. I would have been sorry to miss the chance for a real good-bye."

"Me, too."

I opened my arms, and she stepped forward into them, and the kiss that followed was natural and sweet and said nothing more than good-bye.

Eventually, Shara and Melchior returned, and the kiss *she* gave me said all kinds of things like: Look what you missed out on by being the wrong species, big boy. And, if you ever change your mind, shape-shifter . . .

And then it was just the four of us again, because Shara had to go, and Haemun had said his good-byes hours ago with a plate of cookies and an admonishment to "come back soon," and was now hiding his tears in the kitchen.

So I reached for Occam, though it was hard to find something I was mad enough about, what with all the comeuppances that had been delivered to deserving souls in the past few days and with the promise of Tisiphone waiting for me at the other end. But somehow I managed it, slicing a hole in the wall of our MythOS.

"Pack!" said Fenris.

"Pack," I agreed.

Then I shook Laginn's hand, or really, Laginn, and the moment had truly come.

"Melchior?"

"Ready when you are, Boss."

"You're never going to stop calling me that, are you?"

"Nope."

"Didn't think so."

Then it was time for my exit. Or, if you happen to be looking at it from the other side of the door, my entrance.

**Explore the outer reaches
of imagination—don't miss these authors
of dark fantasy and urban noir that take you
to the edge and beyond.**

Patricia Briggs	Karen Chance	Anne Bishop
Simon R. Green	Caitlin R. Kiernan	Janine Cross
Jim Butcher	Rachel Caine	Sarah Monette
Kat Richardson	Glen Cook	Douglas Clegg